*Praise For*

# INTO THE LIGHT

Christine Anderson demonstrates an incredible talent for drawing readers in from the very first page. Her storytelling is descriptive, immersive, and emotionally charged, making it nearly impossible to stop reading. In this powerful, fast moving narrative Anderson explores the raw, often painful, terrain of human relationships—both romantic and familial—with striking honesty and depth.

What makes this story resonate is its authenticity. The characters don't just face dramatic obstacles for the sake of plot—they wrestle with personal trauma, confront longstanding family tensions, and navigate the fragile yet redemptive nature of love, both human and divine. Through it all, Anderson weaves in a meaningful and compelling exploration of faith, not as a simple solution but as a deeply personal and evolving force that shapes the characters' journeys. This novel is a heartfelt and thought-provoking read, perfect for anyone who appreciates character-driven stories with emotional weight and spiritual depth.

—**Jonathan Camiolo**, Pastoral Associate, *Church of Christ the King*

***

I never cried over a preface before. What an opening! I was immediately captivated by this story. I absolutely loved this book and found myself at the end wanting to go back and read it all over again!

—**Susan Novalis**, Volunteer Eucharistic Minister for Hospital Visitations

***

Christine Anderson's writing flows beautifully, and I quickly engaged with her characters and their story, taking Noel and Jeremy through trauma and ending in triumph fueled by faith. The storyline is fresh and timely. What I came away with after reading Christine's book is how important faith is in our lives. Her message about how one life lived in faith can change so many

others is remarkable. One of the central chapters was so good that I had to read it to my husband.
—**Mary Grace Yost**, Retired English Teacher

***

Simply riveting, wonderfully written! *Into the Light* had me on the edge of my seat with anticipation and excitement. I was overwhelmed with gratitude for the gift of my faith, and it heightened my awareness of the need to share that faith with others so many can be drawn to the Almighty.
—**Vinette Stegura**, Long-time member, *Creative Living Bible Study*

# Into the Light

By

Christine Anderson

Published by KHARIS PUBLISHING, an imprint of KHARIS MEDIA LLC.



ISBN-13: 978-1-63746-361-1

ISBN-10: 1-63746-361-8

Library of Congress Control Number: 2025947146



All KHARIS PUBLISHING products are available at special quantity discounts for bulk purchases for sales promotions, premiums, fund-raising, and educational needs. For details, contact:

Kharis Media LLC
Tel: 1-630-909-3405
**support@kharispublishing.com**
**www.kharispublishing.com**

*For Rodd*

*None of this would have been possible without you. The wonderful life we are sharing and the beautiful family we have created, all the dreams I have watched become a reality. . . it all started with you and me. From that serendipitous blind date to a family flourishing with children and grandchild, we have been blessed by the God who loves us. And though we are far from perfect people, we are perfect for each other.*

# Contents

# PREFACE

A sudden splash, loud and unexpected, sounded in the July air. Jeremy Finnegan spun as a collective scream erupted from the preteen campers in the boat. All their eyes were fixed on the anchor line disappearing into the water. He scanned the group and knew instantly who was missing: Noel, his co-counselor. He'd asked her to lower the anchor over the side as he organized the fishing gear. Now seven campers stared at him with panicked eyes, one voice clear above the rest.

"Her leg got tangled in the rope and it pulled her into the water!"

Had she been wearing a life jacket? He'd told her to put it on earlier, but she was so busy helping the kids with theirs he wasn't sure he'd seen her in the bright yellow jacket the kids all wore. In any case, she wouldn't be able to surface on her own if she was caught in the line. All these thoughts ran through his mind as he screamed for help across the open water. He drew in a deep breath, blew it out, and inhaled again, the next breath deeper like before a race. Then he dove over the side.

The lake's frigid water slapped his bare chest; tiny icicles pricked his skin, the cold so intense it was painful. He checked the impulse to draw in a breath at the shocking temperature of the water, instead directing his attention downward as he followed the rope line into the murky depths. They weren't far from shore, maybe a hundred yards, but the water was deep enough to make for poor visibility. With the momentum from his dive waning, he stroked downward, not wanting to touch the rope and chance making it tighter. His eyes searched for the blonde-haired girl. The small knife he'd been using to cut the tangled fishing line poked his thigh through the pocket of his board shorts as he kicked harder. He was going to need every ounce of endurance he'd learned as a collegiate swimmer to find her and bring her back to the surface.

He'd been a counselor at the camp for underprivileged kids for the past three summers, choosing to stay on campus in California rather than return to his North Carolina roots and dysfunctional family. This was his final summer. He'd been assigned one of the junior counselors, Noel Welsh, a rising senior at the local high school. She was a pretty kid, but Jeremy hadn't given her much thought other than to note she was a hard worker and reminded him of his sister.

He caught a glimpse of something yellow and stroked harder. He realized she was wearing a life jacket as she came into view. The anchor rested in the mucky silt of the lake bottom. A few feet away, Jeremy watched Noel struggle in a panicked frenzy to try and wrench her ankle free from the rope twisted around it. She was using what little air she had in a useless battle. He swam up to her, saw her eyes widen, and placed one finger to his lips in the universal sign for quiet. Her eyes filled with fear and she nodded. Hooking his foot under the anchor line so he wouldn't surface, Jeremy registered the viselike grip the rope had on Noel's ankle, the hemp thick, twisted, and cutting into her skin. The descent to the lake floor had pulled it tight, and the tiny knife in his pocket would never be big enough to cut through it. He looked upward and saw the wide-eyed panic in Noel's eyes. The life jacket pulled upward around her neck, it's buoyancy wanting to break free of the entrapment.

Jeremy's lungs began to burn but he pushed the sensation away just as he had during practice when they were doing endurance drills. A sudden thought gave him a glint of hope. An anchor was only as strong as its weakest link, and although this line was rope and not metal the same principle had to apply. Where was the weakest link? The attachment to the anchor where stress would have been exerted every time it was lowered or hauled up. The camp never had enough money for new equipment and this anchor had probably been with the boat for decades.

Hand over hand he followed the rope to the anchor and then examined the rope's attachment to the metal. It was a simple knot, worn and frayed. Grabbing the knife from his pocket, he wedged the sharp blade between the anchor and the rope and began to saw against the hemp while creating countertraction with his other hand. He didn't know if he had enough breath to cut all the way through, but he resisted the pressure building in his lungs, the undeniable sensation that made him want to take in a breath that would fill his lungs with water. From his training he knew how much time he had before he would need to surface and then try again. He raked the knife across the rope and watched the frayed ends begin to give way; then with one hard pull, it broke free.

The pressure in his lungs was unbearable as he swam back to Noel, just as her eyes rolled back in her head and she lost consciousness. Knowing her lungs were filling with water, Jeremy grabbed her arm and pushed against the lake's bottom with both feet, sending them toward the surface. The life jacket made the ascent faster. Jeremy could see dark spots starting to cloud his field of vision as the light grew closer. He stroked once more and broke the surface.

Coughing and sputtering, he drew in deep drafts of air, the sensation a sweet relief as the scent of pine wafted across the water. Rolling Noel onto her back, he slung his arm across her chest and made a snap decision. The shore was too far. He didn't have time to get her there. She needed CPR now or she wouldn't survive. The canvas-covered float was just a few yards away; turning toward it, he pulled her through the water with a practiced stroke. Reaching the float, he hauled himself up first and then spun, reaching under Noel's armpits and pulling her clear of the water. He opened the life jacket, revealing the pink swimsuit she wore as he felt for a carotid pulse and bent to assess her breathing. Nothing. He opened her airway and, pinching her nose, delivered two rescue breaths. He then placed his stacked hands over her sternum and began delivering chest compressions. He'd done this in CPR class on plastic mannequins, but it felt different on a real person. A part of him wanted to pull back, worried about breaking her ribs, but he knew that for CPR to be effective he had to deliver the compressions just the way he had in class. Hard, fast, and allowing for full chest recoil. He counted the downward thrusts to thirty and then moved back to her head, opening her airway by lifting her chin. Pinching her nose closed again, he covered her mouth with his and delivered two full breaths. Her skin, still wet, felt cold and slippery. As he returned to chest compressions, he saw her lips were blue, her skin ashen with a ghostly pallor.

In the distance he heard the wail of a siren and the purr of a boat engine turning over, but he focused his attention on the rate and rhythm of CPR. With a sudden flash of insight, he knew she was dead. All his efforts would likely be in vain, but that thought, instead of making him pull back made him push harder and increase the strength of his compressions as his energy started to falter. There was a good reason they told you to alternate personnel on a resuscitation. It was exhausting.

Sunlight warmed his shoulders and stole the chill from his skin as the sound of a boat cutting through the water made him look up to see the camp director approaching in the motorboat. Jeremy covered Noel's mouth with his own, catching a fleeting scent of strawberry on her lips before delivering two slow deep breaths. His lips sealed over hers, he felt the muscle spasm begin and his mouth filled with water as she coughed. In one motion he flipped her over onto her side and watched water spew from her mouth.

From the shore, cheering kids screamed as he held her on her side and she continued to cough up spurts of lake water. Her eyes fluttered open as she turned to look at him, her gaze confused but with none of the panic he had seen under the water. She seemed peaceful. Clearly, she was still dazed.

The boat pulled up to the float. Jeremy lifted Noel up, cradling her in his arms as he covered the distance to the float's edge and lowered her into the waiting arms of the camp director. He watched the boat pull around the float and head to shore. Then sheer exhaustion swamped him as the adrenalin rush wore off. He sank to his knees and covered his face with his hands, humbled by the knowledge that somehow, against all the odds, he had saved her. Tears stung his eyes as a wave of relief assailed him. It could have gone the other way. He lifted his gaze, his vision blurry with tears, and saw the paramedics lift her onto the waiting stretcher and wheel it to the rig. And as the ambulance pulled away from the lake, its red and blue lights reflecting off the water's surface, its siren wailing, he wondered if he would ever see her again.

# CHAPTER ONE

The California campus looked much the same as she remembered from her own college tour, the green lawns lush and manicured. Petunias, dahlias, and alyssum, vivid in hues of pink, purple, and white, lined the walkway to the administration building. The refreshing cool of the late September morning was giving way to what promised to be a stifling afternoon. Noel Welsh shivered despite the warmth of the perfect day, a chill working its way across her shoulders and the memories of that summer day on campus wanting to break free. Noel shook off the strange sensation. This day wasn't about her. She glanced over at her younger sister, Mia, her dark hair and skin a sharp contrast to Noel's Nordic coloring. This school was her long shot. She wanted to go here with a fervor Noel found surprising since it was just a few miles from their house. Maybe that was the draw, though. After Mia's adoption into their family at the age of ten, she liked to stick close to home as if having found a stable home with a family who loved her, she wasn't willing to venture far away.

They joined the tour group gathered outside the administration building. A tall, young man with short blonde hair and a pimpled forehead was directing the tour. He greeted them with a bright smile, took their names, and then checked them off his list, telling them the tour would begin in five minutes.

Mia fidgeted from one foot to the other, glancing down at the college map the tour guide had handed her. She'd been walking this campus since she was in middle school; she didn't need a map. But taking the tour was all part of showing interest in the eyes of the admissions department.

Mia glanced over at Noel with an excited smile, her dark eyes pleading. "I know you didn't go here, but don't you know anyone who could put in a good word for me?"

She was dressed in a black skirt, short but not too short, and a blue blouse, the color vivid against her dark skin. The blue beading in the cascade of braids that fell down her back matched her shirt. Noel noted the practicality of the black sneakers Mia had chosen, knowing they were going to cover a lot of ground today.

"Sorry, Mi, I don't think I do. But your grades are strong and your extracurriculars are even better. You have a good shot of getting in on your own."

"But I want to know now."

Noel smiled. "No guarantees in this life, you know that. Well, maybe just one."

Mia looked up at her much taller sister. "What's that?"

"That whether you get in here or somewhere else, you'll always be coming home to the family that loves you." Noel put an arm around Mia's shoulders and pulled her in close, loving the girl who had stolen her heart from the moment they met.

Noel had returned home after college on the East Coast and joined the local chapter of Big Brothers Big Sisters as a volunteer while she looked for a job and contemplated getting her master's degree. She had met Mia the first day of the summer program and the two had been drawn to each other, not realizing the reason until much later. They were both trauma victims haunted by a single incident that had changed their lives. For Mia, it had been finding her mother's dead body overdosed on drugs when she came home from first grade and then being swallowed up into the state's foster care system. For Noel, it had been the near drowning on a perfect morning just like this one. Her memories of the event were vague, but when she slept, she suffered the terror of being unable to breathe. Sometimes in her dream state she was trapped inside her own body, staring outward and feeling the pressure in her chest grow tighter. At other times, she was watching it happen like a movie playing in front of her but feeling the same panic and pain. Her last vision before the darkness descended and she woke up gasping for air was always the same: a pair of eyes, wide with desperation and dread. Blue eyes, just like hers. It was like looking in a mirror, like watching herself die. Post-traumatic stress had been the diagnosis in the years that followed the near drowning, and no amount of counseling had vanquished the nightmares. They didn't happen as often anymore, but the harrowing dreams still accosted her, often triggered by events so unrelated the connection seemed unknowable.

"We're ready to get started," the tour guide called out as a petite undergraduate with a perky smile and wild curls joined him in front of the group. "My name is Ethan and this is Desiree. I am a junior and Desiree is a sophomore here at Langford University. Please feel free to ask any questions as we move through the tour, which should take about an hour. If you'll follow me, please.'

Mia grabbed Noel's hand and maneuvered her way to the front of the crowd, trying to stand out in the diverse group of parents and teens. The tour progressed from the academic centers to the football stadium and past the volunteer center and cafeteria to the new science center, a multimillion-dollar state-of-the-art facility funded by the generosity of an alumni donor.

"If you have some extra time to spend with us today, you might want to check out the coffeehouse and grill located on the main floor of the Laraby Science Center. The food is awesome," Desiree suggested as they walked back to their starting point in front of the administration building. As the group began to disperse, Mia lingered to talk with Desiree and Noel hung back a few steps, allowing her sister to make the most of this in-person contact with a current student.

"Did you pick her brain about admissions tips?" Noel asked as Mia returned to her side moments later, looking pensive.

"Yes, and she was very encouraging about applying early to show interest and letting them know this school is my number-one choice. She did say it would help if I knew any alumni or a current staff member and could get a letter of recommendation from them."

Noel tried to suppress her annoyed reaction to Desiree's suggestion. She had only been trying to help a would-be student, but why did it always come down to who you knew and not who you were? Sensing her sister's despair at hearing this truth spelled out by the tour guide, Noel offered a distraction.

"How about we check out the coffeehouse in the Laraby Center? I'm starving."

Mia's eyes brightened. "Me, too."

Her optimism returning, Mia turned toward the massive science center. With all that had happened to Mia before she became part of their family, she could have been a solemn, angry teenager, but she wasn't. Perhaps that was what Noel had sensed about Mia when they first met, her brown eyes wide and her smile tentative but frequent, her gratitude, for even a small kindness, overflowing. She was intelligent and hardworking and deserved a fair shot at getting into this school of her dreams. Noel pulled open the door to the science center with more force than was necessary, putting her face to face with a man exiting the building. "I'm so sorry… "

The man's eyes grew wide as he stood in the doorway studying her face. "Noel?"

Startled, she looked up at him. He was tall and broad shouldered with brown shaggy hair that fell into his eyes. "Yes, have we met?"

"We have, a long time ago." He stepped beyond the doorway to allow several students to pass. "My name is Professor Finnegan. Jeremy Finnegan."

Noel registered the delight on Mia's face out of the corner of her eye but couldn't place the face until she tilted her head and met his gaze. And then she knew, and her knees buckled beneath her.

* * *

Jeremy reached for her, his hand encircling her arm as she stumbled to right herself. She hadn't fainted. Her eyes were wide open, but seeing him again was a shock and not a pleasant one. He stepped forward, guiding her away from the students headed into the coffeehouse. A pretty, young woman with cornrow braids and ebony skin took her other arm as he settled Noel on the stone bench by the door. He went down on his haunches in front of her. "Are you okay?"

She nodded, then shook her head as if trying to focus.

"You don't look okay," the young woman said, taking a seat beside her. "You're even whiter than usual and that's saying something."

Noel found her voice. "I'm fine, Mia. Just surprised is all."

"So you two know each other?" the young woman asked.

Noel met his upturned gaze. "Jeremy saved my life."

Her words were clear, but her eyes were haunted. Jeremy registered the strange mixture of fear and awe on her face. He had recognized her instantly. She looked a bit older but then she would. He hadn't set eyes on her in fifteen years, since the day he had lifted her in his arms and handed her over to the camp director. That day had changed his life.

A video of the rescue and CPR had gone viral on the Internet, making him an instant celebrity. When Noel's parents refused all attempts to interview her, he became the media's only access to a great story.

"He's the guy who saved you from drowning?" Mia squeaked, her stare bouncing from one face to the other.

"I am." Jeremy squeezed Noel's hand.

"And I never got the chance to thank you." Her gaze drifted downward to study his face, although her eyes did not meet his again.

"I believe your parents did that for you."

"But I wanted to…"

"It's all good, Noel, and over years ago. I'm glad you're okay." He rose to his feet, pulling her with him. "What brings you to campus today?"

"This is my sister Mia." Her head tilted toward the young woman beside her. "She's applying here and we came to take the tour."

Jeremy turned to the would-be student. "What did you think?"

"I think this school is my number-one choice," Mia asserted, taking advantage of the opportunity to speak to a faculty member even as she cast another assessing glance at Noel.

"What do you think you can bring to the Langford community?" Jeremy studied the young woman, interested to see if she would rise to the challenge.

Mia tilted her head, thought for a fraction of a second, and then squared her shoulders. "I don't want to come here to waste four years drinking beer and going to frat parties—don't get me wrong; I love a good party—but for me this school is my opportunity to give back. I'm a child of the foster care system of California, and I was adopted into a wonderful family after meeting my sister as a part of the Big Brothers Big Sisters Program. I have seen what a difference one program—one person—can make, and I want to be a part of making that happen for someone else. I think I can do that here at Langford."

"Nice answer." Jeremy met her gaze. "Send me your application before you submit it, and I'll attach a recommendation."

"You will?" Mia's eyes widened in surprise and excitement. "Thank you so much."

Jeremy glanced at Noel as he reached into his pocket, withdrew a business card, and handed it to Mia. "When you are ready to apply, send me the application at this e-mail. I'll take it from there."

"That is very generous." Noel's eyes met his for no more than an instant. "It was nice to see you again, Jeremy, and thank you for everything." Her hand skimmed the sleeve of his shirt, the touch fleeting and yet somehow purposeful.

Mia grabbed her hand. "Is the food in there as good as I hear?"

Jeremy smiled. "It is. Try the nachos supreme."

"I think I will." The teenager pulled her sister toward the building. Jeremy watched as Noel glanced back at him as if she wanted to say more but then thought better of it.

Jeremy frowned, realizing she'd said very little during that conversation. She'd stepped back and let her sister shine. He couldn't shake the vision of her haunted eyes. It was almost as if she was afraid of him, which didn't make sense. But trauma and memory were tricky things; intricately woven, their pathways not always straight. A part of him wanted to go after her, to pull her aside and speak to her alone, to satisfy his burning need to talk about the day that had changed his life forever. But he stood his ground, fists clenched in frustration, knowing he was already late as she disappeared beyond the tinted glass.

He returned to his office two hours later after finishing his meeting with the Institutional Review Board, better known as the IRB, who'd wanted him to clarify some aspects of his research proposal. How he was soliciting subjects for the study seemed to be the main sticking point. He tried to keep his answers neutral and avoid the condescension he'd been told sometimes crept into his tone. But today his answers might have sounded distracted rather than arrogant as his mind kept returning to his chance run-in with Noel.

He'd never spoken to her after the rescue. She was taken to the hospital and her parents refused to let anyone visit. No friends. No reporters. Even the police got the bare minimum since it came out later that she had few memories of the incident. He learned from the camp director that Noel had quit her job and her parents were taking her out of the country to avoid the crush of reporters encamped outside their home after the viral video.

He opened the laptop on his desk and entered his security code. She wasn't a traumatized teenager anymore, and he just wanted to talk to her. His fingers settled on the computer's keyboard and he typed in her name to initiate the search.

* * *

"She almost fainted when she saw him," Mia exclaimed, bursting with the story as they settled in around the dining room table for dinner.

Noel had hoped to avoid this moment by declining her mother's dinner invitation, wanting to get back to her own apartment. Not happening though. Leaving Marcy Welsh's home without eating was about as doable as building a sandcastle on the shoreline and hoping it wouldn't be washed away by the tide.

Marcy's gaze swung from the platter of pot roast she was placing on the table to the face of her oldest child. Not quite as tall as her daughter, Marcy carried an extra twenty pounds, most of it around her middle, and her sandy hair was a mix of blonde and gray. She had come to the United States from England as a college student and met Garrett her first week here; they married four years later after their graduation. "You ran into the boy who saved you?"

"Not a boy, Mum. He's a grown man and now a professor at the university," Noel clarified.

"Did you recognize him?" Garrett's flushed face matched what remained of his red hair that was now sprinkled with gray. He lowered himself into the straight-backed chair at the head of the table, his new knee replacement needing a few more weeks of physical therapy before that would be an easy process.

"She took one look at his face and almost fell over," Mia piped up, answering for her.

"Very colorful interpretation, Mi. It wasn't that big a deal." Noel's gaze shifted from her mum to her dad, her voice soothing, the déjà vu she was feeling in this moment making her shudder. Her parents had always been restrictive, but at thirty-two and having finally attained an independent life, she wasn't going back. Noel tried to sidestep her father's mounting concern; his cheeks were as red as his hair used to be. "I didn't recognize him until he said my name. He looks very different from the vague memories I have of a clean-cut college kid."

She wasn't about to tell them that Jeremy's eyes had been flashing through her mind like the glare of a strobe light all afternoon. She'd deal with that later. Right now, she needed to get through this meal without awakening the lioness of her mum's fears.

"You won't be seeing him again?" Marcy's eyes narrowed, accentuating the crow's feet reaching out to her hairline as she studied her oldest child.

"No, of course not. Why would I? It was just a chance encounter." Noel directed her attention to scooping mashed potatoes onto her plate and then passing the bowl to her father.

"He did say he'd write me a letter of recommendation," Mia chimed in.

Noel shot her a warning glance and Mia shut her mouth. "Which has everything to do with you and the great student you are and nothing to do with me."

"Don't you have an interview at the university later this week?" Garrett asked.

"I do," Noel admitted. "But it's a big place and I might not even get the job."

"I don't understand why you feel the need to give up a perfectly good job to pursue something new." Her mother passed the broccoli around the table. "I thought you liked working as a PA in the dermatology office. It pays well and its important work."

"Important, yes, but I can't see myself looking at seborrheic keratosis and other assorted skin lesions for the rest of my life." Noel debated asking the question she had wanted the answer to for so many years, but knowing it would only further this discussion, she set it aside. Yet the words almost slipped from her mouth anyway before she bit them back.

How had the parents who'd been willing to adopt a young girl in the foster care system simply because she had asked them to be the same people who had kept her from saying thank you to the young man who had saved her life? Ignoring such a selfless act went against everything she believed about her family. Noel shook her head. She wasn't going there, not tonight. It was so long ago now. Half a lifetime. Trying to dislodge the question from her brain, she tuned in to the conversation that had turned to Mia's travel basketball team and their chances for a championship season.

An hour later, the kitchen clean and her dad settled in his recliner with his legs elevated in front of the television, Noel hugged her mum before Mia walked her to the door.

"Thanks for taking me today." Mia hooked her arm through Noel's, pulling her in closer as she whispered in her ear. "No need to thank me for changing the dinner discussion to my basketball team instead of the lifesaving professor thing."

"You were the one who started it, remember?" Noel countered under her breath, a smile tweaking her lips.

"I know, and I'm sorry. I should have known better. They still can't talk about it, can they?"

"Not without going into protective mode."

"Good thing I joined this family. Took some of the focus off you," Mia teased.

"You're the best thing that ever happened to us." Noel turned at the door to face her.

Mia hugged her, the embrace quick and fierce. "I love having you as my sister."

"Me, too." Noel dropped a kiss on Mia's brow. "Now go work on that college essay."

Out in her car moments later, Noel felt the tension in her shoulders begin to ebb as she plugged her cell phone into the charger. She backed out of the driveway, the bay window of the ranch-style home reflecting the glow of the setting sun as she recalled the day she had met Mia, a vulnerable eight-year-old with distrust in her eyes and a frown to match.

Noel had just returned to California after completing her undergraduate degree at the University of Maine, and she was still readjusting to the change in climate as she stepped into the gymnasium at the youth center downtown. She had volunteered for the Big Brothers Big Sisters Program during college and then sought out a similar program when she returned home. She'd spotted Mia dribbling a basketball, switching from hand to hand with an ease Noel found remarkable in a girl so young. Mia had then attempted a free throw from the line with an overhand shot, but she couldn't make the distance.

"Can I help?" Noel offered, stepping up next to her.

"Can you play?" Mia looked skeptical even as she glanced upward at Noel. "You're tall enough. Don't mean you can play."

"First team all-state in high school and I played four years in college."

"Okay, show me." Mia handed her the ball.

Noel lifted her arms and with a flick of the wrist sent the ball in an arch toward the basket, where it swished through the net.

"Can you teach me to do that?"

Over the years since their family had adopted Mia, Noel had become used to the double take she and Mia often generated when they walked into a room together, Noel's height and pale hair in stark contrast to Mia's compact, wiry build and ebony skin. Noel had developed an innate sense of when the glances were curious versus something more hostile. She still found it hard to believe that kind of bias still existed, but Mia had set her straight about the depth of her naivete and made her realize she had dismissed the hateful prejudice without considering its real-world impact. Mia's lived experience had given Noel an insight into a world she didn't recognize and hadn't wanted to believe existed.

The shrill ring of her phone interrupted her musings. Noel glanced at the screen, noting the university's name flash across the screen. Thinking this had something to do with her interview, she hit the button on the steering wheel to answer. "Hello."

"Noel Welsh, please."

The male voice sounded deep and resonant through the car speakers and a flicker of recognition dawned.

"This is she."

"Noel, it's Jeremy Finnegan."

"Yes," she said, wondering how he had gotten her cell number.

"After I saw you today . . . I wanted to…" He broke off. "Can we get together and talk? We could meet at the coffeehouse, if you're free."

"Why?" Her surprise at the caller's identity was only allowing one-word responses.

"I wanted to talk to the only person in the world who might understand how that day changed my life. Would you be willing to do that?"

A flicker of fear played across her mind and she was unsure if she could sit across a table from this man and look into his eyes again, but there was a part of her that had always wanted the chance to talk with him. "Yes, I can do that. Ten minutes?"

"Thank you."

"I think I'm the one who needs to do that. See you soon."

# CHAPTER TWO

Jeremy sat at a corner table with his eyes on the door. Around him the coffeehouse buzzed with students grabbing a drink before their night classes. Study groups were gathered at the larger tables, many with the coffeehouse's famous nachos in the center of the table. Other students sat alone, open computers in front of them trying to get a little work done. Conversations and light laughter filled the space. He glanced at his watch: seven p.m. This place would be busy until it closed at midnight.

He shifted in his seat, awaiting Noel's arrival and reflecting on his Internet search that had pulled up very little about her. He'd found her parents' home address and phone number but knew he didn't want to go that route to get in touch with her. Then a quick trip to the admissions office solved the problem. The student working in the office had helped him find the tour list from this morning when Jeremy explained he had misplaced the contact information for a student to whom he had promised a letter of recommendation. Noel had given her cell phone and her e-mail when she registered for the tour. Calling her had been the hard part.

The door to the coffeehouse opened and Noel stepped inside, taking a moment for her eyes to adjust to the dark interior. Backlit by the door closing on a setting sun, her blonde hair fell in soft waves around her face. She was taller than he remembered. He recalled that during their encounter earlier in the day, her gaze was almost level with his. Jeremy got to his feet, unsure if she would recognize him. He looked very different from the skinny kid with the crew cut she might remember from years ago.

The movement caught her eye and she blinked before taking a deep breath and starting toward him. Her stride was easy although her eyes were wary as she approached.

"Thank you for coming." He waved her to the seat across from him.

"Hard to resist the chance to thank you for what you did for me. I'm sorry it's so long in coming. My parents were a bit overbearing back then. Still are sometimes."

"They were protecting you."

She looked up at him, but her gaze didn't quite meet his, settling someplace around his chin. A waitress approached the table and spotting her, Noel shook her head. "They told me they spoke to you. Is that true?"

Jeremy nodded. "I called the hospital to see how you were doing, and I spoke with your mother. She thanked me, but when I asked if I could see you, she refused."

"Did she say why?"

"At the time we spoke, the video, taken by one of the counselors on shore, had already gone viral and the reporters were gathering at the hospital. She sounded overwhelmed and said she didn't want you to relive the whole incident by having to talk about it. So I let it go." Jeremy recalled the look of terror in Noel's eyes as he looked at her through the murky water. "Did you ever see the video?"

Noel shook her head. "No. At first my parents didn't allow me access to a computer, but then later I didn't want to see it. I just wanted to forget. I was so grateful for all you did for me, but I wanted to move on and not let that moment define me."

"And has it? Defined you?" Jeremy watched her eyes narrow and her jaw clench.

"No, but it changed me and changed my family. My parents were always protective, but after nearly losing me they went into overdrive. I was a senior in high school with no social life. They wouldn't even let me get my driver's license. They wanted me to go to college close to home until I exploded on a tour of this campus and told them I was going to school as far away from them as I could get." The fervor in her words triggered a flush that tinged her cheeks.

"Did you do that?"

"I did, but not without some help from the psychologist they sent me to after the accident. She told them they needed to let me go or risk losing me for the rest of their lives."

"Wise woman. How far away did you end up going?"

"All the way across the country. I got a basketball scholarship from the University of Maine." Noel's lips lifted in a flicker of a smile before her expression grew somber. "I'm thinking from what you said on the phone that your heroism has had more than a passing impact on your life, too."

The shift in focus from her life to his made Jeremy realize he hadn't thought this through. Was he really about to share the quandary of his adult life with this woman? She was a stranger to him, and maybe that was the draw. He could tell her, and she would walk away, and they would never see each other again. He studied her across the table, her question lingering in the air as he gathered his thoughts and wondered where to begin. Then he plunged in with the truth.

"Saving you was the only unselfish thing I have ever done. And it changed my life." He registered her quick intake of breath at his words, which sparked an irrational urge to reach out and touch her hand resting atop the table. He restrained the errant impulse. "After the video went viral, I became an instant celebrity. Interviews. Talk shows. I was twenty-two and caught up in a media storm, and I enjoyed the ride. The hero angle makes for a great story and there was talk about a book and a movie. Your parents had refused any media contact since you were still a minor, which left all the attention fixed on me. It was heady stuff. People were inviting me to clubs and galas and hanging on every word."

"Sounds addictive."

"Yes, it was." Jeremy ran a hand through his hair, pushing it back from his face as he leaned in closer. "It made me cocky and arrogant—some would say I still am—and when the media moved on to a new story, I was left feeling discarded. It brought out all my worst instincts. The only thing that saved me from myself was being offered a professorship here at Langford after my master's degree program. The university liked the idea of a hero alumni with a social media following being a part of their faculty. I didn't deserve it, of course, but image is everything in academics these days."

"But you're still here. It seems you made the most of the opportunity."

"I did, but…" He broke off trying to find the words to explain a concept he didn't understand himself. He looked at her, wishing she would lift her eyes to meet his, even as the words left his mouth. "The day I saved you was the single best moment of my life. Nothing before or since has even come close to knowing I was in the right place at the right time and without even thinking about it, I put your needs before my own and made the right choice." As if sensing his disquiet, her gaze shifted upward and met his, her blue eyes wide with concern.

"Words are inadequate to explain the feeling," he continued, trying to explain but knowing it could never come close to the awe—the sheer humility—of that moment. "I was one person in a world of billions but with the power to save one girl's life, your life. I've been chasing that feeling for the last fifteen years. I never found it again."

Noel held his gaze for a moment, her quiet words resonant with fear. "Was I really dead?"

Surprised by the question, Jeremy realized the trauma of the drowning might have left her with few recollections of the day. "You didn't have a pulse and you weren't breathing."

She grimaced. "Sounds like dead to me."

"Do you have any memories of what happened?"

A muscle spasm made her shoulders lift even as she tried to shrug it off, her voice reflective. "More like flashes of scenes in my brain. Are they real? I don't know. They could be memories or dreams or… What do you think happens to us when we die?"

"I'm an atheist. I don't think anything happens to us. We cease to exist." Jeremy sensed that was not the answer she was looking for. "Are you a religious person?"

"No, but I do spend a lot of time thinking about it after what happened. I just don't seem to land in one spot. I was brought up in the Christian faith and attended a Christian nursery school, but only because it was the best academic program in town. My parents took me to church on Christmas and Easter until they heard some off-hand remark by a disgruntled parishioner about all the holiday crowds taking their seats. Then we stopped doing even that."

Jeremy frowned. "Christians in name only; they give the whole faith a bad name. In my work here I have met many wonderful Christians living out their faith by serving others. I like talking to them and I enjoy debating them, but I don't agree with them. No one is out there listening."

"What do you do here at Langford?" Noel asked.

"After I completed my master's degree here on campus I went on to pursue my PhD in neurobiology. Now I teach classes about the structure and function of the brain, and I run a research study about the intersection between the physical brain and consciousness."

Her eyes grew wide. "And you're hiring staff for the study."

"We are. How did you know that?"

"Because I have an interview with Dr. McMann on Friday."

Startled by this sudden confluence of events, Jeremy nodded. "David McMann, yes. His PhD is in biochemistry and he will be working with our subjects. He's the physical arm of the study and I'm the coinvestigator on the administrative side. Can I ask what position you applied for?"

Noel sat up straighter and let her hands fall to her lap. "You advertised for a research coordinator to oversee the selection of subjects for the study and serve as their advocate during the study process. I am currently working as a physician's assistant in a dermatology practice, but during the final year of my degree program I helped facilitate a research study that evaluated life style changes versus the use of pharmaceuticals for patients at high risk for heart disease."

Jeremy leaned forward. "I could put in a good word for you with David."

"Please, don't do that," Noel said, her tone emphatic. "I will either get this position because I am the right person for the job or I won't. I prefer to get this job on my own merits."

Jeremy nodded, understanding the feeling. Although he had been the beneficiary of circumstance, the concept of being deserving was one he'd struggled with for years. "I can understand that. Well, good luck, then."

"Thank you." Noel rose to her feet.

Startled by the abrupt move, Jeremy stood, feeling a wistful longing he could not explain. "Can I walk you to your car?"

Noel eyed him with surprise and a touch of humor. "I don't think I have ever had anyone ask me that. Sure, why not?"

"I was brought up in North Carolina. Those southern habits die hard even if I haven't been back there in years." He liked the smile that lifted her lips. He left a tip on the table and followed her out.

Jeremy pulled the door open for her before she reached for the handle. "My grandmother taught me to open doors for ladies. Hope you don't find it condescending or offensive. I've heard both."

"Yet you still do it." Noel's soft smile gave way to a chuckle.

"It's an old habit I can't shake."

Outside the remaining sunlight had faded into the muted purples of twilight. The solar lights along the pathway to the parking lot glowed in the gathering dusk. A light breeze lifted the overhanging leaves in a gentle rustle as they walked in silence, the darkness creating a sudden intimacy. Jeremy glanced over his shoulder to survey the area behind them before returning his attention to Noel.

"Can I ask you a question?" Jeremy ventured, before this woman disappeared from his life again.

"Sure. After all you saved my life," she quipped, the words losing their brightness as they met the dusky night.

"Did you remember me when we met earlier today?"

Her steps slowed and whether she was couching her answer or retrieving her key fob was an open question.

"Not at first, no." She clicked the fob and lights flashed on a small sedan just a few yards away. "But when I looked in your eyes… "

"You almost collapsed."

"That's a bit dramatic." Noel turned to look at him as they stopped by the driver's side of her car. "It took my breath away is all."

"One look at me did that?" He kept his tone light but found he wanted to hear her answer.

Holding the keys in her hand, she opened the door and then turned back to him in the confines of the open doorway. "To tell you the truth, your eyes haunt my nightmares. All blue and grey and filled with terror. For years I believed what I was seeing in my PTSD flashbacks were my own eyes and my own fears. Until today."

Her words drove the breath from his lungs as he took a step toward her. "I'm so sorry."

"It's not your fault. You were trying to help me, but I could see your fear, that flicker of terror as you looked up at me and realized you might not be able to save me. It's one of the only memories I have of that day." She rubbed one knuckle across her lower lip in a curious gesture before lifting her gaze to meet his, her shoulders square and chin strong. "None of that is your fault, Jeremy. You did everything you could to save me. I will appreciate your bravery for the rest of my life."

Jeremy swallowed, his throat tight. He wasn't sure he could find the words to respond, so he didn't try.

She smiled at him, her words a bit wistful but filled with sincerity. "Someday, when I get past the whole PTSD thing, I'm going to tell my grandkids about you, that they get to be here because of you." She leaned into him and dropped a quick kiss on his cheek.

The touch was fleeting. What his mother used to call an angel kiss, more a wish than a kiss. He heard her parting words as if from a distance, lost in the memory and the strange sensation.

"Thank you." She ducked into the car and started the engine. Jeremy stepped back and watched her pull out of the parking space. He had called her to clear the air, to talk to the only person in the world who'd shared that experience with him, thinking it would somehow give him closure, but now he was left with more questions than answers. The car's taillights gleamed as she hit the brakes before making the turn to leave campus. And although he would honor her wishes and not intervene, he found himself hoping David McMann would be as impressed with her as he was.

* * *

Noel glanced in the rearview mirror before making the turn. He still stood in the spot where she had left him. The parking lot's overhead lighting glinted off his brown hair, although his features were lost to the distance.

Why had she told him? She had never told anyone but her therapist about the images that haunted her dreams. The same ones that would assail her waking hours in a blitz of imagery, blotting out the present and sending her back to the worst moment in her life, her heart racing in panic, her lungs ready to explode with the need to breathe. Now she wasn't the only one who would carry that burden. After all he had done for her that wasn't fair to him. Yet in that moment, she had been unable to do anything but speak the truth. That day connected them in a way that could never be severed, an event so elemental it demanded nothing but the truth in its aftermath. Two strangers brought together by a single moment that changed them both forever, and then spun them off in different directions. The world was full of random encounters. Some left lasting impressions and others faded quickly from memory, but that day had never felt random to her, even if that made no sense.

She didn't spend much time thinking about it, not anymore. It had happened so long ago. Fifteen years. She'd been a kid, and he not much more; both tall and skinny, but he with the broad shoulders of a swimmer. Would she have recognized him if she'd passed him on the street? She didn't think so. He looked very different now; his hair was collar length and hanging in his eyes, his shoulders still broad but his torso muscular like he spent a lot of time lifting weights. No, without that face-to-face encounter she would have passed him by without a second thought. But that chance meeting this morning had brought it all back, and she was afraid all the progress she had made would be undone by the simple act of looking into his eyes. Which made the prospect of going to sleep tonight one she wanted to avoid for a few hours.

She had only been able to identify one sure-fire trigger that incited the terror in her waking hours, but that had nothing to do with what happened today. And the nightmares had no recurrent trigger she had ever been able to discern, although looking into Jeremy's eyes today had been as close to a trigger as she could imagine.

She'd managed to get a handle on the aftereffects of the accident with the therapist her parents had sent her to right after the event. Dr. Blake Dempsey was a child psychologist who specialized in treating trauma victims. Right from the start, Dr. Dempsey had insisted that Noel call her Blake. She was young and relatable, and only thirteen years separated them in age. Noel had liked Blake's calm demeanor, so soothing after the constant hovering of her parents in their obsessive need to keep her safe. Noel had met with Blake every week of her senior year. After the first few months they'd included her parents in some of the sessions as Blake began to suspect the trauma of the accident was being compounded by the viselike hold these two loving parents were trying to exert on their daughter's life. Blake had helped her parents see that Noel's desire for independence was a healthy path in her healing process and had encouraged them to allow their daughter to go away to college if that was her choice. Their therapy sessions became virtual visits when Noel started as a freshman at the University of Maine. Knowing the expense had always been a stretch for her parents' finances, Noel had discontinued the sessions in her sophomore year after most of the traumatic aftereffects of the near drowning had resolved.

The two women hadn't seen each other for years after that but in an odd twist of fate, after Noel started her work as a PA at the dermatology practice, she ran into Blake in the produce section of the grocery store. A brief conversation resulted in her referring Blake to Dr. Tess Elliot, her employer, for a suspicious lesion on her arm. The biopsy taken in the office was diagnosed as melanoma and had been followed up by a wide local excision of the cancer by a surgeon. Blake's follow-up call to thank Noel for her referral had been the start of a friendship that had become an anchor in Noel's life. Released from the bounds of their earlier relationship, they became friends, having found in each other a kindred spirit. Noel had worried that might change when Blake met Daniel and they were married on Blake's fortieth birthday, but it never had. Having grown up as an only child, Noel had within the space of a few years found two of the most important people in her life, Mia and Blake, each of them a sister of her soul, one older and one younger, making her the middle child between them.

She used the voice commands on her phone to connect the call.

"Perfect timing. I just got the kids to bed." Blake answered the phone with no preamble.

"Blake, I… is Daniel with you?"

"No. The firm sent him to Nashville for a few days."

"Would it be okay if I stopped by?"

"Of course, anytime. I always have time for you."

"Is five minutes too soon? I'm in the car."

"Perfect. I'll make some tea."

Dressed in black yoga pants and a loose-fitting teal t-shirt that bore the remnants of the twins' spaghetti dinner, Blake greeted her at the door with a warm hug as she pulled Noel into the spacious open floor plan of the renovated split level. At forty-five, Blake looked much the same as Noel remembered from the first day they met, although the glasses resting atop her dark hair were now a permanent addition to her usual attire. They settled on the massive sectional facing the fireplace. Blake handed her a warm mug of herbal tea.

"How do you always know what I need?" Noel wrapped her hands around the mug and took a sip.

"We've been friends a long time." Blake reached for her own mug, relaxing back into the couch cushions. "Tell me what's going on."

"How did you know…"

"Friends, remember?"

Noel smiled, gathering her thoughts as she slipped off her shoes and pulled her legs up, her mug resting atop her knees. "I ran into Jeremy Finnegan today."

Blake's eyes widened. "The man who saved you?"

"Yes. He almost bowled me over on campus this morning with Mia." Noel filled in the details of the college tour and the encounter with Jeremy, ending with the dinner with her parents and the phone call in her car. "Was I crazy to say yes to meeting him? I didn't even think twice about it; I just agreed." She took a sip of her tea, the smooth hint of mint playing over her tongue.

Blake sat up straighter. Turning to face Noel, she crossed her legs in front of her. "Can we go back to the beginning? What you experienced when you realized who he was, that sudden visceral feeling, was it a PTSD event?"

Noel shook her head. "No. It wasn't a flashback; it was more like when someone comes up behind you and yells. My heart raced and I couldn't breathe, then my legs gave way. I might have gone down if he hadn't caught me."

Blake thought for a moment. "Would you have told your parents about seeing Jeremy if Mia hadn't done it for you?"

"No!" Noel responded, her tone agitated. "After all the work you and I did together, I understand why they felt the need to protect me, but I am never letting them exert that much control over my life again. If it hadn't been for you, I might still be fighting to break free. Those four years away at school gave me back my life."

"Okay, just clarifying. So why do you think you said yes when Jeremy called?"

Noel's gaze shifted, watching the tea swirl in her mug as she tried to find the words to explain. "I think surprise was a factor. I couldn't believe he'd found my number. And there was something in his voice, something uncertain and urgent. I answered without thinking, like a part of me had been waiting for the chance to talk to him, too. Which sounds silly…"

"Not silly at all. You never had the chance to talk to the person who shared that experience with you, and the instinct to talk about it, if we don't suppress it, is as natural as breathing." Blake sat forward, her elbows propped on her knees and her hands encircling her mug. "Tell me why you came here tonight. It would seem the chance to talk with this man hasn't given you the closure you thought it might."

"I'm afraid to go to sleep. I haven't had that dream in quite a while and I'm afraid that looking into Jeremy's eyes again is going to bring it all back."

"Understandable."

"There's more. I realized today that the eyes I see in my dreams aren't mine—they're Jeremy's."

Blake sat up straighter and gave her an assessing glance. "Are you sure? We had been working under the assumption that you were seeing a mirror image of your own thoughts and feelings."

"But when I looked into his eyes today, I knew that wasn't the case."

"So a memory then?"

"Yes. Does this mean it's all coming back?" Noel shuddered at the possibility. One image was terrifying enough. She stood, pacing to the window overlooking the back yard where wagons and trikes, balls and mini golf clubs decorated the lawn.

"Your conscious memories of that day stop at getting into the boat with the campers, right? And then nothing after that but the disembodied eyes in the murky water and the sensations of drowning?"

Noel swallowed hard, the backyard scene unfocused as her thoughts turned inward. There was something else. She had never been able to put it into words, a vague memory of intense pressure and weightlessness, of fading light and inky darkness, of waning warmth and bone-chilling cold—a juxtaposition of opposites that made no sense. Was that what it felt like to die?

From behind her she heard Blake's questioning tone. "Is there something else, Noel?"

"Nothing I can put into words right now." Noel turned to face her.

"It is possible seeing Jeremy has triggered something in your brain."

"Maybe I shouldn't have met him tonight. But when I heard his voice on the phone with that flicker of hesitation as if he was asking me a favor, I just responded. So what can I do about it now?

"The problem right now is fear of sleeping, right? So let's get out in front of it," Blake suggested.

Noel's shoulders quivered, the room cold. "We haven't done that in a long time."

It was a form of guided meditation, where the dream was recalled in a controlled setting to create a memory of a different way to respond. They had done this together many times during their professional relationship, resulting in a significant decrease in her nightmares in the months after the near drowning, The technique was one Noel had used on her own during the years that followed to address situations that made her anxious, although she had always felt it never worked quite as well without Blake.

"Would you like to try it?"

Noel nodded, retrieving one of the straight-backed chairs from the dining room and taking a seat. She closed her eyes as the soothing sounds of Blake's voice directed her to breathe in and out to induce a state of relaxation and focus before bringing any images to mind.

"Remember you are in control," Blake said. "You can shut this down at any time, but for the moment just breathe. Feel the sensation of air moving in and out through your nose. If you observe any feeling of tightness in your chest or shoulders, just let them flow away."

Moments later, Blake's words played across her consciousness, recalling the images of that long-ago day. "You are under the water now. See the eyes as if you were watching a movie, feel the emotions echoing through the water as if from far away, the sensation distant. Allow it to flow away from you."

Noel had almost no memories of that day but focused on the one she did have: the blue eyes wide with terror. She registered Jeremy's fear and let it wash away like the waves of a tide. The image of his eyes faded into the murky stillness of the water, a ray of sunlight filtering down from the surface to produce just enough light to see in the greenish depths. A few minutes later, Blake guided her back to the surface of the water and directed her to open her eyes. "How are you feeling?"

"Like I just stepped out of a warm bath. Relaxed. Drowsy and a little cold. That works so much better with you guiding the meditation than it does when I try to do it myself."

They settled back into the couch and fell into their usual exchange of stories about Blake's four-year-old twins and Mia's basketball team.

A few minutes later, Noel retrieved her bag from the floor and Blake walked her to the door.

"Good luck with the interview this week," Blake said, pulling open the door for her.

In all they'd talked about Noel had forgotten to mention the connection between Jeremy Finnegan and the research study, but it would keep. She had already taken up too much of her friend's time, and the twins would be up before dawn.

Noel hugged her. "Thanks for tonight."

"Glad I could help. Can you text me in the morning and let me know how the night goes?"

"I will." Noel reached for the keys in her pocket. "You are a good friend."

"Says the woman who saved my sanity and helped me keep the twins alive during that first year of total madness. I wouldn't have made it through that year without you."

"We're good for each other."

"Yes, we are. Text me tomorrow."

# CHAPTER THREE

"When do we expect to be done with the interviews for the rest of the staff?" Jeremy strode into David McMann's office.

"Good morning, Jeremy. No time for niceties, I see." David raised an eyebrow, looking up from his computer at the sudden interruption. "We should be done by the end of the week. I have several more interviews scheduled for Friday. Did the IRB give us the final approval?"

"No, but they will. They seemed satisfied with my answers." Jeremy hoped that was true after the amount of time he'd spent with them yesterday.

"Did you manage not to antagonize them this time?" David peered over the top of his glasses. His dark hair, peppered with gray, was cut short, buzzed close to his head to detract from his receding hairline. He was ten years older than Jeremy, a friend and mentor, although they had been known to butt heads on academic matters. Both were strong willed and sure of their own positions. "I would think by now you'd have learned the importance of tact with the people who hold your future research prospects in their hands."

"I was never very good at the whole schmoozing thing," Jeremy admitted.

"Tell me something I don't know," David countered. "Yet somehow you're still the wonder kid with the social media following."

"You don't need to be tactful on social media, just bold and out there and…"

"Arrogant? I think you've got that covered then."

Jeremy scowled. He'd heard that a lot. "How many interviews do you have left?"

"Three. I need to find the right person for the research coordinator position. It needs just the right mixture of professionalism, organization, and poise, someone with the ability to put our subjects at ease."

Jeremy was tempted to mention he knew one of the job applicants but managed to keep it to himself. He'd promised Noel he wouldn't insert himself into the process.

"Don't worry. I've got the staffing covered. When the IRB comes through with the approval, we'll be ready," David said. "Shouldn't you be back in your office preparing for your debate tonight? I hear it's close to a sold-out forum."

"I'm ready." Jeremy redirected his thoughts from Noel to this man who had mentored him in his fledgling years as a professor. "This isn't the first time I've done this."

"Yes, I know you're an adept speaker for the atheist point of view, but it's the first time you've debated a Christian with the standing of Patrick Mueller. He's brilliant in the debate setting, so I hear."

"A worthy opponent on the debate stage can take either side and argue it well," Jeremy said, even as David's warning played in his head.

"Could you do that?" David leaned forward, his gaze curious. "Could you argue for belief in Christ with the same fervor as you advocate for atheism?"

"I know all the arguments for belief. You have to, in order to counter their position." Still, it was a good question, and one Jeremy had pondered himself.

"But could you do it so well you could induce a panel of judges to vote for you?" David pierced him with a knowing stare. "That seems to require not just knowledge but fervor."

"It's possible to win a debate on points alone without being on board with the position you're taking. But speaking to something you don't believe in your heart requires some good theatrical skills. I don't think I'm that good an actor."

"Ah, a rare moment of modesty," David quipped. "Good thing for tonight's forum you believe every word you're saying."

"I just let the facts speak for themselves."

"I wish you luck," David said, meeting his gaze. "Just a word of advice from an old friend and fellow academic: Don't underestimate Mueller. Just because you don't believe a word he's saying doesn't mean the judges won't find him convincing."

"I hear you. Thanks for the reminder."

* * *

Noel sat in the upper level of the auditorium as the lights dimmed. As she had toured the campus with Mia yesterday, she had seen tonight's forum advertised in multiple locations around campus. At the time, the name hadn't registered, but after meeting Jeremy last night, she found the idea of observing the man in this anonymous setting to be an irresistible one.

She had slept fitfully last night, waking many times and having a hard time getting back to sleep, which left her feeling tired as dawn brightened the window of her cottage apartment. Thankful for the absence of nightmares, she doubled up on coffee and headed off to work. A flier at the sandwich shop where she'd grabbed lunch planted an idea she kept returning to throughout the afternoon. Interested in learning more about the man she had known as a co-counselor, she had gone online and purchased one of the last available tickets.

As the house lights dimmed, Noel watched the two men step on stage from her perch in the second row of the mezzanine. Meeting center stage, they shook hands before retreating to podiums on either side of the moderator. Jeremy was dressed more casually than his opponent, wearing a navy blazer with a blue dress shirt open at the collar and khaki trousers, his hair combed back from his face revealing chiseled features. At just over six feet, his broad shoulders made him a commanding presence. His opponent, Patrick Mueller, was shorter in stature, his compact body slim and radiating confident energy. He wore an impeccable gray suit and white shirt with a deep purple tie that contrasted with the dark tones of his skin. He appeared to be a good twenty years older than Jeremy, and his gaze was earnest behind wire-rimmed glasses.

The debate began with brief opening statements, followed by the moderator asking a simple question: Does God exist? A discussion of the meaning of the word God ensued. The two men sparred in a relaxed manner that put the audience at ease, dispensing with the antagonism that often characterized these discussions. They were well matched, each familiar with the arguments of the other as the discussion turned to the question of the origin of the universe.

The exchange took a surprising turn when Patrick Mueller offered up an irresistible proposition to his opponent in a measured baritone. "What if I were to grant you the evolution concept just to widen the discussion? I do think the demonstrable science has not caught up with the level of acceptance the theory continues to receive, but I find myself open to the possibility such science may be found in the future."

Jeremy leaned backward, his arms extended and his hands gripping the podium. His expression was wary as he looked out into the audience, taking a moment to assess the softball Mueller had just offered up. Jeremy's eyes narrowed, returning to his opponent as Patrick removed his glasses and squeezed the bridge of his nose before settling the glasses back in place as he continued.

"So if we go all the way back to the primordial soup and the origin of amino acids being synthesized from a pool of elements such as hydrogen and nitrogen, where did the hydrogen come from?" Mueller asked.

"The origin of earth and its elements was the natural result of the evolving universe."

"You would espouse the big bang theory then, a vast explosion of seismic proportions that seeded the universe with the building blocks of life?" Mueller clarified, his tone questioning.

"I believe the images we have received from the Hubble telescope of distant regions of space would substantiate that belief, yes," Jeremy affirmed.

"And the energy for that initial explosion? How was it generated?" Mueller countered.

"All volatile gases are capable of producing explosions in the right proportions," Jeremy responded in an even tone.

"True. Volatile gases could do that. But where did the gases come from? Something cannot be derived from nothing. It's physically impossible in a universe with mass and energy." Mueller's remarks landed with no triumph or undertone of righteousness.

Noel recognized that by accepting the basic premise of the initial question Jeremy had been drawn down this pathway.

"I'm just postulating the hand of a designer who breathed the universe into being at the very start," Mueller continued. "Would you see it as a possible explanation of the quandary?"

"I would not," Jeremy answered. "To assume the existence of a designer simply because we have not discovered the science yet is taking the easy way out of continuing to look for the natural answer that lies out there but is not yet known."

Noel could sense his irritation, although his face was neutral as the rebuttal landed and the debate moved on. After purchasing the ticket for tonight's debate, Noel had done a brief Internet search on Jeremy Finnegan. Avoiding stories of the heroics that had rocketed him to fame, she focused on his published work. Much of it was on the intersection between the brain and the phenomena of consciousness. His declaration that he'd been relegated to the realms of insignificance after his initial media following seemed to be exaggerated. The social media presence he'd maintained in his early career had aided him in getting his work published and establishing himself as an academic force in the world that was now his home. The atheist views he espoused had grown out of his study of the brain's biochemistry and had gained him additional followers for his ability to articulate what so many believed: that religion and God were unnecessary in a time of emerging science. He believed ethics and morality could exist without a deity to guide them. Recently having completed a ten-city tour debating renowned Christian academics, he had won praise for his clear arguments and unflappable manner. His growing recognition had drawn the attention of several fundamentalist groups who had vented their ire on his website.

The moderator posed his next question: Was there a potential benefit to society of belief in God?

"I don't think belief in a deity benefits humanity in any way," Jeremy asserted, the first to speak on this topic. "Our inborn ethics would never lead us down the path to disaster that has been the fallout of religious fervor throughout history. In fact, I would pose a counter assertion to the moderator's question; I believe more harm has been done to society in the name of religion than by any other single cause. The slaughter of innocents by the crusaders trying to reclaim the Holy Land for the church of Rome was an atrocity. Likewise, the hatred of those we characterize as 'other' just because they hold a different view of god is appalling. So many lives have been taken in wars, gas chambers, and bombings, all to rid the world of people who don't believe the same thing we do about a nonexistent god. The world would be a better place, a safer place, without god."

Mueller lifted his gaze to meet Jeremy's, his initial nod conceding some agreement with his opponent. "I will agree that many horrors have been inflicted on the innocent, but here is where we would differ. I don't think those acts were committed for God. I think they were perpetrated by men who, although they had God's name on their lips, had nothing but hatred in their hearts and a lust for power. True believers do not kill to convince others to believe; they serve with humility and meet the needs of the broken. Extremists abound in all belief systems. In Christianity they were called crusaders, in Judaism they were zealots, and in Islam they are jihadists. But the willingness to use violence against others as a means of extermination or conversion is the hallmark of an unbeliever, a soul who knows nothing about the one true God."

"On that point, we agree, Mr. Mueller. Good men can disagree without their personal beliefs infringing on the rights of others." Jeremy met Patrick's gaze, and the two men nodded as the moderator moved on to his next question about the origin of consciousness.

Noel watched a smile tweak the corners of Jeremy's mouth as Mueller got first crack at this one.

Mueller waved a hand at his opponent in a gesture of acknowledgement. "Now, this is much more Dr. Finnegan's area of expertise than mine."

A low rumble of laughter rolled up from the audience. "And because we both know the arguments of our opponent as part of our preparation for tonight, I will tell you that Dr. Finnegan is about to confound you with all the structures, chemicals, and receptors in the brain about which he is an expert. He is going to assert that the phenomena of consciousness is nothing more than the interactions of these physical components that live inside our skulls. Am I right?"

Jeremy smiled, playing along. "Yes, in a nutshell."

"Good, I'm glad I got that part right." Mueller pretended to wipe his brow in a gesture of relief. "With that said, it is my assertion that consciousness can exist apart from the physical brain. For example, some experts would point to the transcendental state achieved during meditation as existing outside the realms of the mind."

"I would agree it is an altered state of consciousness," Jeremy concurred, "but it still derives from a functioning brain. If I were to injure the brain during that meditative state, consciousness would be lost until such time as the brain recovered from the impact. We see this with patients of traumatic brain injury who reemerge from coma. The brain's ability to heal is a remarkable process, but absent a functioning brain there is no consciousness."

Mueller leaned forward with his hands splayed on the podium. "In the past few decades, the phenomena of near-death experiences has changed the way we look at consciousness. These patients were clinically dead with no heartbeat or respirations, all of it documented by their medical records, and yet when resuscitated they report having experiences after their clinical death with a distinct similarity in many of the reported accounts."

Noel shivered, her eyes fixed on stage, Patrick Mueller's words drawing her in.

Jeremy met his opponent's gaze. "They are the final activity of a dying brain. We know that when the heart stops there exists a brief period of time, many would say four to six minutes, where the brain is still alive before the lack of oxygen causes the cells to die. If a person is revived during that time, they can go on to function normally. But the experiences you describe are the final synaptic firings of a dying brain."

Noel clasped her hands together, her palms damp. The utter silence of the audience indicated their interest in the exchange.

"So how do you account for the similarity of experiences described by people from all over the world and of all different religions?" Mueller followed up. "They often describe moving through a tunnel of light surrounded by a feeling of warmth and peace. Some even describe meeting a presence at the end of the journey."

"The subjects of near-death experiences often mention a life review as well as the other images you spoke of, but this is the brain in its last living moments flooded with the memories accumulated over a lifetime. It is a biochemical process as the cells starved of oxygen fire one last time," Jeremy asserted, his broad stance radiating his confidence on this subject.

Noel shook her head, the intrusive tentacles of a memory trying to break free.

"And the out-of-body experience so many describe, of being able to look down from above and see the people trying to save their lives, what are we to make of that?" Mueller continued. "Many are able to give detailed accounts of the resuscitation that brought them back to life."

"Research on coma patients has shown that hearing is still present even in states of deep unconsciousness because the brain is still working on some level. I believe these subjects are hearing the people fighting to save them, and the out-of-body experience is akin to the dreaming state of weightlessness and flight," Jeremy countered. "Again, a return to familiar imagery as the cells die."

Noel realized she had heard all these arguments before, and a memory surfaced, hazy and unclear. Her whispered words upon awakening at the hospital, disintegrating into tearful sobs, that were swiftly shut down by the crisp tones of a no-nonsense physician who had no time or patience for teenage hysterics. Intimidated by his brusque manner, she had relegated the imagery to the recesses of her mind. She chose to mention it only to Blake, and even that had been a glossing over of the event. Noel didn't often think of it in relation to that day, the PTSD images holding sway as her primary memory. Still, sometimes in the drifting moments between wakefulness and sleep, she could feel the warmth of an all-encompassing peace and she would sleep without nightmares.

Mueller posed a final rebuttal. "Some describe the experience of meeting a relative they never knew they had. That couldn't be a dying memory when no foreknowledge of such a person existed. Wouldn't that seem to imply a state of existence beyond what we can see? Especially when most of the subjects of near-death experiences go on to hold a firm belief in God."

"I believe our minds hold more in terms of memory and experience than we even realize on a conscious level," Jeremy said, his tone measured. "Some memories are accessible and others are not, but knowledge of an unknown relative is the trace memory of an overheard conversation, a photo seen or perhaps, in some cases, a genetic remnant carried on our DNA that manifests itself in the last moment of life. All with a physical cause."

"Except the faith," Mueller asserted. "The question is then: Are science and faith in opposition to one another?"

Jeremy's answer was swift. "If I remember your scripture correctly, it says that faith is 'the assurance of things hoped for and the conviction of things not seen.' But I would say hope has no place in the realms of science, and conviction comes from demonstratable facts, which would make faith a choice to suspend the conscious mind and believe in a being you cannot see and whose presence you cannot demonstrate."

"And I would conclude that faith and science are indeed compatible as we continue to discover the mysteries of the universe God set in motion in ages past," Mueller offered with a warm smile. "The exquisite order of mathematics, the perfection of musical harmony—both demonstrate the order and design of the universe. Did man discover the perfection or was it revealed to him? A question for the ages. But I see science and faith, not in opposition to one another but rather as two sides of the same coin. One is the world we have already discovered and the other is the world we have yet to understand but whose explanation is out there awaiting the minds to whom God will reveal the truth so they can explain it to the rest of us."

The moderator spoke up, bringing the debate to a close. The three judges considered their ruling and handed their decision to the moderator, who announced the results. "We have a split decision tonight, with the majority going to Dr. Jeremy Finnegan."

The audience clapped as the two men met at center stage, shook hands again, and exchanged a few words as the house lights came up.

Noel picked up her bag and found herself on the end of a long line exiting the upper level. By the time she reached the ground floor, the remnants of the crowd had thinned, making her exit from the building easier. She wasn't relishing the walk across campus in the dark, though. The sky had been a haze of purple and gray twilight when she had surrendered her ticket at the door, but it was fully dark now.

"Noel."

Hearing her name, she turned. Her eyes widened as she saw Jeremy striding toward her, his blazer slung over one shoulder and his hair returned to the disheveled state she remembered from yesterday. She hadn't thought she would see him in person and felt a bit flustered as he covered the distance between them.

Jeremy stopped in front of her. Their eyes were almost level. "Thanks for coming."

Noel had no idea how to respond; it wasn't like he'd invited her to come, and she felt like a teenager who'd been caught in the act of spying on a boy in high school.

"What did you think of the debate?" Jeremy asked with a smile.

"I thought you were well matched," Noel offered, finding her voice. "Both confident in your positions, well prepared, and able to answer the questions without the arguing tone that makes it hard to listen. You managed to put the audience at ease."

"Interesting. I felt that, too. Patrick is a worthy opponent and a very impressive man. I enjoyed talking with him on stage and off."

"Had you met him before tonight?"

"No, but we had a chance to speak before the debate began. He's one of those people who puts you at ease, the kind of guy you could sit across from at dinner and have the same discussion we had tonight. I had to refocus on the debate before we started, and I was doing well until I spotted you in the audience."

Startled, Noel took a step back and met his gaze. "How could you possibly have seen me among the hundreds of people who were there?"

"Good question. I don't usually look at the audience during a debate, but when I did you were the first person I saw. Maybe it was the seat. The first two rows of the mezzanine are quite visible. Threw me for a minute and then Patrick took advantage and led me down the intelligent design pathway. Shows what happens when you lose focus."

"I'm sorry."

"Not your fault. I was just surprised, is all." He paused. "Have you got time for a drink before heading home?"

Noel knew that having a drink with this man who might soon be her boss wasn't a smart idea. "I've got an early day tomorrow. Seeing patients at seven a.m. in the office. I think I'll have to pass."

"At least let me walk you to your car then."

"Two nights in a row. Chivalry is not dead."

Jeremy's smile faded. "We've had a series of snatch and grabs on campus as well as several incidences of vandalism, so out of an abundance of caution I would feel better if you just said yes."

"Then, yes." She watched the smile return to his eyes as they set off across campus. "Do I need to worry about Mia applying here?"

"No. The police are investigating the situation and campus security have amped up their night rounds. Just being cautious," Jeremy said, matching her stride. "Did Patrick win you over to the faith side tonight?"

"No, although I found some of his arguments compelling." In her peripheral vision, she saw his mouth open, and she cut him off rather than go into the details. "Have you always been an atheist?"

"No, I was raised in the Christian faith, but I always got the feeling my father's decision to join a faith community was more about the contacts you could make rather than the scripture or the service. My father is a superior court judge duly elected by the citizens of North Carolina."

"And your mother?" In the silence that followed, Noel sensed his upbringing had not been an easy one.

"My mother was beautiful and fragile and spent most of my childhood in and out of psychiatric facilities for depression."

"I'm sorry," Noel said, barely able to imagine an upbringing without a mother. "That must have been hard for you."

Noel saw his jaw clench. Clearly, his family was complicated.

"Even when she was home, she wasn't really there." Jeremy's words were dismissive but had an undertone that sounded almost wistful. "Kind of ironic: her name is Hope, and she never had any, not in that household." Jeremy shook his head as if driving the memory from his thoughts. "Can we go back to the debate? I'd much prefer to hear your take on it rather than further this discussion about my estranged family."

Intrigued by the comment, she couldn't help asking, "How long has it been since you've seen them?"

"More than ten years."

Startled, Noel asked, "Do you have siblings?"

"Three brothers and an older sister."

"And you haven't seen any of them?"

"Nope. And barring a miracle from a god I don't believe in, it'll stay that way."

All Noel's life she had longed for a big family, for siblings to talk to and play with and to share the parental attention, but until they'd adopted Mia, she had been an only child. She'd always wondered why, but the pain in her mother's eyes when Noel had asked and the evasive nature of her answers had kept Noel from pursuing the issue.

"Can we talk about the debate now?" Jeremy asked, changing the subject.

"Because you like talking about yourself?" Noel quipped, her tone teasing.

"I've never been accused of modesty," Jeremy responded in kind, "and I do like talking about my accomplishments. But in the interest of learning to be better on the debate stage, what was Patrick's most convincing point?"

Noel's thoughts returned to the debate's final exchange, her pulse racing. The words were on the tip of her tongue, but she bit them back as a tremor shook her shoulders.

Jeremy reached for her arm, his touch gentle, as he pulled her to a stop. "It must have dropped twenty degrees when the sun went down. Here, take this."

He held his jacket open for her and, rather than clarify the misunderstanding, she slipped her arms into the sleeves. Pulling the jacket around her as she turned back to him, she was engulfed in a wave of male scents, of fabric pressed with a hot iron and the remnants of a crisp bodywash that hinted of the beach. A lingering scent of cologne along the jacket's collar flooded her senses as Jeremy leaned toward her and straightened the collar.

"Warmer?"

"Yes, thank you." The jacket's weight settled on Noel's shoulders, the lining silky against her neck and arms, the moment more intimate than the gallant gesture warranted. Flustered by the sensations, she responded to his earlier question with more truthfulness than she might have otherwise. "I think the near-death experiences were Mr. Mueller's most intriguing argument. You could feel it in the audience; they were spellbound. It's the one thing that could almost convince me to believe."

"Sounds like you want to believe?" Jeremy's tone was interested and held no hint of judgment as they resumed their trek across campus

"Maybe I do."

"With so many books written about near-death experiences in recent years that would be understandable. It reinforces what so many people want to believe about an afterlife. Doesn't make it true, though."

Noel glanced over at him. "Perhaps, but if the aim is for you to counter his arguments, then you need to come up with additional points to disprove an event many people want to believe in. Simply reiterating that it's a function of a dying brain only goes so far."

"But it is."

"So you say, but repeating the same argument to hammer home the point does just the opposite. It makes it look like you have nothing else to say while your opponent continues to add fuel to the fire, citing the out-of-body experiences and the meeting with unknown relatives."

"Good point. I'll give that some thought. Very helpful critique." Jeremy nodded. "Are you ready for your interview on Friday?"

Noel slowed her pace. "You didn't speak to Dr, McMann…"

"No. You are on your own, Noel."

Hearing her name on his lips brought back a memory of their chance encounter yesterday and with it a visceral sensation of stomach-plunging shock and warm familiarity. "Thank you."

"I will say you have a bit of competition, though. You are one of three candidates being considered for the job." He stopped short as the Laraby Science Center came into view.

Noel stopped beside him, her gaze riveted to the shining glass façade of the massive building now marred by the bold orange letters from a can of spray paint.

IN GOD WE TRUST.

Noel could feel Jeremy's mounting rage. "Is this the vandalism you were talking about?"

"Yes." His tone was crisp. The single word pulsed with fury held in check.

"This doesn't feel like a random act."

"It's not. It's a message for me." He took her arm, and although his whole body radiated tension, his touch was gentle. He guided her away from the angry letters so in contrast with the message of the words.

"This isn't the first time, is it?" Noel glanced back at the building again as Jeremy steered her toward the parking lot.

"No, twice before. Different message, same theme."

The tension in his hand resting at her elbow was unmistakable. She reached for her key fob as they approached her car. Shrugging out of his jacket, she handed it back to him as the night air chilled her bare skin.

"Drive carefully, Noel, and good luck with the interview."

"Anything I need to know if I'm considering joining your team?" Noel angled her head toward the fluorescent letters still visible between the trees.

"No. It's just a nuisance and time consuming for the custodial staff to clean up. My views seem to have drawn some local ire. Take care, Noel."

She watched his long even gait as he strode away from her toward the building that was his professional home, the disparity between his calm words and angry stride all the more remarkable for the contrast.

# CHAPTER FOUR

The e-mails had started a few weeks ago. Their tone was menacing, and the sender's observations of the campus grew more pointed with each one. Jeremy opened the latest one on his computer the following morning. He'd spent the hours after the debate talking with campus security, the local police, and the university president who had suggested he tone down his atheist rhetoric for a while. Jeremy chafed at the idea that some errant group of thugs could disrupt his first amendment rights to free speech at a university that prided itself on open discussion and diversity.

How could this group of miscreants—it had to be a group given the speed with which they carried out the vandalism—share the same faith tradition as the intelligent persuasive man Jeremy had debated last night? Patrick Mueller was an ardent believer in God, but his belief was based in diligent research and faith, not the twisted zealot beliefs of this crazed group of extremists. He scanned the text of the e-mail again.

**In the beginning God created the heavens and the earth. No primordial slime. No evolution. No big bang. Our country was**

**founded on a belief in the one Almighty God. So many have turned away from this core belief, convinced they can live without the very God who created them. God will not be ignored. The time of reckoning is near for all who have turned from the WORD.**

Whoever had written this had been there at the debate last night, sitting in the same audience with so many of Jeremy's students and colleagues. And Noel. The anger he'd felt last night at the jarring sight of the harsh orange letters welled up in him again. He had been wrong to dismiss this as some random act of vandalism. The tone of these e-mails was growing more strident and unbalanced. Jeremy believed in the arguments he made last night, but his focus had always been more intellectual rather than rooted in some deep core belief. He had become well known for his atheist views because he could articulate the arguments well. He loved the debate stage, the back and forth of well-argued opinions and the testing of a worthy opponent. He found the challenge stimulating, appealing to his competitive nature. But this emotion-driven missive was steeped in rage and the last line was ominous in its tone.

Jeremy forwarded the e-mail to the detective he had spoken with last night who had asked to see the previous two. A computer pop-up asked him if he wanted to include the attachment, drawing his attention to the small box below the bold text. He debated forwarding the message without opening it, but his need to know got the better of him. He clicked on the attachment as a knock sounded on the door.

A tall man, dressed in a pair of khaki pants and a navy golf shirt, stood in the doorway with a pretty dark-haired woman at his side. Startled by the man's familiar features, so like his own, Jeremy shot to his feet to greet his older brother.

"Will! What are you doing here?"

Will let the woman precede him through the doorway and then stepped up beside her. "I don't get to the West Coast often, so I thought I'd take advantage and say hello. Jeremy, I'd like you to meet my wife, Cherie Finnegan." The name lingered on his lips as if he enjoyed saying the words.

Startled by the unexpected appearance of a brother he hadn't seen in over a decade, Jeremy rounded the desk and held out his hand first to Cherie and then to Will. "Very nice to meet you. Have you been married long?"

"Five days," Cherie said with a brilliant smile.

"We're here on our honeymoon," Will added.

"And you're choosing to spend some of that time with me? I'm honored." Jeremy clasped his brother's hand with a firm grip and then waved them over to the chairs opposite his desk. He had no idea what to make of this unexpected visit from a brother he had always looked up to—not physically; they were close in height—but the four-year difference between them had created a bit of hero worship in Jeremy's younger years. That feeling had faded in the years after Will left for college when he, like their sister Maddie, had left home and never looked back, setting up a pattern of abandonment that Jeremy had also repeated. It seemed their father's emotional abuse had taken its toll on all the siblings.

Will and Cherie took the offered seats. Not wanting to return to the far side of his desk as he would with a student, Jeremy shifted backward and let the desk take his weight.

"We don't want to take up a lot of your time during your workday, but we were hoping you might have time to meet us for dinner," Will said. "We're in town for three more days, doing some hiking and taking a few tours of the local wineries. Any of those nights work for us if you are free."

Jeremy's first inclination had been to decline, but Will's leaving the choice of evening up to him made that more difficult.

"We'd love to have you join us," Cherie reiterated. "And bring someone, of course, if you like. A friend or wife, perhaps?"

"I haven't been as fortunate as the two of you." Jeremy smiled. A fleeting image of Noel walking beside him last night and wearing his jacket flashed through his mind before he dismissed it.

"We were thinking Mexican food?" Will suggested. "I seem to remember you liking it, the hotter the better. I checked out a place a few miles from here, Mi Abuela's Casa Grande?"

Clearly, Will had done his homework, doing all he could to get his brother to agree, which made Jeremy wonder why he was reaching out after all this time. "It's great. Hard to get a table, though."

"I already have one. Table for four. Tonight and tomorrow night. Your choice." Will leaned forward.

"Hard to say no to one of my favorite places," Jeremy replied.

"We were hoping you'd say that," Cherie added. "We never get to do Mexican food at home, so this is a treat. The girls hate it."

"Girls?"

"We have three," Will said, with a touch of pride.

"That's quick work, even for you," Jeremy quipped.

"My second marriage. Will's first." Cherie smiled. "He's surrounded by girls now."

"And loving every minute." Will's grin was broad. "We'll tell you all about it over dinner. Tomorrow?"

"Sure, since you went to the trouble of looking me up on your honeymoon. What time?"

"Seven." Will got to his feet with Cherie right beside him. "I'll text you to confirm. Same cell number?"

Jeremy's cell number had been the same since college. "Yup. I'll meet you there."

"See you tomorrow."

The two men shook hands and the couple departed, leaving Jeremy standing in the middle of his office wondering what had just happened. How had he been talked into sharing a meal with a man he hadn't seen since the day he graduated from college? Perhaps in his subconscious mind that was why he had agreed.

The day of his graduation had been stifling, the campus mobbed with graduates and their families trying to find each other after the graduation ceremony. Clusters of people milled about taking pictures on their phones, all with proud beaming smiles for their graduate. Jeremy exited the open-air stadium, the shirt beneath his graduation gown clinging to his skin, a lone figure in a sea of families. It had been a given his father wouldn't make the trip from North Carolina to California for the event and Jeremy hadn't even bothered to ask him. He'd spoken with his mother on the phone last week, knowing Hope would never be able to make the trip alone, her agoraphobia confining her life to the borders of their hometown. His lack of family didn't bother him often; in fact, most of the time he was glad of it—less interference and drama. His father deposited the money for his tuition and living expenses in his account and left him free to fend for himself. He'd been diligent in his money management, knowing there was no going back for more if he screwed up. It helped not having a girlfriend. Or at least, not having one anymore. He'd broken up with Tanya midsemester, knowing she was already making plans for after graduation. He wanted nothing to do with commitments that might lead to marriage and a family. He set out across campus, weaving between the gathered groups, when a hand clasped his shoulder and he turned to find his sweat-drenched brother smiling at him.

"Congratulations." Will's face was flushed but his smile broad. "Nice speech, by the way."

Stunned by the sudden appearance of his older sibling, Jeremy was speechless, the ache in his gut replaced by the sudden sting in his eyes. "Thanks for coming," he said, finding his voice. "How did you know I was graduating today?"

"You aren't the only one with a brain in our sorry excuse for a family. I went online and Googled the date."

Still incredulous at this lone display of loyalty in a family that had none, Jeremy said, "Mom told me you passed the bar exam in New York and got an offer from one of the biggest firms in the city."

"I'm a first-year grunt, working more than sixty hours a week. Nothing glamorous in my line of work."

"But you're here. How did you find the time?"

"We had some client interviews to do in LA, low-level stuff, so I volunteered to do them. I'm taking the red-eye home tonight and I'll be back in the office tomorrow. But right now, I'm taking my little brother out to celebrate his graduation with a few drinks and a good meal." Will clasped his shoulder. "Sound like a plan?"

Jeremy had fond memories of that afternoon eating spicy burritos and washing them down with quite a few cervezas, which no doubt was the reason he'd agreed to this latest invitation. Still wondering what had prompted this surprising encounter, and on their honeymoon no less, Jeremy rounded the desk. It was just one meal. It could be a bit awkward after all these years, but he was sure they had enough to talk about with their careers alone. The addition of Will's new family would keep the conversation moving until the meal was over.

He sat down and touched the computer's black screen. The attachment he had opened just as Will arrived filled the screen. No text. Just a single image that made his stomach clench with rage and fear. A photo. Of him and Noel. She was wearing his jacket as they faced each other on the dark pathway last night, the image cast in the faint shadows of a distant solar lamp.

Jeremy recoiled at the realization that someone had followed them last night. Perhaps they had been waiting to see Jeremy's reaction to the vandalism of the science center but then instead had captured this moment that appeared far more intimate than it had been. A shiver of fear made his neck twitch, the sensation instinctive and ominous.

Jeremy knew he should keep Noel Welsh as far away from this as possible, but as his gaze returned to the image, he knew in his gut it was already too late. Their faces were just inches apart. Had they been that close? He shook his head at that distracting tangent, knowing what mattered. That stroll last night had pulled her into the sights of this threat, and keeping her at a distance now would still leave her a target but an unprotected one.

Jeremy wasn't about to let that happen. He had drawn her into this and felt ethically bound to mitigate any risk to her now. He could think of only one way to keep her close enough to know if she was in danger. It would mean going back on his word and, although he was loath to do so, he justified the need knowing it was for the greater good.

He just had to hope she would never find out.

* * *

Noel sat across from Dr. David McMann in his office and tried to rein in her nerves. She hadn't been through the interview process since she completed the master's degree that earned her the PA after her name. That was seven years ago, before she'd gotten the job in the dermatology practice, and the interview process had changed since then. They had already reviewed her research background and the study she had helped facilitate in the final year of her PA program, and Dr. McMann seemed impressed by her recent pursuit of her certification as a certified research coordinator. Her qualifications established, the interview turned to a series of behavior-based questions.

Dr. McMann straightened his glasses, glancing down at her resume. "I see you have been doing direct patient care for many years now. Tell me about your responsibilities."

Noel relaxed a bit at this straightforward inquiry. "I see patients in the office for annual check-ups as well as more urgent visits for sudden-onset skin conditions. I work independently but consult with Dr. Tess Elliot when the condition is questionable or is something I haven't seen before. Prescribing medications as well as obtaining biopsy specimens to get a correct diagnosis for our patients fall within my scope of practice."

"Do you enjoy working with patients?"

"I do. It's why I decided on the PA program after I finished my undergraduate degree. The knowledgeable care of a good clinician can change the course of a patient's life and give them many additional years of health, free from the pain and deformity of surgeries performed too late in the disease process."

Dr. McMann sat back in his chair, the overhead lighting in his office glinting off the shiny pate of his receding hairline. "I'd like you to give me an example of when your advocating for a patient made a difference in the outcome of their care. Take a minute if you need to think about it."

One patient sprang to mind and Noel knew it was the story to share. "I was seeing a new patient, a woman in her sixties. She was very fit and healthy but had a small painless bump on her arm. It was flesh colored and appeared to be a cyst. She had been to her regular dermatologist who told her it was nothing to worry about, but she told me she knew something wasn't right. I'm in the habit of listening to my patients—they know their bodies better than any medical professional—so I called Dr. Elliot in and advocated for a biopsy. I suspected it might be a rare condition known as Merkel cell carcinoma. She agreed it was a possibility and we went ahead with the biopsy. Later, I discovered that the specimen had been lost somewhere between our office and the pathology department we were using to examine our biopsies. I hounded the pathology office, spoke to the transport driver, and had him scour the vehicle. In the end, a thorough search of our own office revealed that the specimen had not been packed up with all the others that day and had been shoved behind several unused cups of formalin. I drove the specimen over to the pathology office myself."

"What was the outcome of the incident?" Dr. McMann's tone was clinical, but his interest was apparent.

"The patient was diagnosed with Merkel cell carcinoma and referred to a surgeon for a wide excision of the lesion followed by a course of chemotherapy."

"How did she do?"

"It's still a bit too early to know for certain about her long-term prognosis. This type of cancer often metastasizes, but she is several months post-treatment with a clean scan and no sign of any further disease."

Dr. McMann nodded with a satisfied pursing of his lips before moving on to a more mundane set of questions about availability and salary. "Do you have any questions for me?"

"I do," Noel spoke up. "Who is responsible in the study protocol for obtaining the informed consent of the volunteer subjects?"

"I am. The only other people who could do so within the IRB guidelines would be Dr. Jeremy Finnegan, my coinvestigator on the study, and the person we hire to fill the role of research coordinator."

Noel forced herself not to react to Jeremy's name. "And the role of research coordinator, what does that entail in terms of job responsibilities?"

"You would be the liaison between the subjects, the anesthesia team, and the radiology staff administering the MRI. In essence you would serve as the advocate for our subjects at every step in the process. That will necessitate a thorough knowledge of each subject's medical history, allergies, and medications as well as being the go-to person for any problems that might disqualify them from the study or cause them to withdraw. The role will be filled by the person we think has the time management and organizational skills to handle the complexities of the study as well as be the strongest patient advocate."

"I hope I have already demonstrated my ability to do that." She had nothing to lose. Since Jeremy had told her there were two other candidates for this position, she needed to stand out from the pack.

"I agree," Dr. McMann said, looking over the top of his glasses and meeting her gaze. "This interview would be over if that were not the case."

"And I would report any issues of concern to you?" Noel wondered if there were more internal layers in the chain of command.

"Yes, to me or Dr. Finnegan."

"I think I have a better idea about the position now."

"Are you still interested?" Dr. McMann asked.

"I am."

"We'll be in touch once we have made a decision, sometime in the next few days."

Noel stood up, holding out a hand that Dr. McMann took with a firm shake. She paused to deliver one final thought. "I recognize the subjects who are consenting to be a part of your study are in many ways different than the patients I deal with every day. They are, for the most part, going to be younger and healthier, but I believe this puts even more of a burden upon the research team to keep them that way—to first 'do no harm' and to respect their willingness to help us learn more about the nature of consciousness while still maintaining their safety and privacy. I do think I am well suited for that role."

She nodded. "Thank you for the opportunity to speak with you about this important work."

Moments later out in the hallway, Noel drew in a deep breath, knowing she had done all she could to get this job. If they chose someone else for this position, it just wasn't meant to be. Something about that familiar sentiment just didn't sit well with her. She believed in making her own destiny with effort and hard work, although she did acknowledge that sometimes luck played a part in reaching the goal. She'd never been sure if luck was a real thing. The only moment in her life she had been able to attribute to luck was the day Jeremy had saved her. She had been helpless to save herself and only his arrival, his strength, and his stamina under the water had saved her. Had that been luck? Or something else?

She stepped from the Laraby Science Center to find a custodian scrubbing the orange letters from the building's exterior. The only word still visible was the final one. TRUST.

She shivered as she stared at the lone word that felt like a missive.

Not luck, but trust.

But in whom?

* * *

Jeremy stepped through the door of David's office. "Are you done with the interviews?"

David looked up from the papers on his desk with a frown. "Do you ever just step into a room and say hello or good afternoon before jumping right in with whatever urgent matter you want the answer to?"

"I don't like to waste your time or mine." Jeremy stared down at his seated colleague.

"They're called pleasantries for a reason," David quipped. "Because they ease the way into a conversation by creating a 'pleasant' moment before the exchange of information. You should try it sometime."

On any other day, Jeremy would have taken up the challenge and a barbed but congenial exchange of gibes would have ensued, but he had more pressing business today. "I'll think about it. Now, where do we stand with the candidates you interviewed?"

David blinked, having expected the usual verbal jousting. "I think we can rule out the first woman I saw this morning. Not enough empathy and missing the relatable quality I'm looking for in a research coordinator. Our subjects are going to see a lot of the person we choose to fill this role, and she seemed a bit scattered when I asked for a story about being a patient advocate."

Not Noel. She was definitely not scattered." The other two?"

"They're both good candidates. I would weigh them equally after their interviews."

"Anything distinguishing about either one?"

"Other than one being female and the other male, their backgrounds in patient care, their education, and even their work experience were very similar. I'm tempted to take the man just for the possibility of less drama."

"Don't let Human Resources hear you say that." Jeremy kept his tone light. He'd hoped he wasn't going to have to resort to this. "Can I see their resumes?"

David picked up the two pages on his desk and handed them to Jeremy, who took a minute to peruse first the male candidate's resume and then Noel's. He had decided in the hallway to tell the truth as it might come out later. "I knew Noel Welsh years ago. It appears she has worked hard and carved out a successful career for herself."

"Any conflicts of interest I should know about?" David asked, over the top of his glasses.

Jeremy shook his head. "Just a name from the past, but all things being equal, I think we should give her a shot."

David shrugged. "Fine by me. You just saved me the trouble of wading through the minutia of their resumes and spending an hour trying to decide who's the best fit. Ms. Welsh did have a great story about patient advocacy and seemed very confident about her ability to do the job."

"Good. You'll take care of letting HR know. When did she say she could start?"

David glanced down at the notes he'd taken during the interview. "Two weeks. She must have to give notice at her current job."

"Let's see if we can get her in here earlier, since she'll be involved in choosing the subjects."

"I'll see what I can do. Are we still waiting for the final approval from the IRB?"

"Yes, but we should have it by the beginning of next week. Then we'll be ready to jump right in, as you like to say."

"I hope you are going to be more congenial with our research staff than you are with me."

Thinking of Noel, Jeremy answered, "I promise to be on my best behavior."

"I'm going to hold you to that, but since most of their interaction will be with me, I think we're safe. I'm very likable," David said, feigning modesty.

"And I'm not?"

"Well, after your little slipup at the debate, I do find you more human. It took a little sheen off the boy wonder image. We could all use to be taken down a peg, don't you think?"

"You heard about the intelligent design fiasco, I see." Ordinarily Jeremy might have scowled at the reminder, but today he had more important things on his mind. "I did win the night."

"Yes, but in a split decision. Gave all of us in the believer's camp a little hope."

Startled, Jeremy stared at his mentor. "Are you telling me after all the years we've known each other that you're a closet believer?"

David's expression grew serious. "Stranger things have happened."

Jeremy sobered, realizing that perhaps he didn't know his colleague as well as he thought. "Is there a story you'd like to share?"

"Some other time, my friend." David took the resumes from Jeremy's outstretched hand and placed them in the folder on his desk. "I'll notify HR of our decision and have them make the call.

* * *

"Do you think you got the job?" Mia asked as she jumped into Noel's car after school.

"I think I made an excellent case for why I'm the best person for the job, but it's out of my hands now. I should hear something soon. Could be on Monday." Noel pulled away from the high school. She had taken the day off from work for the interview and picking Mia up was one of the perks of a free afternoon. "Want to go shoot some hoops?"

Mia looked at her and then shook her head. "I asked my guidance counselor to take a look at my college essay and she said it needs 'tweaking,' whatever that means. I need to work on it."

Noel glanced over at her as they stopped at a red light. "She must have given you a better idea of what needs changing. She's trying to help you make it better."

"She said it was well written but felt too 'generic,' like there wasn't enough of me in the essay."

"What did you write about?"

"About how much I want to go to Langford, how they're my first choice, things like that."

Noel nodded, understanding the guidance counselor's reaction. "Remember what you told Professor Finnegan when we ran into him on campus, the story about growing up in foster care and wanting to give back? That's the story you need to tell. It won him over, remember?"

Mia hesitated, a frown creasing her brow. "I don't have to tell them about finding my mother, do I?'

"Not if you don't want to. I think if you focus on being a child of the foster care system and then meeting me through the Big Brothers Big Sisters Program and now being a volunteer in the same program that should give them a good idea who you are. They already know how much you want to go there since you're applying early decision."

"It means starting the whole essay over," Mia grumbled as they pulled into the driveway.

"Sometimes getting the things we want most requires a lot of hard work. How much do you want to go there?" Noel already knew the answer.

"Okay, I get it. Now you sound like Mum."

"Where do you think I got it from? We have the same Mum."

Mia smiled as she opened the door. "Yes, we do. Thanks for the ride. Can we shoot some hoops tomorrow, maybe?"

"Done. I'll call you in the morning."

Noel stopped at the grocery store on the way home. She wandered the aisles trying to decide how much work she wanted to put into a Friday night dinner. Not much of a social life going on here. She eyed the frozen pizza and then dropped it in her basket. She wasn't a cook like her Mum and still ate dinner with her parents and Mia several times a week.

Noel still found it remarkable that when she had asked her parents to adopt Mia they had agreed. Noel had been in graduate school for her PA and was living at home with her parents, a necessity after she had taken out loans to pay her tuition. She'd been leery of the arrangement, but the years away as an undergraduate with only brief visits home for the holidays had given her parents a glimpse of what their lives would be like if they didn't recognize their daughter's independence. The move home had started for financial reasons, but as she settled into a more adult relationship with her parents, they found it worked for all of them, perhaps because she hadn't tested its bounds. Or not in the usual ways anyway.

She hadn't been one of those kids who let loose in college, the near drowning and the PTSD having left her a more serious young woman. She could have used alcohol or drugs to still the anxiety of waiting for the next flashback, but on the few occasions she tried it, she found the loss of her natural inhibitions was terrifying. So many things made her anxious back then, dating being the most intimidating. She'd dated very little in college. The intimacy that was so often expected had felt oppressive, and her few attempts to overcome the sensation only reinforced the lack of control she felt as a woman in any physical encounter. Instead, she had tested the bounds of this new relationship with her parents by asking them to adopt the little girl who had tugged at her heart from the day they met at the gym as part of the Big Brothers Big Sisters Program. Mia was eight years old then and over the next few months as they spent time together it became clear that her foster placement was not a good one. Not abusive, but negligent, a home with too many kids, not enough food, and not much supervision. Noel's attempts to try and intervene for Mia had fallen on deaf ears in a foster care system overwhelmed by the sheer number of kids who needed their services. In desperation, Noel had gone to her parents and asked if they would consider adopting Mia. Garrett and Marcy had spent time with Mia on many occasions when Noel had brought her home for a good meal and they'd even started including her in their holiday celebrations. When her parents had agreed to pursue Mia's adoption, Noel had started to see them in a different light, not as the over-protective parents she remembered but as two loving parents willing to do anything for the daughter they loved.

The phone in her pocket vibrated as she exited the market, having purchased a store-made salad to go with the pizza. Retrieving the phone, she glanced at the screen and recognized the university number from earlier in the week. With a surge of hope, she answered the call.

"Noel, its Jeremy."

"I hope you're not calling to let me down gently."

"I'm calling with good news and a strange request. Which would you like to hear first?"

Encouraged by his lighthearted tone, Noel replied. "Easy choice. I'll take the good news."

"You got the job. I just spoke to Dr. McMann. You'll be hearing from HR next week, but I wanted to let you know as soon as he decided."

A surge of pure pleasure made her grin as she crossed the parking lot to her car. "Thank you for not making me wait all weekend to hear the news. So what's the strange request?"

"Remember the other night when we were talking about my family?"

"I do. You said you hadn't seen them in years."

"Until yesterday when my older brother appeared in my office and asked me to join him and his new wife for dinner." The frustration in his tone was apparent.

"That must have been a surprise." Noel placed the grocery bag on the passenger seat and started the engine. The call switched over to Bluetooth and came through the speakers as she pulled out of the lot.

"A bit of an understatement." Jeremy blew out a sigh, somewhere between a groan and a chuckle. "I haven't seen Will since my college graduation, and yet I couldn't seem to say no when he asked about dinner. Now I'm in for an awkward evening talking to a man I barely know and his wife, who I just met. I was looking for a little backup."

"This would be the request part, I'm sensing." A slight smile tweaked the corners of Noel's mouth.

"I was hoping you might be willing to go with me. The whole evening would be more manageable with another voice in the mix."

"How are you planning on introducing me to your brother?" Noel chuckled. "As the girl you saved from drowning half a lifetime ago?"

"As a friend. We could be friends, right?"

The question touched a connection that would always exist between them. It vibrated like a low hum in the background of every encounter she'd had with him, like a bond that bound them together even after all these years. "I think we could, yes."

"I was hoping you'd say that."

Noel hesitated, then gave voice to one thought. "Don't you have someone else in your life you could ask? Someone who knows you better than I do?"

Silence stretched across the Bluetooth connection. "I don't."

That wasn't an easy admission to make. Perhaps they had more in common than just their past. "Then what time are we meeting your brother and where are we going?"

"Thank you," he said, relief evident in his tone. "I appreciate your help. The dinner reservation is at seven at Casa Grande."

"I've always wanted to try that place." Noel glanced at the bag on the passenger seat. Quite an upgrade from what she had been planning.

"Well, tonight's your chance." He paused, weighing a thought. "I could meet you on campus so we could drive over together or I could pick you up, whatever makes you more comfortable."

In any other dating scenario, she would have opted to meet him at the restaurant. But this wasn't a date and she trusted him. She gave him her address. "Six forty-five?"

"Thank you for doing this, Noel."

"Glad I could help," she said, pulling into her driveway and hoping to find the right thing to wear.

# CHAPTER FIVE

Jeremy pulled up in front of the massive colonial. It appeared Noel lived on the pricey side of town, which didn't quite fit with the woman he had met in the coffeehouse earlier in the week. He checked his phone. The address was right. Glancing up, he scanned the wide front door flanked by two circular columns in need of a good paint job. Her parents' house, maybe? Catching a hint of movement down the long driveway, he spotted Noel walking toward him. Her height was accentuated by dark jeans and a loose flowing blouse, aqua in color but with a hint of silver running through it that glimmered gently with each step. Her blonde hair hung loose, barely brushing her shoulders, with one side tucked behind her ear, making for a mix of dressy and casual. Watching her close the distance between them, a smile lighting her face, he wondered if he hadn't been just a little in love with the girl he'd saved all those years ago. Which was absurd, of course. He had never loved anyone in his life. Not family. Not friends. And never any woman he had dated. He shook his head, trying to clear the aberrant impulse to romanticize what had simply been an act of necessity: his saving her from drowning.

Noel pulled open the passenger door before he had a chance to get out of the car and do it for her.

"I forgot to tell you I live around back in the caretaker's cottage, so I thought I'd meet you out here." Noel sank into the low-slung seat of his restored Corvette, the barest hint of lavender scenting the tight space of the coupe.

Trying to shake off his earlier musing, he nodded. "The house did seem big for one person."

"My landlady is an older divorcée. I help her out with some of the gardening and yard work and she gives me a break on renting the cottage, otherwise I'd still be living home with my parents. Rents around here are outrageous." She flashed him a brilliant smile and reached for her seat belt. "Are you ready for tonight?"

"As much as I can be. Thanks for doing this." He shifted the standard transmission into first gear and pulled away from the curb.

"Just my way of thanking you in a more tangible way for saving me," Noel quipped. "Although I did have the thought that since you are about to be my boss this might be outside the employee guidelines for working relationships."

"Technically, I'm not your boss. Dr. McMann manages all the personnel hired for the study." A twinge of guilt mocked his words, the mark of his thumb having shifted the scales in her favor. He shrugged off the wayward sensation. She was equally as qualified as the other candidate. "You impressed David with your patient advocacy story."

"That will be the hard part of leaving my job—the patients I won't get to see anymore." A hint of sadness colored her tone before she changed the subject. "Can we go over a few more details about your family so I can carry on an intelligent conversation? You were raised in North Carolina, and you are one of five siblings, right?"

"Good memory." Will shifted gears, the car accelerating smoothly. The restaurant was just a few miles from Noel's home but the traffic was always a question. Still, they should get there in plenty of time. "My sister, Maddie, is the oldest and lives with her husband and kids in New Hampshire. Will is next; we're meeting him and his wife Cherie tonight. They're here on their honeymoon and they have three girls from her first marriage. Tyler is number three and lives in Colorado. I'm number four. And Mitchell is the youngest.

He lives in Florida." Out of the corner of his eye, he could see her concentration as she filed all this information away.

"You mentioned the other night that your mother has had some mental health issues."

"Yes, although she seems to be more stable on her new meds. She and my father still live in the house where we were raised, and my father still works as a judge although he must be getting close to retirement now."

"What does Will do for a living?"

"Last I heard he was working for a law firm in New York City."

"Still?"

"I'm not sure," Jeremy admitted, glancing over at her as he stopped for a red light. "We're in the same boat tonight. I'm going to be finding things out, too."

Noel nodded. "And you've been living on the West Coast since you graduated from the university."

"You really are a good listener." He watched her eyes widen at his words.

"I suppose so. You mentioned it the other night at the coffeehouse. Why is that so remarkable?"

"Because in my experience most women are busier trying to figure out what they'll say next rather than listening to what I have to say."

"Then you've been hanging out with the wrong women."

Jeremy nodded his agreement as they pulled away from the light. "That's why I stopped dating a while back."

Her brow furrowed at that piece of information, but she sidestepped it, taking the conversation in a different direction. "Tell me one thing you like to do that if we were friends for more than two days, I would know about you."

"I love to spend time outdoors, hiking mostly."

"We have that in common, then. Do you still swim? I remember being very impressed that you were on the university team."

"I don't swim often anymore. I've been pursuing a different form of exercise lately. Little known fact: I hold a black belt in taekwondo." Jeremy downshifted to make the turn into the parking lot.

"Interesting. What drew you to martial arts training?"

"I like the mental discipline that's such an integral part of the practice. And it's great exercise in a different way than hiking or swimming."

"Good to know." She smiled at him as he pulled into a spot and cut the engine. "I think we're as ready as we're going to be." She reached for the door handle.

"Just wait, please." Jeremy exited the car, coming around to open the door and extending a hand to her.

"You really are a throwback to another time." She looked up at him as she placed her hand in his and he pulled her to her feet.

He met her gaze in the gathering darkness, then slowly released her hand as he spotted his brother exiting an Uber with his wife. "Game time."

* * *

Amid the flurry of introductions at the hostess station, Noel made two observations as the restaurant's owner—who did indeed look like someone's grandmother—led them to a corner booth. First, the brothers shared a striking family resemblance although Will was a bit taller and had the slim build of a runner and Jeremy was broader through the shoulders and more muscular. Second, she took an instant liking to Cherie Finnegan, her smile genuine and manner relaxed. She and Will seemed surprised Jeremy had brought someone, but both welcomed Noel warmly as the two women took the inside seats of the circular booth flanked by Will and Jeremy.

The restaurant was not large, a dozen tables in all. The air was rich with the scent of sautéed onions, grilled meat, and melted cheese, mixed with cumin and chilis, coriander and allspice. So much better than frozen pizza. Noel looked over the menu and then glanced over at Jeremy who was doing the same with a concentration that far outweighed the task.

Noel turned to Cherie, starting the conversation off with an easy question. "Jeremy tells me you and Will are on your honeymoon?"

Noel had thought she had a beautiful smile when they'd been introduced, her pale skin contrasting with her long dark hair, but Cherie's smile increased its wattage as she glanced over at her husband. "We were married last Saturday."

"Did you have a big wedding?" Noel knew most women loved talking about their weddings, making this an easy intro to the evening.

"No, very small. Just family and a few close friends under a tent in my parents' back yard."

"Cherie didn't want a big wedding. She couldn't wait to marry me." Will took his wife's hand, his lighthearted banter giving way to an adoring smile.

"That's true," she responded, meeting his gaze.

"How long were you engaged?" Noel asked, feeling like she was witnessing a private moment.

"Two weeks," Will answered, squeezing Cherie's hand.

Jeremy looked up, joining the conversation. "You managed to pull off a wedding in two weeks?"

"You haven't met my mother," Cherie chuckled. "That woman can do anything given the right motivation."

"Had you known each other long?" Jeremy laid aside his menu.

"Depends on what you consider long. Is five months a long time?" Will's words were light but shaded by a more somber note.

"And I was in a coma for a month of that time," Cherie added, her smile fading, her eyes fixed on her husband with a hint of awe. "Will was with me every day. He's the reason I'm still here."

Noel shivered, a chill working its way across her shoulders. Looking over at Jeremy, she saw that the surprise on his face mirrored her own.

Will took up the story, his jaw tight with the memory. "I performed an intubation in the field, but it was Cherie's brother who saved her."

Jeremy leaned forward. "How did you know how to do that? You're a lawyer."

"Not anymore." Will turned his attention to his brother. "I went back to medical school eight years ago and I just finished my residency in emergency medicine."

"You changed your whole career?" Jeremy's tone was incredulous.

"I did, and thank God for that. I never would have met Cherie otherwise. It's a miracle she's here and I plan on enjoying that gift for the rest of my life, for every day God gives me on this earth."

"We didn't need a big wedding. We just wanted to start our life together," Cherie added.

Noel's gaze shifted to Jeremy, who was taking in the momentous changes in his brother's life as well as the fact Will was a believer in God.

"But enough about us," Cherie said, steering the conversation in a new direction. "How did you two meet?"

Jeremy blinked, shifting his gaze to Noel, who offered an encouraging smile. "We met years ago when she was working with me at a summer camp for underprivileged kids. We hadn't seen each other in a while and then we reconnected. We've been friends ever since."

Which was the truth, Noel thought, if you considered a friendship of two days a real thing. It seemed that Jeremy wanted to outline the nature of their relationship so his brother didn't start down the whole dating rabbit hole.

A pretty, young lady who looked like a younger version of the woman who had seated them stepped up to the table. She rattled off the evening's specials without glancing at the tablet in her hand before taking their drink and dinner orders.

"How is the university doing?" Will asked. "I never would have imagined when I left you here on campus after graduation that you'd be here when I came back. It appears the academic life suits you."

"It does," Jeremy responded with a nod. "I enjoy the interaction with the students, watching them refine their thoughts and beliefs as their classes make them take a different look at the world. This generation of students has gotten a bad rap, often being cited as superficial and uninvolved. While I might admit that some of them have a more limited attention span having been brought up in the age of social media, I find they have just as much passion for the things they care about, like the environment and social justice."

"Never underestimate the power of a child to change the world," Cherie said with a smile.

"Cherie used to be a fourth grade teacher," Will said.

"Used to be?" Noel asked.

"I'm hoping to start my new degree program in the winter term. I'm working my way to becoming a transplant coordinator."

"It seems career change runs in the family," Jeremy said.

"Yes, it does," Will confirmed. "Cherie's brother received a kidney transplant this past summer, so she has some firsthand experience of the process." He paused as the waitress delivered their drinks. "What was going on at the campus yesterday? Looked like someone took a can of spray paint to the front of your building."

Jeremy glanced over at Noel, his expression the same as she remembered from Wednesday night as he tried to control his annoyance. "We've had a rash of vandalism on campus. Several buildings have been defaced over the last few weeks. No one has been hurt, but the incidents seem to be increasing in frequency."

"Looked like more than a petty crime, more like a statement of grievance," Will remarked, reaching for the beer in front of him.

Noel recalled the message written in bright orange letters. IN GOD WE TRUST.

"The police are looking into some of the fringe groups on campus and their online affiliations," Jeremy responded, "but so far, they haven't got any leads. They're thinking it's a group rather than just one person because of the dissimilarity in the lettering and how fast they seemed to be able to pull it off."

"The words are familiar, but somehow in that crazy color they felt so menacing," Noel noted. "Jeremy and I were walking back from the debate when we saw it."

"We saw the fliers for the debate on campus," Cherie said. "How did it go?"

"Patrick Mueller was a worthy opponent, well-spoken and likable with well-defined arguments. He didn't make it easy, but in the end, I did win over more of the judges," Jeremy replied.

His attempt at modesty didn't quite ring true, Noel thought. Jeremy was kind and a bit protective, but he wasn't humble. "It was interesting to watch," she added.

"Any chance the two events are related?" Will asked, a note of concern coloring his tone.

"The police are looking into that. It's possible my atheist views may have angered some religious extremists," Jeremy answered. "All the messaging has been directed at buildings, though, not people."

Why did she sense there was more to it than that, Noel wondered. His reaction on Wednesday night? He had said the message on the building was for him. But he couldn't know that, could he?

"The police must be concerned about the escalating frequency," Will noted.

"They are, but more from a malicious mischief point of view."

"But you're being careful," Will stated, his attention focused on his brother. It wasn't a question but a statement of instruction.

Noel found she liked Will even more for this guarded expression of concern. She thought Jeremy might dismiss it out of hand and was surprised when he met his brother's gaze across the table.

"I appreciate your concern, Will, and I am taking this seriously."

Will sat back in the booth. "Good, because I can't deal with any more life-threatening events in the lives of my siblings."

Jeremy's eyes narrowed. "Which implies that someone else is. Who is it?"

"Sorry for the awkward segue, but yes, it's Maddie," Will responded. "She was diagnosed with lung cancer last year."

"Lung cancer? She's only forty-two." The surprise in his words was tinged with annoyance. "Why is this the first I'm hearing about this?"

"I just found out about it a few months ago myself, when she called me out of the blue and asked me to meet her for brunch." Will countered, his words calm.

"Like you did yesterday surprising me in my office." Jeremy's tone was testy. "Anything else you'd like to tell me about our family?"

"Hey, you're as guilty of walking away from our family as I am. We have that in common," Will said. "About time we change that, don't you think? And I wasn't the one brave enough to get it started. Maddie was."

Noel watched Jeremy's wounded pride give way to a hint of remorse in his tone. "How is she doing?"

"Her surgeon removed a lobe of her left lung and followed up with six months of chemotherapy. The possibility still exists that…"

Cherie elbowed him in the side. "…that Maddie is going to live a long life with her husband and beautiful children. She had no metastatic disease on her last scan and has the best attitude about surviving cancer I have ever seen. She's a very special woman, your sister."

Noel watched the loving glance of exasperation and chagrin that passed between the two newlyweds; they'd had this discussion before. Cherie the optimist and Will the doctor.

"Maybe I should call her," Jeremy said.

"I think she would like that," Will responded. "I'll text you the number."

The waitress arrived with their meals, a tall sturdy boy carrying a large oval tray for her and setting it on a stand. With a warning that the heavy white stoneware was very hot she set the oversized dishes in front of them. Scallops with a corn salsa for Cherie. A steaming beef burrito covered in cheese for

Will. A spicy fish taco for Noel. And a sizzling steak with rice, beans, and a spicy salsa verde for Jeremy.

"Looks delicious," Noel offered as the waitress departed.

"Any news about mom and dad since you seem to be a bit more tuned into our family than I am?" Jeremy cut into his steak. The inside was rare, almost purple, provoking a smile.

"Only because Cherie wanted to invite them to the wedding and that required several phone conversations with our father," Will clarified, lifting his fork.

"You talked to him?" Jeremy's tone was incredulous. "I can't remember the last time I had a conversation with him. They didn't come to the wedding?"

The tension in Will's jaw was unmistakable. "No, and talking to him wasn't easy. I had to listen to all his disparaging remarks about my career change."

"He had a problem with you being a doctor?"

"His objection had to do with my leaving the noble profession of practicing law."

"I can remember him holding you up as the perfect son, an example to the rest of us," Jeremy said with a frown. "He thought you were following in his footsteps."

"I went to law school in spite of him, not because of him." Will's words were crisp with underlying anger. "I wanted to defend the little guy. I know how naïve that sounds now."

Noel thought it sounded noble, like a young man who wanted to save the world.

"Just the opposite of our father," Jeremy mused.

Will nodded. "He's always been about the power and prestige. In my more charitable moments, I wonder how he ended up that way."

"Which makes you a better man than I am." Jeremy set aside his fork. "The one person I feel sorry for in our whole awful upbringing is mom. She had five children with him in nine years."

"She tried to make me promise I would bring Cherie and the girls to North Carolina to meet her."

"Did you make that promise?" Jeremy asked, interest in his tone.

"No. I told her I'd think about it. I don't want to take our girls into the home we were raised in," Will responded, his tone tight and controlled.

"We've talked about staying in a hotel and making a short visit to see how it goes," Cherie added, rejoining the conversation, having chosen, like Noel, to let the brothers have this time to talk with each other.

Noel turned to Cherie. "How old are your girls?"

The question turned the conversation from the somber to the chaotic as Cherie and Will regaled them with stories of Molly, Sarah, and Carey and the search for a new home big enough to hold their family. They were living in Will's two-bedroom condo for the moment, the five of them pushing the limits of its closets and toy storage. The conversation continued over dessert and coffee as Noel kept them on this safer track with questions about school and sports. These three little girls were a new addition to Will's life, but it was clear he loved them with his whole heart. Noel decided they were very lucky to have a dad like him.

After splitting the check, the two couples made their way to the parking lot. Standing outside the front entrance, Will turned to his brother, laying a hand on his shoulder. "Thanks for joining us tonight. It was good to see you."

"You as well. And it was very nice to meet your better half," Jeremy said, turning to Cherie.

"Now that we've met, let's stay in touch." Cherie surprised Jeremy with a quick hug.

"I'd like that," he responded, his tone sincere. "You do realize you've married into a dysfunctional family, don't you?"

"Doesn't have to stay that way, though." Cherie met his gaze with a smile.

Will turned to Noel. "I'm glad you joined us, Noel. It was very nice to meet one of Jeremy's friends. I didn't know he had any."

"We're a small but select group. He's a bit of a lifesaver, your brother. I guess that runs in the family." Noel met Jeremy's gaze over his brother's shoulder and watched his eyes widen.

Will glanced over at his brother. "Sounds like there's a story there. I'll look forward to hearing it next time. I'll be back out this way in a few weeks for an emergency medicine symposium in San Francisco. Maybe we could do this again." Will held out a hand to Jeremy as their Uber ride pulled up to the curb.

Cherie turned to Noel. "So nice to meet you.

Noel and Jeremy watched the Uber pull away before he turned to her. "Thank you. That was so much easier with you there. You're a handy friend to have. I might have to keep you around."

"You might, huh?" Noel said. "Do I get any say in this?"

"You do," Jeremy quipped. "Although I'm not above bribery after Will and Cherie took such a liking to you. You are a good listener."

"I can be bribed with really good Mexican food." She glanced back at the restaurant. "Do I get to pick the place?"

"You do," Jeremy responded, his tone no longer teasing as they stepped off the curb. "You can pick the place, the time, and…"

Noel smiled, her shoulder bumping up against his. "Then I think…"

She saw the glare of headlights rushing toward them before Jeremy's arm encircled her waist. He lifted her off her feet, pulling her back against him as he jumped backward onto the curb. A car sped by the restaurant's entrance, its brake lights flashing a bright red before it accelerated and made the turn out into the street. Noel's heart raced, her pulse bounding in her temples as Jeremy's other arm encircled her, holding her fast as he regained his footing. Her mouth dry and breathing shallow, her words sounded breathy and insubstantial despite her sudden anger.

"Who drives like that in a parking lot?"

# CHAPTER SIX

Jeremy's heart hammered so hard he was sure Noel could feel it with her back pressed up against his chest. He'd reacted to the sudden threat without conscious thought, his mind processing the gunning of an engine and the headlights barreling closer. He registered the accelerating speed rather than the squeal of brakes and snatched Noel out of the way, his reaction instantaneous to the danger. He'd thought to get the license plate number, but the sudden flare of the brake lights obscured his view as the vehicle made the screeching turn onto the roadway. His palms slick with sweat, Jeremy released his hold on her.

Noel spun to face him, hands trembling as the adrenalin rush of the near miss began to abate. "That didn't feel like an accident."

Jeremy's hands settled on her shoulders, running down the length of her arms before taking her shaking hands in his. He had a momentary impulse to downplay the incident to protect her but dismissed it. "I don't think it was. Are you all right?"

She nodded, meeting his gaze. "Does this have something to do with the incidents on campus?"

She appeared unharmed but her eyes were wide with fear, and her pupils were dilated. The fight or flight reaction would take some time to wear off.

He wasn't surprised she had put the pieces together. "I think it does. I'll explain, but let's get out of here."

Holding onto her hand, he glanced both ways before leading her across the parking lot to his car. Inside, he started the engine and pulled out of the parking lot as he handed her his phone. "Can you pull up my recent calls?"

Noel found the phone app and opened it. "What am I looking for?"

"John Santino. Should be close to the top. He's a detective investigating the vandalism on campus."

Noel located the number and put the call on speaker. It was answered on the third ring.

"Detective Santino."

"John, it's Jeremy Finnegan. I think we have an escalation in our vandalism case. A friend and I were having dinner at Casa Grande and when we came out of the restaurant a car tried to run us down in the parking lot."

The detective followed up with questions about the make and model of the car, which Jeremy couldn't answer. He'd been more focused on Noel than the car.

"It was a black SUV," Noel spoke up. "Large like an Escalade."

I'm going to send a patrol car by the restaurant to see if anyone saw anything, and I will need a statement from the two of you."

"Tonight?" Jeremy asked.

"Yes, before the details are lost. I'm assuming you're not still at the restaurant by the sound of the engine I'm hearing. I could meet you somewhere or you could come down to the station."

Jeremy glanced over at Noel, letting her choose the location. She spoke up and gave the detective her address with instructions to pull down the side drive to the cottage in the rear of the property.

"I'll meet you there," the detective responded.

Glancing in the rearview mirror as he had been doing since they left the restaurant, Jeremy saw no one behind them. He never should have asked Noel to come with him tonight. This was not the time for a new relationship, friendship or otherwise. And the idea that keeping her close to him would keep her safe now seemed appalling. He had pulled her into this mayhem. "I'm sorry, Noel."

"This isn't your fault, Jeremy." She turned to him in the tight confines of the car as he negotiated the sweeping curve of her driveway, where motion sensors activated lights at the back of the house. A small dwelling, its front entrance lit by a single bulb over the door, was accessed by a walkway that skirted the pool's fencing. Bigger than a poolhouse and about the size of a garage, the small A-frame was cast in the shadows of the lighting from the main house.

"I shouldn't have asked you to come with me tonight …" His words trailed away as they exited the car. "I need to show you something. You have a computer in there, right?"

"Of course." Noel unlocked the door and disarmed the alarm system. She led the way into the open room that served as both kitchen and living room, the space divided by the clever placement of furniture to delineate each space. The overstuffed love seat and matching chair looked comfortably worn. They sat at a right angle to each other, facing the flat screen TV on a table in front of the window overlooking the pool. The kitchen, with a small butcher block island at its center, was separated from the living room by a rectangular table with bench seating. Her computer rested on a desk under the loft's overhang, creating the illusion of a small additional workspace. Noel powered up the computer and entered her password.

"May I?" Jeremy stepped closer to the keyboard at her nod. "I need to access my e-mail on something bigger than my phone."

Noel sidestepped in the confined space as he leaned over the computer and opened his Gmail account. "I started receiving these e-mails a few weeks ago. At first, they were just weird, but since they coincided with the vandalism on campus, I sent them to Detective Santino."

"How many have there been?"

"Three. I received the last one yesterday, the morning after the debate. Here, take a look." He leaned back so she could read the message. Standing beside her, the near run-down in the parking lot still fresh in his mind, the words seemed even more menacing.

"You think this is the reason for what happened tonight?" She turned to face him. "How could anyone know where you would be?"

"Wait, there's more." He clicked on the attachment and heard Noel's swift intake of breath as the image filled the screen. The picture of them standing on the university path, their faces just inches apart, evoked a feeling of expectation and desire although the actual moment had been quite innocent.

"Someone's been following you." She lifted her gaze to meet his in the darkened alcove.

A knock on the door stilled Jeremy's reply. Noel crossed the room in a few quick strides, then used the peep hole before she opened the door to Detective Santino, who had his badge in hand.

A tall man in his early forties with short dark hair, he carried himself with a quiet confidence. Noel and Jeremy sat on the small couch across from the detective, who pulled out his phone as the interview began. "Mind if I record your statements? Makes for a more accurate report having your actual words so soon after the incident."

They both nodded as the detective took them through the personal data needed for his report: name, address, phone number.

"Are you two dating?" the detective asked.

Noel glanced over at Jeremy before shaking her head. "No, we're friends."

The detective's eyes narrowed as he fixed them with an assessing stare. "I only ask because the attachment in that last e-mail makes it look otherwise. If I thought that, maybe someone else did, too."

"Jeremy and I have a bit of history, but we just met again a few days ago."

"What kind of history?"

Jeremy took up the explanation, giving Santino the abbreviated version of Noel's near drowning fifteen years ago.

The detective responded with a nod. "I remember that day. I was new to the force and that was one of my rookie runs. They put me on crowd control outside the hospital." He then led them through a series of questions designed to prompt their memories. Any other people in the area? Lighting in the parking lot? Sounds? Unusual smells? Jeremy was able to give very few specifics; the rushing lights and their imminent danger had been his focus at the time. Noel had a few observations, though. A streetlight out at the entrance to the parking lot. The scent of burning rubber. The rev of the car engine. The large size of the vehicle. But without a license plate number it was going to be hard for the detective to identify the car.

Santino concluded the interview by handing Noel his business card. "If you remember anything else, please call me. Even small details can be helpful." He glanced over at Jeremy, then stood. "You already have my contact info from our last few conversations."

Jeremy nodded, gaining his feet as Noel did likewise. "Any luck tracing the IP address of the e-mails?"

Santino shook his head. "Based on the last e-mail we were able to obtain a warrant for the e-mail server, but it didn't give us any pertinent information. The sender is using a program that reroutes their messaging through international servers and maintains their anonymity. I've got one of our IT guys working on tracing it back to the source, but so far, no luck."

"Which leaves us where?" Jeremy asked, walking him to the door.

"Still investigating."

"I don't understand how, on a campus full of students, someone hasn't seen something. It takes time to leave a message that size," Noel said, pulling open the door for the detective.

Santino turned to her. "We sent out an e-mail to all the students through the university asking for anyone with information about the incidents to contact us. Got a few prank responses but so far nothing helpful."

"He was at the debate. That was clear from the message," Jeremy stated.

"We thought of that, and with this escalation tonight, we'll be running down the names of all the people who purchased their tickets online, but the tickets sold at the door are untraceable." Santino stopped in the doorway, noting the security panel with a brief nod. "It would appear that Jeremy is the target of these incidents, not you, Ms. Welsh, but I would suggest you use the security system."

"I already do, detective. Every night."

Jeremy closed the door behind the departing detective and turned to Noel. "I'm sorry I dragged you into this. When I saw the photo on my e-mail…" He broke off, noting the firm set in her jaw and knowing the only way forward was the truth.

"I don't remember that moment being so… intimate." Noel's quizzical frown almost masked the heightened color in her cheeks.

"It wasn't," Jeremy insisted, even as a memory belied his words. As Noel had slipped her arms into his jacket, he'd had the sudden impulse to wrap his arms around her. When she'd turned back to face him, that thought still lingered as he'd leaned in closer to straighten the jacket's collar just as the photo was taken. "It was an innocent gesture. One any man with a southern background would do for a woman shivering in the cold. But when I saw the picture on my computer, I knew someone had been watching us and I thought…" His hands dropped to his sides, fists clenched.

"Come sit for a minute." Noel waved him over to the couch, her expression unreadable as she sank into the corner. "Explain to me, what were you thinking."

Jeremy tensed. "That I needed to keep you safe."

"That seems to be a bit of a pattern with us. You coming to my rescue." She met his gaze, her expression growing more animated, her tone strident. "Don't you think you should have mentioned this to me?"

She broke off, weighing a thought before Jeremy watched her eyes narrow and her chin lift. "Is that why you asked me to go with you tonight?"

Startled by the inconvenient truth, Jeremy squared his shoulders and met her stare. "In part, yes."

"I don't need you keeping tabs on me," Noel asserted, her annoyance clear in the crisp tenor of her words.

"I did it for your protection," he countered, hearing his defensive tone.

"I am so tired of people trying to protect me!" Heat rose in her face, flooding her cheeks with an angry flush.

Jeremy knew he had set off a tsunami of emotions by withholding the truth and he steeled himself for the consequences.

"I'm not sure whether to be annoyed at your arrogance or flattered at your gallantry," Noel continued, her exasperation clear in her crisp diction. "You're just one man, Jeremy, and although you are very handy to have around, it would appear this threat is well beyond your skill set. I'm not a teenager in need of saving, not anymore, and I can take care of myself."

"Yes, you can. Point taken. I apologize. I should have told you." He admired her directness as he got to his feet. Staring down at her, he extended his hand to her. "Although I am glad you find me handy to have around."

"Don't let it go to your head." She placed her hand in his, letting him pull her to her feet.

"Still friends?" he asked, holding onto her hand just a moment longer.

"Yes, but only because I like your brother. He and Cherie are fun, and they seem to care about you." Her anger receded as quickly as it appeared as she walked him to the door.

"I'm still processing the whole sibling reunion and wondering why he reached out in the first place." Relieved at the change of subject and the forgiveness implicit in her tone, Jeremy released her hand, not wanting to push his luck.

"Maybe it's a God thing," Noel offered, her words light. "This could be the miracle you mentioned the other night."

At her reminder of his flippant remark, Jeremy shook his head. "Just a coincidence. There's no one out there listening."

"You don't believe in miracles?"

"No, I don't. Why? Do you?"

"I don't know…" Her words trailed off as she pulled the door open for him. "Sometimes I wonder what I'm supposed to do with this life you gave back to me. There has to be a reason I'm still here."

"You are here because a terrified kid with strong lungs happened to have a knife in his pocket the day you fell into the water."

"Sounds so random. And it doesn't explain the after…" Noel shook her head.

"What after?" Jeremy turned to her in the open doorway, watching her search for the words to explain.

"There are things about that day that still terrify me, flashes of images and strange sensations." Her finger lifted to her lips as if she was trying to stop herself from saying the rest. She shook her head and then met his gaze. "But the warmth and the peace when I opened my eyes . . . seeing you again has brought all that back. I feel like we're still connected somehow. You can feel it, right?"

Jeremy nodded. "Yes, but there's nothing supernatural about it, Noel. We have a shared experience no one else has but us. It ties us together." That sounded so clinical, and looking into her eyes he wondered if there was more to it than that. Because the connection he felt to her was more than just an attraction to a beautiful woman, more than just an incident cemented in his memory by terror and triumph. It had an intangible quality he couldn't put into words. It made him want to wrap her in his arms and hold on tight.

Noel took one step toward him and placed her hands on his shoulders. His arms encircled her waist of their own volition, settling at the small of her back as he linked his hands.

"Thank you for saving me again," she said her gaze earnest and words soft.

His brain, lost in the hormonal response to her nearness, responded on autopilot. "You're welcome."

"Let's try not to do it again, though."

"I'll do my best." Stepping back, he pushed open the screen door. "You'll set the alarm?"

"As soon as you leave. And you'll be careful?"

He nodded. After the door closed, he waited on the far side for her to set the alarm. Hearing the beep, he turned toward his car, knowing the connection between them was more than a shared memory, that it existed in the here and now and was growing stronger with each hour they spent together.

* * *

Blake flipped the pancakes high into the air to the delighted shrieks of her twins. Noel smiled behind the mug of coffee Blake had handed her when she came through the door this morning. They were going to take the kids to the zoo after breakfast.

"When do you start the new job?" Blake stepped away from the stove to retrieve a basket of strawberries from the refrigerator.

"I haven't spoken to HR yet, but Jeremy said they would be calling me with an official job offer this week. I'm excited about getting started, although it's going to be hard to leave my patients." Noel took a seat at the table next to Eric and Lyla, who awaited their Saturday morning feast.

"I was surprised when you told me you wanted to step away from the practice. I thought you enjoyed direct patient care."

"I do, but I'm also missing the intellectual stimulation of tackling larger issues."

"Can I make a suggestion?" Blake flipped the pancakes onto two plates and carried them over to the table for the twins. When Noel nodded, she continued, "You've been with the dermatology practice for seven years and you have a solid career there. Why not ask them for a leave of absence instead of resigning?"

"Like a sabbatical in teaching?"

"It would give you a chance to try the academic route for the length of the study but still leave you with options if it doesn't work out." Blake poured syrup over the pancakes to smiles of pleasure from Lyla and Eric."

"What are you really worried about?" Noel sensed her friend was making her way to a larger point.

"I'm concerned about you working with Jeremy. You already share more than a working relationship given your history and that doesn't seem like a stable foundation on which to launch a new career."

"I won't be working with him, though. Dr. McMann is overseeing the subject end of the study," Noel replied as Blake placed two plates piled high with strawberry-covered pancakes in front of them and took a seat.

"Eat up. You'll need it for the zoo. Many miles to go this morning." She spooned some strawberries onto the twin's plates before reaching for her own fork. "Now I want to hear the rest, the part your face says you're debating whether to tell me."

Blake knew her so well, which was both a blessing and a drawback of being friends with the woman who had once been her therapist, even if that was years ago. Couching her language in case the kids were listening, Noel filled her in on the call from Jeremy yesterday afternoon, the dinner with his brother, and the near miss in the parking lot, concluding with the interview with Detective Santino.

Blake listened with care as her breakfast disappeared. After the kids had cleaned their plates, she wiped their hands before they ran into the family room. Then she grabbed the coffee pot to refill their mugs. "Okay, here's my question: Why did you say yes when Jeremy asked you to go with him?"

"That's what you want to know after hearing all that?"

"I do, because it's the root of everything that follows. Why did you go?"

Noel got to her feet and started clearing the dishes from the table, placing them in the sink as Blake remained quiet. "Because when I asked him if he had anyone else to go with, he said no. And I realized we were alike in many ways. It isn't just the past that connects us. That one event changed us both. It seems to have left us unable or unwilling to make a deep connection with the people around us. Yet we still seem to have that link to each other." Noel leaned back against the counter. "I know that doesn't make any sense..."

"Maybe it does. The two of you share a unique experience. It couldn't help but change you."

Noel paused, gathering the courage to say the words. "There's something else there, too. It's like seeing Jeremy is bringing back little pieces of my memory, at least I think it's a memory. A feeling of being safe and warm, which doesn't make any sense when there wasn't anything safe or warm about what happened that day."

Blake lifted her gaze to meet Noel's. "Does this have something to do with what you told the doctor in the emergency room after the accident?"

"I don't know. Maybe."

Blake cleared the rest of the plates from the table as Noel opened the dishwasher and began to load it. "You were never able to tell me the details about that. How much of what you told him do you remember?"

"Not much. It's like trying to recall a dream from a decade ago. Just some disconnected images."

"For years you haven't been ready to think about what you experienced that day, but seeing Jeremy again may have triggered something…"

"I've been thinking about it more in the last few days," Noel admitted. The clink of silverware punctuated her words as she loaded the last utensils and then closed the door.

"And when did that start?"

"At the debate when I listened to Patrick Mueller talk about near-death experiences."

"Then maybe you should look into that, do a little research," Blake responded as they headed into the family room to get the kids. "There's much more information out there now, so many books written about the phenomena in the last fifteen years. Maybe this is the final piece to putting what happened behind you." Blake retrieved the kid's sneakers from the bin by the door and handed a pink pair to Noel. "You might consider contacting Patrick Mueller. I believe he's pastor of a church near here. I think it's in Bakerston."

Noel remembered reading his bio in the debate program. Although he had a national reputation as a speaker on Christian apologetics, he lived in the next county. Noel sat down on the floor, gathering Lyla into her lap and putting her sneakers on.

"Too bad you didn't write it down," Blake said, doing the same with Eric and then reaching for their jackets.

Startled by her words, Noel pictured the slim black volume she'd buried in the box of high school textbooks still residing in her parents' attic. A flicker of fear and anticipation made her shiver.

Because she had.

# CHAPTER SEVEN

Jeremy drew in a deep breath and blew it out as the taekwondo class moved through one of the more complicated forms. When he had started taking classes three years ago, he had done so for the power and precision of the self-defense practice. He had hated the forms, a structured series of punches, kicks, blocks, and stances done in a precise pattern, the difficulty increasing with each belt level. At first just remembering the order of the moves was a challenge, like a dance with too many steps. But over the years as he progressed through his training, he found the precision of the forms increased his focus and generated a mental clarity as his body moved through the required elements. Completing the black belt form, the group then donned their chest pads, headgear, and gloves for the sparring that concluded the class.

The master paired them off based on belt level. Jeremy bowed to his opponent before the sparring began, knowing he was going to have to step up his game with Lance Petroff as his sparring partner today. Lance had become a friend as they'd progressed through the belt levels in tandem. As sparring partners, the two were a good match physically, of equal height and similar age. Lance's blonde hair was cut close and he donned the protective headgear easily, chiding his friend about needing a haircut so he would be ready faster. Jeremy took the good-natured ribbing in stride, securing the chin strap before they faced off. They bowed to each other as the master called for the session to begin.

His guard up, he assessed Petroff's stance, noting his almost military precision as they circled around each other before making their first move. Spotting an opening. Jeremy threw a quick jab followed by a cross, but Petroff blocked both and then resumed his bouncing stance. Lance had an innate sense of knowing what move his opponent would use next. Watching him spar against others, Jeremy had tried to learn Lance's technique, but he'd never quite mastered the skill Petroff now used to his advantage to block the punches Jeremy threw in quick succession. Jeremy's competitive nature surged at the parry, his annoyance fueled by the events of last night, creating an anger that had no place in class. He tried to dial it back as he threw a roundhouse kick that Lance dodged with ease, leaving Jeremy vulnerable to the uppercut to the gut that handed with a solid thud on his padding. They both pulled back, bouncing from one foot to the other, arms raised in a guarded stance as they assessed their next opportunity. Jeremy knew Lance had a tendency to drop his guard after a series of punches, a flaw in his delivery that was nowhere to be seen this morning. Frustrated by his inability to make any solid contact, Jeremy attacked with a flurry of punches that did nothing but leave him winded. Lance blocked the blows and then spun into a back kick and landed a solid blow to Jeremy's midsection that drove him backward to land on the mat as the master called time on the session

Lance stepped forward, taking off his gloves and offering his hand to Jeremy. "Hey, what's up? You're off your game today."

Jeremy reached up and let his friend pull him to his feet. "Sorry, I think I was letting the rest of my life make its way into class."

"Yeah, no kidding. Good thing you were paired with me. You might have hurt someone else," Lance said, with a hint of concern before his usual bravado won out. "You can't handle my skills when you're focused, much less distracted. Now I know all I need to do is get you mad to mess with your timing."

"Point taken and you're right," Jeremy replied as the two bowed to each other and then turned to the front for the end-of-class ritual of acknowledging the master with a traditional bow and salutation.

"You want to talk about it?" Lance asked, a hint of his upbringing in the deep south evident in his tone as they stripped off their gear and shoved it into their gym bags.

Embarrassed by his lack of control, Jeremy kept his answer short. "No, thanks."

"How about a beer and a ball game, then?" Lance asked.

"Much more my speed. Meet you later at the Brew Pub?"

"Sounds good. Text me a time."

Out in the parking lot moments later, Jeremy opened the door of his red Corvette. No modern bells and whistles in this car. No key fob or navigation system. And no Bluetooth, either. When he'd bought the 1984 Corvette ten years ago, it was in rough shape, which is how he'd gotten it for a reasonable price. He'd had to put some money into restoring it, but he loved the shiny red exterior of the two-seater coupe. He checked his phone as he settled into the seat, half hoping he would have heard from Noel but scoffing at the idea. Her anger with him last night had been short-lived and they had parted on good terms, but that didn't mean he was going to be hearing from her anytime soon. Hitting the icon for his e-mail with one hand, he started the engine with the other. He glanced down at the screen as the powerful motor roared to life and then settled into a steady purr. Spotting an e-mail address similar to the one he'd shown Noel last night, he opened it, noting with relief its lack of an attachment. Its message was a simple one.

**The WORD of God will not be mocked.**

Jeremy's eyes went to the time signature. It had been sent within an hour of the near miss in the parking lot. Had the attempted hit and run been intended to scare him or had his reaction time been the reason he and Noel were unharmed? This e-mail with its bold but simple message was one more Detective Santino would attempt to track. That effort had produced no tangible results so far, but each message gave them more information and increased the likelihood of identifying the sender. He forwarded the e-mail to the detective just as the chime of a text message pulled his gaze to the top of the screen. A follow-up from Will after their dinner.

**Good to see you last night. We enjoyed meeting Noel. Here's Maddie's cell number if you want to touch base with her.**

Grateful for the distraction from the ominous e-mail, Jeremy added Maddie's number to his contacts. He marveled at the turn of fate that now had two of his siblings' contact information residing in his phone when a few days ago he would have been content to never hear from either one of them again.

Glancing at the dashboard clock, he calculated the time difference. Eleven fifteen on the West Coast. Two fifteen in New Hampshire. No time like the present. He put the call through.

A melodic voice answered on the second ring. "Hello."

"Maddie, it's Jeremy. Thanks for not sending me to voicemail."

She laughed, the sound clear and lilting. "Will gave me a heads-up you might be calling. How are you?"

"Very well, thanks. but the better question is, how are you?"

"Will told you about the cancer diagnosis, I suppose. He's a bit of a worry wart, but I am more than a year posttreatment now and feeling great. He mentioned in his text that he and Cherie had dinner with you last night. And on their honeymoon, no less."

"I had no idea he was a doctor, much less a husband. It was nice to meet Cherie. They seem very happy together."

"He's crazy about her."

"I got that feeling, yes." A sudden question came to mind. "Did he invite you to the wedding?"

"He did. They kept it small, since they did it on such short notice. Scott and I took the kids, but we weren't sure we were going to make it until the last minute," Maddie said by way of explanation.

"Don't worry, I'm not offended he didn't invite me. I'd have been more surprised if he had. Will tells me you're the peacemaker in our dysfunctional family. How's mom doing?"

"Better. She hasn't had an inpatient stay in years, and she's doing well on the new medications her psychiatrist prescribed. Dad has mellowed a bit, maybe because he's realized the reason he never sees you boys is because of how he treated you. He built his own little dynasty in that town and now he's got nothing to show for it. No real friends and a family who doesn't want to be in the same room with him."

"Don't you wonder why she stayed with him all these years?" Jeremy mused aloud, siding, as he always did, with his mother.

"She almost never leaves the house, much less the town. It's a weird codependency thing they have going on and I think in his own way he loves her."

Jeremy scoffed at the notion. "That man isn't capable of loving anyone."

"I don't know," Maddie's tone was doubtful before she changed the subject. "I hear you have left the faith of our youth behind you now."

"How do you know that?"

"When Will mentioned he might try and see you, I did a Google search, of course. You've got quite a following in atheist circles as a counterpoint to Christian apologetics. Is that a matter of conviction or do you like the debate arena?"

"Both," Jeremy replied, flattered by her interest. "The whole faith element never made sense to me. Faith isn't a provable concept, although the pastor I debated the other night did about the best job I've seen of laying out what passes for facts in the belief arena. I got the sense Will has returned to the believer's side of the equation after what happened to Cherie."

"She came very close to dying from the fall." Maddie exhaled, her words filled with tension. "Will was terrified. He'd finally fallen in love at forty years old and he came within a hair's breadth of losing her. What saved her was all the people praying for her. Hundreds of people from her church, her family, her job."

"It could be a coincidence—the convergence of prayer and recovery—don't you think?"

"I am ill equipped to debate you on this topic," Maddie laughed. "Although I would note the study out of Harvard on remote prayer and its positive outcomes on patient recovery."

"Which I hear cited often from my debate opponents. You're in good company. Not going to win me over with that one, but I am glad Cherie made a full recovery."

"When I was searching the Internet, I was reminded of an article I had read long ago about you saving a young girl's life with CPR. Did you really breathe her back to life?" Maddie asked with a hint of awe in her tone.

Jeremy recalled the cold lifeless feel of Noel's lips still wet from the icy lake as his mouth sealed over hers and he filled her lungs with his breath. "I was in the right place at the right time."

"How did you feel when she opened her eyes?"

Jeremy recalled the confusion in Noel's eyes. "I felt small and grateful and humble. And believe me when I tell you that may be the only humble moment I have ever experienced." He wondered why he could tell Maddie the simple truth he kept hidden from everyone else. Maybe because she wasn't just any woman. She had grown up in the same family that had shaped him, and she might be the only woman in the world who would understand the arrogant chip on his shoulder that had protected him, then and now.

"When I reread the article the other day, I was so proud to be your sister."

Her words touched him, producing a lingering ache in his chest. He'd almost never heard such declarations in his youth. On occasion a teacher or a coach had said they were proud of him for completing a project or winning a meet, but he'd never heard those words from his parents. In the years since, he'd convinced himself that he didn't need that kind of affirmation, but the sting in his eyes at Maddie's words spoke the truth louder than any inner conviction.

"What ever happened to that girl? Do you know?"

Jeremy found his voice again. "I do. She's grown into a beautiful intelligent woman. She's been working as a PA caring for patients in a dermatology practice. We reconnected in a random encounter a few days ago."

"Maybe not so random?" Maddie said in a teasing tone.

"I don't believe in fate or faith, but I do believe in the random nature of the universe and its ability to confound us with coincidence." Jeremy could hear a crowd's cheer in the background.

"I'm so sorry. I have to go. Kylie's team just won their field hockey game. Let's stay in touch."

"It was good to talk with you, Maddie. And, yes, let's talk again."

Jeremy tossed the phone on the passenger seat as the call ended. He started the car and shifted into reverse. He'd foreseen a more awkward exchange with his sister, but Maddie was easy to talk to and as busy with her life as he was with his. If he was going to wade back into the family waters, then this quick conversation with his sister had set just the right tone. Family waters, he mused at the ironic thought. Those waters had been more like a swamp.

* * *

The attic was hot. Afternoon sun heated the roof, making the close space beneath suffocating, the smell dusty and arid. Her feet still on the creaky ladder she'd pulled down from the hallway ceiling, Noel knew she needed to be quick. She lifted a hand and pulled the chain on the single bulb that lit the space and scanned the corner where she'd placed the box, not seeing it. Dust motes lifted in the air to swirl in the limited light as she moved across the plank flooring, having to stoop to avoid the cross supports.

"I thought we were going to shoot some hoops," Mia called from the bottom of the ladder.

"We are. I just need to find something first."

"Can't you do it later?"

Noel wasn't about to explain to Mia that she wanted to retrieve the book before Mum returned from the grocery store. She'd already invited Noel for dinner and hadn't waited for an answer before grabbing her shopping list and her purse. Noel figured she'd have ample time to find the box, even if it had been moved since she stowed it up here years ago.

She'd packed up her high school books before she left for college, intending to leave her turbulent senior year behind her. The arguments with her parents that year had been grueling. They'd kept her from doing so many things every other senior took for granted, like driving a car and working a part-time job. With Blake's help, Noel had gotten them to agree to let her go away to college, and then she had chosen to apply only to schools on the East Coast. Her acceptance to the University of Maine with a full athletic scholarship to play basketball had been life changing. She'd had to sit through three days in the car with her parents when they insisted on driving her there, an absurd compromise but one that gained Noel her freedom.

Navigating around the Christmas decorations and old clothes, she pushed aside the other boxes of childhood memorabilia she'd piled in front of the one hidden under the eaves. It was sealed with packing tape, and the University of Maine sticker still rested perpendicular to the tape. It had remained untouched for more than a decade.

"It stinks up here." Mia appeared through the opening, standing on the ladder's rungs.

"It's really dirty, too." Noel knew that would deter Mia from venturing further. When she'd first come to live with them, they had discovered her aversion to anything dirty. Her social worker had said it was likely due to the squalor she lived in with her mother, but the aftereffects lingered for years. Mia was a meticulous child who always wanted to wear clean clothes, a near obsession that had gradually faded but had never gone away. "I found the box, so I'll just be another minute. You can wait for me downstairs."

Mia retreated down the steps as Noel reached for the box and peeled the packing tape back, tearing the sticker as she did. Reaching inside, she lifted the calculus book and the Shakespeare anthology before finding the volume she was looking for near the bottom inside a folder marked "class notes." She plucked the slim book from the folder and then covered it with the anthology before closing the box and returning it to its corner.

"Got it," Noel said, coming down the ladder and turning to find her father looking red faced and sweaty after finishing his yardwork.

"What was it you needed up there?" he asked as she lifted the stairway and watched it fold inward, disappearing into the attic.

"Just a book on Shakespeare that has some of my old notes in it."

"Are you thinking of taking a class at the university?"

Noel recalled the name of the show the Shakespeare arm of the drama department was doing for their fall production. "No, going to see *The Tempest* later this fall. I was going to brush up on the plot."

"Please don't tell your mum that. She'll want us to go." He dropped a kiss on her cheek and headed for the shower.

Out in the car moments later, Noel tucked the books under the driver's seat as Mia climbed into the car.

"Where are we going?" Mia asked, buckling her seat belt.

"To the park on Cedar Street. We can play one-on-one or try and get into a pickup game."

"When was the last time you played ball?"

"A few weeks ago. With you, remember?"

"And I beat you by how much?"

Mia played on a travel team as well as being a starting forward on the high school team. Noel was no match for her sister anymore. Although she wasn't tall, Mia was agile and fast, with a spot-on shot from the key and a three-point percentage that had earned her first team all-county as a junior.

"Since I'm not much of a challenge we could just turn around..." Noel feigned a turning motion on the steering wheel.

"No, no, I was just kidding," Mia countered. "Can't lose my skills before the season starts."

"How's the essay coming?" Noel changed the subject, watching Mia shoot her a sidelong glance.

"Finished it last night."

"Can I read it?"

Mia shrugged. "If you want to. Couldn't hurt to put another pair of eyes on it. Then can I send it to Dr. Finnegan?"

"The early admission deadline is November 1, still weeks away. So how about you run it by your guidance counselor before you send it to him?"

"It's pretty much a sure thing with his letter of recommendation, right?" Mia asked, her words eager.

"Your grades, your extracurricular activities, and your board scores all make you a great candidate for admission. Jeremy's letter is just icing on the cake."

"Jeremy, huh? What happened to Dr. Finnegan?"

"He's my contemporary. I think I can call him by his first name."

"Because he's old like you, you mean."

Noel grinned, responding to her teasing tone. "Yeah, really old. So what does that make Mum and Dad?"

"Ancient!" Mia laughed, grabbing the ball between her feet as they parked across from the court.

# CHAPTER EIGHT

Noel turned into her driveway and followed it around to the back of the house, triggering the perimeter sensors and flooding the yard with light. It had been a long day. The zoo in the morning with two tireless kids dragging her and Blake from one exhibit to another. An afternoon of basketball with Mia playing a pickup game with kids half her age, followed by a full load of carbs from mum's fettucine carbonara with garlic bread. Exhausted, she made her way along the path to her door before remembering what she'd left in the car. Turning, she retraced her steps and retrieved the books from underneath the front seat.

Inside moments later, she set the alarm, closed the curtains over the bay window, and put on some hot water for tea before settling on the couch. She reached for the Shakespeare anthology and set it aside. Studying the slimmer volume beneath, she hesitated, glad she had retrieved the book from her parents' attic but unsure whether she wanted to read it or hide it again where no one would find it.

Did she want to read the words she'd written so long ago? She had come through the drowning with no lasting physical injuries. Her inability to stop crying and her gasping speech had annoyed the elderly doctor who had treated her in the ER, and he'd turned away from her muttering under his breath about an ER full of patients. His manner had been curt, although in her more forgiving moments she wondered if he was just an old man who felt helpless in the face of her tears. But whatever the reason, she had never shared those memories again. Her parents had gotten a recommendation for a counselor from their pediatrician and Noel had started seeing Blake just days after the accident. In one of their first meetings, Noel had alluded to the images stirring in her head but had given no details. Blake had suggested she write down what she could remember as a bridge to the time when she might be ready to talk about it. That day never came as the PTSD nightmares emerged soon afterward and became the focus of their time together, their terrifying nature superseding any other images from the near drowning. But the journal her grandparents had given her for Christmas that year now rested in her hands. It held her memories of the events leading up to that day and what she could recall about the actual event, all written within days of the accident.

The whistle of the tea kettle pulled her from her musings. Noel rose to turn off the stove and make the chamomile tea, before carrying it back to the couch. Setting the mug down on the table next to her phone, she reached for the black book, running her palm over the leather cover. She hoped reading its words wouldn't trigger the images that had haunted her dreams ever since. The thought made her hesitate, her hands closing around the slim book. But she was no longer a terrified teenager. She was a grown woman who had moved beyond the single event that defined her life. She opened the cover, the sight of her own handwriting, so neat and precise, taking her back.

*I guess I should start at the beginning, from the day I started working at the camp. I don't know if this writing thing is going to help but Blake thinks it might. Feels weird to call her Blake but she said that's what she does with her patients, that first names just work better. It does make it easier, not so much like talking to a doctor because we know how well that goes. Ugh!*

*I loved the kids in our group. They were like a pack of puppies always clamoring for attention, especially the girls. And they weren't getting that from Jeremy who was nice, even cute, but kind of distant. The boys seemed to like him and some of the girls were crushing on him, which made me laugh. The camp director must have put us together on purpose since this is my first year as a counselor and Jeremy has been here for the last three summers. He's got the experience, and I've got . . . I don't know what I've got but I love these kids, so open and enthusiastic, and for the summer, at least, the little sisters and brothers I never had.*

*Now if mom and dad would let me take my driver's test, the summer would be off to a perfect start. I think I hold the world's record for the longest time with a learner's permit without taking the test to get my license. Eighteen months! What are they waiting for? Mum keeps saying we'll schedule the test soon, but she doesn't want me to drive cuz then I might be able to go places without her. All part of the cocoon I've been living in my whole life. I could have gone wild, I guess, like some kids in my class—wild parties, getting arrested, drinking, drugs—but why risk it? I want to go away to college and I don't want to do anything to mess that up and make them think they need to keep me at home. And when I leave, I might never come back.*

*Back to the point. I'm sure this wasn't what Blake had in mind when she told me to write down what happened. Could be I'm just stalling? Maybe so.*

*The day of the accident was the end of the first week of camp. The morning was sunny but cool. Jeremy and I started with the kids in arts and crafts. We were teaching the kids how to make lanyards, braiding the plastic strips into a loop they could wear around their necks. The girls were having an easy time, but the boys were hopeless and Jeremy wasn't much help in teaching them. So we switched places. I taught the boys how to braid and Jeremy supervised the girls who all seemed to think this was a good chance to try and make him laugh. Afterward everyone changed into their bathing suits and we headed over to the lake to take them fishing. Jeremy was checking the fishing poles and untangling the lines while I was helping the kids into their life jackets when he looked over his shoulder and told me to put on my life jacket. I wanted to finish with the kids first but the way he said it, kind of like an older brother looking out for me, made me stop and put it on before I finished with the kids. Then he pulled the cord on the engine and we started to pull away from the dock. The kids were SO excited you could feel it. Most of them had never been on a boat before.*

The phone's shrill ring made her glance at the clock in the kitchen. Ten p.m. Who could be calling her this late? Glancing at the phone, she recognized the number from yesterday and put the call on speaker, a smile tweaking the corners of her mouth.

"Noel, it's Jeremy. Am I catching you at a bad time?"

"No, just doing a little reading. Are you checking up on me after last night?"

"If I am, are you going to be annoyed and hang up on me?"

In the background Noel heard the commotion of talking and televisions before the clamor faded as if he'd stepped outside. Recalling the words she'd just read, she said, "You do always seem to be looking out for me, but I'm fine, and you must have better things to do on a Saturday night than check on me."

"None that I can think of. Just finished having dinner with a guy from my marital arts class and I'm headed home. So what are you reading?"

Noel glanced at the book in her lap and thought about dodging the question but instead wrapped her hands around her warm mug and settled back onto the couch. "Actually, I was reading about you."

"Me?" He sounded surprised and pleased. "Did you pull up one of my obscure publications on the Internet?"

"Nothing quite so formal. Something from when you were a lot younger. And you aren't the author; I am."

"Now, you're just confusing me." He chuckled, playing along. "So what is it?"

"A journal entry from the summer we met."

"You kept a diary back then?"

"Not a diary, more like a therapy journal. I retrieved it from my parents' house today."

"And I'm in it?"

"Of course. We worked together. I was just reading how the little girls in our group had a crush on you."

"How about you?" he asked, his tone teasing.

"Nope. Brotherly was the way I described you."

"Oh." He sounded disappointed, which made her smile. "Good thing, I was way too old for you back then. And you did remind me of my sister, who I talked to today, by the way."

"Making inroads back into the family. Your brother would be proud."

A flash of light in the driveway framed the closed curtains across her front window. Noel got to her feet and pulled back the edge of the curtain, the perimeter sensor having flooded the pool area and driveway with light. She stood for a moment studying the well-lit yard, knowing her landlady was away for the weekend visiting her daughter. It could have been a deer or a loose dog, she thought, before she saw a figure slip around the side of the house, his dark clothes contrasting with the backyard lighting.

"Noel, what's going on?" Jeremy's voice came through the phone's speaker sounding loud in the sudden stillness.

"I just saw someone outside in the yard."

"Hang up and call 911. I'm on my way."

The sound of an engine starting up was cut off as Noel ended the call with a touch to the screen. The concern in Jeremy's tone after the events of last night was clear and she dialed 911. Standing at the window again, she pulled back the edge of the curtain as the call was answered. She gave her address and a quick description of the situation to the 911 operator, who dispatched a patrol car to her location. Thinking this might be overkill when the sensor lights would have scared the would-be burglar away, she scanned the yard and spotted the outline of a dark figure hiding behind the pool pump on the edge of the cement surround.

Noel's pulse raced. What was he waiting for? Why not just run away? In an effort to save money, her landlady had installed perimeter sensors on the exterior of the property but no motion sensors in the back yard with the exception of the alarm on the pool gate and the water sensor meant to keep teenagers from helping themselves to the pool on hot summer evenings. The main house had an alarm system, as did her apartment. Any attempt to break in would set off an ear-splitting racket and wake the whole neighborhood, making it harder to get away. For now, it was a stalemate.

Until the lights went out.

Noel dropped the curtain and reached for the light by the couch, turning it off and plunging the room into darkness. Resuming her stance by the window, the illumination now doused inside and out, she could make out the outline of the man just starting to move in the dim light of a quarter moon. He appeared to be using the pool fence as a shield, moving toward the main house. How long did it take for a patrol car to respond? Never having accessed the 911 system before, she had no idea. Not more than a few minutes, right? She hoped some other call with higher priority wouldn't delay their arrival. The man stood to his full height on the far side of the pool and gazed at the tree line to his left, his calm demeanor sending a shiver across her shoulders and down her spine. Given his distance from her, she moved to the table by the front door where she usually tossed her keys and mail. Sliding open the drawer, she retrieved the taser gun her father had bought for her when she moved in here. The plastic felt cold against the sweat of her palm as the weight settled into her hand. She stepped toward the window before a moaning squeak from the porch just outside her door made her freeze. That was impossible! He couldn't have crossed the yard that quickly. A shiver of pure fear made her clutch the taser tighter.

There were two of them.

Her pulse racing, she stared at the solid door that stood between them, even as she heard a distant siren. Too far away. She gripped the taser in her right hand and stepped forward, triggering the security alarm with a touch to the keypad. A high-pitched wail split the night, the automated voice shrill with its mechanical intruder alert warning. Noel stepped back, extending the taser at arm's length when all she wanted to do was cover her ears to shut out the ear-splitting shriek. A minute passed and then two before a loud pounding on the door and the flashing blue and red lights beyond the curtain announced the arrival of the police.

Her hands shaking, she managed to disarm the alarm before opening the door to find two police officers on her porch. Coming up the path behind them were Detective Santino and Jeremy. The doorway was crowded but Jeremy managed to navigate around the officers, who were having a word with the detective.

His hands gripped her shoulders as his gaze met hers. "Are you all right?"

She nodded, hands still shaking,

Taking the taser from her, he set it on the table and drew her into his arms. "Good to see you can take care of yourself," he whispered in her ear, holding her a moment longer before Detective Santino spoke up.

"This is feeling a bit like déjà vu with you two. Let's sit down and you can walk me through it." Santino's words were all business, but his tone was edged with concern. "I have the patrol doing a perimeter check."

Seated on the couch next to Jeremy, Noel recounted the events of the evening. The phone call with Jeremy. The activation of the perimeter lights. The realization that the man she'd seen by the pool was not alone. She wasn't able to give much of a description to the detective beyond the fact the dark clad figure was tall and male.

"You seem very certain there were two of them," Detective Santino observed.

"I saw the first one on the far side of the pool and then seconds later heard the noise on the porch. I've stepped on those creaky boards hundreds of times since I've lived here so I know the sound varies with the weight of the person stepping on them. The noise I heard was like when my dad comes to visit."

"Doesn't rule out the possibility of a burglary." The detective held up a hand when he saw Jeremy open his mouth to protest. "But I grant you the poolhouse doesn't look like much of a target. No guarantee there's anything in it but extra lounge chairs and pool toys. Why not just go for the main house?" The detective glanced through his notes before pocketing the pad and getting to his feet. "I'm glad you called 911 so fast. With what happened last night, it might be time to consider staying somewhere else for a few days until we sort this out."

Noel grimaced. "Do you think that's necessary?"

"Out of an abundance of caution, yes. Let us work the case and find out what we can. We'll do a canvas of the neighborhood and find out if anyone saw anything."

"Did that latest e-mail I forwarded to you give you any new leads?" Jeremy asked.

"I've got my IT people working on it, but so far, no luck. If you get any more, send them my way."

"Will do."

The detective stood. "Just one last question: Do you own a firearm, Ms. Welsh?"

Noel could feel Jeremy's assessing stare as they both got to their feet. "No. I've never even held a gun. I have the taser because my dad gave it to me."

"Are you suggesting she needs one?" Jeremy asked the detective.

"No. Just assessing for the presence of firearms in the home."

Jeremy's jaw clenched. Clearly he didn't like the answer. "You'll let Noel know what you find?"

"I will. Call me if you remember anything else."

"I will, and thank you." Noel shivered in the draft from the open door as she closed it behind him. Turning to Jeremy, she met his gaze. "You didn't have to run over here tonight, but thank you, I'm glad you did."

"When I heard…" He shook his head, his brow furrowed. "I thought… well, I wasn't thinking. I just jumped in my car. I wanted to be here."

"To save me again?"

"I wanted to be here for now, for the after. I thought maybe you could use a friend, even a new one."

Her arms encircled her waist as the adrenaline of the last few minutes dissipated, leaving her weak and trembling. "Do you have time to stay for a few minutes?"

"As long as you need me to." He placed a hand on her elbow, leading her to the couch and watching her settle in. "You look a little shaky."

Her eyes met his as he sat beside her on the love seat, which was just big enough for the two of them. "Feels that way, too. That fight or flight reaction is a real thing." She held up a hand, the fingers still trembling, even as she felt her pulse returning to normal.

Jeremy covered her hand with his own, his grip gentle and warm. "Yes, it is, I remember the first time I felt it. I thought my heart was going to beat right out of my chest."

"When was that?" Noel let her hand rest in his, the touch strong and calming, knowing he was trying to distract her with his words.

"I was ten, and I got the bright idea of cutting school with two of my friends and trying to sneak into the county fair. We scoped out this massive tree on the rear side of the fair and climbed up, dropping one by one over the fence. I was the last one and a cop spotted me and chased me half a mile before catching me."

"He didn't arrest you, did he?" Noel smiled, trying to picture a ten-year-old Jeremy, his hair shorter and lighter after a southern summer.

"Oh, he gave me a good talking to and threatened to call my parents. I didn't want to give him my name, but when he got it out of me and realized my dad was a judge, he escorted me to the entrance, gave me a stern warning, and let me go."

"Did your parents ever find out?"

"Yes." His eyes were narrow, his expression grim. "When I got home my father was standing on the porch waiting for me, bigger than life and every bit as scary. One of our neighbors had spotted me walking home in the middle of the day and called him."

Noel felt the tension in his hand. "I'm thinking if he left work, he wasn't too pleased with you."

"A bit of an understatement when it comes to my father. He was furious and in full judge mode by the time he sat me down in the living room and made me explain every detail, like I was being cross-examined on the witness stand. My father never shouted, never even raised his voice. But his rage was an icy blast and his judgment was menacing, like I was just another criminal in his courtroom."

Noel could see the tension in his jaw and the wariness in his eyes, as if just the telling was taking him back decades to his North Carolina home. She leaned toward him, her shoulder touching his, a solid presence at his side. "What did he do?"

Jeremy lifted his arm and wrapped it around her shoulders, pulling her closer. "He sentenced me to one month of solitary confinement. I could go to school but had to come right home after, and no one in my family was allowed to speak to me for thirty days. I ate alone in my room. No television. No video games. And no talking."

"But you were ten!" Noel protested, turning her head to look at him, a quiet anger filling her chest. "How could any parent do that to their child?"

"He did the same thing to all of us if we stepped out of line. A month is a long time to live with that kind of silence."

"Oh, Jeremy, I am so sorry." Her heart ached for the boy he had been.

He blinked, looking over at her. "I don't know what it is about you… about us, but I have never told anyone that story."

Noel nodded, feeling the same connection as she met his gaze. "How is it you can make me feel so safe after knowing each other for just a few days? It doesn't make sense, but it's true."

The wonder in her words was reflected in his eyes as he studied her upturned face for a moment and then slowly bent his head to kiss her.

His lips met hers, the touch gentle, and she had the fleeting thought that maybe this time she could do it, that this time it would be different. Jeremy drew her closer, deepening the kiss with a subtle increasing pressure that made her heart race. She tried to stay in the moment, tried to savor the safety of his arms around her, before the flashes of light appeared behind her eyelids, pulsing like a strobe light. She couldn't breathe. Her heart hammered against her chest, but not with desire. Fight or flight. She shook her head from side to side, cringing backward and pressing a hand to his chest.

He jerked back. "Noel, I'm sorry, I…" The remorse on his face was clear as his hands settled on her shoulders and kept her at arms' distance.

"No, it's not you. It's me." She shook her head, unable to meet his gaze, her eyes fixed on her hands folded in her lap. "I should know better by now."

"What does that mean?" Jeremy angled his head to try and get her to look at him.

She couldn't look into his eyes, not now, but he deserved an explanation. She didn't know if she could find the words, though. She'd never spoken to anyone about it but Blake.

He waited, and although she could feel him studying her face, she sensed his concern, not his judgment.

"You're going to think I'm crazy…" She felt the words trip over each other as they left her mouth.

He squeezed her shoulders, his hands gliding down her arms before he covered her hands with his. "No, I won't."

She drew in a deep breath. She was so tired of carrying this around inside her. If there was ever a safe place to let it out, she knew it was here with the one person who had been there from the beginning. She lifted her eyes to meet his. "I have never successfully kissed anyone, not since the accident."

His eyes widened, but his gaze never wavered. "Is that a PTSD reaction?"

She nodded. "Yes. Before the accident I had only kissed my high school boyfriend, but afterward I couldn't do it with him or anyone else. I tried a few times in college—because isn't that what everyone does in college—but I never got any further than we did just now. It's the only consistent trigger for the PTSD I have ever been able to identify."

"Is kissing the only trigger?" he asked, his tone gentle.

She covered her face with her hands, embarrassment making her cheeks flush with heat even as a cold sweat broke out on her forehead at the memory. "No, any prolonged physical contact where I feel restrained will set it off. I tried taking the kissing out of the equation with one man I was starting to get serious about, but I couldn't do it."

"Can you tell me what happens to you?"

She had come this far; she might as well tell him the rest. Her finger grazed her lower lip, and she could tell from the narrowing in his eyes that he recognized the gesture she could never seem to control in the few instances when she had come close to talking about it. "It always starts with the feeling of pressure on my mouth. It makes my heart race and then I start seeing images like the ones in my nightmares, flashes of light followed by disembodied eyes glowing behind my eyelids. Then my chest tightens like someone is pushing on it and I can't draw a full breath. Then I panic and wake up screaming."

She watched the color drain from his face at her words. "Noel, that was me. All those things. I did that to you." His words resonated with guilt and pain. "During the CPR. How can you remember that?"

At his words, the memory surfaced. Fingers pinching her nose closed. The pressure of his mouth sealed like a vise over hers. The sharp downward thrusts against her chest. Of course, she couldn't breathe when he was doing it for her. Just a moment ago she had been unable to look at him and now her eyes searched his face, seeing the distress in his furrowed brow. She reached for his hands. "It isn't your fault, Jeremy."

"I don't understand how you could have that memory. You had no pulse. You weren't breathing," he said, his voice just above a whisper. "You were dead, Noel. I didn't make that mistake. I checked to be sure. You were gone."

She knew every word was true. She had watched him do all of it. Check her pulse and breathing before starting CPR. She had seen it from above and not known what she was seeing, not then. The memory, vivid and clear, lingered in her consciousness until her gaze met his and she saw the fear in his eyes. She'd already said too much. She knew she had hurt him, destroying his memory of the one good thing he thought he had ever done. She leaned toward him, resting her head on his shoulder and trying to return to him what she had stolen. "You saved my life. Gave me back the years I would have missed."

His arm lifted, resting with a light touch around her shoulders. "And traumatized you in the process. I'm just glad you're still here."

His words faded and Noel had none of her own to offer. Minutes passed in silence with her head resting on his shoulder, his arm around her but barely touching her. A part of her wanted to feel him pulling her closer, but she wasn't risking a repeat of moments earlier, not tonight. As if sensing her thoughts, Jeremy shifted to his feet and pulled her up as well.

"You can't stay here, Noel. It's not safe."

She sighed. "I know, but I can't show up on my parents' doorstep at this time of night without answering a lot of questions, and I'm not ready to do that. It's just one night. I'll set the alarm."

She was surprised and a bit disappointed when he didn't put up a fight but just studied her for a moment and then nodded. "All right, but tomorrow you'll pack a bag and go stay with your parents."

"I will."

"Then I'll let you get some sleep." Releasing her hands, he turned toward the door. "Call me if you need anything."

Rounding the couch, he reached for the door even as Noel fought the urge to call him back and ask him to stay. The words died on her lips, though, as the door closed behind him.

* * *

Jeremy settled into his Corvette, studying the cottage as the light changed from the brightness that framed the curtains in the front window, to the dimmer light from the small loft window, and then vanished.

He wasn't leaving her alone. He would never abandon her when the danger that stalked her tonight had started with him. But he couldn't stay in there with her, even if she had wanted him to. He couldn't look into her eyes knowing he was the cause of her nightmares.

How had a random encounter outside the university's coffeehouse upended his life in a matter of days? Before he ran into Noel and Mia on Tuesday, he hadn't thought about her in years. Then, suddenly, she was there, driving any thoughts of his meeting with the IRB from his mind as his eyes settled on her face. He'd recognized her instantly, although that had not been a mutual event. He'd stood riveted in place and had given her his name, then sprang into action when it looked like she might fall to the ground. Crouching down, her hand ice cold in his, the instinct to protect her had been visceral. He'd never believed in fate or destiny or any of that other nonsense but that left him no way to explain the connection he felt to her. Yet it was his eyes she saw in her nightmares. His hands pressing on her chest that suffocated her dreams. His lips that induced a panic she still lived with and had kept her from any relationship that might lead to marriage and a family. Not that he wanted any of that for himself, but most people, most women, wanted a family. He had taken that from her.

The area around the poolhouse was quiet, the cool night still with only a quarter moon to diminish the darkness. In moments of stillness like this, his thoughts often turned to the very nature of the musings going on in his head, to the nature of his own consciousness. Such thoughts naturally led to the research he was about to undertake to explain how consciousness was generated by billions of interconnected cells in his brain. His thoughts drifted to the more practical aspects of the research as he made a mental note to touch base with David on Monday about the anesthesia portion of the study. He grabbed the legal pad and pen he kept under the passenger seat and began to brainstorm solutions to the remaining obstacles to getting the study up and running. Setting the work aside hours later, he saw the first hint of dawn begin to banish the night. As the light bloomed, changing from muted grays to whispers of pale blue, the assurance of a new day let him close his eyes and he slept.

A knock on the window awakened him. Bright sunlight streamed through the windshield as he rolled down the window.

Noel handed him a mug of coffee, the aroma pungent and strong. "You stayed."

"I wasn't leaving you here alone." He took the warm mug from her hand, the steam rising to tickle his nose. "Thanks."

"It's the least I could do when I saw your car was still here. I left it black. Hope that's okay."

"Just what I needed." He took a sip. She liked her coffee strong just like he did. "What time is it?"

"Nine."

"Are you packed to go to your parents?"

She nodded. "Headed over there later today. After last night, though, I have a stop to make first."

He was going to ask her where she was going but the look on her face suggested she wasn't ready to tell him. "How did you sleep?"

"I woke up a lot, but no nightmares. After our conversation last night, I count that a win."

"Can I call you later to see how you're doing?" He sipped the dark brew, the sharp, almost bitter, tang playing across his tongue.

"To check up on me? Kind of like the older brother I never had?" she quipped but with no rancor in her tone.

"I'm not interested in being your brother." Jeremy hid a smile behind his lifted cup.

"A kissing cousin, then?"

Startled, he watched the corners of her mouth lift in a quirky smile. "Good to know we can joke about this now."

"You're the only person I've ever told about this, besides Blake, so there's no point in dancing around it. It felt good to let it out. Made me feel not so freakish."

"If you ever manage to work this through, I'm volunteering to be your first test case," he responded, only half in jest.

"How gallant of you, ever the southern gentlemen, I see. I'll file that selfless offer away for later." She laughed, the sound light and clear in the morning air as she stepped back from the car.

"What are you going to tell your parents about why you need to stay with them?"

Her expression sobered, all laughter gone. "I was going to go with a fumigation story, but I think the bare-bones truth might work better. A near miss on the burglary should be enough of an answer to explain however long I need to stay without setting off too many parental alarms. Gotta go. I'll be late."

Jeremy watched her lift her suitcase into the trunk of her car as he turned the ignition key, pressing the clutch to put the Corvette into reverse. In tandem, they backed out of the driveway. She waved at him and then made the turn toward the highway, leaving Jeremy to wonder where she was going at nine a.m. on a Sunday morning.

# CHAPTER NINE

Noel stepped through the rear doors and found a seat in the back. The church was packed, with ushers leading last-minute arrivals to the few remaining empty seats. Pews spanned outward, forming a semicircle around the altar where a group of musicians took their seats and lifted their instruments.

The woman seated next to her smiled. "Are you new to the Calvary community?"

Noel nodded. "Yes, it's my first time."

The woman's smile grew broader. Her pale skin and auburn hair set off a pair of beautiful brown eyes as she held out a hand to Noel. "Welcome. We love to see new faces. I think you're going to enjoy the service. Pastor Mueller always has a good story and a powerful message."

"I heard him debate the other night at the university. He's a gifted speaker."

A screen came down into view from the vaulted ceiling, stopping over the altar. The words to the opening song appeared on the screen as the musicians began to play the opening bars. A male cantor stepped up to the podium to lead the congregation in song. The music was upbeat and the melody catchy as everyone sprang to their feet and began to sing. Noel couldn't remember ever seeing this level of enthusiasm in a church. Her memories of the few times she had attended with her parents were of a more solemn service with slow organ music and very little singing. This felt more like a concert than a church service, with men and woman of all ages clapping their hands, some with raised arms, and many singing with unrestrained voices. The woman beside her had a beautiful contralto voice and began to harmonize to the song's refrain.

Last night, lying in bed in the loft, the fearful and embarrassing events of the evening had kept sleep at bay. Blake's words from earlier in the day about Patrick Mueller having a church in the area had settled over the bedlam of her thoughts like a calming mist washing away her disquiet as she drifted off into a restless sleep. During the many awakenings of the night, she had refocused on the calming fog and when she woke up just after dawn, she knew what she needed to do. She'd gone online, found the address and time of the Sunday service at Patrick Mueller's church, and then packed her bag for the move to her parents' house. Holding the slim volume she'd been reading last night she'd debated bringing it with her and then decided against it. She could wait a few more days to read it. The decision made, she hid the journal in the tiny closet just outside the bathroom door, slipping it under the folded sheets on the lower shelf.

Noel watched the formal procession move down the center aisle. Pastor Mueller wore the traditional vestments of worship, a long white robe with an overlay of green and gold. Noel hadn't been to church in years, but the order of events was similar to what she remembered. The readings were followed by the gospel, a story about a shepherd who goes in search of one lost sheep, leaving the other ninety-nine behind. Pastor Mueller closed the Bible in front of him on the wooden lectern, the final words lingering in the air.

On Wednesday night, dressed in his gray suit, he had looked very much like an academic, but here in this church, with his smile wide and his dark skin contrasting with the white of his vestments, he radiated joy. During the debate, he had been focused and purposeful, but this morning he seemed eager and spoke with no notes on the podium in front of him. Noel settled back against the pew to listen before his booming question came through the speakers.

"Have you ever been lost?"

A few of the parishioners knew this was not a rhetorical question. A sprinkling of voices answered, "Yes."

"Now I might need more of an answer than that," Pastor Mueller responded with a smile. "Let's try that again. Have you ever been lost? As a child in a department store. On a long road trip. When the lights went out in a blackout. Have you ever been afraid and didn't know what to do?"

The response was immediate and much louder. "Yes."

"Me, too, in all those places and a few more." He chuckled. "I'm not a betting man, but I believe I might be willing to wager that everyone sitting here has felt lost at some time in their lives."

Noel's thoughts raced in tandem to an old memory and a new one: to the accident that had left her deep underwater and to standing alone in the dark last night after calling 911.

"Who was it that came to save you? Who found you and made you feel safe? Now I know your mind goes to your mom who found you under the clothing rack or to the guy in the service station who gave you directions when your phone died, but I'm here to tell you that God knew where you were every minute, and He sent someone to save you. Those people who came to your aid may not have realized it, but they were sent by God, our Father who loves you more than you can even imagine."

Noel felt a smile touch her lips at the irony. Jeremy had been sent by a God he didn't believe in to save her. The thought was as surprising as it was satisfying.

"Today I want to focus not on the sheep but on the shepherd, because we have all been the sheep lost in some aspect of our lives. But after the shepherd found you and saved you and brought you home, rejoicing over you, what then?" Pastor Mueller gazed out at his congregation, leaning forward. "The story isn't over. If you have ever been on the receiving end of saving grace, then you have the responsibility to be that grace to others. You were saved for a reason. It may have felt random, but I assure you, it was not. You have carried that grace inside you ever since, and it is your turn to share it with others."

Noel felt the pastor's words settle into her soul. She had been saved for a reason. It wasn't a random act of chance that she was still here. She had known this. Yet here it was, spelled out with clarity. For years she'd thought asking her parents to adopt Mia and saving her from a life of foster care might be the way to balance the cosmic scales when by all rights she should have been dead. And while she still considered loving Mia the best thing she had ever done, the pastor was suggesting there was still more to do.

"Now, I'm not going to pound the point home," he said, making a fist and pretending to strike the podium but stopping just an inch short. "But I think you see where I'm going with this. As with so many things in scripture, there is a dual meaning. Yes, we are talking about a physical rescue of someone who is lost in the darkness…"

An image flashed through Noel's mind of an eight-year-old Mia, wide-eyed and quaking with fear, as she told Noel the story of finding her mother dead in their apartment when she came home from school.

"But we are also talking about the spiritual rescue of those lost in the darkness of lives without faith," Pastor Mueller continued. "If you have ever felt God's hand lifting you up and drawing you to him, if you have ever envisioned the shining light of his countenance or gleaned the breadth of his love for you and then stepped out in faith to accept Jesus as your Savior, then you know the power of that transformation." His voice rose in a swell of passion, the words flowing from his heart.

Every muscle in Noel's body quaked at his words, the vision from last night pulsing like a strobe in her mind: Jeremy checking her pulse before stacking his hands in the center of her chest and starting compressions. A sudden sensation of weightlessness made her shift in her seat just to feel the solid pew beneath her.

"Who knows?" the pastor continued, his tone mellowed to just above a whisper but amplified by the speaker system. "You may even be called upon to share that grace with the very person who saved you. The child rescued from the clothing rack may become the caretaker of the person who rescued them all those years ago. The friend who pulled you from the darkness of grief might be the one who needs your words years later when they are confronted by a terminal diagnosis. God has a plan for you. Never doubt you are here for a reason, that one life lived in faith can change the course of a family, a community, even a nation." He took a step back from the podium and turned to the cross, bowing low as music filled the silent space with an interlude of poignant notes before the communal prayers were offered.

Noel sat in silence, a familiar warmth spreading outward from her core to her limbs, the same warmth she felt when she was drifting off to sleep. Was it that simple? She had been saved from drowning for a reason. For years she had been content to have no memories of that day. In fact, she hadn't wanted them, fearing the turmoil and trauma they would cause. But last night she'd caught a glimpse of those memories returning, had watched Jeremy fighting to save her as she had been drawn upward away from the scene of his heroism. The sensation permeated her mind, the weightlessness, the freedom from struggle, the light that grew stronger as she began rising toward it. Had she been given a glimpse of what lay beyond this life?

The rest of the service passed in a blur of familiar imagery until the notes of the final hymn faded into silence and the congregants flooded from the church.

"Did you enjoy it?" The woman next to her smiled as she lifted her oversized handbag.

"I did,' Noel replied. "Lots to think about."

The woman met her gaze, her brown eyes assessing. "I don't often do this, but have you met Pastor Mueller?"

"Not in person, no."

"Would you like to? I'm his administrative assistant, Amelia Kelleher."

She held out a delicate hand and Noel shook it, feeling like an awkward teenager next to this elegant woman. "Yes, I would, very much."

"Follow me, then."

Startled by the unexpected offer, she followed Amelia weaving her way through the departing crowd. Pastor Mueller was greeting the last of the congregants as they approached.

"Patrick, we have a first timer here," Amelia said.

Noel stepped up and introduced herself. "First timer to the church but I heard your debate the other night at the university."

The pastor's grin was wide and welcoming. "Dr. Finnegan was a worthy opponent. I love few things more than a discussion with a prepared speaker."

"Jeremy is a friend of mine. He told me he enjoyed speaking with you, both before and during the debate."

"I don't agree with his reasoning, of course, but I found him to be a thoughtful young man. Are you a churchgoer, Noel?"

"No, I consider myself to be more in line with Jeremy's mindset than yours…" Her words drifted off as she realized that might have sounded rude.

He wasn't put off by her words. "But you're here this morning when you could be sleeping or drinking a latte, so I suspect you have a question for me. Have you been thinking about something we discussed on Wednesday?"

Noel nodded. "Yes. The one place I think Jeremy fell short was his explanation for near-death experiences. He didn't have a good answer, and I couldn't stop thinking about the commonality of people's experiences all over the world."

"He didn't have a good explanation because there is none—except God, that is. Why don't we sit down?" Patrick turned to Amelia and thanked her before leading Noel to a seat in the last row of the church.

"Is this more than an academic argument for you?" Patrick angled his body toward her, his manner open and inquiring. "Do you know someone who has had this experience?"

"Yes, at least I think so." Noel watched the pastor's eyes widen. She had been expecting an eagerness to hear all the details, but his response was unhurried. He didn't speak right away, his eyes seeking the cross over the altar before he turned back to her with a nod encouraging her to continue.

"It happened years ago when I was a teenager. I drowned in a boating accident and Jeremy was the one who saved me. The things I saw were like a dream or a hallucination. But when I tried to tell the doctor in the emergency room, he dismissed my words as the ravings of a traumatized child. It wasn't until I met Jeremy again a few days ago that I knew for certain I had died that day. My parents told me I had been unconscious but not that my heart had stopped beating. Now it's all coming back to me in bits and pieces, and I think your words the other night set it off."

The pastor nodded, his words soft and filled with awe. "You were given a gift, Noel. One few people get to see."

"Jeremy would say it's all the images of a dying brain planted there by a Christian nursery school."

"Have you told him about the memories you're experiencing?"

Noel shook her head. "I'm just starting to remember, and I don't want to hear another man tell me I'm traumatized and crazy."

"That doctor did you a great disservice," the pastor asserted. "Because of him, you've suppressed an experience very few people get to have, but those memories want to be seen and heard. Let them come back to you, a piece at a time. God will reveal what He wants you to know."

"Why me? Why would He save a kid who never gave Him more than a fleeting thought? Why allow me this glimpse of something beyond the here and now when all I have ever believed in is the ground beneath my feet?"

"It's what I talked about earlier; you were saved for a reason. First and foremost because God loves you, Noel, and second because He has a purpose for you and all the lives you will touch."

"I'm not that important; truly I'm not."

Pastor Mueller leaned forward. "I can assure you, that is not the case. No one knows you better or loves you more than the God who made you."

"I wrote it all down," she said, lifting her eyes to meet his gaze as the unbidden words met the still air. "In the days after the accident, I thought it was a dream, but it was so beautiful that I wanted to hold onto it."

"Have you gone back and reread what you wrote?"

"No, I was starting to last night but then the phone rang and the whole night just got crazy…" She broke off, not wanting to go into the whirlwind that had become her life in recent days. "Now I'm not sure I want to. Read it, I mean."

"Then leave it for now. Let the memories come back to you on their own. Right now, your brain is giving you all you need to know. Can I pray for you, Noel?"

She nodded, clasping her hands in her lap to still the trembling.

"Heavenly Father, a simple prayer for this your child. Give Noel your guidance as she recalls what you have shown her, your protection from the forces that would dissuade her from getting to know you, and your peace in the process. Amen."

She had been prepared for the droning prayers of so many ministers she had heard over the years, but the brief, straightforward words of this man were soothing and made her wish she could take them out into her life.

He touched her hand. "I am available any time you need to talk." He slipped a business card from his pocket and handed it to her. "Call me anytime and please say hello to Jeremy for me when you see him." He got to his feet. "And, Noel, when you are ready to share those memories, I would be honored if you would consider doing so with me. But for now, stay as long as you like, think, pray. He is speaking to you. Maybe it's time to listen."

* * *

On Monday afternoon, as work piled up on his desk, Jeremy tried Noel's number. Her phone went to voicemail again, the second time in as many hours. Just like last night. His concern for her grew with each attempted contact, and frustration gave way to anxiety at being unable to reach a woman that a week ago he'd forgotten existed.

A short conversation with Detective Santino an hour later assuaged some of his fear. The detective called to ask if he'd received any new e-mails after the incident Saturday night. Jeremy acknowledged he had not, which led Santino to fall back on his theory about an attempted burglary in the high-end neighborhood. He mentioned he'd spoken to Noel who was now in residence at her parents' home. Moments later, Jeremy received a call from Human Resources confirming Noel Welsh had responded to their offer of employment and would be starting at the end of the week. Feeling disgruntled at her unavailability, Jeremy hit the gym on the way home and spent an hour redirecting his frustration into upping the weights on his tracking app.

Wednesday morning the IRB granted final approval for the study. While he should have been elated, he found this professional win was not what held sway over his thoughts. He'd stopped calling Noel yesterday, feeling a bit like a stalker. She wasn't just missing his calls. Her unavailability felt deliberate. After her embarrassment Saturday night about his attempted kiss and her explanation of the origin of that trauma, perhaps she needed some space. He didn't care if he ever touched her again; he just wanted to see her and talk to her, to know she was all right. And while the first part of that thought was a total lie, the latter was entirely true. If space was what she needed, he could do that—he wouldn't like it, but he could do it.

He'd managed to keep his distance from any serious relationship with a woman for his entire adult life, having no inclination toward marriage and wanting to avoid the subject even coming up. He'd been interested in a few women over the years and even sought after them, but he always walked away when the subject of a future together reared its head. Yet somehow all his usual barriers had fallen victim to a girl from his youth, a woman now, whom he'd spent the better part of last week thinking about.

Sitting in his office Wednesday night as he prepared for the onboarding of the study employees, he reached for his phone, then put it back down with a firm thud to the desktop. He could walk away, he told himself, but then shook his head as his fingers closed around the cool surface of the phone.

If she wouldn't talk to him, perhaps there was a less intrusive way to find out what she was thinking. Keep it short, he thought as he opened the message app.

**Tried calling you earlier in the week. Are you all right?**

He set the phone down, wondering if she would even respond as he looked over the folder on the final hire for the study. David had decided to hire the candidate Noel had been up against for the job as it now looked like they would be able to recruit a larger number of subjects for the study based on their funding grant. Too much work for one research coordinator, hence the final hire, Dwayne Rawlins. He and Noel would be working together.

The phone at his elbow vibrated with a new message and he grabbed it.

**Busy week. Heard from HR and accepted the job. Starting Friday.**

All information he knew already, and he wanted more.

**Good to hear. Now my main concern: How are you?**

He waited, staring at the screen. At least she was talking to him.

**I'm fine. No worries. My parents are glad to have me home. Mia, too.**

**I feel like you're avoiding me. True?**

He hoped she wouldn't shut this down now.

**Maybe. I need some time to think.**

In a sudden flash of insight, he knew when that had happened, and it had nothing to with his attempted kiss.

**Where did you go on Sunday?**

This time the response took longer.

**To Patrick Mueller's church. He said to say hi. Called you a thoughtful young man.**

**Why did you go there?**

**I have questions he can answer and memories I can't explain.**

A shiver of fear shot up his spine, making his shoulders twitch.

**From the drowning?**

**Yes.**

**Can I help?**

**No.**

The finality of that last statement left him staring at the screen, wondering if he was about to lose this remarkable woman to a God he didn't believe in.

# CHAPTER TEN

Noel stepped through the door of the Laraby Science Center and spotted David McMann seated by the window talking with a dark-haired man. Both men got to their feet as she approached.

"Noel, welcome." David extended his hand and shook hers. "I'd like you to meet Dwayne Rawlins. He is coming on board for the study as well."

Noel didn't often meet a man she had to look up to, but her chin tilted upward as they shook hands. Dwayne had a good six inches on her, maybe more. Broad-shouldered with short dark hair, he sported a five o'clock shadow at nine a.m., which could have been the scruffy look so many men seemed fond of these days but felt like more of a genetic trait than a choice. He smiled, clasping her hand. "Nice to meet you."

"Today, we'll get you oriented to the building," Dr. McMann began, wasting no time. "Then we'll send you over to HR to complete the necessary paperwork so we can hit the ground running on Monday, when you will meet the rest of the staff. Follow me."

Dwayne held out a hand, indicating she should lead the way as they fell into step behind their new boss. The science center was an impressive building with state-of-the-art laboratories and classrooms along with a massive lecture hall. Throughout the tour, Noel found herself half expecting to see Jeremy around the next corner.

She was doing the right thing by keeping him at a distance. She couldn't pay attention to what God was trying to tell her with the warring sentiment of disbelief being whispered in her ear. She would never be able to reconcile the two. The flesh and blood presence of this man she felt connected to would win out over the tenuous hold she was trying to find with a God who was bringing back the memories she'd lost. And she wanted them back—needed then back—to move on with her life. Noel had used that mental argument many times in the last few days, but that hadn't made it easier each time her phone lit up with his number. Then, as if thinking could make it so, he stood handsome and imposing in the lobby as David returned them to where they had started.

David performed the introductions as Jeremy held her gaze, his manner formal. He gave the tall man at her side an assessing glance, shaking his hand before dismissing him with an arrogance Noel had heard about but never seen. His hand clasped hers in a professional manner, but the eyes that studied her face were searching before he turned to his colleague. "David, if I might have a word with…"

"Yes, of course." He turned to Noel and Dwayne. "Can you two find your way to the administration building? HR is on the top floor."

"I know where it is. I can show Dwayne." Noel saw the narrowing of Jeremy's eyes as if he'd been about to say something but then thought better of it.

"Thank you. We will see you both on Monday," David said with a distracted smile as he turned to Jeremy.

As Dwayne held the door for her, Noel glanced back at the two men who were now her employers. As if sensing the scrutiny, Jeremy lifted his eyes and met hers over the head of his colleague, his expression unreadable. Her initial instinct to keep her professional and personal lives separate had been the right one. She found herself hoping Jeremy's role in the study would be as administrative as he had made it sound.

"Is this your first research study?" she asked, making conversation with the man at her side as they crossed the campus. During the tour she'd discovered that Dwayne had graduated from the same high school she'd attended, although he'd been two years behind her.

Dwayne shook his head. "No, I did a research internship in my final semester of nursing school."

Noel tried to hide her surprise but missed the mark.

"That's everyone's reaction," Dwayne chuckled. "Not the traditional body type or gender, I know. But I come from humble beginnings where a steady job was the difference between feeding your family and going hungry. My mom was a nurse and she always had a job. Sometimes two. She worked hard, really hard, but she kept us fed and saw that we all got a good education."

"You're a nurse practitioner then?" Noel clarified, knowing the research coordinator role had called for an advanced degree. "I went the PA route, but they're two ways of getting to the same place."

"I started my career after high school with a stint in the military as a medic. That set me up to get through the RN accelerated program in two years. The master's degree was the obvious next step. These days I also have a side gig as an RNFA, which is a whole lot of initials for a nurse who is certified to first assist in surgery."

"You mom must be very proud of you." They mounted the steps to the administration building, an imposing brick structure that dated back to the university's inception.

A touch of melancholy played across his intriguing features: strong jaw, a bit too square, and a nose that looked like it had been broken a few too many times. "She was. She died last year. Colon cancer. She was fifty-one years old."

Standing in the open doorway, Noel turned back to him. "I am so sorry."

"Thanks. I appreciate that." He pointed to the sign in front of them. "Looks like the elevator is out. Hope you aren't opposed to taking the stairs."

Noel smiled. "It's only six floors. I think we can make it."

* * *

Jeremy had watched Noel exit the science center, his view of her obscured by the massive shoulders of the guy she would be working with on the study. He bristled at the thought of them spending so much time together. Distracted, he almost missed David's question.

"What was it you wanted to talk to me about?" David asked.

Annoyed at this misunderstanding when he'd wanted to speak with Noel, Jeremy shelved his displeasure behind a question. "I saw some paperwork come across my desk about a possible new addition to the IT team. I thought we had all the people we needed. We're going to be tight for money if we keep hiring extra people." He inclined his head toward the door, indicating the man who had just left with Noel.

"The job of research coordinator is too big for one person with the number of subjects we're recruiting. Dwayne is a necessary addition to the team. We talked about this, remember?" David's tone stopped short of irritation as he adjusted his glasses.

"And the IT guy?"

"I thought I was doing you a favor since he used your name as a reference. Lance Petroff. I'd assumed you asked him to apply."

Surprised at the mention of his taekwondo classmate and friend, Jeremy had a vague memory of telling Lance they were hiring staff for the study. They didn't often talk about work, preferring to stick to sports when they'd gotten together outside class. Lance knew his way around computers, though this study seemed a bit academic for him. Maybe he just needed the money.

"I didn't ask him to apply," Jeremy clarified. "But I did mention we were looking a while back. If we need another body, he's a good man."

"Done. You'll get a chance to meet all the staff on Monday. You are doing the opening presentation, right?"

"Yes. I just want to set the right tone from the outset and delineate our roles, so they'll know you're the up-front guy they'll report to. Good to play to our strengths."

"Admit it, you just don't like talking to people and you're letting me handle all the new hire inquiries."

"You are much better with people than I am."

"Perhaps because I try to be nice." David's tone was needling, although the chuckle that followed made the banter just another sniping conversation between colleagues.

When they'd parted ways, instead of returning to his office, Jeremy made his way to the administration building. He waited in the shadow of the monolith monument that marked the founding of the century-old university. It rose from the center of a bordered garden, the surrounding trees creating a shady gathering place for many who came to campus and a favorite spot for students to enjoy a drink before heading to class.

Thirty minutes later Noel descended the steps with her colleague. Jeremy waited until they parted before calling her name. His tone was sharper than he'd intended, designed to get her attention, and it did its job.

Her even stride faltered, and she turned at the sound of her name. A smile lifted her lips before her mouth creased into a firm line. She stood in place, meeting his gaze, and then crossed the path to him. Her steps slowed as she drew near, as if considering whether talking to him was a good idea.

"You waited for me." She stopped a few feet from him.

"I did. Can we talk for a minute? I think we need to clarify a few things if we are going to be working together." He waved her over to the bench that rested in the shadow of the surrounding trees.

She nodded, sinking down onto the wrought-iron bench, her features a mask of neutrality so different from the woman who had slipped into his car Friday night with a breezy air of expectation. In the last few days, as she'd kept her distance from him, she'd confirmed the true nature of their relationship, putting it in its rightful place. He took a seat beside her, allowing ample room for her to place the stack of paperwork she carried between them.

He cleared his throat, wanting to reach out to her, to touch her one last time. What he was about to say was the right thing to do, but he dreaded the distance it would put between them. "I have been working on this study and its funding for the last several years. It is important work that will increase our current knowledge about the workings of the conscious mind, where it begins and where it ends. It has the potential to impact the study of consciousness for decades to come."

The tenor of his words seemed to soften the set of her jaw as she nodded. "I agree. It's one of the reasons I wanted to be a part of it."

Jeremy leaned toward her, his words earnest. "I have a hypothesis about what the study will find. All scientists start out with one, but I am open to whatever our subjects will reveal to us. This research is a chance to learn more about a topic that has fascinated me since I was kid in North Carolina and spent long summer afternoons in a hammock wondering where thoughts came from and where they went."

Jeremy watched her eyes widen, his honesty cracking the veneer of her distance, and although that had not been his intent, he was glad it still could. "You and I will always be connected by the experience we shared. It changed us both, but I've realized in the last few days I was getting lost in it, that by trying to protect you I was seeking to recreate the feeling of worth and satisfaction I had so long ago with you and only with you." The last phrase slipped from his mouth before he could stop it. "Saving you is still the best thing I have ever done, but I can't chase after that feeling anymore. I have work to do here on campus, good important work, and I want to thank you for giving me the time to realize that what we have is a past and, yes, now a friendship, but we can't let it overshadow the work we are about to do."

Noel met his gaze. He thought he detected a glimmer of sadness in her eyes, although perhaps he was reading too much into her simple affirmation. "You're right, of course."

He paused, wanting to ask a question and then giving it voice. "I am curious, though. What made you decide to go to church on Sunday?"

Her shoulders tensed, but she didn't look away. "I'm starting to remember what happened after the drowning. Just fragments so far, but seeing you is bringing back things that never surfaced in all the years since. Listening to Pastor Mueller at the debate started helping me put the pieces together."

His curiosity won out over the distance he was trying to put between them. "Would you be willing to tell me about the memories?"

Noel shook her head. "No, because you won't believe me."

"Because they have to do with God?"

"Yes, and we both know what you think about that."

Jeremy nodded. "Did taking time away from me this week clarify any of this for you?"

Her brow furrowed in a look of frustration. "No. I thought it would, that once the memories began they would just continue . . . "

"But they didn't," Jeremy asserted, knowing by the look on her face it was true.

"No, they stopped completely." A look of confusion tinged with annoyance glinted in her eyes. "It feels like you're the catalyst."

Startled by her words, Jeremy remained quiet, working through a thought. "When I have a hypothesis, I am open to wherever the facts lead me. Sometimes that means forming a new theory. Would you be willing to try an experiment?"

"To prove what?"

"Your catalyst theory. I'm willing to help you find whatever you are looking for without weighing in with my opinion either way."

"You could do that?" Noel eyed him, her tone reflecting her suspicion.

"For you, yes, because this is about your needs, not mine. I will always help you, Noel." He meant every word but wondered if he was just trying to do anything to keep her close.

"How does that jive with keeping our professional distance?"

"Two separate avenues of scientific investigation. One professional and one personal. We're friends, linked by a common experience. I would like to help you if I can."

"Thank you for the offer. I'll think about it," she replied, reaching for the paperwork on the bench.

"Noel, one more thing." He was unsure if what he was about to say was courageous or the ultimate in stupidity. "I need to apologize to you. I never should have kissed you the other night and your bravery in explaining the origin of your fear caught me off guard. When I had time to think about it, I realized—and you're not going to like this—you need to work this through. With Blake. With Patrick Mueller. With someone you trust. If you ever want to have those grandchildren you told me about the first night we met, then you need to see this through to its conclusion so it won't hold you back from the things you want in your life."

She lifted her eyes from her folded hands. He'd thought she might be angry with him or embarrassed at the mention of their kiss, but the set of her jaw and narrowed gaze spoke of sheer determination as she stood. Her words were unnecessary, although they soothed his regret.

"I think you might be right about that."

* * *

"You know he's right." Blake pushed the swing higher as Lyla sailed into the sky. "It's the reason I encouraged you to find a new therapist."

Noel had called her after speaking with Jeremy, and Blake had invited her to join them at the park.

"I tried, several times, but I never felt comfortable with anyone else." Noel pushed the swing to Eric's chants of "higher, higher" as the twins swung in tandem, enjoying the fall afternoon. She brought Blake up to date on the events of Saturday night and her decision to attend church on Sunday.

She followed with Jeremy's words this afternoon and his offer of help. "I know this is asking a lot, but would you be willing to work with me on this?"

Blake gave the swing one last push. "I think you're dealing with two separate issues here: the repressed memories from the accident and the PTSD reaction triggered by intimacy. They both have their origin in the same event but solving one won't necessarily solve the other. Which would you choose to tackle first?"

"The memories because they feel like the key to all of it."

The swings slowed to a stop and the kids jumped off, running over to the elevated play structure that looked like a barn with slides coming off the upper levels. Noel and Blake took a seat on the closest bench as they watched the twins clamor up the ladder.

"Are we going to do this with or without Jeremy's help?" Blake asked.

Relieved by the implication that they were in this together, Noel turned to her. "What do you think?"

"I think your relationship with this man is complicated." She considered a thought. "Just to clarify, did you want Jeremy to kiss you?"

Noel felt the blush warm her neck and cheeks. "Yes."

"You were fully consenting?"

"Yes."

"Eager?"

"Yes. Why is that important?"

"We'll get to that in a minute. What were you thinking?"

"That maybe this time, I could finally do it." Noel's wistful tone was edged with frustration at the memory.

"Which implies a significant level of trust. Are you ever afraid of Jeremy?"

"No, never. He makes me feel safe."

Blake nodded as if Noel's tone had affirmed her own conclusion. "I think in this case there might be some benefit to including Jeremy in a controlled session. We've never been able to move further than the floating images in your nightmares, and yet seeing Jeremy again seems to have cracked open the door to what happened that day. Can you tell me a bit more about what you recalled in church on Sunday?"

"It's coming back in pieces, like snatches of a dream. I remember being lifted up, more like floating away from my body and watching Jeremy on his knees next to me checking the pulse in my neck."

"So you knew it was you?"

"Not at first, but then I recognized the pink bathing suit I wore that day."

"Were there any sensations?"

"Yes, but not the ones I expected. I knew I should be freezing after coming out of the water, but I wasn't. I felt warm and calm when I saw Jeremy compressing my chest. It was like watching a movie with a weird camera angle from above. I could see the back of his head."

"Were you afraid?"

Noel shook her head. "No. Curious would be a better word. This boy I barely knew was using every ounce of his strength to save me."

"And could you hear anything?"

Startled at the question, Noel remembered the sounds. "Children screaming for help. A boat engine turning over and churning the water. The whine of a siren in the distance."

"By the look on your face, I'd say pieces of this memory are still coming back."

"More like getting clearer, like a digital camera with auto focus where the images were blurry and then they sharpen."

"Is there more, Noel?"

"Only the sensation of being drawn upward." She struggled to find the words to explain what happened on Sunday listening to the pastor's words. "It was like muscle memory, because for a split second I felt like I was leaving the pew just remembering." Noel turned to Blake. "This isn't a dream or some kind of hallucination, right? These feel like real memories to me."

"To me as well. They follow a logical sequence with none of the weird segues of dreams. And they are very much in keeping with the experiences of others who have died and been resuscitated."

"I'm not crazy?" Noel asked, an undertone of relief shading her words.

"No, not now and not then. It's an unusual but well-documented phenomena."

"It feels like there's more."

"There may be. It's not unusual to have memory loss in the wake of trauma and your brain probably did suffer some degree of hypoxia during the event," Blake asserted. "Then add to that the trauma of the ER doctor dismissing your words and your young traumatized brain chose to relegate the memory to the importance level of a dream. But now there's a part of you that wants to remember."

"Will you help me, please?" Noel asked, as the twins ran over to grab their water bottles from Blake's bag.

"Yes, of course, I'll help you. We might consider using hypnosis. I know you weren't comfortable with it when you were younger because you didn't want to remember. Now you are looking for the answers; it might be a way to get the memories to return." Blake paused, clearly weighing a thought as she handed the kids snacks from her bag before turning back to Noel. "One final thing. I would like you to consider what you want from this relationship with Jeremy. It would be good to be clear about that before we begin."

"To be honest, I don't know." A series of images flashed through Noel's mind, of the caring man ready to defend her at every turn juxtaposed against the controlled academic she had spoken with just an hour ago. "He feels like a part of my past but perhaps not my future. I would trust him with my life, but we are very different."

"Maybe he's the man who opens the door to your future, not the man who steps through it," Blake suggested.

Noel's thoughts lingered on those words as they parted an hour later. What did she want from Jeremy? She was attracted to him—more attracted than she had been to any man in a long time—but their lives were diverging. She could feel it. Something momentous had happened to her the day of the drowning. A part of her had known it but buried it deep because she was afraid to relive the terror. But the way forward lay in a straight line through the trauma. Beyond it lay something more important, someone she had glimpsed and now wanted to know more about.

She could think of only one place to find the answers.

# CHAPTER ELEVEN

"Noel, so good to see you again." Pastor Mueller's eyes were warm as if it was truly important to him that she had returned this Sunday. "How was your week?"

"Thoughtful, with a few conversations that are pointing me forward."

"And they led you back here."

"Yes, felt like the place I needed to be today," Noel responded, the truth of that statement evident in the calm she felt.

He held her hand a moment longer as the departing church members veered around them. "You are welcome anytime. The church is always open for quiet reflection, and I am here every day if you want to talk. Have a good week."

Crossing the parking lot to her car, Noel was struck by the sincerity of the pastor. With a church this size Patrick Mueller must have many things to do: hospital visits, classes to teach, budgets to scrutinize. Yet it felt like he would drop everything and find time for her. It was a rare gift in this busy world to find someone willing to set their plans aside and just listen. She reached for her car door.

"Noel."

Turning, she saw Dwayne Rawlins striding toward her. Casually dressed in khaki pants and a striped button-down with the sleeves rolled up, his smile was a mixture of surprise and pleasure as he stopped in front of her, his tall frame towering over her. "I thought I spotted you during the service. Are you new to Calvary? I don't remember seeing you before."

"Yes, just my second time here. I take it you're a regular?" Noel tilted her head to look up at him, noting the strong lines of his recently shaved face.

"Every week, since I was a kid. I came today with my sister and her family. Spotted you from the balcony. Are you changing churches?"

"More like exploring something I haven't thought about in a long time."

"Well, this is the perfect place to do it then. Maybe next week I can introduce you to a few of the people in our service group. We've got a project coming up helping homebound seniors with repair projects in their homes. We could use another set of hands." Dwayne smiled, trying to recruit a new volunteer.

"How big is your group?"

"About thirty, a mixture of retirees with home improvement experience and quite a few people our age willing to help. A few high school and college kids, too. We usually send a trio out to assess what the homeowner needs done and then return later with the necessary supplies for the job, like roofing and plumbing."

"You have some hidden talents, then." Noel leaned back against her car and looked up at him, the midday sun making her wish she had her sunglasses.

"I've been with the group since high school, so I've developed a few skills over the years. I'm great with dry wall and painting, and not too shabby with roof repairs." Dwayne's gaze met hers as he stepped to the side, creating a shadow that fell over her. "But the most important part is building a relationship with the homeowner. We spend a lot of our time just talking and listening, letting them know they're heard. Will you join us next week?"

Impressed by his commitment to the project, Noel nodded. "Sure, sounds like a good way to get involved."

His smile was brilliant, its wattage far exceeding the simplicity of her reply. "Great. Listen, I have to go meet my sister and her family for lunch." He lingered just a moment as if he wanted to say something but then thought better of it. "I'll see you tomorrow."

Turning, she pulled open the car door, impressed by this man who seemed so committed to helping others. Not a trait you found every day in this world consumed with self-interest. If he was an example of what the Calvary community had to offer, then continuing to come seemed like a good idea.

* * *

The staff for the study begin to gather in the science center's amphitheater, finding their seats in the first few rows. Jeremy felt the hum of their conversation vibrate in his chest, excitement and expectation making him smile as they began this research that had been two years in the planning. This would be the only day they would all be together before assuming their assigned roles. Some specialized in IT and data security, others were anesthesiologists, still others were research assistants and ancillary staff. Jeremy spotted Lance Petroff, his jaw shaded by a day's growth of beard as he took a seat toward the back of the new hires. Jeremy's gaze shifted as he saw Noel standing in the doorway. Her blonde hair was pulled back away from her face. She wore a navy skirt with a peach blouse, her professional attire in keeping with her role managing subject recruitment. She settled into a seat in the third row.

He'd meant what he said on Friday about the importance of the study and their need to maintain a professional distance. What he hadn't foreseen was the wave of longing that flooded his senses at the sight of her. He had only spent a few days with her. Why couldn't he let this go? All weekend he'd fought the urge to pick up the phone and call her, not knowing if she would answer even if he did. He found her captivating in a way he couldn't explain. As a scientist he was interested in the reemergence of her memories and as her friend he would do whatever he could to help her regain them, although he was skeptical of her assertion that they had to do with God. There had to be a logical explanation for what she was experiencing as these traumatic memories surfaced. She assumed it was a higher power, and he knew it was not. Still, a part of him reacted without conscious thought as he watched the tall man he had seen Noel with on Friday settle into the seat next to her. Jeremy squelched the wave of annoyance that washed over him as she turned to Dwayne and smiled.

David stepped to the podium and the light chatter in the room stilled. Although he was not tall in stature, he had a presence that defied definition, a mixture of congeniality and professionalism that Jeremy had never been able to master. David welcomed the group with enthusiasm, gave them an overview of the day ahead, and then took care of a few housekeeping items like the location of the restrooms and the availability of the coffeehouse for food and drinks. He paused with dramatic effect and waved a hand at the table behind him that was covered with thick documents, each with a number and name assigned to it. "Now I'd like to introduce my coinvestigator, Dr. Jeremy Finnegan, who will give you an overview of the study protocol."

Jeremy stepped to the podium, his thoughts focused on these carefully chosen individuals who were about to help him with the biggest scientific endeavor of his life. He felt uplifted by the sheer possibility of what lay ahead, the subject so much a part of him that he needed no notes.

"I have been fascinated by the origin of consciousness since I was a kid in North Carolina, where summer days were too hot to do anything more than laze in a hammock and stare at a sky so blue it hurt your eyes to look at. That simple thought—the contrast between origin, observation, and analysis—has held me captive ever since. Very simply put: Where do thoughts come from and where do they go?"

He met Noel's gaze across the room and saw her smile, having given her a preview of his thinking when they spoke on Friday.

"In this document behind me is our approach to search for the answer. The mapping of the brain in recent years as a way to treat various neurological disorders has delineated areas of the brain and their function. We're going to take it one step further by using MRI data to narrow the threshold between consciousness and unconsciousness, to map its return given the exact same set of stimuli, the same words, the same smells, the same sensations."

"The protocol is four hundred pages long and all of you need to have read it by Friday. We will give you ample time to do so this week. You will each have your own copy of the protocol, which you will study in this building. It will be returned to Dr. McMann at the end of each day and will be stored in a secure location, as will the documents concerning our subjects who we will begin selecting a week from today."

"The exclusion criteria for the study are well laid out. Our subjects will be young and healthy without the disease processes that might impair consciousness, and as such we bear an overriding responsibility to do them no harm. They are volunteering to undergo anesthesia and, although many in our world have come to view anesthesia as routine, there are inherent risks involved in such an undertaking."

The room was still, each of them listening with rapt attention. Jeremy could feel their interest and he drove home the final point.

"Each of you has been chosen by Dr. McMann and me for the same reason, for your commitment to patient advocacy. You all answered the same question during your interview, and you are sitting here today because we trust you to speak up for our subjects if you sense a problem. Any break in protocol, any untoward event, you must err on the side of safety for our subjects. If you see something, you must say something. Research is meaningless without first caring for the individual, not only because failing to do so would compromise our study but, first and foremost, because it is the right thing to do to protect each other from harm."

Then retreating a step, he exited the stage to a void of sound, knowing he had left the impression he intended. The exit was dramatic and meant to be so. David stepped into the silence and began the PowerPoint presentation on the exclusion criteria for the study. From the wings of the stage Jeremy's eyes were drawn to Noel, registering her soft smile. He'd impressed her with his words as he had meant to do for all of them. Why was it her face he sought then as he looked out over the group, her reaction that mattered most to him?

He couldn't have it both ways. His words on Friday had been the right ones. Yes, they'd become friends, but her life and his were now veering off on opposite tracks like two trains leaving the station, one headed east and the other west. He had to keep his focus on his work. He didn't want any distractions in the weeks ahead.

Noel Welsh was a part of his past, not his future, and he wanted to keep it that way.

He watched the man at Noel's side lean closer and whisper in her ear. Turning away, Jeremy fumed, knowing his assertion was a complete lie.

* * *

Noel's vision blurred and her head bobbed, her eyelids closing before she woke up with a start. She pulled her black sweater closed around her and shook off the disorientation at the bright classroom lights, her eyes returning to the protocol. Monday she had made it through the first one hundred pages, yesterday as well, but today she'd pushed to finish since she was planning on leaving early tomorrow to make it to Mia's travel team game. Dr. McMann had given her permission to stay until he was ready to leave since all copies of the protocol had to be locked in his office overnight.

The writing was dry and professional. Many of her new colleagues had sped through the assigned pages for the day and returned their copies to Dr McMann's office early. Noel had found herself staying later and later each evening, reading each page carefully and trying to digest all the information. Beyond the classroom's window, the waning light of evening faded as darkness gathered in the forested areas leading down to the lake. Solar lights along the pathway on the building's perimeter flickered on. Refocusing her attention on the page in front of her, she reread the section she'd been studying when she dozed off. The labored prose and long unwieldy sentences made her wish the writer had been clearer. This section about disqualifying factors leading to a halt in the study seemed contradictory, and after reading it several times Noel decided she was too tired to keep at it tonight. She filed the page number away for reference tomorrow and gathered the pages, placing them in the box. Standing, she saw her reflection in the windows, the light from the classroom now holding at bay the darkness beyond. She patted her pockets for her cell phone and keys and grabbed her bag from under the chair.

On the second floor, she knocked on Dr. McMann's office door, surprised when he pulled it open immediately.

"Ms. Welsh, your timing is perfect. I was just about to come get you."

"Then I saved you the steps." She handed him the protocol.

"I must say you are either a slow reader or extremely diligent about understanding the material. Most of your colleagues left a while ago."

"A bit of both, I think," Noel answered. "Who wrote the protocol?"

"Both Dr. Finnegan and I did. Why? Did you need help with something?"

Noel shook her head, glad she'd refrained from commenting on the ponderous prose. "No, I just like to be thorough. I was wondering why we aren't using digital copies of the protocol. That's a lot of paper." She waved a hand at the file cabinets lining the wall.

"We were concerned about unauthorized access. A digital copy could be opened anywhere and by anyone who had the log-in and password. We felt a face-to-face sign-in would be more secure. Not environmentally friendly, I know, but safer in the long run. Will you be finished reading by the end of the week?"

"I should be done tomorrow. Not much left to read."

"Wonderful. Then have a good evening." He turned, carrying the box over to the filing cabinets and reaching for his keys as Noel closed the door.

A construction detour at the end of the hallway sent her down the back staircase to exit the building on the rear side. A pathway encircled the massive building, leading to the parking lot. It wasn't a long walk, about two hundred yards, but the solar lamps were dimmer due to the encroaching tree line that bordered the path. She buttoned her sweater, the temperature having fallen after dark, glad she had jettisoned the formal attire she'd worn earlier in the week. Her look had grown more casual each day, right down to the black pants and sneakers she'd stepped into this morning. Off to her right she could hear two students laughing, their approach visible in the diffuse cones of solar light. They crossed in front of her, one holding out a cell phone to show something to the other. At least she wasn't alone out here. Noel recalled Jeremy insisting on walking her across campus after the debate as she descended the stairs and gained the path.

The blazing lights of the parking lot were partially obscured by the building's height but it wasn't far, she thought, trying to push aside a growing unease as she heard footfalls behind her. The events of the last two weeks had left her a bit suspicious. She glanced over her shoulder and saw a lone figure, young and male, a good distance behind her. It was a college campus, she reminded herself, turning back and increasing her pace until she noticed the pair in front of her had slowed their steps and the gap between them was dwindling. Was she being paranoid? Looking back once more, she registered the rapidly diminishing space; the man behind her was closer than she would have expected. She knew in her gut that paranoia wasn't always crazy. With no time to think, she made a snap decision and stepped off the path into the tree line. The sound of pounding steps behind her confirmed her fears as she broke into a run. She didn't need to look back to know they were following her. She tossed her bag into the woods. If that was all they wanted they could have it. She heard cursing and the slap of sneakers breaking branches as they plunged into the woods behind her. Fear drove her forward as her eyes adjusted to the darkness. The dense mixture of evergreens and firs made the footing slippery, even as she heard the crash of a body going down with a cry of pain. Her heart racing, she increased her speed and wondered how long she could keep up this pace. Although she cross-trained at the gym, she wasn't a runner.

They would expect her to turn left toward the parking lot, so she veered right, knowing it was her only chance of losing them. Minutes later she caught the faintest glimpse of shimmering light through the trees, patches of moonlit water from the lake beyond. She knew then where she was going, although the thought made her joints ache with bone-chilling fear.

She slowed her pace, trying to move without any sound through the wooded terrain even as she tried to listen for noises behind her. The snap of branches under foot seemed distant now, although perhaps they were doing just what she was and stopping to assess rather than plunging forward without thinking. She reached for the phone in her pocket and crouched down, shielding the phone's light with her body. She pulled up one name and fired off a one-word text.

**Boathouse.**

It wouldn't mean anything to anyone else, but he would know, and he would come. She knew it in her soul. But it wouldn't be soon and knowing that a crazy plan crystalized in her mind even as she wondered if she could pull it off.

She caught the faintest hint of cologne mingled with pine on the breeze and resumed her pace, trying to keep her footfalls from giving her away. The trees thinned as she approached the lakeshore. It was the only way to get beyond their reach. Noel knew the university had built a large boating center further down the lake to house the sculls for their championship rowing team, leaving the old boathouse unused. She just hoped the university was still as lax about securing the boathouse as they had been. Using the tree line for cover, she circled the boathouse and approached from the far side, keeping an eye out for any movement. Off to her right a narrow unpaved roadway led back to campus, but it would leave her exposed. She was tempted to take it, but her gut told her it was the wrong move. She pulled open the door to the boathouse, feeling a wave of relief as it yielded under her hand. Inside the darkness was not total. The three-sided structure, open on the lake side, allowed a view of moonlight shimmering on the lake's black surface. The small building's walls were lined with assorted oars, and an open lane of water ran down the middle. An old-fashioned rowboat rested on the side of the platform, its oars crossed on the floor of the boat. Lifting the end, she tested the weight of the aluminum boat and tilted it toward the water, even as she wondered if she could do this.

The soft splash as it hit the surface of the water sent a chill of fear up her spine. She hadn't been out on open water since the accident. She could swim; she had made sure of that in the years since, doing lap after lap in indoor pools trying to tackle her fear. She knew how to row from her hours of cross-training at the gym, but she had never tried it in a boat. She'd been working up to it slowly, too slowly she thought now, stepping into the boat and feeling it shift under her weight. The rocking motion was unsettling but she found her footing and used the oar to push against the platform, moving her closer to the open water.

The door flew open and a man appeared in the doorway before he barreled toward her. Still standing with the oar in her hand, she knew she had one shot at stopping him from joining her in the boat. She pulled the oar back and swung at his knees, hearing the crack of wood impacting bone as she powered through the backswing and watched his legs fly out from under him. His head whipped back, and he hit the platform hard as Noel made one final push against the wood planking and cleared the boathouse. She sat quickly, hefted the other oar, and set it in place, stroking hard and fast and hearing the oars impact the water's surface with a chaotic splash. She kept her eyes fixed on the unmoving man on the boathouse deck, hoping he would stay that way. He wouldn't be letting anyone know where she was if he remained that still. Was he badly hurt? A skull fracture, maybe? She shook off the speculation and focused her attention on angling the oars to enter the water with a clean edge, decreasing the splash and increasing the power and distance of each stroke. She pulled hard again and again until the shore was a distant tree line, murky in the distance. Trying to keep her eyes fixed on the area so she could come back in close to there, she was left wondering how she would know when to do that.

Around her the quiet lap of the oars and the gentle movement of the boat stilled as she rested the oars, allowing the boat to drift. Her heart rate began to slow, the sweat from her exertions chilling her skin. She crossed her arms over her chest, rubbing her aching biceps. The rowing machine had prepared her for the sensation of pulling weight through the water, but the real thing made her muscles ache in different places. Reaching for her phone, she pulled it from her sweater pocket and saw it light up with the answer to her desperate message.

**On my way.**

Her eyes stung as she closed them and lifted her face to the night sky, feeling a wave of gratitude surge through her body. She had known he would understand her message. A shiver of relief coursed up her aching legs as she wrapped her sweater around her and waited.

A flare of red light waved in an arc from the shoreline a short time later accompanied by the rotation of red and blue lights pulsing in the night. Noel lifted the oars and started to row toward shore. Stroking evenly, her muscles rested now but still sore, the steady movement of the boat cutting through the water soon replaced the chill on her skin with a fine sheen of sweat. As she neared the shoreline, she could see Jeremy waiting, the flare still in his hand. His stance was wide and his eyes were fixed on the boat moving toward him. The boathouse was now brightly lit as campus security and local police worked the scene.

Jeremy didn't wait for the boat to land. He dropped the flare, stepped into the water, and pulled the boat up onto the shoreline. Noel stood and he lifted her over the side of the boat. His arms closed around her in a fierce embrace as she buried her face in his neck, her tears flowing freely.

"You came," she whispered and felt the tremor in his shoulders as he pulled her closer.

"Always." He turned his head toward her, his lips skimming her forehead and settling at her hairline.

"Don't let go," she said as she savored the feel of his breath on her skin. Her senses filled with the clean scent of his skin, the abrasive feel of a day's growth of beard against her cheek, and the rhythm of his racing pulse beneath her ear.

He pressed a lingering kiss to her temple and held on tight.

"Where were you?" She pulled her head back to look at him.

"At home. Broke a few speed limits to get here." His palm cupped the back of her head as he met her gaze, his eyes as shiny as her own.

"You knew I needed you."

"Felt it in my gut." His hands moved to the sides of her face, his thumbs caressing her jawline. "I have never been so scared in my life."

Looking into his eyes, Noel knew it was true. As scared as she had been for herself, she could feel his panic just starting to recede, the tremor in his arms replaced by a gentle embrace as his arms closed around her again. And although their words in the last week had kept them distant, Noel knew with certainty the answer to the question Blake had posed at the park. What did she want from this relationship with Jeremy? She hadn't known then, but she did now. Jeremy Finnegan wasn't just her past. She wanted him to be her future, a thought as unsettling as it felt right. "Thank you."

Her words whispered into the curve of his neck were suddenly eclipsed by a flash of brilliant light, an image both distinct and beautiful superseding all her thoughts. The face of a young girl. Joyous. Welcoming. Her blue eyes wide, strawberry blonde hair framing her face.

Celeste.

At the name, her knees buckled beneath her. Sensing the sudden shift, Jeremy swept an arm under her knees and lifted her up, cradling her against his chest as he strode up higher on the shore. He set her down on what remained of a sandy beach. Kneeling in front of her, he met her gaze. "You remembered something, didn't you?"

She nodded, her chin quivering with sadness and awe.

"Tell me, Noel."

She could no more deny the vision than she could tear her eyes away from his insistent gaze. "I wasn't alone. The day you saved me. The day I died."

"Who was there?" Jeremy's finger tilted her chin upward, stilling the tremor. His eyes were riveted to hers.

"My sister," Noel said, her words alive with wonder.

He frowned. "But you didn't even know Mia back then."

"Not Mia. My sister Celeste."

"I thought you only had one sister." Jeremy's brow furrowed with concern.

Noel reached for his hand, her fingers closing around his and willing him to believe what she now knew to be true. "One living sister, yes, but Celeste was the stillborn baby who died three years before I was born."

* * *

Jeremy held her gaze even as his mind raced. She was alive and safe and finally talking to him. He wasn't about to shut her down with all the logical assertions flooding his brain right now. Instead, he squeezed her hand and shifted to sit beside her. His arm encircled her shoulders and he drew her to his side. "The memories started coming back that night in your apartment, didn't they?"

Noel nodded. "When you tried to kiss me. Yes."

"Will you tell me about them?"

"I need you to believe me." She looked over at him, her tone calm and earnest. "Can you do that?"

He could see in her face how important this was to her, and that alone was enough to keep his thoughts unvoiced. She was a trauma victim with long-buried memories of a day that had changed both their lives forever. That she was willing to share those memories with him was a display of trust and intimacy he would never violate. "Yes. I promise you I will believe every word you tell me."

She stared into his eyes a moment, then nodded. Her lips parted to speak as a voice called her name.

"Ms. Welsh?" Detective Santino stood over them, the bright lighting from the vehicles surrounding the boathouse casting a shadow over them. "I'm going to need you to answer a few questions for me."

Frustrated with the interruption, Jeremy clamped his jaw shut as he got to his feet. Holding out a hand to Noel, her skin cold in his warm grasp, he pulled her to her feet. "Can we do this tomorrow, John?"

The detective shook his head, addressing his words to Noel. "I'm sorry, but I need to get a statement from you about what happened tonight. Can you do that?"

Noel nodded, glancing at the boathouse. "Of course. What happened to the man in there?"

"He's unconscious. Looks like a skull fracture from the drainage coming from his ears. The ambulance just left. Can we start from the beginning, please?"

Noel tightened her hold on Jeremy's hand as she described leaving the Laraby Science Center and realizing the men in front of her and the one behind were narrowing the gap between them.

"I thought I was being paranoid, but it just felt wrong. When I stepped off the path, they were chasing me before I even made it to the tree line."

Jeremy felt the sweat of her palm against his as she described the chase, the moment she lost them, and the one-word text she sent him.

"You were the one who called it in?" Santino turned to Jeremy. "And you knew from that one word where to find her? How?"

"We told you about Noel's near drowning when you responded to the 911 call at her house. This is where it happened." Jeremy waved his free hand at the lake. "I knew exactly where she was, and I knew she was in trouble."

Detective Santino returned his attention to Noel. "What prompted the escape out onto the water? Why not just take the road back up to campus once you lost them?'

"Too much of a chance they might find me if I did the obvious thing. I needed to buy some time. I knew Jeremy would understand and I knew he would come, so all I had to do was keep myself safe until he did." She squeezed his hand and turned to look at him. Jeremy felt his chest tighten at her words.

"You two seem to have an uncanny connection," the detective remarked.

"Yes, we do." Jeremy met her gaze with a feeling of awe welling up inside him, knowing it was true.

"The guy in the boathouse was one of the assailants?" Santino looked at Noel.

She nodded. "He came charging through the door and I swung the oar and took his legs out from under him."

Jeremy felt a wave of relief and pride at her prowess as the detective lifted his phone and made a call, confirming that the patient en route to the hospital needed to be placed in custody. He turned back to them. "I've got what I need for tonight. Now that we have a suspect, I hope we can move this case forward. You two seem to be the intersection between the vandalism on campus and the escalation we've seen this week. Call me if you remember anything else," Santino said in parting, leaving them alone on the beach.

"Let's get you out of here." Jeremy's arm around Noel's shoulders, he led her over to his car, parked haphazardly off the rutted roadway amid the trees. He bundled her into the passenger seat and watched as she wrapped her arms around herself. Her shoulders trembled but whether from the cold or the aftermath of the attempted assault was an unanswered question. In the car, Jeremy turned the heater on full before he navigated his way around the remaining police vehicles. Casting a sidelong glance at her troubled expression, he knew he didn't want her going home until they talked this through.

"Are you still staying with your parents?"

"Yes. I was planning on going back to my place this weekend. Now that doesn't seem like the best idea."

"I agree." Pulling into the parking lot, Jeremy glanced at the clock. Ten thirty. "Can we talk in my office? I'd like to finish the conversation we were having."

Noel studied his face in the darkened car. "You made me a promise back there. Think you can keep it?"

"I can," he assured her.

"Might not be as easy as you think."

His office space was filled with books, the shelves behind his desk crammed with mismatched volumes and file folders. The room had a sense of cluttered order. The desk, however, was clear of everything but a laptop. Noel turned to him, extending her hand as she leaned back against the desk.

Her fingers were cold, the chill of the October evening still lingering. He warmed her hand between both of his, choosing to wait for her to speak.

"I am about to challenge everything you believe to be true." Her words were quiet and earnest. "I don't understand all of it myself, but I do know it wasn't a dream or a hallucination. What happened to me the day I drowned was as real as this desk I'm sitting on." She boosted herself up to sit on the polished surface and patted the wood next to her with her hand.

Jeremy sat beside her, a shiver of anticipation and dread making his hand twitch as he covered her hand with his, one shared point of contact he would need as she began to speak.

"You asked me how I could remember the CPR you used to save me," she began, turning her palm upward beneath his. "I didn't remember it, I saw it. I watched you do it. From above. I saw you pressing on my chest and breathing for me. I could see the top of your head with this small bald spot just barely visible back then."

His free hand lifted to the crown of his head, to the area of thinning hair that was not so small anymore. He kept his words neutral, his promise to her holding sway over his thoughts. "Patrick Mueller would call that an out-of-body experience."

"He would, but it was much more than that. I watched you and I knew I should have been scared, but I wasn't. I felt warm and peaceful and drawn away from the sight of you struggling over me, like I was being pulled upward. Then everything was getting smaller and smaller like looking at a car on the highway from the window of an airplane. And I knew in my soul there was something better ahead of me than behind."

He could hear the awe in her words, as if even in the telling she was experiencing it again. He had no idea what to say, so he remained quiet. He had read the books about near-death experiences as part of his debate prep. Noel's memories were well in keeping with those accounts, and yet he had always attributed the phenomena to the biological degradation of the hypoxic brain. "And your sister? Where does she fit in?"

Noel's voice warmed, her tone filled with surprise and wonder. "Then I wasn't alone any longer. This beautiful girl was moving at my side, her smile brilliant. She was overflowing with happiness to see me. She didn't speak, not with her mouth anyway, but it was like I was inside her thoughts. She was my mother's firstborn, and she died in utero with the umbilical cord wrapped around her neck."

"You remembered this tonight on the beach?"

"Standing there in your arms, yes. And I didn't remember; I learned it for the first time. I never knew my mother had another child." She glanced at him, her eyes wide. "It feels like you're the link between fear and revelation. How is that possible?"

Jeremy shifted to his feet, his restless unease needing a physical outlet, knowing the obvious answer was the right one. "Because I was there with you that day, under the water in your moment of desperation, and I'm still here with you now in one of the most terrifying moments of your adult life."

She lifted her gaze and studied his face with an intense scrutiny. "There's more, I can feel it, and I want to know the rest. Will you help me do that?"

"Of course," he said without hesitation, his concern for Noel winning out over the warring convictions trying to take control of his thoughts.

"Do you believe me?"

"I do, every word." Jeremy drew her to her feet, his hands settling on her shoulders. He wanted to pull her into his arms but was afraid that in the aftermath of earlier it might trigger not a memory but a PTSD event.

As if reading his thoughts, she stepped closer to him, her eyes studying his for a moment before her arms encircled him and she rested her head on his shoulder. "Thank you."

He believed her words and believed she had experienced this in the aftermath of the drowning, but the origin of this phenomenon was still an open question. The scent of her hair filled his senses as his arms encircled her in a possessive hold and he knew he had never felt as committed to anyone as he did to this girl he had saved, now a woman trusting him with her most intimate fears. Her breath on his neck when she spoke sent a quiver of tenderness and desire coursing through his body.

"How do we go back? To working as colleagues like we talked about last week?" she whispered.

"I don't want to go back." He tilted his head, his cheek resting against her hair. "I thought I could walk away from you, but it wasn't true then and it's not true now. We can find a new way forward because I'm not losing you again." He felt her answering smile and the warmth of her words against his skin.

"So we're in this together?"

"Feels like we always have been. Let's get you home."

As they walked to their cars, Jeremy secured a promise from her that she would tell her parents about what happened. Although she was reticent to do so, his logic won out over her worries. He walked Noel to her car and then found his own. Inside he started the engine and then called John Santino to ask if he would increase routine patrols around her parents' neighborhood. The detective, still working the incident tonight, agreed. Following her car as they navigated the empty streets between the university and her temporary home, Jeremy downshifted to make the turn into her parents' street. As Noel pulled into the driveway, he idled by the curb and waited for her to walk up the path and unlock the front door. She turned back to him and waved, and he flashed his lights before watching her close the door.

Jeremy shifted into gear and headed home. His life and everything he believed had been upended in the span of a few hours. Helping Noel would challenge everything he thought he knew, but he remained committed to helping her find the truth. Everything in him wanted to argue the impossibility of God being the origin of her memories, but his belief in Noel left him ready to make this journey with her. In the recesses of his mind, he could feel the pull to try and dissuade her from this search for a deity, but he knew that was selfish and wrong. He wanted her to find the future she'd told him about on that first night together. A sudden thought made him punch the brakes as he stopped for a traffic light. She wanted to be a wife, a mother, and someday a grandmother, and although he had never considered the possibility, he knew he wanted to be the man who made that happen.

# CHAPTER TWELVE

"You got in late last night." Garrett glanced up from the stove as Noel came into the kitchen. He stirred the oatmeal, his usual morning fare, while Marcy pulled berries from the refrigerator.

"I stayed late to finish reading the study protocol since Mia has a game tonight." Remembering Jeremy's words, Noel steeled herself for the moments ahead. "Did she leave already?"

"Yup, just made the bus."

"I need to talk to you both about something. Can you come sit down?"

Settled at the small kitchen table moments later with coffee mugs in front of them, Garrett's concern was evident. The flush that colored his skin was a stark contrast to Marcy's sudden pallor; the butterflies on her pajamas were a touch of whimsy against the fear in her eyes. Noel knew that look; she had seen it often over the years.

"Did something happen last night?" Marcy leaned forward, pushing her mug aside.

Noel couched the truth in words designed to shield them from the panic of being chased through the woods and floating alone on the dark water. Unfortunately, the incident rather spoke for itself, and Noel watched their concern grow. Marcy's fear escalated into a near panic and her hands shook on the table.

Garrett covered her hand with his own, his tone tense but measured. "But you're all right? They didn't hurt you?"

"I'm fine, Dad, just a little shaky this morning." Noel knew that trying to deny the aftereffects of the incident would only make them want more details. Better to stick with the truth.

"This man you texted, who called the police," her father continued, "is he the same man who rescued you the summer you were working at the camp, the professor you mentioned at dinner?"

Noel nodded, unsurprised that her father had put the pieces together.

Startled, Marcy glanced first at Garrett and then at Noel. "Jeremy Finnegan? He was there?"

"You remember his name?"

"I'm not likely to forget the man who saved my daughter's life." Marcy's tone was indignant, her panic beginning to subside as she met Noel's gaze.

"We've become friends since I ran into him on campus with Mia."

Garrett gave her an assessing glance. "Do the police think this incident is related to the attempted burglary last week?"

Noel nodded. In for a penny, in for a pound. Wasn't that the expression her grandmother used to say? "Most likely, yes."

"Is Jeremy the target or are you?"

"It started with Jeremy, and now it seems to be both of us."

"I suppose it's already too late to ask you to stay away from him," Garrett said, his tone thoughtful. "By the look on your face, I don't think you would do it anyway. He's more than a friend, am I right?"

"We're still working that out," Noel answered, not trying to be evasive. Her words were simply the truth. "He wanted me to tell you so the increase in police patrols wouldn't alarm you and so we could all look out for each other."

"Would you have told us if Jeremy hadn't asked you to?" Marcy sat up straighter, her tone direct.

Noel froze. "Yes, eventually. I was hoping the police would solve this before I had to."

"Why would you try and keep this from us?" Garret's words held an undertone of urgency as he leaned toward her. "I know you've always thought we were too restrictive—I believe overbearing was the term you used—but you are no longer a teenager, and I would like you to look at this from our point of view. What you thought was restrictive was our parental caution after the accident. What you perceived as overbearing was our worry for your safety from reporters harassing you. And what you saw as our obstinate refusal to let you go was our fear that someone would try and exploit your trauma by taking advantage of a heart-wrenching story just to make a few bucks."

The sincerity in his words was clear, but still the old grievance rose to Noel's lips. She felt like she was seventeen again as the words rushed from her mouth. "Why didn't you let me get my driver's license? You refused to let me take the test!"

"Because we didn't have the money to pay for another driver on our insurance policy, much less the money to buy another car," Garrett admitted with a touch of chagrin. "We should have told you. We had thousands of dollars in credit card debt and were just starting to get ourselves out of it. Sharing out financial mishaps with our teenage daughter was not something we wanted to do. I admit that was a mistake."

Startled by his honesty and never having considered that time in her life from any perspective but her own, Noel had to agree mistakes had been made on both sides. Honesty going forward was the only way to keep that from happening again. "Will you tell me about Celeste?"

Garrett's eyes filled with anguish and he lifted his hand to massage his chin.

Marcy sat back in her chair, her eyes glistening. "How can you possibly know about that?"

"Tell me how she died, Mum," Noel said softly. "You've hidden her from me all these years, but she was my sister, the only biological sister I will ever have."

Reaching for Garrett's hand, Marcy wove her fingers through his, seeming to draw strength from his touch. "We had struggled with infertility for years, when against all the odds, we conceived a child on our own. Those months of my pregnancy were the longest of my life, just waiting to meet our baby, a little girl we found out by ultrasound. We were just days away from our due date when I went to the office for a checkup and the nurse couldn't find a heartbeat. At first, they thought she was just in a position that made it hard to hear, but then the obstetrician did an ultrasound and I knew by the look on her face that our baby was gone. The rest of that day was a blur. The trip to the hospital. Another ultrasound. And then finally an induced delivery of our precious girl. The umbilical cord was so tight around her neck that they had to cut it to even get her out." Tears streamed from Marcy's eyes before she dashed them away with the back of her hand. "We named her Celeste, just as we'd planned and had to say goodbye to her before we even had a chance to meet her."

Driven by the pain in her mother's voice, Noel stood and wrapped her arms around Marcy. "I'm so sorry, Mum."

Marcy looked up at her daughter. "How did you know about her?"

Noel sank to her knees, taking her mother's hand and reaching for her dad's.

"Because I saw her. She's beautiful, Mum." Noel looked up at them. "Beautiful blue eyes, strawberry blonde hair, and a birthmark shaped like a heart just under her ear."

Every day she seemed to remember more about the experience, as if having opened the gates last weekend the images were flooding back with a clarity that increased each morning when she opened her eyes. Today she'd remembered the birthmark.

"How can you know that?" Garrett gasped.

"Because I met her, Dad. The day of the drowning." Noel paused, her next words a query, not an accusation. "Why didn't you ever tell me I died?"

Marcy's face grew even paler. "Because we didn't want to scare you. We knew about the CPR but in the aftermath of the hospitalization, you seemed to have no memories of that day. For a long time afterward, you were a very different child, quieter and more anxious, like you didn't fit into your own life. It's why we sent you to Blake. You do have memories now, though, don't you?"

"Only recently. They started coming back a few weeks ago."

"The day you met Jeremy Finnegan again," her father clarified.

"Yes."

"I would very much like to meet this man," Garrett said. "Thanking him seems the least I can do."

"I think we can make that happen." Noel squeezed their hands and then got to her feet. "But for now we need to talk to Mia and keep her close until this whole thing is resolved."

"She's not going to like that." Marcy looked up at Noel with a knowing glance.

"You're right, she won't. But it's for her safety," Noel added, the irony of her words not lost on her. "How about I meet you at the game tonight and we can talk to her afterward?"

"We're picking Mia up from school and getting on the road from there. How about we swing by the university so we can all go together?" Garrett suggested with a raised eyebrow and upward tilt of his chin.

Noel had always known her parents loved her. That was never in question, but what she had perceived as the need to fight for her freedom had turned out to be an illusion. How had she let that adolescent view of her parents linger so long into her adulthood, a perspective that now turned out to be a tainted version of the truth? They hadn't been holding her back but trying to protect her in the same way she was trying to protect Mia. The insight lingered as she replied, "I think that's a very good idea."

* * *

Noel read the last page of the protocol, her eyes skimming over the citations and references in the index that followed. She had finished in time to meet her parents for the drive to Mia's game and was contemplating getting them drinks from the coffee bar before she remembered the mental note she had made last night. She flipped to the page and started at the top, trying to remember what had caught her attention. Some kind of discrepancy with the exclusion criteria. The wording was ambiguous but suggested that any inclusion of a subject with an exclusionary condition would void the study. But that couldn't be right. In most cases the discovery of additional information would result in the subject being dropped from the study but wouldn't impact the subsequent findings. She must be reading into it too much and misunderstanding the awkward wording. She made a mental note to bring it to Jeremy's attention when she saw him, which in the course of her regular workday was not often. He'd told her he was not hands-on with the staff, and she hadn't set eyes on him at work since Monday. Dr. McMann would be an easier avenue to a timely answer.

Noel placed the protocol in its box and gathered up the handbag the police had returned to her this morning, having found it in their search of the woods between the science center and the lake. She met Dwayne in the upper-level hallway as they returned their materials to Dr. McMann's office.

"Heading out early?" Noel asked, trying to distract herself from the sudden wave of déjà vu brought on by walking down the same hallway as last night and for the same purpose.

"I'm trying to sneak in a few site visits before the meeting on Sunday. You are coming, right? After the service?"

"I'll be there." Having forgotten about the meeting with all that had gone on this week, Noel was glad of the reminder. Helping local seniors would be a good diversion from the rest of her life.

"How about joining me now to take a look at some of the homes we'll be working on?" Dwayne asked, as they stopped outside Dr. McMann's office.

"Sorry, I can't. I'm leaving early to go watch my sister play basketball this afternoon. Did you ever play?" Noel looked up at him with a smile.

"I get asked that a lot. Yes, I played but I never made the all-county rankings like you did." He laughed at the look of surprise on her face. "We went to the same high school, remember? I was a sophomore when you were a senior. Although I don't expect you'd have any memories of a lowly underclassman."

Especially during her senior year after the accident, Noel thought, recalling how she'd thrown herself into practicing as a retreat from her parents' hovering after they returned from visiting her grandmother in England.

"Actually, I do have a vague memory of watching a tall, gangly kid playing in a JV scrimmage while I was waiting to watch my boyfriend's game."

"I've filled out a bit since then, but I was never anywhere near as good at basketball as everyone expected me to be." Dwayne knocked on the door. "What ever happened to the boyfriend? Was he a keeper?"

Noel cringed. "He dumped me midway through our senior year." Not that she blamed him. What guy in high school wanted to date a girl he couldn't even kiss?

"Bad move," Dwayne said as the door was opened by Dr. McMann, who seemed to be on his way out.

"Good, I'm glad you two finished up." He took the boxes from them and laid them on his desk before returning to lock the door behind him. "I've got a meeting with the IRB about some last-minute issues with the protocol. You would think we would have cleared all this up last week. We have subject interviews scheduled for Monday."

Noel's question died on her lips as she watched him hurry off. Maybe the IRB had found the same problem she had. If so, it was going to get addressed today.

"He seems a bit frazzled," Noel said.

"This is a big undertaking. There's a lot of money involved, not to mention the academic expectations of the university. He's a man with a lot riding on the outcome of this study," Dwayne said. "I'll see you tomorrow."

Pondering his last words, Noel realized David McMann wasn't the only one with a lot riding on the study outcome.

* * *

Sitting in his office Friday afternoon, Jeremy picked up his cell phone and called John Santino. He hoped it wasn't going to go to voicemail like earlier.

"Detective Santino. How can I help you?"

His voice sounded weary like he hadn't slept much since the incident on campus last night. "John, it's Jeremy Finnegan. Were you able to get any information from the man transported to the hospital last night?"

"He's unconscious after a lengthy surgery and still needs a ventilator to breathe. They're calling it critical but stable. We won't be able to interview him for a few days, and the surgeon said his memory may be affected by the injury."

"He is under arrest, though?"

"Technically, yes, based on Ms. Welsh's statement about him trying to harm her. We have a guard stationed outside his room. But we can't ask him any questions until he has been read his Miranda rights."

"Did you get his name, at least?" Jeremy heard the detective's weary sigh.

"No ID on him; he's a John Doe for now."

"Fingerprints?"

"Not in the system. I'll keep you posted but I expect you to do likewise."

"Got it." Jeremy laid the phone down next to his computer. His gut roiled with frustration, knowing they were no closer to finding the others who had threatened Noel. His irritation grew when he opened his e-mail and caught sight of the now-familiar address. His fury mounted as he read the subject line.

**This was never about her. It's about you.**

Jeremy clicked on the e-mail, his fury chilled by fear as a picture appeared on the screen. The photo showed a couple walking across the university's well-lit parking lot. Jeremy remembered the feel of Noel's shoulder brushing against his and the self-control it had taken not to draw her into his side in what for them was a professional space.

He pulled his gaze from the image to the text below.

**God created them, man and woman, for each other and for his glory. His WORD speaks about sacrificial love. One man sacrificing his life for another, for a world of others that pay him no honor. What would you sacrifice to keep her safe?**

Jeremy's anger flared as he forwarded this latest e-mail to Detective Santino. He reread the e-mail and noted the strange capitalization of WORD. He seemed to recall that being the case in all the e-mails he'd received and quickly checked, confirming that conclusion. Was it a name or an abbreviation of some kind? He'd have to ask Santino if they were looking into it.

His eyes shifted upward to the subject line again. **This was never about her. It's about you.** Although he was relieved Noel was not their target, the threatening tone of the message left him doubtful about the truth of that statement.

What would he sacrifice, Jeremy asked himself, the answer as clear to him as the words on the screen. Before he could think twice, his hands settled on the keyboard and he typed a reply to the warped missive.

**What do you want from me?**

He knew Detective Santino would never condone communicating directly with the source of the threat, but he dismissed the cautionary thought and hit send.

The phone at his elbow rang. Startled by the interruption, he glanced at the caller ID. Blake Dempsey. He didn't recognize the last name but the first made him swipe the screen to take the call.

"Jeremy Finnegan, please." The woman's voice was soft but assertive.

"Speaking," he answered. The e-mail was still lingering in his thoughts as he tried to refocus.

"Jeremy, thanks for taking my call. I'm thinking you recognized my name."

"Noel has mentioned you several times. You are an important part of her life."

"As she is in mine. We have been good friends—best friends I like to think—for many years. As you know, I'm her former therapist."

Jeremy waited, knowing she'd called for a reason and giving her time to spell it out.

"I have agreed to help Noel as she tries to recover her suppressed memories from the drowning and its aftermath," Blake began, her words measured, her tone crisp and professional. "I received a call from her earlier today asking if we could set up an appointment, and she told me she would like you to be there. Normally, I do not include nonfamily members in our sessions, but after she told me about what happened Wednesday night, I agreed."

He could hear the leeriness in her voice. "Can we talk about this in person?"

"My thoughts exactly,' she replied. "Could you stop by my office in thirty minutes? I'm just a few miles from the university."

"That works for me."

She gave him the address, one he recognized. Her office was in the medical suites across from the hospital.

"I appreciate you looking out for Noel," he said. He knew from her tone that he was on shaky ground with this woman who loved Noel like family.

"I hope you still feel that way after we talk. I'll see you soon."

The stark message on his computer screen converged with the memory of Noel shaking in his arms. He knew the tenets of the Christian faith. He had studied them extensively in his debate preparation, and the logic of the e-mail was twisted. The Bible did speak about sacrificial love but not as a bludgeon to be used to blackmail others into belief but rather as a choice. And there was no choice here. This was a threat, a threat of harm to the innocent. It was a bit more subtle than the last one but was a threat nonetheless. Still the question lingered: What did they want from him? After patting his pocket for his keys, he locked the office and headed for the parking lot.

"Jeremy."

He looked up to find David bearing down on him as he descended the steps from the science center. Jeremy glanced at his watch; he didn't have time for a lengthy discussion.

"Good, I'm glad I caught you." David's face was flushed from the heat of the day, his breathing labored as he stopped in front of his colleague.

Jeremy tried to squelch his impatience as he waited for David to catch his breath. The man needed to spend some time at the gym. He wasn't as young as he used to be. If he wanted to be around to see his son and daughter graduate from college he was going to need a bit more self-care.

"It seems the IRB found my answers acceptable yesterday."

Jeremy's focus sharpened. "Is there a problem with the study?"

"Not anymore. Apparently, some of the board members didn't have the final copyedited version of the protocol, while others did. There was concern we had changed the protocol without telling them."

"But you took care of it?"

"I did. Every board member now has the final copy. And the section they seemed concerned about has been read and approved."

"Why didn't I hear about this yesterday?"

"Because I was taking care of it for you, like any good coinvestigator does. It doesn't take two of us to solve a minor problem. I must say the gossip in the meeting was more interesting than the actual reason they called me there. Apparently, your hero status remains intact, at least for the foreseeable future." David's eyebrow arched with a knowing glance.

"What are you talking about?" Jeremy asked, sneaking a look at his watch.

"Apparently you saved some woman from being attacked on Wednesday night?"

Jeremy stilled. That the story was making its way around campus shouldn't have been surprising. "More like she saved herself. I just called the police."

"Is it true she's one of our new hires?"

Jeremy gritted his teeth. "Yes. Is that a problem?"

"Not for me. I'm glad you were able to help her." David eyed him with a hint of a smile. "You'll never live the hero thing down now, though. The undergraduates are all buzzing about it. Just wanted to give you a heads-up, since you might hear about it in your classes this afternoon."

"Thanks for the warning."

In his car moments later, Jeremy glanced at the clock with a wave of relief, realizing he would still make it to Blake's office on time.

Blake was waiting for him in the reception area as he came through the door. She was short in stature, with dark hair bundled into a bun atop her head and her glasses at a slight angle amid the mass of curls. She wore little makeup. Her black pants and white shirt were a nod to professional attire, although the loose fit of the pants looked comfortable. She stepped forward and extended her hand. "Thanks for coming."

"Of course. I want to help Noel in any way I can." Jeremy shook her hand, surprised at the strength of her grip.

She waved him into her office, where a comfortable couch of burgundy leather sat across from two wing chairs. "I gathered from my conversation with her that she thinks you are the nexus to getting her memories back."

"You sound skeptical." Jeremy noted how she waited for him to sit. He chose the wing chair and she chose its mate, changing the angle so she faced him.

"I'm reserving judgement for now, trying to keep an open mind." Blake met his gaze, her eyes assessing. "Before we begin, I think you should be aware that I know a great deal about you from Noel. I have not seen her in a professional capacity for over a decade, but we are friends and she tells me almost everything. I know about the recent attempts to harm her and your part in saving her, for which I will be eternally grateful because I love her like a sister."

"I'm sensing you don't trust me."

"What you are sensing is my fear for her. The traumatic moment the two of you shared makes her vulnerable and you have the capacity to hurt her in a way no one else can. I don't want that to happen."

"What can I do to reassure you that I would never hurt Noel?" Jeremy leaned forward and clasped his hands between his knees.

"She told me about your conversation Wednesday night and the fact that you said you believed these latest revelations about her sister."

Jeremy nodded. "I do."

Blake studied him, her gaze unwavering. "But I'm afraid, given your background, your words are just platitudes and your belief won't stand up to the onslaught of what she is about to tell us. You've read the books on near-death experiences, so you know where this is going."

Jeremy heard the concern in her measured words. "I have read them, and for right now I am setting aside the origin of the experience and choosing to believe in Noel's understanding of the occurrence."

"I don't think that's enough." Her eyes narrowed, lips pursing in a shift from the professional to the personal. "She'll know if you are shading the truth. She seems to know you very well and she trusts you in a way I find surprising. Frankly, I'm afraid you are going to violate that trust."

"I would never do that," Jeremy asserted with conviction, trying to keep the steel from his tone.

"If that's true, then I think you have to set aside everything you believe and listen to her with an open mind."

"About God, you mean?" Jeremy understood her concern but still felt blindsided by her sudden adamancy. "You can't force me to believe in God, Blake."

"Of course not, but I am asking you to be open to the possibility …"

"Do you believe in God?' Jeremy interrupted.

Blake blinked. "That's not relevant…"

A wave of annoyance drove the next words from his mouth. "Why is it relevant for me but not for you? We both love her!"

Even as the surprising admission exploded into the silent room, Jeremy knew it was true. He sank back into his chair with an awestruck feeling of having settled on the obvious.

"Have you told her?" Blake asked, her eyes wide.

"Just coming to terms with it myself." He met her gaze. "You are talking to a man who has never loved anyone in his entire life… until now."

Her lips curved upward in a subtle hint of a smile, although he thought he detected the return of her professional demeanor at his words.

He spoke up before she could. "Someday, when we know each other better, I'll tell you the story of my growing up in a punitive, silent household. But for now all you need to know is that I will do everything in my power to help Noel recover her memories so she can move on with her life. A life I very much hope includes me, but that will be up to her, of course. I told Noel recently that I am a scientist who is never above modifying my thinking in the face of new evidence, so I will give Noel all the support she needs to discover the truth and myself the room to understand it."

His answer seemed to satisfy her as she relaxed back into her chair. Her eyes were curious rather than assessing.

"Can I make a personal observation?" Blake ventured and, at his nod, continued. "It is clear to me now that you care deeply for Noel, and I know you are aware of her ongoing problem with intimacy."

"She told you about the kiss in her apartment?"

"She did."

"Then you know it's likely the CPR that provoked that reaction."

"I agree that was likely the instigating event. But I believe it was the additional trauma of her attempting to share what happened to her and being soundly rejected that cemented it in place. A physical trauma followed by a psychological one. Afterward, she trusted no one with that experience and buried it deep. She's been suffering the consequences ever since, both physically as an aversion to intimacy and psychologically as an aversion to trust. She has chosen to trust a very small group of people, and it appears you are one of them."

Jeremy leaned forward. "If I want to help her move beyond both those issues, what would you suggest?"

"I think you know. Believe what she tells you and move slowly with any physical encounter. This is a game of inches with an end zone in sight but far down the field."

"But well worth the wait." Jeremy met her gaze.

"I'm so glad you think so." Blake got to her feet and shook his hand.

In the car moments later, headed back to the university for his final class of the week, his declaration still rang in his ears. He'd told Blake the truth. He had never loved anyone in his life. He'd wanted his father's approval and longed for his attention, but he never loved his cold and distant father. As a young boy, Jeremy had longed for his mother but rarely felt comfort in her arms, her many admissions to the hospital precluding the normal maternal/child bonding. He had vague memories of his grandmother, sweet memories of hugs and cookies and bathtime, but she had died when he was in kindergarten, which made those memories precious but fleeting. His childhood home had isolated the siblings from each other, and although he recalled looking up to Will as a role model, he wouldn't call that love. In fact, he had resigned himself to living a life without that messy emotion, so sure it would never reach the depths of his hardened soul. Now here it was, triggered by a girl from his youth who captured his imagination and left him wanting things he had never dreamed of having. The image on his laptop flashed through his brain and he knew in an instant the terror and vulnerability of loving Noel. The emotion was new to him, yes, but he recognized its power and he knew with clarity that he would do anything—anything—to keep her safe.

# CHAPTER THIRTEEN

Noel sat in the last row of the spacious auditorium, where earlier in the week she had started her new job with a gathering of all the study employees. On stage Jeremy was giving an interactive lecture to his sophomore biology students. Although it was late afternoon, he held their attention while delivering the details of the physiology of the brain. His use of analogies sparked an exchange of questions and answers that helped to reinforce the concepts they were discussing. Watching him, Noel wondered if many of the young women in the class weren't just a little in love with their professor which, while quite possible, had more to do with her own fascination with this man who had become an important part of her life. As the class began to disperse, a few students lingered to talk with him. Jeremy tapped out a quick message on his phone and Noel felt the accompanying vibration in her pocket as he turned his attention to his students.

**Wait for me, please.**

A chill of anticipation made her shoulders quiver. In a room filled with students, he had known she was here. There was no denying the uncanny sense they had of one another, like a fine-tuned inner hum that sounded whenever the other was near. A sudden thought took her by surprise.

Was she a little in love with him?

Noel shook her head. How was that possible after such a short time? Admittedly, there had always been a part of her that was in love with the boy who saved her, but that was more an idea than a reality. Early on, she had fantasized about meeting Jeremy again, but the emergence of the PTSD events drove all thoughts of him from her mind as she strove to give no mental landscape to the day of the drowning. With no practical experience of falling in love as an adult, she had only the memory of a high school romance as a point of reference—and look how that had turned out. Not the best comparison.

She watched Jeremy stride up the aisle, stepping into the row of seats in front of her and standing over her with a warm smile. Leaning forward, he clasped the seat back in front of her. "Have dinner with me."

He looked like he was getting ready to convince her as he leaned in closer.

She got to her feet, bringing them eye to eye. "Where are we going?"

His grin was brilliant with just a hint of mystery. "I've been thinking about this all day."

"Good to know I've been on your mind," she quipped.

"Lately, you are all I seem to think about," he said, his tone light but his gaze direct.

His words stole the response from her lips. Her earlier musings returned. Is this what it felt like to fall in love?

"I've come up with the perfect place," Jeremy continued, oblivious to her thoughts. "A place where I won't have to worry about your safety and we can just enjoy each other's company. I don't think we've ever done that."

"Aside from the dinner with your brother, you mean?"

"And though I did enjoy the beginning of that evening, tonight is about us. Not two kids who shared an experience long ago, but two adults getting to know each other. You game?"

"I am," Noel replied, her tone infused with an emotion she barely recognized. Joy. She glanced down at her clothes, wondering where they were going. Dark jeans. Yellow sweater. Sneakers. "Do I need to change?"

He gave her an assessing glance, which seemed to take a long time before his eyes met hers again. "Perfect."

"Where are we going?"

He touched her hand, sending a warmth radiating up her arm. "Do you trust me?"

"Always."

"Then let's go."

He kept a professional distance between them as they made their way to his car. Settling into the sporty coupe, Noel savored the feel of this man at her side. She glanced over at him. His hair was disheveled as always and his plaid dress shirt was a bit rumpled, open at the collar with the sleeves rolled up. He turned to meet her gaze and smiled. She didn't care where they were going. She was happy just to be in his company, the strained relationship of last week banished by the terror of Wednesday night. It seemed to have clarified for both of them that the road ahead would be traveled together.

They talked easily of superficial things like Mia's high-scoring basketball game and the state park Jeremy had hiked last weekend. He navigated a series of back roads to keep them off the highway on a Friday afternoon as he told her more about the taekwondo class he loved and she spoke of the cross-training class that had taught her how to row.

Jeremy made a turn onto the main street of a local farm community. He followed the road to its end in an open field where a carnival had sprung up for the weekend. A banner above an archway of balloons in rainbow colors announced the carnival would benefit the Widows and Orphans Fund for families of police officers killed in the line of duty. Finding a parking spot in the adjacent field, they exited the car to the smell of buttery popcorn, sweet cotton candy, and roasting hot dogs. A hint of spiced cider and fresh hay bales gave a seasonal scent to the autumn air as they started for the midway.

"This place is swarming with cops and their families. I couldn't think of a safer place to spend the evening," Jeremy said as they made their way to the carnival entrance.

"You seem very intent on the safety angle. Any reason for that?"

He slowed his pace. "In the interest of full disclosure, you should know I received another e-mail after what happened Wednesday night. It included another photo of us."

"Someone is watching us?"

"Looks that way, yes, although the e-mail did say this was never about you, Noel. It's about me."

Noel stopped short just outside the carnival entrance and turned toward him. "I don't think I buy that. They were trying to do more than scare me."

Jeremy pulled her toward him as the crowd of carnival goers swerved around them, like a stone in the river diverting the flow. "I agree. The escalation in their actions rather negates their assurances."

"What exactly do they want from you?"

"Unclear, although I broke with police protocol and asked them directly."

"Detective Santino's not going to like that."

Jeremy nodded, stepping toward the ticket booth at the start of the midway. "I went back and reread all the messages and found a strange similarity. A single word was capitalized in all of them. W-O-R-D."

"Like a name?"

"I was thinking more like an abbreviation, but it could be either one." Jeremy tightened his hold on her hand. "Now can we forget about it for just a few hours and make this evening about us?"

She leaned toward him, her shoulder bumping his. "I think we can. Now—rides or games? What's your first choice?"

"Games. Most of these rides are of the little kid variety."

"Except for that huge swing." Noel inclined her head toward the circular swings spinning out like the spokes of a wheel as the passengers squealed with a mixture of fear and delight. "I love that ride. Will you do it with me?"

Jeremy took her hand. "How about we start with our feet on the ground?"

Walking the midway, they tried their hand at tossing rings onto bottlenecks, catapulting rubber frogs onto lily pads, and shooting down moving cardboard clowns. The air hummed with cheers and groans as prizes were won or nearly missed. They played cornhole, which Jeremy won, before Noel smiled in delight at the archery setup at the end of the midway. She stepped up to the attendant, who helped her pick a bow and then gave her a quiver of arrows.

The weight of the bow felt familiar in her hands as she tested the bowstring, checking the tension before notching the arrow. Squaring her stance with her left shoulder to the target, her eyes narrowed as she sighted the center of the bull's-eye. She pulled back on the bowstring, feeling the remembered tension in her shoulder before letting the arrow fly. It landed just outside the bull's-eye.

"You've done this before, I see." Jeremy chuckled behind her.

"Back in college. I was part of the archery club until it conflicted with my basketball scholarship. Have you ever tried it?" She notched another arrow and took aim, letting it fly with more accuracy than the first. It landed in the red zone, although not in the center.

"Back in high school. I remember thinking it was harder than it looked."

"Here, give it a try." She turned to him, holding out the bow with a smile.

"You are going to help me so I don't make a fool of myself, right?" Jeremy stepped toward her.

She met him halfway. "Do you trust me?"

He looked into her eyes and echoed her earlier reply. "Always."

"Then show me what you remember."

Hefting the bow, he notched the arrow as he had seen her do. Noel stepped up behind him and squared his shoulders, feeling the tension in his muscles melt away at her touch. She wrapped her arms around him, and they pulled back on the bowstring together, holding it for just a second. "That's the right amount of tension. Can you feel it?"

"Oh, I can feel it all right," he whispered under his breath as they let the arrow fly.

Laughter bubbled up in Noel's chest and she pressed her cheek against his back. "How about you try that without my help?"

He landed the last two arrows in the bottom third of the target.

A whistle from behind made them both turn to find Lance Petroff standing with a pretty brunette watching from the sidelines. His hair was as light as hers was dark. They were an attractive pair. "Nice work."

"I had a good teacher." Jeremy winked at Noel as the two men shook hands and Lance introduced his date, Eden. "What brings you out this way?"

"My dad was in law enforcement for twenty-five years. He's retired now, but taking care of the families of those who served is a cause close to his heart, and mine." He turned to Noel with a quizzical stare. "We've met, yes?"

Noel nodded. "Not formally. I believe we have the same day job, working at the university. Noel Welsh." She held out a hand to him.

He engulfed her hand in his, nodding. "Don't you get enough of this guy at work?" He angled his head toward Jeremy with a joking smile.

"We're old friends," Jeremy replied, giving an answer before she could come up with one.

"Then maybe you should show her what you've learned from me in class. They've got a heavy bag and a dunking tank set up back there." Lance turned his head to glance back down the midway.

Noel followed his gaze, wondering if they had missed it or if Jeremy had chosen to take a pass on it.

"There's a sweet spot in the bag. When you hit it with the right amount of force it sends the guy into the tank," Lance explained.

"He was dry until Lance dunked him," Eden added, a touch of pride in her tone. "By the look on his face that doesn't happen often."

'You could show off your spinning back kick," Lance joked, elbowing his sparring partner.

"I believe that move is your specialty, not mine." Jeremy took a step back, glancing over at Noel. "Didn't you say you needed to grab something from the car?"

Reading the set of his jaw, she responded. "Yes, just a headache coming on and I wanted to head it off with the medication in my purse."

After they parted ways with the couple, Jeremy kept his distance until they melded into the crowds on the Midway. "You don't really have a headache, do you?"

"No, but I knew you wanted out of that conversation, so I made something up."

"Lance is a good man but he was probably going to ask us to have a drink with them…"

"And that wasn't what you had in mind for tonight?"

"Not even close. I want to spend tonight with you." He squeezed her hand and then let go.

"Is this going to be a problem for you?" Noel asked. "Being seen with an employee away from work?"

"Lance is a friend, so I don't think he's going to mention it. But I suppose in public we do need to be discreet." He turned to her, the look in his eyes in direct opposition to his words. "Ready to eat?"

They wandered down the midway, collecting barbequed ribs, corndogs, gooey cheese fries, and funnel cakes and finally grabbing two homemade lemonades. Finding a picnic table where they could watch the rides, they sat across from each other and shared the carnival feast.

Noel sized up the food, knowing there was no way to enjoy this without making a mess. She reached for the cheesy fries and a napkin as Jeremy started in on the ribs. "What's a spinning back kick?"

"It's a power move that uses a stance reversal to generate force and take down an opponent."

"Can you show me sometime?"

"Sure. Just not tonight"

"Don't like showing off?"

"Not particularly. If I need that to win you over tonight, I haven't done my job very well." He lifted one eyebrow in a questioning glance. "How am I doing so far?"

"Let's just say that I don't need to see your taekwondo skills." Noel smiled as both the sticky and the sweet fare began to disappear as quickly as the napkins. "Blake called me after the two of you spoke this afternoon. How did your conversation go?"

Jeremy's eyes narrowed as he reached for a piece of the funnel cake between them. "She asked a lot of questions, but in the end all I had to do was tell the truth."

Noel saw the color rise in his face and wondered just what Blake had said to bring about that reaction in this usually composed man. "She has time to see us at noon tomorrow if that works for you. Her husband, Daniel, is going to watch the kids."

He nodded. "At her office?"

"No. She asked if we could meet at her house. I used to do a lot of my sessions at her home office. I'll text you the address."

"How are you feeling about going after something your mind has kept hidden for more than a decade?" Jeremy pushed the remnants of their meal aside, giving her his full attention.

"The hypnosis is making me nervous," Noel replied, her throat suddenly dry at the thought she would be surrendering her conscious mind to someone else. Blake had told her she would be in control of her own journey, but she still found the myth hard to shake. She reached for the lemonade and took a gulp, feeling the icy sweetness play across her tongue and soothe her throat. "But I want the answers now. I want to put this behind me so I can move on with my life, and the only way to do that is to walk through those memories. It scares me to think what would have happened if I hadn't met you again that day on campus. Would I have continued to accept half a life to avoid reliving the terror? But seeing you changed everything."

He nodded, his eyes fixed on hers. "For me, as well."

"Good to know I'm not the only one. It feels like the ground is shifting under my feet."

"Seismic would be a good word for it."

"Exactly, but…"

"Let's just deal with one life crisis at a time. Yours for now. Mine we'll talk about later." His smile was disarming, covering a note of uncertainty in his tone. "What changed when we met?"

"I did. Right from that first conversation in the coffeehouse, I told you things I never tell anyone and I didn't even think twice about it." She stopped, then frowned, before the words tumbled from her mouth. "I rarely touch anyone outside my family and that night in the parking lot it felt like the most natural thing in the world to thank you with a…" She felt the blush rise in her cheeks and hoped in the fading light that he wouldn't notice.

"My mother used to call that an angel kiss," Jeremy said, his words warm.

"In my family we called it a butterfly kiss," Noel continued. finding her voice. "A touch so light it's barely there. I trust so few people in my life but right from the start, I've trusted you. You make me bold, Jeremy. You make me want to grab hold of things I never thought I could have."

"And what if I told you I not only want those things for you, I want them…" His words faded away and Noel sensed his hesitation, the air between them tinged with expectation and longing. "But first, how about we try those swings?"

* * *

He had almost told her last night. Navigating the route to Blake's house the next morning using the GPS on his phone, he ran a hand through his hair still damp from a shower. The images of last night played in his mind as he recalled the exhilaration of conquering his own fear of heights to take that ride at Noel's side, the arc of the swing spinning slowly at first, her laughter infectious as the ride began to spin faster and faster. With feet on the ground moments later, she dragged him over to the dunking tank and asked him to teach her the spinning back kick.

Somewhere in his apologetics research he'd read a quote by Thomas Aquinas who described love as "to will the good of another." At the time he had thought it simplistic, stripping away the trappings of romance to focus solely on motivation, but the reality of that statement rang out with clarity in his thoughts this morning. He'd never had a relationship with a woman that wasn't driven by his physical need to get her into bed, to sate his passion in the arms of the current object of his desire. He had never put the needs of another before his own—until he met Noel. His desire for her hummed like an undercurrent in their relationship, muted by his longing to free her from the prison of memories that had held her bound for too many years. He wanted her free to decide if he had a place in her future, and by whatever definition he could come up with that felt like love.

Stopped at a red light, he rested his forehead on the steering wheel, his mind filled with images of last night. They had returned to the university to get her car and he had followed her home. But instead of driving away, he pulled in behind her and exited his car before she'd turned the engine off. Opening her car door, he extended his hand and she wove her fingers through his, her smile soft in the moonlight filtering through the overhanging trees. She closed the door behind her and leaned back against the car, the night surrounding them as the car's headlights faded into the darkness. Looking into her eyes almost level with his own, all he'd wanted to do was kiss her. Instead, he gently pulled her into his arms, his desire burning like a bed of smoldering coals but his will ironclad as he pressed his lips to her forehead.

A horn blared and he shook off his musing, hitting the gas. Ten minutes later he pulled into Blake's driveway and parked. He drew in a deep breath, steeling himself for the hour ahead. Blake's words from yesterday pulsed in his brain. "You have to be willing to set aside everything you believe and listen to her with an open mind." He believed he could do that, yet like smoke beneath a doorway signaling the blaze beyond, he could feel skepticism seeping into his thoughts. Forcefully, he pushed aside his qualms, knowing that whatever happened in the next hour he needed to believe her, because if he could not he was going to lose her.

Noel answered the door at his knock. Dressed in black yoga pants and an oversized sweatshirt, she reached for his hand. "Are you ready for this?"

Her hand was cold. He noted the quirky half-smile that turned her lips upward but never made it as far as her eyes. "Better question: are you?

"As ready as I can be, I guess."

"Then lead the way."

He followed her to the lower level of the split-level home. Blake's office was an extension built off the back of the house with its own entrance and waiting area. A comfortable mixture of seating options from the overstuffed couch and straight-backed chairs beside it, to a beanbag chair in one corner and a small table and play area in another reminded Jeremy that Blake was a child psychologist.

Noel chose a seat on the couch. "Will you sit with me?"

"I will do whatever you want me to do." Jeremy took a seat beside her, watching Blake study their interaction.

Noel looked up as her friend pulled a chair over to sit in front of them. "Having never done this, are there any rules I need to know about?"

Blake shook her head with a smile. "You just need to get as comfortable as possible."

"Can I hold onto something?"

"What did you have in mind?"

She extended her hand to Jeremy, who covered her hand with his own. "Will this work?"

"Whatever puts you at ease is what will work." Blake leaned forward with her palms pressed together and her elbows resting on her knees. "I do want to say before we begin that there is no guarantee we will be able to retrieve your memories. The fact you are highly motivated to remember will work in our favor, but there is some empirical evidence to suggest that memories retrieved in this manner may not be entirely accurate. You should know that going in."

Noel nodded. "Will I remember what I see when the session is over?"

"Yes. You should have full recall of what we discover here. Do you want to continue?"

"Yes, I'm ready.' She turned to Jeremy and smiled. Her expression was more confident than the sweat against his palm would imply, although he wasn't sure whether it was his hand or hers that accounted for the damp connection.

"Then close your eyes, Noel. Some of this will seem familiar in the beginning, but even as it changes just relax and follow my voice."

Jeremy watched spellbound as Blake began the hypnotic induction.

"Remember that you are in control," Blake said softly. "You can shut this down at any time, but for now take a deep cleansing breath and blow it out."

Over the next few minutes, Blake used a body scan to induce a state of relaxation. Jeremy could feel Noel's hand relax beneath his. He eased his grip, his hand resting atop her open palm.

"Now I want you to visualize steps leading down into a pool," Blake continued. "There are five of them and, as you descend, each will bring a deeper level of relaxation. As you step off the final one the water will cover your head, and we will continue downward."

The scientist in Jeremy was interested in Blake's induction technique, but the man who had just become aware of his capacity to love could feel his anxiety ramping up.

Blake's voice was gentle. "You are relaxed and standing beneath the water inside your own body looking outward. You recognize feelings from the day of the accident, but they are in the background, just a faint hum like a bee flying by your ear, the sound there but then gone. Tell me what you see."

Noel's relaxation was evident in her slack jaw, creaseless brow, and rounded shoulders, but her words were clear, soft, and unhurried, her lips barely moving. "I see Jeremy."

He stiffened at her side, berating himself for not anticipating he would be an integral part of her memories. Like an uppercut to the jaw, he felt blindsided leaving him stunned and breathless.

Noel's words whispered into the quiet room. "He's looking up at me through the water. His eyes are so blue and he's terrified he won't be able to save me but that doesn't stop him from trying."

Jeremy flinched at the memory, her soft emotionless delivery triggering a flood of despair at her words.

"He swims to the anchor, then pulls a small knife from his pocket, the one he'd been using to cut through the tangled fishing line. He starts sawing the blade against the rope's connection to the anchor. It's never going to work, not in time. But he's trying so hard, using every ounce of his strength against the weight of the water. This boy I barely know, who treats me like a little sister, is going to drown trying to save me."

Jeremy's eyes stung with tears, but he forced himself not to move or do anything that would disrupt the state of relaxation that allowed Noel to remember. "Then the line breaks free. A miracle, had to be, but I see the dark spots gathering before my eyes, just a few at first and then a cloud so dark I can barely make out Jeremy rushing toward me, grabbing me by the arm, and sending us upward toward the light. But it's too late."

Blake met Jeremy's gaze, her expression filled with sympathy. He was sure she could see the angst in his eyes and he didn't care; he had never felt so vulnerable in his life as in this moment when Noel was recalling her own death.

"You are safe now, out of the water and on the deck of the float." Blake's words were calm and whether they were meant for Noel or for him, they worked. "Tell me what you see and feel."

Here we go, Jeremy thought, feeling the exhale that chilled his lips.

"I feel like a hummingbird, warm and safe, hovering over the float. I can see my arms and legs, yet I'm floating in the air staring at the back of Jeremy's head and thinking he's much too young to have that bald spot. He's leaning over a girl in a pink bathing suit, her wet hair a tangled mess. Then I recognize her. It's me. I know I should be scared, but I'm not. His face is close to mine, his fingers are on the side of my neck, and he's watching to see if I'm breathing. Then he pinches my nose closed and breathes into my mouth. He straightens and the weight of his wet shorts makes them ride low on his hips, so he hitches them up before placing one hand on top of the other in the middle of my chest. He pushes downward, over and over. I know what he's doing. I took the class, too, to be a counselor. It's kind of fascinating to see, like watching kids play on a playground from a tree high above. Kind of distant and surreal. I see how hard he's working and how tired he's getting, but he keeps going as I drift upward, slowly at first and then faster and faster, the ground falling away beneath me as I move toward the light."

Noel fell silent, a look of awe lifting her features even as her eyes remained closed. Jeremy shivered. A part of him wanted to end this before it went any further, but he couldn't steal this moment from her any more than he could stop loving her. "To will the good of another," the phrase flickered through his mind. He held his tongue and listened.

"Then what happened?" Blake prompted.

Noel's voice grew animated and her still countenance was tinged with a soft smile. "Then I'm not alone. This beautiful creature is there with me, her perfect face glowing. Her cheeks are pink and her eyes are pale blue. Her hair is the color of sunrise on the ocean when it first breaks the horizon. She speaks into my mind, and I understand her perfectly. She's my sister, Celeste. She's so excited to see me, and says she's been waiting for this day to come but didn't expect it to be so soon. She is the first baby born to my parents and she tells me how devastated they were when she died in utero."

"She wasn't an angel then?" Blake clarified.

"No. She's an escort for the journey. Up ahead a tunnel appears. We plunge into it moving faster and faster, the light increasing in brightness all around us. It surrounds me, drawing me closer, enveloping me in warmth and peace and love. Celeste giggles just watching my face."

Jeremy had read many of the accounts of near-death experiences in his debate preparation, and Noel's words were well in keeping with what he recalled.

"Where are you going?" Blake asked.

"She's taking me to meet the Father. That's her job, to show me the way."

Jeremy stifled a cringe, his instinctive response to the word Father. All Blake's attention was on Noel, but he knew she hadn't missed his response.

"We exit the tunnel into the most brilliant place I've ever seen. Green and vibrant. Flowers of every color so vivid that what I'd known before felt like a shadow by comparison with this view before me, like a painter had thrown a bucket of colors up in the air and it had covered the landscape, making it shine. It looks like earth but clearer somehow, all the lines sharper in focus."

"Then He is there, waiting for me, all the light from every corner of this beautiful world condensing into this one being, this Father who radiates love from every aspect of His being. Celeste hums with joy beside me, her body bursting with happiness for me as she steps backward to give me this moment."

Jeremy heard the shift in her tone, a soft reverence infusing the timbre of her words. "I can't even describe what I see, only what I feel. Love. The purest most blissful form of love standing in front of me in a man shining with light and radiating this love that surrounds me, pulses through me and in me, a man who knows everything I have ever done and has loved me through all of it."

Jeremy watched tears fall from Noel's eyes and roll down her cheeks. Her smile was brilliant, like nothing he had ever seen before. He knew the love he wanted to give her would pale in comparison to what she had already known. He was going to lose her to a God he didn't believe in and a love he could never come close to matching. He looked up at Blake and found her gaze fixed on him. She shook her head, reading his thoughts, a silent admonition not to go there as Noel began to speak again.

"I want to stay with Him forever, but in my mind, I know He is giving me a choice because He loves me so much—a choice to return to earth. I don't want to go, not at first, but then Celeste appears beside me, and I know I can't put my parents through the agony of losing another child. She holds out her hand and I take it. I look up at the Father and feel His words in my heart. 'It will only be a little while. Remember how much I love you.' Then we start back the way we came. Celeste whispers something softly into my mind but before I can grab hold of the words, I'm suddenly coughing and water is gushing from my mouth. And I am looking up into the eyes of the boy who has saved my life."

Jeremy's eyes stung at her words as Blake guided Noel back to the surface of the water, where she directed Noel to take a deep breath and open her eyes. As she did, she turned to him, her face damp with tears. Her hand lifted to touch his cheek and her words were clear and heartfelt. "Thank you."

"Do you remember?" he asked, meeting her gaze.

"Yes, it's still overwhelming but I know it's true. I don't know how I could have suppressed such a wondrous place." Her eyes searched his face. "You do believe me?"

"I do. I don't understand it, but I believe you." He brushed the tears from her cheeks, relishing the smile that lit her face.

"I can't explain it," Noel said, looking back and forth between Jeremy and Blake. "Words aren't big enough or clear enough to explain. It's like a different state of being, and just like you know the difference between a dream and being awake, the comparison so obvious you would never mistake the two, that's the distinction between the earth we are living on and the heaven we will see. And the only thing that links the two is love."

Jeremy didn't know what to say, so he let Blake take the lead, wondering how this fellow nonbeliever was dealing with the words they had just heard. Blake's professionalism was front and center as she stood and held out her hands to her friend, her words tinged with amazement. "I think you've been given a gift, Noel."

Standing hand in hand, Noel tilted her gaze downward to her much shorter friend. "Feels like that to me, too. Like I'm supposed to do something with it, but I have no idea what that is."

"I think for now it's enough to just know. What to do about it will come later. For now, just let the memories settle and see how you feel," Blake suggested. "You've never been a religious person, and this is a lot to take in."

"Feels like I'm back in middle school when Kathy Barsto convinced me to go to sleepaway camp with her youth group from church. I didn't know it was a bible study camp, but I remember the campfire on the final night, the praying and the elation. It felt like this." She turned and held out a hand to Jeremy.

He took her hand and got to his feet, a lingering question rising to his lips. "Did you pray with them that night?"

"I did." She met his gaze. "It was the end of a wonderful week with none of the backbiting of middle school girls or the hovering of my parents. In my twelve-year-old heart I wanted it to go on forever."

That explained it, he thought. Although a few of the near-death experiences he'd read about had no acknowledgement of God prior to the occurrence, in most there was an underlying awareness of who Jesus was, even if they'd learned it as toddlers too young to understand.

His mind was reeling. Everything he believed was being turned upside down by this beautiful woman at his side. He believed she was telling the truth as she knew it, but Blake's comment as they began the session now held sway over his thoughts. Memories recalled in this way were not always accurate; therein lay his dilemma and perhaps his salvation. He grasped the possibility like a drowning man, well aware of the irony. Was there a way to believe Noel and not believe in the God she spoke of with such awe? He had to find a way. He couldn't lose her now. Maybe at least some of what she'd told them had been an inaccurate recollection.

He met Blake's gaze as Noel bent to retrieve her purse from the floor beside the couch. Blake's eyes narrowed in a flash of warning, like she knew what he was thinking. She had undoubtedly looked into the faces of many people trying to hide their greatest fears and her professional instincts, honed over many years, could see the truth.

Her next words, spoken in a neutral tone, were directed at both of them but meant for him. "We've covered a lot of ground here today. I began this session with a disclaimer, but I want you to trust yourself and your feelings. You don't need proof to believe in the memories we have uncovered here."

Noel grew still, her eyes wide as she turned to Jeremy. "But I have proof."

It took every ounce of self-control he possessed to voice the words evenly. "What kind of proof could you have?"

"I wrote it all down years ago, a few days after it happened."

Jeremy remembered now. "That's what you were reading the night of the attempted break-in at your house."

She nodded. "After I was discharged from the hospital, I convinced myself it was a dream, but it was so beautiful I had to write it down."

"Have you read it?" Blake asked.

"No. When I spoke to Pastor Mueller he suggested I let the memories return naturally, and although we chose to give them a push today, he was right. I don't need to read it. I know the truth."

Jeremy's gut clenched in fear. There would be no going back now that she'd remembered, no turning from the belief that now lived in her heart. He had to be all in or walk away, and he could no more imagine doing that than he could believe in the God she spoke about with such awe. And that left his heart about to be torn in two as he wrapped his arm around her shoulders. "Let's get you home."

# CHAPTER FOURTEEN

Noel settled into the bucket seat of Jeremy's Corvette, feeling his disquiet in the small space between their shoulders as he backed out of the driveway. She'd had her dad drop her off at Blake's this morning, knowing that she might be too shaky to drive in the aftermath of their session. As Jeremy shifted into first gear and pulled away from the curb, she knew that had been the right move. Not for her, but for him. In the confined space of his car, she could feel the tension radiating off him like a heater blasting on an icy morning. He'd said he believed her, and she was sure he wanted to, but the pull of his academic knowledge was waging a war inside him. She didn't want to leave him alone with his own thoughts right now. She wanted to help him process all he'd heard, but she knew in her heart that ultimately this battle was one he would have to fight alone. No, not quite alone. He and God would have to wrestle this one out.

"Can you take me home? Not to my parents' house, but to mine?" she asked softly, breaking the silence that had settled over them.

He glanced over at her. "I'm not going to leave you there alone."

"I know. That's why I'm asking." She reached out a hand and brushed the back of his where it rested on the gear shift.

A soft smile lifted his lips. "Home it is then."

They drove in silence, each with their own thoughts about the morning. As they neared her house, Noel broke into the quiet. "I know this is hard for you."

"I do believe you," he reiterated.

"I know you're trying to. I can see that and I lo…" Noel bit back the words that had nearly slipped from her mouth. Did she? Love him for it? To her surprise, she found she did love him and not just for the struggle warring inside him to try and see the world in a whole new light. She loved him for his willingness to do so for her, to put aside his own beliefs and consider hers in the light of all they had learned.

He looked over at her, waiting for her to finish the interrupted thought as he made the turn into her driveway and pulled around to the A-frame cottage she hadn't seen in two weeks. He shut off the engine and turned in his seat to face her, his eyes troubled but his words clear. "I believe you, Noel, but I'm struggling to find how this fits in my life."

"I'm trying to find the same thing. Maybe we can do it together?" She brushed back the hair that fell across his forehead. "But right now, I'm starving. How about lunch by the pool?"

His brilliant grin took her breath away. "Lead the way."

Inside, they worked together with the remnants of what was left in her refrigerator and freezer to produce a lunch of hot dogs on English muffins, chicken noodle soup, and frozen berry smoothies. They talked easily of inconsequential things over lunch and then sat under the umbrella sipping their drinks and swapping stories of long-ago college adventures and childhood dreams as the afternoon waned. As the sun began to dip toward the horizon, they gathered the dishes and carried them inside. Standing side by side, they washed and dried the dishes together in a domestic scene Noel wanted to repeat many times.

She folded the dish towel and hung it up after they were done, then crossed the room to the closet by the bathroom. She noted Jeremy's quizzical stare when she opened the door, reached under the pile of folded sheets, and brought out the black volume that had rested there since the morning she left.

She saw his expression shift from questioning to apprehensive as she extended the book to him.

"You don't have to do this." He took a step closer, his eyes fixed on hers. "I don't need proof . . . I just need you."

His words stole her breath away, making her pulse race as she closed the distance between them with the book in her hands. "I don't know what's in here, either. I was hoping we could read it together?"

He took her hand, leading her over to the couch. Sitting down, he lifted his arm and she curled into his shoulder as he rested his feet on the coffee table.

"Can you read it aloud?" she asked. "I'd like to just listen."

Jeremy nodded, opening the book.

"I guess I should start at the beginning, from the day I started working at the camp," he began, his deep voice and academic cadence a sharp contrast to the words of a teenage girl. Noel smiled against his shoulder, loving the sound of her words on his lips. "I don't know if this writing thing is going to help but Blake thinks it might. Feels weird to call her Blake but she said that's what she does with her patients, that first names just work better. It does make it easier, not so much like talking to a doctor because we know how well that goes. Ugh!"

Noel felt the rumble of his laughter beneath her cheek as his lips brushed her forehead. "Sounds just like the girl I remember, spunky and sweet. Made me want to look out for you and our campers."

He shifted his weight, getting comfortable before he returned to the text. "I loved the kids in our group. They were like a pack of puppies always clamoring for attention, especially the girls. And they weren't getting that from Jeremy, who was nice, even cute, but kind of distant. The boys seemed to like him and some of the girls were crushing on him, which made me laugh. The camp director must have put us together on purpose since this is my first year as a counselor and Jeremy has been here for the last three summers. He's got the experience and I've got . . . I don't know what I've got but I love these kids, so open and enthusiastic, and for the summer at least, the little sisters and brothers I never had."

Noel felt the resonance of his words beneath her ear, his manner relaxed at first. The tension in his arm increased as the words of the story turned to the boat leaving the dock. She drew in a deep breath. This was as far as she had gotten the night of the attempted break-in.

From here, it would be new for both of them.

Unsurprisingly, she'd written nothing about the actual accident. Instead the text went to hovering over the float and watching Jeremy perform CPR. The description was similar to the one from this morning, but the tone was younger and the word choice was simpler. She hadn't had the words to describe what followed any more than she had just a few hours ago, but the sequence of events played out in the same order.

At the final page, Jeremy's words grew softer. His breath whispered by her forehead as he tilted his head to touch hers.

"Then I woke up, wet and coughing, still warm but wondering if I passed out and fell in the water. My lips were stinging and my chest hurt. I looked up at Jeremy and the relief in his eyes was so obvious it made me want to smile, but I couldn't seem to remember how. He lifted me up in his arms and held me close as he carried me over to the waiting motorboat. His hold loosened and I knew he was handing me over to someone else, but I didn't want him to let me go." His words fell away as if recalling the moment before he read the final paragraph, his tone hushed and uneven.

"It must have been a dream, but it's the best dream I ever had. Sometimes when I'm falling asleep, I can still feel the warmth surrounding me like the softest comforter I have ever touched. And for a minute I can feel the love again, a love so deep you could drown in it and go willingly—a weird thought after what happened but there it is—and I wonder if I'll ever feel that love for real, not just in a dream. How can I dream something I've never felt? Where did it come from? And what about Jeremy? What happened to him? I wanted to thank him but Mum and Dad wouldn't let me. It made me mad at first, but the part of me that's been too scared to talk about it won out and I just left it alone. I wonder if I'll ever see him again, ever get a chance to thank him for saving me. I suppose not, but I hope so."

Jeremy closed the book, laying it on his chest with his hand splayed across the cover. "I felt that, too. For a split second while I held you in my arms, I didn't want to let you go. But the camp director was waiting and they needed to get you to the hospital." His arms enfolded her as he drew her to him. "But I am never letting you go again."

She rested her hand on his chest, turning toward him. "I'm not going anywhere."

He met her gaze, one finger lifting to graze her lower lip. "You tasted like strawberry ChapStick that day."

A tremor of desire pulsed through her at his touch. "Will you kiss me?"

His eyes widened and he released his hold on her, sitting up to face her. "Are you sure you want to do that?"

"Very sure." She reached for his hand. "You are the only man I would ever trust to do this."

Jeremy cupped her cheek in his hand. "A lot has happened today. Do you think this is the best day to try this?"

"I don't know if there will ever be a best day," she replied. "I'll admit I'm a little scared, but I haven't wanted anyone to kiss me in a long time… and now I do. I want it to be you."

She registered his quick intake of breath and the flush that colored his face.

"Blake told me to take this slowly." His words were just above a whisper.

"At the moment, I don't care what Blake told you." Her lips curved upward.

"Still, I think we should start with something familiar." Lifting her chin with his knuckle, he leaned forward and touched his lips to her cheek.

His touch was gentle and fleeting, a kiss reminiscent of their first night together and yet somehow so intimate it made Noel shiver with longing. Pulling back, he met her gaze. "Good so far?"

She nodded, unable to voice a coherent reply, caught in the chasm between desire and fear and not knowing which of those potent emotions would win out. She didn't want to hurt him again, to end up cringing away from him. Blake had been right about going slowly, she thought, worried more about her own failure than her fears. She wanted to be normal like other women, able to experience love and desire without disintegrating into a mass of trembling terror.

"You okay?" Jeremy asked, seeing something in her face that made him hesitate.

She nodded. He studied her a moment and then closed the distance between them. Her eyes flickered closed as his lips met hers, the touch gentle and sweet and then gone.

The fear was palpable now, a smoldering ember igniting into a flame as if the fear was feeding on itself despite Jeremy's gentle touch. She trusted him completely, so it wasn't him, and in a sudden flash of insight she knew the only way through the fire was to walk right through it as she had this morning. Meeting his gaze, she noted the lines that furrowed his brow and knew he was going to put an end to this to save her from the fear. She fixed her eyes on his, on the blue depths that had once made her afraid to even look at him. Her words cut through the withdrawal she sensed was coming. "Can you let me do this?"

"Are you sure you want to? We don't have to do this today."

"I want to. I need to do this." She'd thought he might smile at her insistence, but his eyes only narrowed with increased concern.

"Okay." He reached for her hands, his reply tinged with more doubt than desire.

This was why she loved him, the truth suddenly so clear to her. Because he put her needs before his own. The thought washed over her like a sprinkler on a hot summer afternoon, its droplets falling to stave off the heat and quench the flames of fear in a shower of relief. She didn't think twice but leaned forward with her hands still resting in his as she kissed him. When she felt nothing but a deep longing, she pressed her lips to his more firmly and found his answering pressure as he returned her kiss.

A smile touched her lips as she lifted her head to look at him. Joy bubbled to the surface as he pulled her into his arms, whispering into her ear. "I love you, Noel."

"You do?" Pulling back in surprise, she met his gaze.

"And here I thought you might have figured that out by now." A warm smile lit his handsome face as he smoothed her hair back from her forehead, tucking it behind her ear. "I think I have loved you since the first night you got into my car looking like a shimmering sky on a summer morning and then told me I was dating the wrong women. I knew then that the only woman I ever wanted to date, the only woman I would ever love, was right in front of me. I have never loved anyone in my life, Noel, which gives me a poor track record on the subject, but I do love you."

He drew her to him and Noel saw in his eyes the same longing that radiated through her like a warm pulse. More than physical desire, it was an aching need to connect with the one person who made her whole, who touched the loneliness in her soul and banished it from her life. She had waited a lifetime to find him—to find him again—and when their lips met she felt no hesitation or fear, the connection between them complete. She answered the increasing pressure of his kiss, wrapping her arms around him and pulling him closer, her heart racing with exhilaration.

She sensed the subtle shift first in herself and then in Jeremy, the longing taking on a more physical drive, overwhelming her senses with its power to push all rational thought from her mind. As if in answer, Jeremy lifted his head and looked into her eyes before gently pulling her head down against his shoulder. She could hear his heart racing in a cadence that riveled her own.

"As much as I enjoyed that, Noel, there are many reasons we need to go slowly." His voice was hoarse, his breathing rapid. "But the most important is this: I don't want you to feel any pressure from me to go any further than we did right now. I want to do the right thing for you. We have years ahead of us to enjoy each other. It doesn't have to happen now."

Noel turned her head, her lips brushing his ear. "This is why I love you." She felt the quiver in his shoulder before she lifted her head and saw his pupils dilated with desire.

"Because you always put my needs before your own. I have never felt as safe and cared for and loved as I do right now."

"Good to know we're in this together."

"Yes, we are," she said with a smile. She felt the sharp edge of the black book wedged between them in the couch cushions. Lifting it up, she set it on the coffee table.

"It doesn't have to change anything between us." Jeremy reached for her hands, covering them both with his.

"It doesn't have to, you're right, but I'm afraid it will. I do love you, Jeremy. I'm just wondering how you're going to deal with the woman you love being a believer."

"And are you? A believer?" His eyes never left her face, and she could sense the tight rein he had on his tone as he awaited her answer.

"After all we learned today, how could I not be?" Noel replied. "Blake was right earlier. I've been given a gift. I don't know how I ever suppressed such a beautiful memory. God and heaven are real. I could no more deny that now than I could forget my own name or yours."

Jeremy lifted her hands and kissed them before holding them against his heart. "I am going to make you a promise and I want you to make one as well. You know how firmly I believe in atheism, but as a man confronted with new evidence, I am forced to examine those beliefs in the light of all I know now. Perhaps there is a God, and because I do believe you, I am willing to go back and look at the facts. I can't promise you I will believe on the other side, but I will promise you a diligent search for the truth."

"You would do that for me?" Noel's eyes stung with unshed tears, knowing how much such a promise would cost him.

"I would do anything for you," Jeremy replied, his gaze fixed on hers and his tone certain.

"What do I have to promise you?" She couldn't fathom what she could possibly give him that would be as important as what he was giving her.

"Promise me you'll talk to me about all of it, all the things you're thinking. Don't shut me out because we hold different views. I want to hear it all. Can you do that?"

"I believe I'm getting the easier end of the deal, but yes, I promise. No secrets, everything out in the open."

She thought she detected a flicker of doubt in his eyes before he drew her to him. Resting in his arms, she prayed the love they shared would be enough to weather the journey ahead.

* * *

Jeremy drove to his townhouse after dropping Noel off at her parents' house. His mind replayed the day in a sensory mix of images and feelings that were both exhilarating and terrifying.

Noel's beautiful face covered in tears as she spoke of the Father of light.

The comfort and ease of lunch by the pool, talking about nothing more important than his ten-year-old dreams of swimming in the Olympics and hers of being an astronaut.

The warmth of her body against his as she allowed him to read her words, a bold display of trust that spoke of her love for him as clearly as the words she voiced just moments later.

The icy fear in his heart that his love for her would pale in comparison to the love of a God he didn't believe in.

He had so many reasons not to believe—the extensive research he had done, his professional reputation as an atheist speaker, his firm belief in the fallacy of an all-knowing God—and only one reason to consider the merits of belief: his love for Noel. He shook his head, one thought so clear. He wanted to marry Noel, to be the father of her children, and to grow old at her side. His hands gripped the steering wheel, knuckles white, as he pulled into his driveway knowing his future happiness lay in reconciling these two opposing viewpoints.

Taking the stairs to his townhouse two at a time, he unlocked the door and threw his keys in the bowl on the entryway table, the loud clash of metal on glass reverberating in the silent space. Glancing at the professionally decorated living room, the cool gray of the streamlined couches was a jarring contrast to the comfortable jumble of furniture in Noel's cottage. Her little home was much more appealing than this sterile space around him that could easily have been a hotel suite. He was nowhere in this space, except in the awards that rested on the pristine bookshelves. Even those were evenly spaced between leather-bound books, not one volume of which he had ever read.

Reaching for the mail he'd retrieved yesterday from the mailbox, he shuffled through the bills and junk mail before coming to a cream-colored envelope at the bottom of the pile. Noting the return address in New Jersey, he flipped it over and opened the card. Will's bold scrawl made him smile. He even wrote like a doctor now. Jeremy carried the card into his study, sinking into the desk chair in front of his laptop.

**Jeremy, it was good to see you on our trip to California. We enjoyed the wineries and the quiet of a few days away together, but seeing you was one of the highlights of our trip. I've missed you, brother, and didn't even know it until I laid eyes on you again. Thanks for meeting us for dinner. I hope we can do it again soon. Say hello to Noel for us. She is a very special woman, but I think you already know that. Be well and God bless you.**

Cherie's addition at the bottom made Jeremy smile.

**PS It was nice to finally meet one of my new brothers-in-law. I thought you might like a picture of your expanding family tree.**

Jeremy studied the photo of Will and Cherie with Molly, Sarah, and Carey, all dressed in their wedding finery with smiles to match the joy of the day. A touch of envy coursed through Jeremy's veins until he recalled the mountain of pain they had scaled to get there: the fall, the coma, how close Will had come to losing the love of his life.

Jeremy glanced at the clock. He shouldn't call, not with the time difference. He'd spent most of his life being independent, not needing anyone, and now all he wanted was to hear his brother's voice after the day he'd had. Giving in to the impulse, he pulled up Will's number and hoped he was still awake.

Will answered on the second ring, his words warm and welcoming. "Nice surprise. You got our card, I'm thinking."

"Just read it. Hope I'm not calling at a bad time. I know it's late."

"No worries. Cherie and I usually stay up after the kids go to bed so we can have some time alone, but I'm sensing from your tone and the late hour that you have more of a reason for calling than just to catch up."

Jeremy massaged his forehead, placing the phone on his desk and putting it on speaker. "I need your help."

"Of course, whatever I can do. Is this about Noel?"

"How did you know?"

"I'm a doctor with good powers of observation," Will chuckled before his tone grew somber. "I could tell by the way you looked at her she was more than a friend. Tell me what you need."

Jeremy started from the beginning, filling Will in on the near drowning, the CPR that saved Noel's life, and the near-death experience she had only today recalled. He finally concluded with the promise he had made just hours ago. "I love her, Will. And now she's a believer."

"Clearly you know what that means in terms of a future for the two of you?"

"I do, but this is all new to Noel. She has no idea many sects of the Christian faith won't allow a marriage between a believer and a nonbeliever."

"You didn't tell her?"

"No, it's an antiquated belief system, built around a nonexistent God, with rules to insulate its followers from being drawn away from the faith. Besides I don't think she'll care."

"But you need to care," Will said, a hint of condolence in his tone.

"Why?" The single word was filled with all the anger and awe of a day that had upended his life. "It's an absurd concept. A marriage isn't doomed from the start because the couple hold different views about religion."

Through the phone's speaker, Will's words were measured and his empathy clear. "It isn't that a marriage is doomed, but there's only so much wear and tear any marriage can take. Being at odds about a core belief will produce repeated conflict. How do I spend my Sundays? At church, or watching my spouse run a marathon? How about kids? How will we raise them, with a belief in God or not? And if you choose belief for the kids, then one partner is left doing all the heavy lifting. All these conflicts are like stones in the road, eventually forming a wall too steep to climb."

"I know the statistics are against us, but we can make it work. It feels like we were meant to be together," Jeremy asserted

Will's tone was gentle. "With your history, I can understand that, but here's my question: Who gets caught in the middle of the tug of war between a spouse they love and the call of a God they believe in?"

Jeremy flinched. "Noel does."

"Exactly. I know you are an ethical man; I've been reading some of your published work about how ethics can exist without religion. That's still your stance, right?'

"Yes." Jeremy was unsure where this was heading but sensed he wasn't going to like it.

"So if you know what Noel believes, how can you be the cause of her violating her own beliefs, waging a battle for the heart of this woman who has literally seen God face to face? Is that an act of love?"

Jeremy felt his heart crack at the words.

"It isn't a matter of what you want, Jeremy, or even what Noel says she wants. Ask yourself, what is the ethical thing to do?"

"To keep my promise to Noel," Jeremy responded. "And I have every intention of doing just that, but I'm not sure where to start."

"You have a lot of knowledge, brother. You've read the historical texts and examined the Bible but only to refute it. Right now, what you need is a new perspective. My best advice is go back and start from the beginning with Christ himself, and ask yourself this question: What if it's true? You have always assumed it was false, perhaps even thought that believers were fools for embracing what you saw as fantasy. But if you are going to keep your promise to Noel you need a new starting point: What if it's true?"

Jeremy let the words sink in, knowing it was a mantra that would need to be repeated many times in the coming days. "As I remember, you were nearly as hard core on this subject as I am. How did you find your faith?"

"On my knees on a cold bathroom floor after a colleague asked me if I was too angry or too proud to pray for Cherie. Stopped me in my tracks, that question. I had done everything in my power to save her, been with her night and day for nearly a month, but I refused to pray for her. Then this surgeon I respected stood in her room and told me she was unlikely to ever have any meaningful recovery. I had nowhere to go. I was losing the woman I loved more than my own life, and in a desperate plea I asked God's forgiveness for my pride and prayed for Him to heal her."

"And He did?"

"Yes, but the irony of how He did it is a story for another time."

Jeremy heard the lift in Will's tone, a lightness akin to reverence. "So where do you suggest I start my promise keeping?"

"The Gospel of John is foundational; I would start there."

"Talk about irony. I've probably read those lines more than many believers. I've studied them and dissected them, and now I don't know how I'm going to see them any differently than I have in the past."

"A little prayer wouldn't hurt, but I don't think you're quite ready for that so I'm going to do that for you," Will said, fraternal warmth flowing through the tinny cell phone speaker. "Cherie and I will be praying that God gives you new insight into those familiar words."

"I'll take all the help I can get." Jeremy leaned forward, his head in his hands. "I can't lose her, Will. It's only been a few weeks since she stepped back into my life, but I can't imagine my life without her."

"I've been there, believe me. The men in our family fall hard and fast for the women they love. You know the right one when you find them and it sounds like you and Noel found each other a long time ago. Don't worry about the future. Just take the next step. One at a time. God's going to show you the way."

"You know I don't believe that, right?"

"I do, but God never turns away a seeker. Let's see how much progress you can make before I see you again and we can talk face to face."

Startled, Jeremy remembered Will's parting words at the restaurant. "When is the symposium?"

"This week. I was planning on calling you in the morning. Think we can find some time to get together?"

"I'll make time," Jeremy responded. "Thanks, Will. It's good talking to you."

"You can call me any time, little brother."

The sincerity in Will's tone shaved the edge off Jeremy's desperation as the call ended. He hadn't ever missed having a family until now, and Will's straightforward advice was just what he needed to move forward.

He opened the laptop in front of him, realizing he hadn't checked his e-mail since running out to meet Blake in her office yesterday afternoon. One at the bottom of the screen caught his attention. Recalling the hasty reply he had sent before leaving to meet Blake, Jeremy opened the e-mail and steeled himself for the contents.

No picture this time. Just text.

**We want a public denouncement of your greatest belief. But are you willing to sacrifice your atheist WORD to keep her safe?**

# CHAPTER FIFTEEN

Noel got to her feet with Mia at her side as the service began. She'd been surprised when Mia flew into the kitchen earlier and asked to come with her to the ten o'clock service. Noel had explained she had a meeting afterward about outreach to the elderly in need of home repairs, to which Mia nodded and asked if she could help, too. With the opening hymn pulsing through the speaker system, Noel glanced over at Mia, noting her enthusiasm at the music and her surprise at the diversity of the congregants. Pastor Mueller's church was a true reflection of his faith, a mixture of old and young, those with much and those with little, migrant workers and local farmers, all standing with voices raised to worship their God.

After the readings and the gospel, Patrick Mueller closed the Bible. He walked to the center of the worship space and took a seat on the steps leading down from the sanctuary, a hand-held microphone clasped in his hands.

"I'm going to ask any children who want a better view to come and join me for this sermon, which is going to be short and sweet and all about you."

A rustle of movement and whispers hummed in the quiet church before a steady trickle of children made their way down the aisles. The Pastor invited them to take seats on the steps surrounding him, the semicircular stairway accommodating the fifty or so brave enough to take the pastor up on his offer.

"I had a sermon all planned, but God is nudging me this morning and telling me we need to talk about faith. And when He talks, I try to listen. So here goes: What is faith?" he asked the kids, his gaze moving over them and waiting for an answer.

"It's believing in something you can't see," an older child of about twelve responded.

"Almost exactly right." Pastor Mueller gave a wide smile to the child who had spoken up. "We're just going to change one word. It's believing in someone you can't see. Who is that someone?

"God," one of the younger kids answered with a shout, making the congregation laugh.

"Exactly right. Has anyone ever seen God?"

"Moses did, I think?" The answer sounded like a question from a girl of about ten with a long braid hanging down her back.

"Good answer, and you're right. God was there in the burning bush, but Moses still needed faith to see Him. Has anyone ever seen God in a human body?"

The children were silent for a moment before a little boy wearing torn jeans and a ragged sweatshirt spoke up. "Jesus had a body."

"How do we know Jesus is God?"

'Because He said He was God," the same boy answered.

Pastor Mueller grinned, his gaze sweeping over the group. "Now I could say I'm a rabbit, but that doesn't mean I have long ears and white fur. How do we know what Jesus said was true?"

"Because of the miracles. He did things only God can do," a young boy with glasses replied.

"How do we know that all these years later? Did anyone write it down?" The pastor followed up.

Several children nodded vigorously before one spoke up. "Yes, you just read it in the Bible."

"Those men who wrote the gospels, were any of them there to see the miracles?"

"Yes. Two of them," an older girl answered. "The Gospel of John and the Gospel of Matthew were written by Jesus's followers."

An older boy raised his hand. "Wait, don't some people say the gospels were written long after Jesus died? Wouldn't the apostles have all been dead by then?"

"Great question." Patrick Mueller reached out a hand to high-five the young man. "A lot of smart people have argued over when the gospels were written. They didn't have printers like we do today, and scribes had to write every word by hand. What they did have was a tradition of oral history where stories were memorized, repeated, and passed along to others. As the apostles grew older, they realized they needed to write those stories down so they wouldn't be lost or altered. They exist today in the gospels, the eyewitnesses telling of how Jesus made the blind see, the deaf hear, and the lame walk. Did the eyewitnesses need faith?"

"No, they saw it," a little girl answered, the bow in her hair large and pink.

"They did see it. But later, after Jesus died, did they need faith then?"

"Yes, because they couldn't see Him anymore," the boy with the glasses replied.

"Then what happened after Jesus died?" Pastor Mueller asked.

"God made Him be alive again," a little girl answered.

"Did the disciples see Him then?"

"Yes," several of them answered at the same time,

"So did they need faith when Jesus was with them?"

"No!" They all shouted.

"But later, when God took Jesus back to heaven and they couldn't see Him anymore, did they need faith then?"

"Yes!" The outcry was loud and certain.

"Okay. Here's the most important question of all: Do you have faith that Jesus is God?"

"Yes!" the kids shouted as the congregants broke out in a wave of applause.

As the uproar faded away, Pastor Mueller spoke into the silence. "Faith in a nutshell."

* * *

Could it be that simple?

Jeremy stood in the far corner of the church listening to Patrick Mueller conclude his unusual sermon. There had been no soaring oratory. No quoting scripture. No stories or analogies. Just a simple question and answer with a group of kids straight out of central casting for the Hallmark channel. He leaned against the wall by the restroom and watched the children return to their seats. Kids of every race and color, from toddlers to middle schoolers, some dressed in their Sunday best and others still sporting the clothes they probably wore yesterday.

Jeremy had spent the early morning with a cup of coffee at his side trying to read the Gospel of John as Will had suggested, but he had no new insights. He felt like he was being torn in two, the e-mail from last night trying to force him in a direction he very much wanted to go but for a totally different reason. His love for Noel was a powerful incentive to continue his research, but did ensuring her safety come at the cost of everything he believed? His frustration and unease growing, he'd decided to take a different approach.

He'd come to Pastor Mueller's church because he wanted to know what Noel was hearing on Sundays. He knew after her proclamation of faith yesterday she would be more open to the persuasive words of the pastor. Jeremy had been to many churches over the years, to the Catholic church as a child with his father and siblings and later to a series of churches, synagogues, and mosques as he sought to sharpen his atheist rhetoric with solid facts about the claims of various world religions. He'd found many of them staid and cold, their rituals leaving little room for faith. But as he exited the church with the sound of voices raised in song washing over him, Jeremy felt the difference in this congregation. This church was alive with energy and pulsing with belief, led by a man whose faith was on full display. Pastor Mueller didn't just believe; he lived his faith and its mission to serve.

Will's words filled Jeremy's mind as he reached his car.

What if it's true?

* * *

Noel and Mia followed the crowd, descending the stairs to the church's all-purpose room. The scents of cinnamon and coffee drew them through the doorway into a space partitioned off into a dozen classrooms. Children darted around the refreshment table, grabbing munchkins and donuts. Noel dodged the small bodies and filled two cups of coffee, handing one to Mia before spotting the sign for the Helping Hands Program. Dwayne stood inside the doorway welcoming the volunteers. Some were families with teenagers, a fair number were young adults, and a few people were old enough to be the project's recipients rather than its volunteers.

"Great! You made it!" Dwayne's welcoming smile grew wider as he spotted her. "And you brought a friend. My kind of girl."

"My sister actually." Noel watched the double take play across his features. She should be used to it by now, but still she fought her disappointment at his reaction to their family relationship.

"Welcome! We take all comers." Dwayne covered his surprise with a warm smile as he turned to Mia. "We have quite a few people your age volunteering this year. What college do you go to?"

"I'm still in high school, but I'm hoping to get into Langford early decision," Mia answered, beaming at the suggestion she was already in college. "Actually, there's a guy in my class right over there." She lifted a hand to wave and then turned to Noel.

"Go. I'll find you afterward." Noel waved her off, watching Mia's excited grin as she ran off to join her friend.

"I was going to try and get you to join me on a few site visits this afternoon, but I can see you probably have other plans." Dwayne's tone was warm as they watched Mia blend into the group of young volunteers, one young man wrapping his arm around her and introducing her to the others.

"I have to get her home. She needs to finish her college essay." She watched Mia laugh at something one of the girls said. After her years in the foster care system, Mia could have been guarded and shy but instead she was outspoken and honest—sometimes too honest, which had on occasion gotten her into trouble. If Noel had to bet, her sister would be friends with half that group by the end of the meeting.

"Have you got time for coffee later?" Dwayne's sudden question was as straightforward as the piercing glance he directed her way.

Surprised by his question, Noel tried to pivot the conversation back to safer territory. "You're just trying to reel me in as a volunteer, aren't you?"

His eyes narrowed as a smile lifted his lips. "I might be trying to reel you in, but it has nothing to do with securing your help as a volunteer."

"Oh." Noel stilled, at a loss for what to say. "I don't think…"

"Don't think, just say yes." He leaned toward her, meeting her upturned gaze.

"I'm seeing someone," she explained, feeling a wave of unease with this man she had been eating lunch with for the better part of a week. Maybe that was the problem. She should have seen this coming after spending so much time together.

"Anyone I know?" Dwayne's eyes narrowed with a glint of amusement.

"That depends on how many people you know," Noel responded, not wanting to disclose the nature of her relationship with their boss.

"Since you haven't mentioned it before, I'm thinking this is a recent event. I can see I should have spoken up sooner. My mistake." Dwayne turned to the people filling the room, holding the clipboard aloft. "Before we get started, can anyone who hasn't signed in do so now? Please include your e-mail and cell number." He handed the clipboard to an older man with dark hair and gray temples before turning back to Noel. "Now after this awkward moment, no bailing on me as a volunteer. We've got a lot of work ahead of us in the coming weeks. We're good, right?"

"Of course." Noel looked up at him, the firm set of his jaw somewhat at odds with his casual words before he turned and strode to the front of the classroom. She took a seat in the front row, accepting the sign-in sheet from the older man with silver sideburns. When she looked up Dwayne had opened a PowerPoint presentation on the large screen behind him.

Noel's cell phone vibrated and she slipped it from her pocket. The single sentence made her smile.

**Early dinner tonight?**

She smiled, typing a simple reply. **Yes.**

**Pick you up at five.**

She grinned, slipping the phone back into her pocket, and then looked up to find Dwayne's eyes on her as he continued his explanation of the Helping Hands Program. She tried to focus on his words as a series of images faded in and out on the screen, pictures of volunteers kneeling on roofs, painting railings, and replacing floorboards. The work crews' comradery with the grateful homeowners was readily apparent.

Out in the car later, Mia was eager to join her new friends as a volunteer.

"You do know it's going to be hard work, right?" Noel teased, trying to ride the wave of her sister's enthusiasm in to shore with the reminder.

"Yes, but I've never been afraid of hard work," Mia stated, her smile wide. "Tanner said it's even fun."

"Tanner?" Noel noted the slight change in Mia's tone when she said his name.

"He's a junior at my school, transferred in last year. We're both taking the same lit elective. And he's going out for the basketball team. He worked on a Helping Hands crew last spring and said they made a big difference."

Noel smiled at the wealth of information elicited by one simple question.

"Did you see the faces of those people they helped?" Mia continued. "It's like they thought it was a miracle or something when it was just some kids giving them a new roof."

"When you're used to living with rain falling inside your house, a dry room during a storm is like an answer to prayer." Noel made the turn out of the church parking lot.

"I don't think I've ever heard you talk about prayer before." Mia turned in her seat, the seat belt stretching across her shoulder. "I overheard Mum and Dad talking about what happened after your accident."

"Is that why you wanted to come with me this morning?"

"Yes. Why didn't you tell me?"

"Because I'm just starting to remember. I was going to talk to you after I worked through how I'm feeling."

"Did you really go to heaven?" Mia's tone hinted at her skepticism.

"I did, yes."

"Was it as good as in the movies?"

"So much better." For a moment Noel's mind lingered on the images she had recalled yesterday. "But I'd say you and I have some living to do here before we get a chance to explore it together."

"And does your living include that guy Jeremy?"

"It does."

"He is still going to help me get into the university, right?"

"Yes, he is. Is your essay done?"

Mia nodded, flipping her braid back over her shoulder. "I know you're going to want to proofread it, but it might be hard for you to read."

"Because you talk about your mother?"

"You said to tell the truth and that's what I did."

"Can you tell me about it? We haven't talked about that in a long time."

"I don't have a lot of memories of my mother." Mia picked at her fingernails as she spoke, a gesture Noel hadn't seen her use since the early days of her coming to live with them. "I remember people coming and going through our apartment. There would be a knock on the door and she would let someone in, some of them dressed like the people on television and some that looked like she did, all pale and thin, with hair that never got cut. They'd stay for a minute and then she'd peek out the door first and they would leave."

Noel knew some of this from their social worker, but she'd never heard Mia speak about it so openly. Mia's mother had been dealing drugs, selling to others to pay her rent and feed her child. Somewhere in those years she had become a user herself.

Mia's voice grew softer. "Sometimes one of the men would stay longer and they would go into the bedroom and close the door, and I knew I was supposed to turn the sound up on the TV and just keep watching until they came out." Her tone held a remnant of the little girl who'd lived that life.

"Then I came home from school one day and I didn't see her right away. Usually, she was waiting for me in the living room, watching some show on TV, but that day I found her in the bathroom, on the floor. Her skin was a weird gray color, and she had a syringe in her arm."

Noel stifled an instinctive flinch at her sister's words. "What did you do?"

"I did what she'd told me to do. I didn't touch anything. She'd told me never to touch the white stuff cuz it could hurt me, even kill me. So I went downstairs to get the landlady and tell her my mom was dead."

"And you knew to do that because your mom had prepared you?" Noel asked, barely able to imagine a mother having that conversation with her child.

Mia nodded. "It's one of the only conversations I can remember having with her because we talked about it a lot. Just in case, she would say. That's how I came to think about it: what to do, just in case."

"She was looking out for you because she loved you."

"She used to tell me that all the time. That she loved me and she wished she was strong enough to get clean. I didn't know what that meant then, but I do now."

"Did you put this in your essay?"

"A shorter version and without the bedroom part."

"I'm proud of you for being brave enough to do that, and now I'm even more interested in reading it if you'll let me."

Mia nodded slowly. They rode in silence for a time, the conversation clearly weighing on them both. As they approached the house, Mia spoke up quietly. "Did you really have another sister?"

"I did." Noel made the turn into their neighborhood.

"I'm kind of a little jealous since I heard that. I know that's stupid but…"

"It's not stupid. I'm the only sister you've ever had and on this earth you are my one and only sister, Mia. But now I think we both have a heavenly sister looking out for us."

"Well, I guess that's not a bad thing. Do you think she'll like me?"

"I think she loves you already."

"How do you know that?"

Noel recalled the whispered words Celeste had spoken just before leaving her. "Because she told me to take care of our sister."

# CHAPTER SIXTEEN

Jeremy parked in the driveway and unbuckled his seat belt, glancing back at the zippered cooler he'd tucked behind the seat. He'd texted Noel earlier about the attire for the evening—a blue jeans kind of dinner he'd told her—and although she had wanted to know where they were going, he'd dodged the question. Stepping from his car, unease roiled in his gut as he looked up at Noel's childhood home.

He was thirty-six years old and he had never met the parents of any woman he'd dated. He'd eluded attempts to make that happen in previous relationships and had always taken it as a sign it was time to move on. He had told each one at the start that he wasn't looking for a serious relationship; most of them thought they could change his mind. No one ever had. The example of his own parents had made him shun the kind of attachment that would leave him shackled for a lifetime. He'd felt bad at the inevitable breakups, regretting the loss of companionship and sex, but none of that had ever moved the dial on his commitment to remain single. Until he met, or rather met again, the most memorable girl of his life. Now he was attempting many firsts because he loved Noel, and meeting her parents was just the beginning. He rang the bell.

Mia opened the door, her smile wide and mischievous. "Nice to see you again, Professor Finnegan. Come in."

The living room of the ranch-style home was an eclectic mixture of formal and comfortable. A sectional sofa faced a large screen TV hanging over the fireplace, while a more traditional seating area in front of the bay window paired two straight-backed chairs with a small parlor table like the one his grandmother used to rest her book on when he ran into the room to find her. Shaking his head at the bygone memory, he watched Noel's father get to his feet, the movement slow as he shifted his weight to the knee that bent more easily. Standing beside him, Noel beamed, meeting Jeremy's gaze. "I'd like you to meet my dad."

Her father stepped forward and held out a hand to Jeremy. "Garrett Welsh. Nice to finally meet you, young man."

"Not so young anymore, sir, but it's an honor to meet you." Jeremy returned the man's warm smile, his flushed coloring matching his thinning red hair and his grip firm as they shook hands.

Jeremy turned toward a noise in the kitchen before being engulfed in a woman's hug. The scent of a floral perfume mingled with the aroma of roasting meat; her embrace was fierce and unexpected. Jeremy didn't know what to do but chose the easy option and hugged her back, meeting Noel's gaze over her mother's shoulder. "And this is my mum, Marcy to her friends."

"Of which you will always be one because you saved my daughter's life." Her British accent, softened by many years of living in the States, was warm and lilting as she leaned back, her hands settling on his shoulders. "I can never thank you enough for all you did for Noel and for us."

"It was my pleasure." Jeremy looked into her eyes, meaning every word. "Your daughter is a very special woman. She was then and still is today."

"We're glad you think so," Garrett injected.

"I do, sir." Jeremy turned back to Noel's father and let Garrett take his measure. He had nothing to hide. He had never loved anyone the way he loved their daughter.

"I can see that," Garret replied with a nod.

"Are you sure I can't talk you into staying for dinner with us?" Marcy's grin was playful.

Garrett stepped forward, placing a hand on his wife's shoulder. "They already have plans for this evening."

"But I would love to join you for dinner later this week. Maybe Friday?" Jeremy suggested and won an adoring look from both mother and daughter.

"Wonderful!" Marcy beamed. "It's a date, then."

Mia hooked her arm through Noel's, leading her over to Jeremy and giving them both a push toward the door. "You better go while you can."

After a flurry of goodbyes, Noel laughed as she buckled her seat belt. "I haven't introduced a boy to my parents since I was in high school."

"I've never been the man introduced to a girl's parents."

Noel turned to him in surprise. "Never?"

"Never," Jeremy reiterated, leaning toward her in the close confines of the vintage car. "I've spent my whole life running from commitment, until now." He watched her eyes widen, transfixed by the smile that lifted her lips upward. He had every intention of kissing her until the sun's reflection in the glass of the windshield made him realize their every move was visible from the bay window of the house. He inclined his head toward the open view. "I think we'd better go."

"Good idea. Where are we going?" she asked as Jeremy backed out of the driveway.

"This is the last night of the carnival we went to on Friday. It ends with blue grass music and a sky full of fireworks." He fell silent for a moment, the hum of the engine the only sound as he shifted into a higher gear. "One of the only good memories I have of being a kid was the night my parents took us to see the fireworks at the county fair. We rarely went anywhere together, except to church. But that night my mother surprised my father with a picnic dinner, and surprisingly he agreed to go. We were quite a group—five kids ranging in age from twelve to four. I have this vivid memory of running around with my friends until dark and then sitting with my parents and watching the sky light up with bursts of color. In my six-year-old brain, it felt like a magical evening, like we were just a regular family. No stony silences. No crying behind closed doors. It's the only time I ever remember seeing my parents touch each other."

"Are we recreating that memory?" Noel asked softly.

"No. We're starting new ones." Jeremy reached over, extending his hand to her, palm open. She placed her hand in his and he gently squeezed, his words soft. "Memories to last a lifetime.

They found a parking space in the trampled field filled with pickup trucks. Chairs and pillows in the cargo areas awaited the evening to come.

Jeremy turned to Noel as he shut off the engine. "Wait, please."

Noel smiled, reminded of his southern chivalry as he rounded the car and opened her door. Extending a hand to her, he drew her to her feet and then pulled her into his arms, his whispered words just loud enough to hear. "Why is everything in my life better with you in it?"

Noel felt the sting of tears behind closed lids as she rested her head on his shoulder, her chest tightening with joy at his words. "It feels like we were meant to be together, like right from the start you were my other half."

"Because I am," Jeremy said, his smile infectious. "Now how late can I keep you out tonight?"

"You can keep me out as long as you want." The tone of her words made his hands twitch against her back.

"Remarks like that are exactly why we are spending this evening in a very public place. After meeting your father, it's the right thing to do." He met her gaze, the smile fading from his lips. "I don't have a very good track record when it comes to relationships, Noel. I've done things backward my entire life. I skipped over the relationship building and went straight for the instant gratification."

"I don't need to know this." Noel saw the angst on his face and heard the honesty in his words.

"I think you do."

"But that's all in the past."

"It is, but it's the reason I want to do things differently for you. For us."

She brushed back the unruly hair from his forehead. "There really is an us now?"

"Oh, yes." His words were long and drawn out, making her smile. He reached for a soft-sided cooler behind the passenger seat and slung the strap over his shoulder, handing her a folded picnic blanket. They headed toward the music coming from an open field to the right of the carnival as the October sun sank toward the tops of the tree line. A brisk wind lifted the tree's branches, making Noel glad she'd grabbed a jacket.

In the field, a series of risers had been used to create a stage. Cables coiled like snakes, black against the autumn grass, supplying the speakers with power as the air filled with the rollicking beat of a seven-member band. The pulsing melody had drawn dancers to the area in front of the stage, kids spinning in circles with their parents while couples danced.

Choosing a spot on the fringe of the crowd, Noel eyed Jeremy as they spread the blanket on the ground. "If we're an us now, there's a few things I need to learn about you. Can you dance?"

"I can, although I prefer the cover of darkness. How about we eat first?"

"That either means you are very good or very bad." Noel quipped. "Which is it?"

"I'll let you make that call later." He opened the zippered cooler and began to cover the blanket with a selection of finger foods. Mini sandwiches, spring rolls, skewered shrimp. "I talked to Will last night. I needed some advice if I'm going to keep the promise I made to you."

Her chest tightened at his determination to keep his word. "Was he able to help?"

"He wants me to try a new starting point in my research," Jeremy said as they sampled the dinner fare.

"Sounds logical. What did he suggest?"

"He wants me to start with a new question: What if it's true? Instead of assuming it's a fallacy, to start with the premise of possibility."

"Could writing down your thoughts from that new vantage point help?"

"Like the book we read yesterday?"

"I didn't know what any of it meant when I wrote it down, but in the end those words let me see the truth," Noel responded.

They ate in silence for a time, each with their own thoughts as the twilight faded and a smattering of stars flecked the sky. As the band transitioned into a set of slower songs with country lyrics, Jeremy stood and held out a hand to her. "Dance with me?"

Draw by the intimacy of darkness, they joined other couples in front of the stage as the singers blended into a tight harmony on the song's refrain. Jeremy drew her into his arms, and although she had never been much of a dancer, Noel found his lead easy to follow. It felt exhilarating to be enjoying the simple pleasures that had so long eluded her, the intimacy she had shunned now vanquished by the touch of the one man she had always trusted. He held her close in a classic stance he must have learned from dance lessons as a kid, with his right hand encircling her waist and his left hand clasping hers. He drew their hands in closer, resting them against his chest, his words warm against her cheek.

"My brother thinks you are a very special woman. I told him I agree. Then he reminded me how the men in our family fall hard and fast for the women they love."

Noel smiled, seeing in the depth of his gaze the truth of his words. "How fast exactly?"

"Well, Will and Cherie were about five months, minus the coma, of course. Tyler and Abby eloped after two months."

Her eyes widened. "They got married after knowing each other for eight weeks."

"Told the family in an e-mail after the fact."

Noel's laughter was light. "We're not trying to break any records, are we?"

"That's exactly what I want to talk about." Jeremy pressed a kiss to her forehead.

"You want to talk about our future here? Now?"

"Right now, with you here in my arms."

"You sound like you're afraid I'll run away," Noel ventured.

"I just might be."

Noel lifted a hand to touch his face. "Nothing could ever make me run away from you."

Jeremy leaned forward, touching his forehead to hers, and Noel could feel the increased pressure in the arms that held her. "As a new believer, you don't know this yet," he whispered. "But you can never marry me."

A chill of apprehension ran from the base of her skull to the tip of her spine. She tried to step back but his arms held her firmly. "I don't understand. What does one thing have to do with the other?"

A sudden gust of wind bore an acrid whiff of burning grass before the speakers on stage blew out with a loud screech. The crowd parted, falling backward as fire engulfed the risers, swept outward, and caught the overhanging branches of a nearby tree. The autumn grass around the stage ignited, sizzling with sparkling light. Band members abandoned their instruments and jumped through the flames, most of them smart enough to hit the ground and roll as the dancers ran for their cars. The bass player, an older man with long white hair, was the last to jump through the fire. He emerged on the other side with his hair and shirt on fire. In a panic, he began to run before Jeremy tackled him to the ground and Noel used her jacket to smother the flames. They helped him to his feet and set out for the parking lot already jammed with exiting vehicles and blaring horns.

After a hot, California summer and an equally dry start to the fall, the field and surrounding trees were a tinder box. With a quick word of thanks the bass player veered off, and wind gusts drove the fire behind them into a smoky cloud that threatened to engulf them. Jeremy grabbed the picnic blanket and the cooler as they ran past, the abandoned food spraying out in a wave of debris as he tossed the blanket over his shoulder. He reached for Noel's hand as the visibility decreased, and they ran in a direction perpendicular to the fire.

"Where are we going?" Noel shouted, glancing back at the open field and the flaming dry grass.

"We'll never get the car out of here with that logjam of vehicles." Jeremy followed her gaze and picked up the pace. "There's a hiking trail not far from here that leads back down to the highway. I've done it a few times. The terrain is rugged, but with the smoke gusting we need to head downhill."

Noel nodded, pulling her shirt up over her nose and mouth and breathing through the thin cotton as she watched Jeremy do likewise. "Do we need to keep the blanket? It could slow us down."

"It's the only protection we have from the embers and debris. We may need it later."

"And the cooler?

"Has water and a flashlight."

"I'll take one of them, then," she said, meeting his gaze.

"No arguments here." He handed her the cooler, then took the lead, searching for the trailhead and skirting around the fleeing cars and people. He found it within a few hundred yards, the entrance marked by a wooden trail marker. With a quick glance, Jeremy turned to assess the fire behind them before deciding this was still the best way out. Waving her in front of him, he stopped just long enough to pull down the shirt covering his mouth.

"You set the pace but keep it steady and not too fast. We've got a long way to go."

"How far is it?"

"Four miles to the reservoir and three beyond it to the highway."

He leaned forward and pulled down the shirt that covered her mouth, dropping a quick kiss on her lips. "I love you."

She echoed his words, hoping he'd heard her with the blare of car horns coming from the clogged roadway.

The trail cut an angled path away from the meadow with a downward slope that increased as they moved away from the trailhead. The packed dirt pathway was an obstacle course of rocks, some of which would have been ideal footholds on the way up but presented a dangerous challenge on the way down in the dark. She unzipped the cooler and pulled out the flashlight. Sweeping the light across the path, she focused all her attention on her next step, knowing Jeremy was choosing his way as carefully as she was. She couldn't chance glancing back at him. A twisted ankle or a fall would only slow them down. She wondered if choosing this escape through the woods with a fire at their backs had been the right one. But the narrow roadway they had taken an hour ago would not have been a better choice with large crowds fleeing on foot and the likelihood that many vehicles had been abandoned in the logjam of trucks trying to exit by the only viable egress. Emergency vehicles were going to have a hard time getting to the injured or close enough to assess the fire.

The air around them began to clear as they headed downhill, the moon shrouded by eclipsing smoke as a gust of wind brought a new wave of smoke and ashes. Noel stepped up the pace, offering a silent prayer for their safety to the God she had ignored for too many years. The remarkable memories she and Jeremy had read together last night had created a clarity about her future. But what about Jeremy? She refocused her attention on the task at hand, her anxiety replaced by a determination to help the man behind her learn what she knew with certainty.

Overhead the night sky grew darker, obscured by what she thought might be rain clouds before the scent of burning leaves dispelled that hope. Up ahead the pathway forked and Noel slowed before feeling Jeremy's hand on her shoulder veering her to the left. Not wasting any words, she took the left fork following the trail's meandering route. On a sunny day the hike would have been challenging, but in the dark it was treacherous. Behind them the distant crackle of burning wood and the occasional snap of branches punctuated the air, the scent of smoke heavy on the wind. They continued for more than an hour before a shift in the wind cooled her cheeks and the air around them cleared a bit. Ahead she saw a break in the trees and the lighter hues of an open space. Minutes later she realized the trail was headed down to skirt the perimeter of a reservoir, the flat black surface open and smooth beneath clouds of a similar color.

Jeremy appeared at her side, taking her free hand and leading her over to a large rock with an eroded shelf that created an alcove just off the trail. "Water break."

Glad of the reprieve from the constant vigilance of navigating the terrain, Noel took a seat beside him on the narrow ledge. Reaching into the cooler, she retrieved two water bottles. Handing one to Jeremy, she watched him lower the shirt from his nose and mouth and take a long sip as Noel did likewise. "How much further to the highway?"

"Another mile to the reservoir and then three to the highway. We're making good progress."

She started to stand and he pulled her back down, his arm around her shoulder. "Let's just rest a minute. We've still got a way to go."

Noel nodded, taking another swig from her water bottle. "What did you mean before when you said I can never marry you?"

Jeremy blinked, his expression grim. "It comes from a concept in the Christian faith called being unequally yoked, a biblical reference to the pairing of two animals who then move forward as a team. But if one is strong and the other is weak the pairing won't work because they will constantly be fighting each other."

"That impacts us how?" Noel questioned, not understanding the farm animal reference.

"Since you are a believer, you can't yoke yourself to an unbeliever like me."

She could see the frustration in his eyes as he explained a concept he didn't believe in. "We aren't living in biblical times. I can do what I want. I have free will."

"You do, but according to your new faith, God believes that being so far apart on a core issue like faith produces a constant wear and tear on a relationship because it causes too much disagreement, particularly when you add children into the mix. Long term it will cause the union to fail."

"But I love you," Noel said, her heart aching as she glimpsed the tenderness in his eyes.

He pulled her closer to him. "I'm afraid that doesn't matter."

"Do you find it ironic that you have to explain this to me," Noel asked, her frustration growing.

"I do, since I believe we belong together."

"Me, too. How can we make that happen?"

"I have to become a believer."

Noel shivered at his words. "That's the only way?"

"It is."

"Can you do it for me?" Her voice just above a whisper, she knew the answer before he said the words.

"No. Everyone has to make that decision for themselves. True belief in God must come from a place of faith, not just because you want something from Him. And we both know I'm a long way from that." Jeremy kissed her head resting on his shoulder.

Noel considered his words, feeling her autonomy rise within her. "We can't possibly be bound by such an outdated concept. This is a new millennium. People have changed and evolved since the Bible was written. We can make it work. I know we can."

"Yes, we are living in a different time, but people haven't changed that much. Their emotions and decision making are still rooted in their core beliefs. It seems like it won't matter, but in the day-to-day living, it will cause disagreements and erode the foundation of even the best relationship." Jeremy turned her to face him, his hands on her shoulders. "I may not be a religious man, but I am an ethical one. I cannot let you violate your own beliefs for me because in the end it will tear us apart."

"Then I'll wait." Noel met his gaze, her tone firm.

He touched her cheek with one finger. "This is why I love you, because you think I'm worth waiting for. There's a part of me that thinks I should just let you go, so you can find a believer to share your life with, to have the family you've always wanted."

She was about to protest, but his thumb caressed her lower lip. "But I am so selfish and flawed, I can't let you go." He drew her into his arms, his words and his kiss lingering just long enough to make her forget how they had ended up sitting on a cold stony ledge in the dark, until a sudden flicker of sparks flashed in the night sky. "We'd better keep going."

She nodded, stowing the water bottles in the cooler as she settled the strap across her chest. They'd been resting for less than five minutes but the night felt dense around them as they resumed their downhill trek.

Jeremy's words echoed in her head. He loved her, and holding onto that thought, she pushed aside all the obstacles to a life together. As the trail took a steeper descent, Noel slowed and chose her steps carefully, the flashlight's beam their only beacon. Thirty minutes later, they approached the reservoir. The pathway flattened to a circumferential route around the large body of water. On a clear day it must have been beautiful, but here in the darkness the black water seemed ominous. A sudden wind shift increased the scent of smoke and charred wood. Noel waited for it to clear as it had earlier, tensing at the realization it wasn't lifting as they began their counterclockwise trek around the water.

Up ahead, she spotted flickers of light amid the treetops, like a cluster of fireflies gathered in one place. Remembering the shower of embers earlier, she slowed to give them time to assess as the scent of smoke grew stronger. Jeremy's hand on her shoulder stilled her progress as the trees in front of them burst into flames. He pulled her back against him, his muffled voice close to her ear. "Once we start down that trail there's no way out for more than a mile. We can't go that way. We'll be walking into a firestorm."

"But we can't go back." She turned to him, seeing the firm set of his jaw and the resignation in his eyes.

"I know." His hands settled on her shoulders.

"So what choice do we have?" The question left her mouth even as the answer became obvious.

Jeremy tilted his head toward the water. "We don't have a choice. It's less than a mile across. You can do this, Noel."

Her eyes widened, fear pulsing through her like a bass vibration on repeat, so loud she could barely hear his next words.

"I know you can swim. You passed the test to be a counselor, and you must have done some swimming since then."

"Only laps in a pool. I was working up to an open water swim." Her stomach roiled with terror as she glanced out over the black water.

"I'll be right beside you, but we have to go now." He took her hand and drew her off the trail, leading her through the sparse brush to the water's edge. He moved quickly, taking off his sneakers and stripping off his jeans. She followed suit, knowing the dense fabric would weigh them down in the water. Reluctantly, she shed the jacket and felt the night air chill her skin.

"Keep the shirt for now. If we have to we'll lose them later." He grabbed her sneakers. Unzipping the cooler, he ditched the water bottles, stuffed both pairs of shoes inside, and zipped it closed. The cooler bulged with its new cargo. "We're going to need these on the other side to make it out of here."

Noel shivered, her bare legs cold in the smoky air. She was glad the button-down shirt she wore covered her from shoulders to hips, its warmth the only barrier to the night air. It wouldn't be warm for much longer, though, she thought as they stepped in tandem into the water's shallows.

Jeremy squeezed her hand. "Slow and steady, just like before. You take the lead. Pick a point on the far shore and keep it in sight. I'm right behind you." He pulled her to him in a brief hug and then secured the shoulder strap across his torso with the cooler resting on his hip. "If you get tired just roll over on your back and float. We can do this together, Noel."

She nodded, drawing strength from the certainty and the love she saw in his eyes. She stepped deeper into the water, felt the chill rise over her knees and thighs, and gasped as the cold hit her belly and chest. Fear impaled her and paralyzed her for a split second before she plunged into the water. Jeremy couldn't be looking out for her the whole time. She recalled him admitting that he rarely swam these days. He needed to look out for himself, and with the weight of the cooler he had a much harder journey ahead than she did.

Still, panic threatened to overwhelm her as icy water splashed her face and a chill permeated her limbs. Just stroke and kick, just like in the pool, she told herself, even as a wave of terror made her heart race and her breathing shallow. Lifting her head, she glanced backward and spotted Jeremy off to her right about a body length behind as if they were swimming in adjacent lanes. If he could do it, so could she. Turning back, she stroked with her head above water, her eyes fixed on an oddly shaped tree on the far shoreline. Backlit by a touch of moonlight, the tree's squared-off top and its outstretched branches made it look like a cross. It would be a good reference point and a reminder that she needed to lose the panic and seek the help of the God who had loved her unconditionally even when she paid Him no mind. Her free-style stroke was slow but steady, the prayer rising unbidden to her mind as she recalled yesterday's revelations.

*Lord, guide us with your light. Strengthen us with your love. Protect us with your might. And bring us both safely to shore. Amen.*

Her stroke found its rhythm as happened so often in the pool, lap after lap. Granted there was no solid wall to use as a touchstone to mark the distance, but her usual twenty-five strokes per lap gave her an approximate measure. As she counted, she found the numbers strangely calming. Her steady pace soon drove the chill from her limbs; the only parts of her still cold were the tips of her ears and her toes.

Jeremy had said the distance was about a mile. Seventy laps in a pool. A swift calculation brought the unwelcome conclusion they were less than halfway. Glancing back at Jeremy, she saw he had fallen further behind, about the distance of a full lap. She rolled over and floated on her back, noting his uneven stroke and splashing kick. He was getting tired. A wave of fear pulsed through her as the smell of smoke grew stronger across the water. She rested and let him swim to her, knowing that with his level of physical conditioning, it must be the weight of the cooler that was making him work so hard. She tapped him on the shoulder and he lifted his head, rolling over to float beside her. Though she could sense the wall of encroaching smoke, she kept her words calm.

"You need to rest for a minute." She caught his hand and squeezed, feeling his answering pressure. "Give me the cooler. It's my turn now."

He blinked and turned his head to meet her gaze, his breathing heavy. "That bad, huh?"

"Your stroke's a mess. You're tired. You need to give it to me or let it go."

The ease with which he surrendered it spoke louder than any words about his level of fatigue. He closed his eyes and floated for a moment. "I'll take it back in a bit."

Feeling the weight of the strap in her hand, she could understand his exhaustion. Unzipping the cooler, she saw the problem. Not only were the sneakers wet but the cooler itself had filled with water. Reaching in, she rested the sneakers on her stomach, tied the laces together, and did the same to Jeremy's. She released the cooler and watched it sink, then rolled over, looped the laces behind her neck, and tucked them under her shirt collar. The scent of smoke was getting stronger. She tapped him on the shoulder. "We have to go."

He rolled over, meeting her gaze and nodding at her improvised carry system. "I should have thought of that. Thanks." He flashed her a quick grin and started to swim.

Finding her rhythm after the break was harder and the addition of the flopping sneakers around her neck made breathing harder as she kept an eye on Jeremy, who was keeping pace with her. The shore was still a long way off. She hazarded a look behind them and offered up a silent prayer.

*You can do anything, Lord, so I'm asking you to change the direction of the wind so we won't suffocate in a cloud of smoke. I know if this night goes badly that I am coming home to you but Jeremy doesn't know you, Lord, not yet. Please save us today so he will have the time to know you as I do. I love him, Lord, and I know you do, too."*

The sneakers were a constant source of irritation, but rather than linger on that thought, she challenged herself with a reward for her efforts. Twenty strokes face down, breathing every other one, then ten strokes with her head above the water, eyes on the cross. It reduced the pace but helped her breathe easier. A quick glance assured her Jeremy was still at her side. The scent of smoke seemed to recede as the shore grew closer. What had been an indistinct mass of darkness save for the huge tree soon took on the distinction of individual trees as a glimmer of moonlight bled through the shifting cloud cover. Glancing upward she could see a portion of the night sky and the welcome beacon of the moon's light.

The final hundred yards seemed to take longer than the distance warranted. The tentacles of sheer exhaustion spread outward along her limbs as if the only thing sustaining her had been sheer determination. Or was it answered prayer? Her feet touched the mucky bottom of the lake and she stood as Jeremy gained his feet. Her legs weak and shaky, her breathing heavy, she felt his hand under her elbow supporting her through the shallows. At the shoreline, he drew the sneakers over her head and dropped them to the ground before pulling her into a fierce embrace, his chest heaving as he drew in deep gulps of air. Her eyes brimming with tears, she buried her face against the cold skin of his shoulder. She pressed her lips to his neck, feeling the pulse just beneath the surface as his arms tightened around her. The sense of déjà vu was unmistakable at this lakeside scene before an explosion of light behind her closed eyes make her gasp.

Celeste's final words rang in her ears with the clarity of a flute's high note. "He needs you to save him."

Noel shivered, her body quaking with fear. Clearly, Jeremy thought her trembling was a response to cold air on wet skin as he briskly ran his hands up and down her back.

Then meeting her gaze, he cupped her cheek in his hand, his thumb wiping away the tears flowing from her eyes. "When I tell this story in years to come, you will always be its hero."

"We did it together," she insisted, quelling one final shiver by scrunching her shoulders upward.

"We did, but you confronted one of your greatest fears to do it."

Still reeling from the sudden memory of her sister and not understanding what it meant, she knew she needed to tell him the truth. "I didn't do it alone. I promised you last night that I would tell you everything." She paused just a moment. "God was with us out there, Jeremy. I know it with certainty. I never could have done that swim on my own."

She saw the impact of her words in the narrowing of his eyes, although his reply was carefully neutral as he reached down and delivered her wet sneakers into her hands. "Thank you for telling me. The only way we can make it through this is to talk to each other, but right now we need to keep moving."

She had been hoping for more from him, for some recognition of the impossible task they had just accomplished, even as she realized his strongly held beliefs were going to be a challenge for them, maybe for a long time. She freed her improvised knots and donned the wet sneakers, feeling the icy squish of water between her toes as they set out. The chill night air knifed through her wet shirt, making her shoulders shiver. The flashlight gone, they could just make out the path that was wider than the one they had traveled earlier.

Jeremy reached for her hand. "Not long now. We're almost there."

Noel's hand tightened around his, her skin covered in goose bumps. But whether that was from the breeze against her wet shirt or her fear for the man beside her would remain, for now, an open question.

# CHAPTER SEVENTEEN

They emerged from the end of the trail to find a parking lot filled with emergency vehicles: fire trucks, ambulances, tow trucks. Local authorities were using the lot as a staging area for the disaster response. Jeremy and Noel found themselves surrounded by medical personnel and, after a thorough exam determined they were uninjured, they were given dry clothes and blankets and directed to the green zone of the triage area to await transport home by the police.

A volunteer handed them each a cup of hot coffee and Jeremy watched Noel wrap her hands around the warm paper cup. He lifted his and took a sip. Hot and sweet, it tasted wonderful, the warmth on his lips a sharp contrast to the chill of his feet. "Are you okay?"

She rolled the cup between her palms. "I'm fine physically, grateful to be alive and safe and together." She paused, leaning into his shoulder. "But I saw something again when we stepped out of the water—another vision or memory or whatever you want to call it."

"I thought we'd uncovered all your memories yesterday." Jeremy's surprise was mixed with a hint of apprehension at her words.

"I thought so, too." She looked worried and though the swim they had just survived could have been the reason, he sensed there was more to it than that.

"Tell me the rest, Noel."

"I have no idea what it means."

"Maybe we can figure it out together." A guardedness in her tone made him suspect the only reason she had brought this up was because she had promised him she would.

"I saw Celeste again and heard her whispered words to me before I regained consciousness on the float."

"What did she say?" Jeremy suspected he wasn't going to like the answer.

"She said, 'He needs you to save him.'"

"And you think that him is me?"

She nodded, setting aside her coffee and reaching for his hand. "I do."

"I think you just did that." Jeremy lifted their joined hands and kissed her palm.

"I don't think that's it." Her words trailed off. "We were out of the water and the danger was behind us when I saw this. What else could it mean?"

Jeremy bent down to place the coffee cup on the ground before turning to face her. "In the Christian faith the word 'saved' doesn't refer to a physical rescue. It means being saved from eternal separation from God."

"But I can't do that for you. You have to do that yourself."

"Even in a disaster you were listening to me." He lifted her chin and their eyes met.

"I don't always like what you say but I'm listening." Her focus remained undeterred by his attempt at levity.

"I think the simplest explanation is the right one. You saved me tonight; I might have drowned if not for you."

"Sounds too easy." Her eyes narrowed, her disbelief obvious. "I think it's something in front of us, not behind."

"Even if it is, you can't be with me every minute of the day, right?" He raised one eyebrow in an assessing glance, choosing humor in a situation over which he had no control.

"Try me." Her chin tilted up, annoyed at his flippancy.

"I believe your new faith has a few things to say about cohabitation." His tone took on a more sober note as he leaned in closer. "But even if this is some celestial balancing of the scales after fifteen years, we are two adults with separate lives. We can't spend every minute together, much as I might want to."

"Now you're patronizing me."

"No, I'm not. I'm just being practical. Whatever is in our future is unknowable and as much as I want that future to include more conversations like this one, we can't live our lives waiting for the next disaster to strike."

A young police officer stepped up to them before Noel could respond and directed them to a waiting squad car parked along the roadside. They rode in silence in the back of the cruiser, and with the steady motion of the car Noel soon fell asleep against his shoulder, succumbing to sheer exhaustion. He held her in his arms and felt the regular cadence of her breathing, his thoughts consumed with how close they had come to losing their lives to a natural disaster that came out of nowhere. Selfishly, he wanted to take her home with him, to hold her in his arms for the rest of the night, and to wake up with her next to him in the morning, but he directed the officer to Noel's parents' home where they were met with tears of relief and words of gratitude.

Alone in bed after a hot shower, sleep proved elusive despite Jeremy's fatigue. His mind kept replaying the swim through the frigid water, a cloud of smoke at his back and no way to go but forward. He had to admit he'd been scared, and he wasn't a man who scared easily. He'd always prided himself on his intellect and physical strength, but tonight had given him cause to doubt everything he considered foundational about who he was as a man. He'd doubted his judgment in sending them into the water, although rationally he knew it had been his only choice. He'd doubted the strength of his own body, wondering whether it would be enough to save them. Had it not been for Noel and her assessment of his fatigue, he might have held onto the cooler and expended all his energy, with no reserve left to finish the journey. She was the one who had saved them by conquering her fears. She had credited God, which in any other situation he would dismiss out of hand, but he had seen the terror in her eyes when she looked out over the black water and somehow she had found the strength to persevere for herself and for him. Was that love? Or was that God? Or were they, as he'd heard so often from his opponents on the debate stage, one and the same?

He tossed and turned throughout the night, dozing off only to awaken in a wave of terror as frigid water scented with woodsmoke closed over his nose and mouth. He got up in the early hours of the morning, his body exhausted but his mind rebelling at the idea of closing his eyes again. Settling in at the desk in his study with a cup of black coffee at his side, he returned to the research he'd started yesterday morning. It had been less than twenty-four hours but seemed so much longer.

Noel's words about God being with them last night had chilled him to his core. She wasn't just a new believer because of her near-death experience, she was a true believer and becoming more so each day. She wasn't going to sit quietly on her faith and not mention it and, in his heart, he feared that belief would tear them apart.

Placing his hand on the open Bible in front of him, the words of John's Gospel blurred in his sight, whether from fatigue or despair he couldn't be sure. He knew these words better than many believers. He'd analyzed them while preparing to argue against them, and he knew he needed to start in a different place. He turned pages randomly until he came to the next section, The Acts of the Apostles, a book far less familiar to him. He heard Will's words in his head as he began to read.

What if it's true?

* * *

Noel pulled open the door to the Laraby Science Center, catching a glimpse of her reflection in the glass door. She looked tired and felt worse. Her muscles ached, but there was no way she was calling in sick to a new job. She'd managed to get a few hours' sleep after calming her parents' fears, a cup of chamomile tea in her hands to sooth her own. But despite the warm drink, what little sleep she'd gotten had been fitful and filled with images of fire and darkness.

Trying to shake the fatigue, she stopped at the coffeehouse and grabbed the largest coffee they had. She hoped it would keep her focused as they began to interview the volunteers for the study. She and Dwayne had finally been assigned a workspace on Friday, a small office with two cubicles on the main floor. Noel came through the door to find Dwayne already hard at work reviewing the study protocol.

"Good morning," she said, glancing at her watch. Eight twenty. They had interviews scheduled to start at nine a.m.

Dwayne got to his feet and rounded his desk, his expression somber. "Good morning. We've got a long day ahead of us, so I want to begin by apologizing for yesterday."

Noel looked up at him. "For what?"

"For asking you out yesterday and then backing you into a corner where you felt you needed to tell me you were seeing someone. Clearly, I wasn't taking no for an answer and I'm sorry," Dwayne responded, his tone sincere. "We're colleagues and I never should have put you in that position."

"I appreciate your apology." Noel put her coffee down on the desk. With all that had happened, she'd forgotten about going to the meeting with Mia yesterday. "Perhaps I should have mentioned it sooner."

"No. I was totally out of line. You have no responsibility to announce your dating status to a colleague just to get him to stay out of your business."

"Thank you," Noel said, trying to bring this awkward discussion to a close. "You were reviewing the protocol?"

"Specifically the exclusion criteria, yes, so its fresh in my mind as we start the day. Still want to do the interviews together?"

"Of course. That's what we decided on Friday, and two sets of eyes on each candidate seems like the best idea. At least to start. Less chance of making a snap judgment about someone and excluding them without cause."

Hours later, Noel knew Dwayne had been right about the day being a long one, but they now had ten candidates accepted into the study. She spent her lunch hour making phone calls to report her lost credit cards. Sipping her third coffee of the day at a corner table in the coffeehouse, she followed the automated prompts while she managed a few bites of the sandwich she'd purchased.

The loss of her purse in the fire paled in comparison to Jeremy's losing the car he loved. A wave of regret washed over her as she recalled the comfortable confines of his sleek car. The thought made her glance up and scan the crowd around her. She wished she could talk to him, but they rarely saw each other during the workday. He'd texted her early this morning to check on her, a message she'd gotten when she woke with a start after finally falling asleep in the early hours of the morning. Knowing she was going to be late, she'd shot off a quick reply, wishing she had time for more. The fire was the day's big story; it was still only partially contained. Mandatory evacuations had been issued for homes in its path and state officials had called on the federal government for assistance.

After lunch, an afternoon of interviews produced fifteen more volunteers accepted into the study. At five p.m., Noel offered to return the study protocol to Dr. McMann before heading home. Dwayne handed it to her as he finished organizing the paperwork from their interviews. Taking the stairs to the upper floor, she knocked on the office door and followed the directive to come in.

"Ah, Ms. Welsh, thank you." Dr. McMann stood, coming around the corner of his desk and taking the protocol from her. The fading sunlight of the October afternoon streamed through the window and glinted off his glasses. "How did the first day of interviews go?"

"Very well. We now have twenty-five subjects for the study and interviews are scheduled for the rest of the week."

"That's a good start. You and Mr. Rawlins seem to work well together." He turned toward the filing cabinets to secure the document.

"We do. We've been doing the interviews together to eliminate any chance of bias or misinterpretation in our decision process."

"I'm glad the budget allowed us to include a second coordinator," he said over his shoulder as he reached into his pocket and withdrew a key ring.

"This job was originally slated for just one person?" Noel found it hard to imagine all the work they were doing falling on the shoulders of one person.

"Yes. Initially our funding only allowed for one coordinator and we had three qualified candidates."

"So how did you decide who to hire?"

"I let Dr. Finnegan make the call." His back was still to her as he slipped the key into the lock and turned it, pulling open the drawer.

His words landed like a punch. "And he chose me?"

"He did, and then when the funding came through, we were able to add Mr. Rawlins to the team as well."

Noel barely heard his response, realizing Jeremy had done the one thing she'd asked him not to do. Not only had he weighed in on her getting the job but he had also made the final choice. Nausea roiled in her gut even as her eyes stung at his betrayal. She'd been hired weeks ago, and he'd kept this from her all this time. She stepped backward, a breeze from the open doorway chilling her back as Dr. McMann turned to her.

"Now that you have a handle on the interview process, do you think you and Mr. Rawlins could each do your own interviews? We could get the full complement of subjects much quicker, and I know Dr. Finnegan is eager to get started."

Noel nodded, unable to find her voice, her thoughts ablaze with anger and disappointment. "Yes, we'll have to move up some of the interviews, but…"

"Excellent. I appreciate your flexibility. Jeremy knew what he was doing when he chose you. Have a nice evening, Ms. Welsh." He turned back to his desk but then shot her a curious look before she turned, feigning composure, and fled from his office. Her face was flushed with a mixture of embarrassment and anger, and she slowed her stride to an indoor pace.

How could Jeremy have done this? And then kept quiet about it? The rational part of her brain knew he'd been trying to protect her after seeing the photo of them in his e-mail. But he'd had any number of chances to tell her the truth and he'd kept silent. She had told him things she'd never told anyone and all the time he'd been lying to her.

Her mind reeling at the betrayal, she hurried down the stairs. She had to get out of here. Had to think. A sudden thought hit her. A week ago, it would never have occurred to her, but the revelations of this weekend had changed her. She was different now, stronger, more purposeful, a woman deeply loved by the God who had been waiting for her to remember His place in her life. She knew what she needed to do was to pray.

She pulled open the door to the lower floor with more force than was necessary and ran straight into a pair of strong hands that gripped her shoulders.

"Whoa! Where are you going?"

Surrounded by his now familiar scent, she lifted her gaze to Jeremy. Seeing his welcoming smile, she twisted away from him in the hallway where a few students still lingered after their late afternoon class.

"Noel, what happened?" Seeing the look on her face, he took her by the elbow and drew her down the hallway into an alcove by the window.

"You lied to me." She watched the color drain from his handsome face, any hope she had been harboring about it being a mistake vanquished by the dread she saw in his eyes. "You gave me this job."

"Yes." He reached for her hand before she snatched it back. "We had two equally qualified candidates in you and Mr. Rawlins, and when David asked my opinion, I chose you."

"I asked you to stay out of it!" Noel stared into his eyes, but his gaze never wavered, the sincerity in his tone mirroring the intensity she saw there.

"I was confronted with a professional dilemma." Jeremy's words were deliberate. "Your resumes were practically identical in terms of schooling and work experience. I wasn't about to choose Mr. Rawlins just because you had asked me not to weigh in. I knew you would be perfect for the job, so I made a choice. I will always choose you, Noel."

She could feel her anger begin to ebb at his heartfelt words. How could she let go of it so easily? Instinctively she knew the answer. Because she loved him. As the anger receded, she recognized the underlying emotion: bitter disappointment. The man she loved was a man of honor, a man of his word—or so she'd thought until a moment ago.

"I need to get out of here." She turned from him, craving time to think and to pray.

"You can't walk away every time we disagree." Jeremy blocked her path and gently took her arm. "I'm sorry Noel. I know I should have told you and that's on me. I was trying to avoid just what is happening here, but I should have spoken up from the start." His hand drifted up her arm, then cupped her cheek. "We'll never be able to make it if you shut me out like you did two weeks ago, like you are ready to do right now. We've got bigger issues in front of us, and this will only work if we face them together."

The sincerity in his apology was clear, but a part of her wasn't ready to let it go. She'd had people making decisions for her for too many years, and while she knew he loved her, his betrayal stung, the pain sharp and deep.

Jeremy glanced at his watch. "Okay, now I'm the one who has to go."

"Where are you going?" she asked, noting the downward pull of his eyebrows and the firm set of his jaw.

"I'm going to keep my promise." He took a step closer to her, his face just inches from hers. "Can you tell me you'll do the same?"

Her eyes met his, and although her disappointment lingered she couldn't deny the truth. He was a man working to keep his promise and she owed him no less than the same. "I will."

His back to the hallway, he kissed her softly. "Wish me luck?"

"How about I say a prayer for you?"

"Now you sound like my brother," Jeremy quipped, a hint of warmth and ease returning to his eyes.

"Then I'm in good company. I would say we've got you covered."

"I hope so."

Noel watched as he strode away, wondering where he was going and who he had an appointment with this late in the day. She offered up a silent prayer that the meeting would give him clarity as she headed for the parking lot.

To her surprise, she found Dwayne leaning up against her car, his features solemn and his jaw defined by a dark shadow of beard. "Did we forget to talk about something for tomorrow?"

He pushed off her car, straightening to his full height and looking down at her, a stance she found unnerving since few men in her life were tall enough to do it.

"Do you think it's a good idea for you to be dating our boss?" His tone was firm and his answer to that question apparent in his demeanor. "I saw you arguing with him. Clearly you have more than a professional relationship."

Noel's earlier anger returned with a vengeance at another man who wanted to weigh in on her life. "I thought we established that who I'm seeing is none of your business, Dwayne."

"Do you like your job, Noel?" Undeterred by her clipped tone, his eyes never left her face.

"I do."

"Then I suggest that getting involved with our boss is a bad idea. He has all the power and if things don't go well, you could end up unemployed." His words were terse, his arms tense as if he wanted to reach out and touch her but was holding the impulse in check.

Noel wasn't about to defend her choices to this man she barely knew. "This discussion is over, Dwayne. The better side of my nature is going to chalk this up to a friend trying to look out for me. I hope we can leave it at that!"

"I'm trying to save you from a world of heartache," he responded, his tone so earnest it stole the angry retort from her lips. "You can't pursue this relationship, Noel. He's an atheist and you're a Christian. He denounces at every turn the God you believe in, and more than that, he tries to convince others to turn away from God as well. You can't be a part of that. If you are serious about your faith, your relationship with him has no future."

Deflated by a truth she had only just discovered, her reply was quick and firm. "I know that."

"Then what are you doing?" he asked, his tone filled with alarm for her.

She looked up and met his unwavering stare. "I'm trying to save him."

# CHAPTER EIGHTEEN

Jeremy pulled up to the address on his GPS, checking it against the number on the mailbox. He parked in front of the Cape Cod-style home, the yard still bright with blooming flowers of every hue, their color fading into the autumn evening. He had left himself ample time to get here and had arrived early. Not wanting to intrude on this man he'd asked for a favor, he chose to check his e-mail for a few minutes before keeping their appointment.

He sat back in his rental car, wishing for the sleek fitted seats that had molded to his body and mentally bemoaning the loss of the car he treasured. On the news this morning, he had seen the wildfires were still raging and the authorities had called in air support to try and douse the flames. The little town through which they had driven yesterday had been destroyed as had thousands of acres of forest in the surrounding hills. Homes had been engulfed by the blaze and several people had lost their lives fleeing the inferno.

Jeremy hit the e-mail icon on his phone, a wave of apprehension tightening his shoulders as he scanned the dozens of e-mails he'd received since yesterday. The subject line of one near the bottom of the screen caught his attention.

**Fire.**

He touched the screen to open it, steeling himself for the contents.

**Are you ready to heed our WORD?**

The single sentence drove the breath from his lungs, like a roundhouse to the solar plexus. The implication was clear. The fire had been a purposeful event, set because he hadn't responded to their demands to publicly denounce his atheism. No! That couldn't be true. People had lost their lives in that fire. Homes were destroyed. The depravity of that mindset was almost incomprehensible, and yet there it was in black and white, the claim bold and cruel. He knew it was possible that some militant fringe group was trying to use a natural disaster to scare him into complying with their demands. But even that implied a level of degeneracy far afield from rational thought, using the terror and misery of the innocent to force his hand to their will. His natural inclination was to push back and refuse to give in to their demands as they went against everything he believed.

He drew in a deep breath. Only one thing could motivate him to keep moving forward on this impossible quest to keep the promise he had made: his love for Noel. He would never be a part of her life unless he found the faith she now embraced. He hadn't promised her that outcome, but he had promised her a diligent search for the truth and that was exactly what he was about to do. He opened the car door with a hard push and strode up the walkway, his hand reaching out to ring the bell.

The door was opened by Patrick Mueller. His smile was wide until he saw the look on Jeremy's face and then he simply said, "Welcome. Please come in."

"Thank you for seeing me on such short notice." Jeremy shook the pastor's extended hand as they stood in the entryway of his home. The open space was comfortable and lived in. An open book rested on an end table by the floral couch with a half-finished cup of tea beside it. Shoes and rainboots were lined up under the foyer table. He could hear a dishwasher running in the kitchen and smell barbeque emanating from the crock pot on the counter. "I hope I'm not interrupting your dinner."

"Not at all. My wife is over at the church teaching a teen bible study. Monday is always a late dinner for us. I'm glad of the company. Come sit. Can I get you something to drink?"

Jeremy shook his head. "No, thank you." Now that he was here, he didn't know where to start. He followed the pastor to a pair of chairs separated by a table with a Bible resting on the wooden surface.

"To what do I owe the pleasure of seeing you this evening?" Patrick settled onto the padded seat of the straight-backed chair.

"I need you to convince me that everything you said the night of our debate is true."

Sitting back against the chair, Jeremy could hardly believe those words had just come from his mouth.

"Sounds like you're searching," Patrick mused, with a soft assessing stare.

"I am, sir. But for what exactly, I'm not sure."

"I'm sensing you have a new motivation here. Am I right?"

Jeremy nodded. "I'm in love with a woman who is a true believer."

"Love is a powerful motivator." The pastor leaned forward with his elbows on his knees and his hands clasped together as he gave Jeremy his full attention. "Tell me, how can I help you?"

"I've read your scripture more than most of your congregants," Jeremy began. "I've dissected its language with no aim other than to dispute it."

"I'm sure that's true," Patrick said. "You've accumulated a lot of knowledge over many years."

"My brother, also a believer by the way, tells me I have to change my approach to the words and ask a new question: What if it's true?"

"Sounds like a good place to start. Have you tried it?"

"I have, and I can't seem to see the words of the gospel any differently than I have for the last decade. This morning I started reading the Acts of the Apostles, hoping my own prejudices weren't so firmly entrenched."

"I admire your openness to a new way of thinking. Did anything you read intrigue you, perhaps raise a question?"

"Just one." Jeremy leaned forward. "How did the group of disciples who deserted their friend and leader on the night he was arrested, who never showed their faces the day Jesus was crucified, how did those sniveling cowards become a band of brothers who went to their deaths declaring Jesus as the long-awaited Messiah? I know the history. All those men died terrible deaths. Stoned. Run through with a sword. Burned to death. What changed them so much they were willing to die rather than denounce their Lord?"

"You know the answer, Jeremy." Patrick lifted his head and met Jeremy's gaze.

"The resurrection." His tone reflected all his unbelief in that event.

The pastor nodded. "They didn't die for a lie."

"I think I've heard that before," Jeremy responded, his tone grim.

"I'm sure you have, maybe even from me. The belief those men demonstrated after the death of Jesus came about because they saw Him alive. His mother had watched Him die with the apostle John at her side, so we know He was dead. Then just days later, they saw Jesus whole and completely well. No weakness from the massive blood loss of the flogging. No healing wounds from the crown of thorns. Only the holes in His hands and feet, and the evidence of the spear thrust through His side. They saw Him alive and they believed. And on that cornerstone they built a church that still stands today."

Jeremy studied Patrick and saw the clear conviction in the pastor's eyes. His words in this casual setting were far more persuasive than all his oratory on the debate stage. "It's the one thing I can't explain. I've tried to brush it aside as misguided zeal, but if the resurrection never occurred at least a few of them would have recanted their claims about Jesus under the persecution and torture they endured. But none of them did. Not one." He massaged his jaw with a shaky hand and then looked up at the pastor. "It's the argument I could never counter. That and the near-death experiences. In the interest of full disclosure, I should tell you the woman I'm in love with had a near-death experience after a near drowning."

Patrick blinked in surprise. "Is her name Noel?"

"So you've talked with her."

"Yes. She started coming to church a few weeks ago, but at that time she didn't have any clear memories of the event. I take it she does now?"

"Her suppressed memories returned this past weekend and then were confirmed with a journal entry she'd written right after the accident."

"She told you all of it?"

"We read the journal together, so I believe I got a firsthand look at her journey. She is a true believer now, so you can see my dilemma."

"I can." The pastor's eyes narrowed as he considered his next words. "I'm sensing there's more, though, more pressure on you right now than just your love for Noel."

Startled, Jeremy stared at the older man, wondering how he could possibly know that. "I am being threatened—no, extorted—into publicly denouncing my atheist beliefs to protect Noel. At first it was just e-mail threats, but then a car tried to run us down in a parking lot, which set off a series of near-miss attacks on Noel. The latest e-mail implies they started the fire last night to force my hand. How could men who use God's name justify this violence against the innocent?"

"Fanaticism has always existed on both sides of the religious spectrum, but those who employ violence in the name of God are seeking their own will, not God's. His name may be on their lips, but their actions demonstrate He is far from their hearts. In their zealotry they have wandered far from the path of righteousness. God doesn't force people to love him. He offers a clear choice: to believe in Him freely or to turn from Him. No violence. No rhetoric. Just a simple choice." Patrick paused and then drew in a deep breath as if to calm his soul. "Is the God you and Noel read about in her journal, the God she has seen with her own eyes, does that God have anything in common with the threats you've been receiving?"

"No, of course not. Noel speaks of a God of pure love and what I'm seeing here is pure…" He broke off, unsure if he even believed in the opposite concept.

"Evil, that's the word," Partick injected, completing the thought. "It does exist in this world. It is far more plentiful than we want to contemplate. Love is what changes people's hearts, not fear or coercion, only love. True believers spread the word through acts of kindness and generosity; they are known by their love. They make mistakes and are sometimes too adamant and prideful, as we all are, but what underpins their lives is love for God and love for others, and that is a far cry from what you are describing." The pastor leaned forward, his voice urgent and yet somehow soothing. "I can see the pressure this has placed on you, but you need to leave the extremists to the police and focus on what you can control: your own journey and your love for Noel."

Jeremy heard the passion in the pastor's words and knew he had come to the right place seeking answers. "So where do I start? What's the one passage from scripture you would want me to consider."

Patrick met his gaze squarely. "Joshua 24:15. Because it starts where you are right now and ends where you want to be."

Jeremy reached for the Bible on the table but Patrick spoke the words aloud.

"'But if serving the Lord seems undesirable to you, then choose for yourselves this day whom you will serve, whether the gods your ancestors served beyond the Euphrates, or the gods of the Amorites, in whose land you are living. But as for me and my household, we will serve the Lord.'" The pastor paused and let the words settle into the stillness.

"Right now, Jeremy, you are living in the first phrase of that scripture. You have spent years denying God's existence, seeing it as undesirable to even contemplate, much less serve, Him. But we all have gods in our lives, things we give our time to and invest our wealth in. And whatever that is for you, that is your god. For the ancient Egyptians it was idols made of gold, but today we worship other things. Some people spend their time gathering wealth and hoarding it, and in so doing they make money the lord of their lives. Others bend their knees to worship celebrities, flawed human beings just like us but elevated by our envy. Some praise their own accomplishments, taking enormous pride in their intellect and superior wisdom, and elevate themselves to the status of God."

Jeremy winced, a shadow of his adamancy and ego flashing to mind as he studied the pastor's calm demeanor, his words ringing with purpose and sincerity.

"Each of us must make a choice whom we will call the God of our lives. Noel has made that choice. With her example, her family will choose to believe, and they will live out the rest of that verse, 'but as for me and my house, we will serve the Lord.' Now she stands on the opposite side of a chasm you want desperately to cross, and you know there is only one way to do that," the pastor concluded, his eyes fixed on Jeremy.

"I have never loved anyone in my entire life, only Noel." Jeremy clenched his fists in frustration, the truth of that statement emanating from his core. "But I can't toss aside everything I believe, the principles I have founded my life on, and just say I believe… because it wouldn't be true."

"God knows your heart, Jeremy."

"Does he?" The challenge in his words was unmistakable.

"Yes, He does. And any profession of belief must come from a place of faith and truth."

"I know that, and I have none."

"An honest answer, and right now that may be true, but it doesn't have to stay that way. You are on the right path. Coming here to speak with me was the humble act of a seeker. If you seek Him, you will find Him. Of that I have no doubt."

"What if I can never find it?" A cold sweat broke out on Jeremy's palms. "I can't make her wait for me forever. There's a part of her, the strong independent, modern woman who doesn't understand the constraints of her new faith. She wants to toss aside what she sees as antiquated and just take our chances as a couple, even knowing the odds would be stacked against us. And I am almost selfish enough to let her do it." Jeremy took a moment to gather his thoughts, half expecting the pastor to weigh in and surprised when the man remained silent. "But at the same time, I feel ethically bound not to let her violate the tenets of her faith for me. It's a bad precedent to set, to build our new life on an unstable foundation, which means I may never be able to give Noel what she wants, a husband and a family. How do I live with wanting her so badly and never being able to share that life with her?"

Jeremy watched the pastor's eyes shade with sorrow, his brow furrowed and his frown deep. He looked up at the mantle above the fireplace to a photo of himself standing beside a lovely Asian woman.

"When my wife and I married thirty years ago, our one desire, besides serving God, was to have a big family. We wanted to fill our home with children's laughter and love. We tried for a long time to make that happen, spending years of our lives and money we didn't have on infertility treatments. None of it made a difference and the stress of wanting it so badly almost tore our marriage apart. Finally, we came to understand after years of misery that a natural-born family was not in God's plan for us, that in fixing our eyes on that one goal we were missing the other opportunities God had for us to serve."

"So what did you do?" Jeremy asked, intrigued by the story but fearing the ending.

"We prayed and we cried and we stopped trying to fill our lives by our own power. And when we did, a teenager showed up on our doorstep, dripping wet and sick with fever from living out on the streets. We took her in and fostered her until she aged out of the system. And then we took another child no one wanted and did the same. One at a time, giving them all the love we had in our hearts. We're six kids in now. All grown and out of the house, but still our family, all of them brothers and sisters."

"You gave up your dream."

"And found something better." He clasped his hands between his knees as he did when they first sat down. "Can I ask you a question?"

Jeremy nodded, the story Patrick had told piercing his heart.

"Can you remember a time in your life when you acted with no thought for yourself, no ulterior motive, where your only purpose was the good of another?"

"A pure selfless act," Jeremy murmured under his breath, closing his eyes and feeling the sting of the memory. "Yes, just once. I was the one who saved Noel from drowning."

After that the words came of their own volition, drawn from his soul as he spoke of the day he dove into the icy water to save a girl he barely knew. Of the struggle to free her from the anchor and his terror that he would not be able to save her. Of the fire in his lungs as the line broke free. And finally of the CPR he'd performed that brought her back to the land of the living.

"It's the only selfless thing I have ever done. I was one person, so small, so insignificant, but with the power to save Noel's life." Jeremy felt the agony building in his chest and bowed his head, his face resting in his hands. "I can't lose her again."

Patrick's hand touched his shaking shoulder as the raw emotions held him captive, tears spilling from his eyes just as they had on that morning so long ago. The pastor's words came to him from far away, slipping through his anguish to be heard by a battered heart.

"You weren't the only one at work that day, my friend. God sent Noel back to earth because His plan for her had not been completed, and you, Jeremy, are a part of that plan. You were then and you still are now. Give yourself the time and space to see the God who has been drawing you, teaching you, and loving you your entire life and wanting nothing more than for you to turn to Him and say only two words, 'I believe'."

Jeremy looked up at him, his cheeks wet and raw. "But I don't."

Patrick didn't argue the point. "Can I pray for you and Noel?"

At the sound of her name, Jeremy bowed his head, not for himself but for her. He needed to get out of here. Patrick was a good man, but they would always be worlds apart when it came to belief. Nothing would ever change that and, while he'd thought coming here would give him some new insight, he was about to leave as confused as ever. Maybe more so.

Patrick's words filled the room, making Jeremy recall the closing prayer yesterday as he'd watched from the back of the church.

"Oh, gracious God, you have heard every word spoken and unspoken here today. This man has come seeking a new path, a way to bridge the span that now separates him from the woman of his heart. I pray that you will give him peace and the time it takes to find you. I ask for clarity and the time to ponder it. And I ask that you in your time will reveal your great love for him. Bless Noel in her new-found faith and grant her your protection. You have given her a glimpse of heaven and of you, and now I pray that you give her time to live out your plan for her life and to hold the hand of the man she loves while she does it. Give them both the grace and time to work this all out, in Jesus's name. Amen."

Jeremy lifted his head and scrubbed his face with his hands, having heard the words but taking no comfort from them. "Thank you for seeing me today. I can't say that I have any more clarity than when I stepped through the door though."

"Give it time, my friend. It's not a race to the finish line; it's a journey with a wondrous end in sight."

"You really believe that, don't you?"

"I do, and I pray someday you will, too." The pastor walked him to the door. "You can call me anytime, Jeremy. Whenever you want to talk, I will make time for you."

"Thank you. I just might do that."

"I hope you will."

As Jeremy stepped onto the darkened walkway and covered the distance to his car, he felt an ease that shouldn't have been there. He had just poured out his heart to a virtual stranger and he should have been second-guessing his decision to come here today, but instead he felt strangely calm. He had no more in the way of answers than he had an hour ago, but he had a verse to start him down a new path and a word that seemed seated in his consciousness. Time.

He would make no snap decisions. He would diligently study and keep his promise. He just needed to give it… time."

* * *

Mia met Noel as she came through the door. The scent of basil and garlic hinted at the pesto Mum had been talking about making for dinner when she left this morning.

"My guidance counselor read my essay and she says it's good to go." Mia's dark eyes brimmed with excitement. "Can I go ahead and e-mail it to Dr. Finnegan so he can attach the recommendation?"

"It isn't due for another two weeks. How about we sit down with him and go over it together so we're sure we haven't missed anything?" Noel deposited the results of her shopping trip on the table by the door: a new purse, wallet, and phone to replace the ones she'd lost in the fire. She wasn't looking forward to tomorrow's trip to the DMV to get a new driver's license.

"Okay, but can we do it soon? I don't want to wait until the last minute."

"Let me talk to Jeremy tonight and see what the rest of his week looks like. I'm sure we can work something out."

"Nice to know we have your new boyfriend on our side," Mia quipped with a teasing smile.

Noel's hands settled on her sister's shoulders. "Jeremy's help has nothing to do with me. He offered to help you the first day he met you because he listened to your words and knew you would be an excellent addition to next year's freshman class."

"Doesn't hurt that he loves you." Mia turned toward the dining room as Mum called them to dinner.

"How could you possibly know that?"

Mia shrugged her shoulders as if the answer was obvious. "You can see it when he looks at you. Even Dad noticed."

Noel didn't know whether to cringe or laugh at the thought of her father discussing her love life with Mia.

"Don't worry," Mia called over her shoulder, intent on the food appearing on the table. "He's good with it. He said any guy who can save you twice in one lifetime gets his vote."

"You got that right." Garrett appeared from the kitchen carrying the vegetables he'd roasted on the grill.

Marcy joined them. They took their seats around the dining room table that had hosted their dinners since Mia had joined their family, making the kitchen eating area no longer an option.

Noel looked around the table, taking in her father's thinning hair and her mother's deepening wrinkles. No time like the present. "Can we say grace?"

Mum held out her hands to her daughters. "I'd say we have much to be thankful for today."

"Can I do it?" Mia asked, surprising them all.

Instead of bowing her head, she glanced around the table and lifted her gaze upward. "Thank you, Lord, for saving Noel and Jeremy last night, for keeping them safe, and bringing them home. And thanks for the food. Amen."

Noel smiled. Short and sweet. Hopefully the first of many.

Hours later, exhausted both mentally and physically, she stepped from the bathroom, ready for a good night's sleep. She heard the telltale vibration of her cell phone where it rested on the nightstand and scooped it up. Propping the pillows up against the headboard, she hit the icon connecting the call in real time.

Jeremy appeared on the screen, his handsome face looking weary and apologetic. "Noel, I'm sorry. I know you're angry with me."

"I was angry—furious actually—but now I'm just disappointed," she answered honestly. She watched him cringe at her words and noted the bookshelves behind him, knowing he was still at work.

"I think that might be worse." Jeremy massaged his forehead, shielding his eyes from her gaze.

"Where did you go today?"

"To talk with Patrick Mueller. His words at the debate started you down the path to finding your memories. Seemed like the right place to start my new research."

"You know he's the pastor of the church I'm going to?"

"I do. In fact, I went there yesterday morning because I wanted to hear what you're learning. He's a gifted speaker."

"You were there?" Surprised, Noel tried to picture Jeremy among the crowd of worshippers at the service, amazed at the depth of his commitment to her. "Did sitting down with Pastor Mueller give you any new insights?"

"He gave me a lot to think about, a new verse to study, and the gift of his time." Jeremy's next words were measured and clear. "I have no idea how long it will take or if I will ever find the belief you have embraced."

"I'm going to wait until you do. You know that, right?"

"I do, but you can't wait forever. I would never want you to set aside your dreams for me." His tone was resigned. His eyes sought hers through the screen that connected them.

"Don't you see?" Noel responded, her words gentle but firm, trying to make him understand. "You are the only man I want to live out those dreams with. If we learned anything last night, it's that life can change in an instant and we are better together than apart."

"Even though I sometimes make you furious and disappointed?"

"Yes, even then." Noel sensed in him a vulnerability she had not seen before, knowing that in choosing to love her he had opened himself up to all the heartache that could come from that decision. "I am never giving up on you, Jeremy. You are the man, the only man, I want sitting beside me when we tell these stories to our grandchildren."

"I want that, too, more than I can tell you."

"Then keep your promise and maybe it won't take as long as you think." She hoped with all her heart that would soon be true. "And now for a self-serving change of subject. Is there any chance you have some time this week to sit down with Mia and look over her application?"

"If we do it Thursday, you could get a chance to see Will. He'll be in town for the symposium on emergency medicine and we're meeting at the coffeehouse at four."

"It will be nice to see him again. I like your brother." She paused, debating the wisdom of sharing a thought she had been pondering all day. "I'm thinking about moving back to my place this weekend, Jeremy."

On the screen, she could see his surprise followed by his deepening concern in the firm set of his jawline. "I don't think now is the time to do that, Noel, after all that happened with the fire."

"But that had nothing to do with us." She watched the muscles in his neck tighten and his lips thin in a grimace. "Did it?"

"That's what I was calling to talk about. I opened another e-mail shortly before meeting Patick. That fire was meant for me."

"People died last night, Jeremy." Noel's mind raced at the depravity of setting an entire landscape on fire to silence one man. "What do they want?'

"They want me to denounce my atheism." He massaged his forehead with one hand. "I contacted Detective Santino earlier. He had the same thought I did, that maybe this group is taking credit for a natural disaster to force me to do what they've wanted all along."

"Are you considering it?"

"I am, to protect you and me." He met her gaze squarely. "But even if I do, it won't change the situation for us. I'll be saying the words, but you and I both know it's a lie."

Noel's mind reeled, awash with fear at the sheer malice of setting a fire to bend one man to their will. Noel wanted Jeremy to come to genuine faith, not be bludgeoned into it to protect her. "I don't think that's a good idea. You'd be letting them win, rewarding their actions and driving them back into the shadows for now. But for how long? They'll just find another target and next time the loss of innocent lives could be worse. I think you have to stand your ground."

"If I do, will you stay with your parents for a bit longer?"

"I will," Noel answered. "Do you find it ironic that this group is trying to blackmail you into doing the very thing you are trying to do on your own, for me and for us?" She watched him cup a fisted hand in front of him like a warrior wanting to do battle but not knowing which way to turn or where the danger would strike next.

"Ironic would be one word for it." His eyes fixed on hers, the depth of his gaze as earnest as his words. "I just want this to be over so you and I can move forward together. So I can have the time to find true faith—if that's even possible—and claim the life that I want with you, to be your husband and the father of our children."

She gasped, her eyes stinging at the realization that he wanted to marry her. She had known it last night, but hearing it spelled out so clearly made the urgency real. A sudden thought made her ask, "The verse that Patrick gave you, can you tell me which one it is?"

"Joshua 25:14. He said he chose it because 'it starts where you are and ends where you want to be'."

"Do you remember the end?" She waited, a shiver of anticipation running up her spine, a message from the God she had seen and now believed in.

"But as for me and my house, we will serve the Lord," Jeremy answered. "I only hope someday that will be true."

# CHAPTER NINETEEN

Mia pulled open the door to the Laraby Science Center, her eyes wide with anticipation.

"Are you nervous?" Noel asked.

"This is only the most important meeting I've ever had. So, yes, I'm a little nervous."

"Jeremy is on your side, remember? He wants you to get in. That's why he's writing the letter of recommendation."

"Look at this place." Mia waved her arm at the room bustling with students. "I want to be a part of this next year."

Noel smiled. The coffeehouse was a scene of commotion and connection. Friends greeted each other with hugs, groups gathered at the larger tables for project planning, four burly football players shared two orders of the nacho supreme, and an awkward couple by the window announced with their body language that they were on their first date. The din of conversations, punctuated by an occasional burst of laughter, filled the room with energy. Noel scanned the room and took note of Dwayne waiting in line at the counter before she spotted Jeremy and Will sitting at a table against the back wall. She nudged Mia in their direction.

The two men got to their feet. Both were tall and broad shouldered and had an obvious fraternal resemblance. Jeremy didn't reach out and touch her—this was still their workplace—but Will had no such qualms. He enveloped Noel in a warm hug before shaking Mia's hand as Jeremy made the introductions.

"It's good to see you again," Will said to Noel as they took their seats. She and Mia sat on one side of the table and the brothers on the other. "Cherie said to say hello and to tell you the girls are looking forward to meeting you."

"I'd love to meet them; let's make that happen soon. How's the symposium?"

"I'm learning a lot about the latest innovations in ER medicine, but the sessions are long. This is a welcome break." Will addressed his next question to Mia. "I hear you're applying early decision?"

Noel shifted her gaze to find Jeremy studying her with a soft smile, the conversation at his side seemingly unheard and his eyes never leaving her face. How could one look hold so much love and concern, admiration and resolve, and all without a single word being spoken? She remembered sitting in this room just a month ago and being afraid to meet Jeremy's eyes, and now all she wanted was a lifetime to do so. The urge to reach out and touch his hand where it rested on the table was tangible, but she restrained the impulse. She saw his fingers twitch against the wood surface. Lifting her gaze to meet his, she knew he had been thinking the same thing before a crash of metal against glass rent the air.

The doors of the coffeehouse burst open and a cadre of men in military gear blocked the entrance. An additional pair appeared behind the service counter, blocking the only other egress. They wore army camouflage gear with work boots and wide belts arrayed with tools and hand grenades. Each carried a weapon, no two alike, as if each man had brought his own weapon of choice.

Noel reached for her phone and saw Jeremy do likewise. But when she tried to call 911, she had no signal and the call wouldn't go through. Looking up she saw Jeremy and Will exchange a pained glance and heard Jeremy whisper one word. "Jammer."

"Phones in the middle of the table. They won't work. We took care of that."

A man strode to the center of the room, his company at his back. His stance was wide. A day's growth of beard shadowed his jaw. His blonde buzz cut was short, almost military. Noel recognized him instantly from their encounter on Friday.

Lance Petroff.

She glanced over at Jeremy and watched his surprise harden into fury.

The group of men behind Lance were four in number. One was quite young by the look of him and another was pushing seventy and built like a rock climber, wiry and strong. They looked familiar but Noel couldn't place them; the thought was fleeting. Two others, both the size of professional linebackers, rounded out the group. She placed her phone in the middle of the table with the others, but at the last moment opened the voice memo app and started recording. If they didn't live to see the end of this day, it would document what had happened here.

"Stand up! Hands where I can see them! Do it now!" Petroff ordered as a rustle of chairs scraped the floor and almost eclipsed the whispers of fear. "Back up to the nearest wall. No bags, backpacks, or jackets."

Noel reached for Mia's hand, glancing over at Jeremy as they stood. She watched as he and Will used the general commotion to cover the sound of them pushing the table to the side, which gave them some room to maneuver. They took up positions as ordered, but each was a step away from the wall, using their bodies to shield Noel and Mia. The crowd moved backward in an expanding circle to the limits of the room's perimeter, the first-date couple now holding hands and the football players obscuring a good portion of the window behind them. Noel heard the clink of metal on metal and watched as the youngest man secured the door closed with a linked chain and padlock before rejoining his unit. They shifted their positions, guns drawn, as two of them joined their fellows at the service counter, reinforcing their position at the one remaining exit point.

Noel recognized their strategy. Students, now hostages, were fanned out around the room with their backs to the windows, obscuring the view and serving as human shields.

"Men in back. Women in front," Petroff barked.

She saw the reluctant glance the brothers exchanged before complying as Jeremy stepped behind Noel and Will stood behind Mia. Noel glanced over at her sister, expecting to see tears, but when Mia met her gaze, she saw not fear but confusion tinged with anger. She reached for Mia's hand even as she felt Jeremy's breath warm against her ear.

"Hold onto her," he directed, having seen Mia's demeanor and knowing that any rash action would only call attention to them.

Lance Petroff's voice reverberated in the quiet room, the deep register of his southern drawl somehow more pronounced as he spoke into the silence. "No one will be hurt if you stay where you are. We have one reason for being here and it has nothing to do with all of you. We will fire, though, if you choose not to listen. Fair warning. Your choice."

Noel felt Jeremy lean forward, his chest against her back. "Stay put. We know what they want."

"Professor Jeremy Finnegan, step forward!"

Noel heard Will gasp and felt the tension emanating from him as he took an involuntary step forward before Jeremy restrained him with an extended arm. Looking over her shoulder, she saw the determination on Jeremy's face meet with a nod of admiration from his older brother. Jeremy squeezed Will's forearm and stepped around Noel, blocking her from view.

Lance Petroff spotted him immediately. "Professor, I believe we have some unfinished business."

Jeremy nodded. His shoulders were tense, his hands fisted at his side.

"Then join me so we can tell the world about your change of heart." Petroff's words rang out in a commanding tone.

Visibly relaxing his shoulders as if to shake off his earlier anger, Jeremy strode across the room. Noel knew what he was doing. He was going to comply to protect them all and end this nightmare, but she feared it would not be so simple. Will's whispered prayers behind her spoke of his concern as well. Noel echoed his petition with one of her own as she watched the man she loved face off against his friend.

*Lord of light, please save him.*

The words rang in her head, calling to mind Celeste's final declaration as Noel had stood wet and trembling in Jeremy's arms Sunday night on the shore. "He needs you to save him."

Bewildered, she wondered what she was supposed to do. She felt helpless to do anything but watch.

*Show me, please. You need to show me.*

Jeremy stood in the center of the room, his back straight and shoulders square. No fear clouded his features. He had stepped forward without hesitation, and the determination that radiated from him was as palpable as the malice and darkness that seemed to envelop his former friend. Noel's eyes grew wide and tears blurred her vision. She remembered Jeremy telling her about the one thing he'd been searching for since the day he saved her, to find again the awe and wonder of one selfless act. Now he stood at its center.

The oldest member of the cadre stepped forward, lifted his cell phone, and pressed the screen to start recording as he used two fingers to zoom in on Jeremy. Petroff's voice pierced the silence as the camera captured every word. "Jeremy Finnegan, do you believe in God?"

"I do." Jeremy answered, his voice strong and clear.

"Do you believe in Jesus Christ, the only Son of the living God, who died on the cross to save you?"

"I do."

Noel shivered. As much as she wanted to believe his resounding declaration, she knew he was lying. He had told her so on the phone Monday night.

"Do you denounce your atheist beliefs?"

"I do."

Petroff eyed him with a snarl of disbelief. "Tell us now. What changed your mind?"

Jeremy's chin lifted, his presence commanding. With every eye in the room on him, he didn't hesitate. "It tells us in Joshua 24:15 to choose this day whom you will serve. It's a verse that calls us to set aside the lesser things we so often put above God in our lives. Our worship of money and fame, our pride in our own intellect, our lust for power." He turned away from Lance, sweeping his gaze over the crowd and coming to rest on Noel. "I have worshipped all those things in my life, but in the last few weeks I have been shown a different way. Now I choose, as an act of my will, to walk in that way and to worship the one true living God, so I can live out the end of that powerful verse: 'But as for me and my house, we will serve the Lord'."

His eyes met hers and although she knew he was repeating what he'd learned from Patrick, he spoke with assurance and almost convinced her.

"Now, the final question." Petroff spit the words out into the hush of the crowd. "Are you willing to die for your faith?"

"No!" Noel screamed the single word, muffled by the sudden gasp of the onlookers. Even the men behind him looked stunned at the question.

Jeremy turned back to face Petroff, his tone firm. "You have what you came for. Post the video and let these people go."

"You are in no position to make demands," the blonde commander said. His temper flared, reacting to Jeremy's calm demeanor with rage. "You have done more damage to the minds of those seeking the path of righteousness than any man in recent memory. You will pay with your life for that sin."

Noel shivered, her muscles trembling with fear. She wrapped her arms around herself, watching the scene, helpless to do anything to stop it. A real-time version of the debate was playing out in front of her, but this time with deadly consequences.

"The God you claim to believe in," Jeremy responded evenly, "is not a God of retribution. His name may be on your lips, but your heart is far from Him if you think that coercion and violence can bring about His will. He is a God of unfailing love, and no sin can ever put us beyond the reach of His forgiveness."

"Which applies only if we are truly repentant for our actions." Petroff stepped backward. "I don't think that's what we're looking at here. You're lying to me and to everyone here and with God as your witness."

"Scripture tells us no one can judge the heart of a man but God himself," Jeremy countered, his eyes narrowing but his words resounding.

"You are citing the WORD of God to me!" Anger rose in Petroff's chopped words. "The Warriors of Righteous Deliverance will not allow such blasphemy!"

Petroff held out a hand to the youngest of the men behind him and the kid extended his weapon. Beside her, Noel heard Mia gasp as Will stepped forward to call attention to himself, but he never got the chance. Mia broke ranks and hurled herself toward the trio, her scream reverberating off the walls. "No, Tanner, don't do it!"

Petroff grabbed the weapon and leveled it at Mia, squeezing the trigger twice in rapid succession just as Jeremy dove in front of her, shielding her from the bullets' path. He collapsed to the floor as the room erupted in pandemonium.

Will and Noel raced to Jeremy, flashes of the fallout making a vague impression as she focused all her attention on reaching him. Two brawny football players tackled Petroff as his men tried to flee but were confronted by local police.

Will dropped to his knees beside his brother, nodding at Noel who helped him roll Jeremy over so they could assess the damage wrought by two bullets fired at point-blank range.

Blood was everywhere. Noel pulled off the light sweater she had been wearing over a tank top and used it to wipe his face and neck. "Jeremy, talk to me."

Will ripped open the front of Jeremy's shirt, sending buttons flying as he assessed the chest and abdomen.

"The bullet nicked his carotid, Will." Fear coursed through Noel as she used a corner of the sweater to press a finger against the oozing wound in his neck that pulsed with each beat of his heart.

"You know the drill, Noel. Firm steady pressure to occlude the vessel and you can't let up for even a second."

"Where did the other shot hit?"

"Looks like a through and through to the abdomen. Hard to know what kind of damage it did. Abdomen is still soft for now."

But for how much longer? Noel heard the concern in his tightly controlled words, the undertone of fear held in check by Will's years working in the ER.

A campus security officer dropped a jump bag of medical supplies at Will's side, and he ripped it open to find the BP cuff just inside the flap. "Mia, I need you to go through the bag and find dressing material for the abdominal wound and a pulse ox monitor. It looks like a clear band-aid with a string attached."

With her eyes fixed on Jeremy's face, Noel saw his eyelids flutter. "Will, he's awake."

"Keep him talking if you can. If he can hold a conversation, we know he's getting adequate blood supply to the brain."

"Jeremy, talk to me, please."

His eyes opened just a sliver at her words but then grew wider. His expression was dazed. "Noel."

He knew who she was. That was a good sign, although the single word was weak and just above a whisper.

"You saved Mia."

"Couldn't let you lose another sister." His words were choppy but clear.

"BP 86/50," Will said aloud. "He needs an IV start and a bolus of fluid."

"You do know I love you, right?" Noel phrased it as a question that required an answer. She knew he would respond if he could.

"I love you, too." His words faded. The last one so soft, it was almost lost.

"Jeremy!" She shouted to get his attention. "Stay with me. Focus on my face and talk to me."

"Always… focus… you."

"O2 saturation eighty-eight," Will announced.

Fear pulsed through Noel with every heartbeat. Her finger started to cramp with the constant pressure to Jeremy's neck. All her attention was on this man she loved with every ounce of her being. "Did you mean what you said, about believing?"

"Don't… know… maybe."

"You have to keep your promise, Jeremy," she said loudly, trying to keep him in the present moment even if she had to annoy him to do it.

"Tried." The single word was weak and thready.

His confident words from just moments ago rang out in her mind with all the clarity of a church bell on a summer morning.

"Then choose now who you will serve. Make a choice to believe," she pleaded. Her eyes wet with tears, she shook her head to clear her vision, her finger cramping against his neck.

"Choose?"

His eyelids drooped down over those blue eyes that had for a time scared her and now were the only thing she wanted to see for the rest of her days here on earth and into eternity. She had to reach him! But how?

*Lord, help me please. I can't do this alone.*

The words rose in her consciousness like the lyrics of a long-forgotten song.

*Not perfect, just present.*

The urgency of her words made her tone loud and strident. "Life is full of things we don't understand, but we use them and choose them every day. Faith doesn't have to come from perfect understanding. It comes from turning to God and saying two words, 'I believe.'"

His lips parted and his eyes closed. "I… believe."

Was he just repeating her words? "Jeremy, talk to me," Noel cried, desperation piercing her tone even as she heard Will's words.

"No palpable pulse, starting CPR."

Mia was at her side as if knowing what Noel needed her to do. Noel took her sister's strong hand and placed it over the carotid wound with firm steady pressure as she rolled her finger off, the transfer seamless. "Press hard, Mia."

Scrambling to Jeremy's other side she opened his airway, watching Mia follow her movement and adjust accordingly. Looking up at Will she saw him nod, his compressions strong and flawless. A line of students with Dwayne at its head formed behind him, waiting to relieve Will when he grew tired. CPR compressions needed to be fast with full chest compression and recoil. No one, no matter how strong, could keep that up for long. She heard Will counting the compressions aloud and when he reached thirty, she pinched Jeremy's nose closed and covered his mouth with her own, just as he had done for her all those years ago. She exhaled two breaths in quick succession as she shared with him the breath of life.

* * *

Noel watched the ambulance pull away, knowing she had made the right call. Only one of them could ride in with Jeremy and she knew Will could help the medics far better than she could. They had gotten Jeremy back on the second shock. The arrival of the paramedics and their quick work of intubation, IV access, and medications had stabilized him for transport. The trauma team would be waiting to take him to the operating room as soon as he came through the ER doors. Her arm around Mia's shoulders, Noel offered up a silent prayer to the God she knew was listening, a prayer of thanks for His deliverance and a prayer of healing for the man she loved who had saved them all.

Now she needed to find her car key, drop Mia at home, and get to the hospital. Her sister's slender shoulders trembled and her muttered words were almost incomprehensible. Discerning their meaning, she spun Mia to face her. "It's not your fault. You were trying to save him."

"When I saw Tanner with the gun, I had to stop him." Mia's words faded into a wave of tears. Noel enfolded her distraught sister in her arms as she lifted her gaze and saw her parents rushing toward them.

"We saw the news about a hostage situation on campus." Mum's eyes were anxious but held a hint of relief now that she had eyes on both her girls.

Noel had energy for only the briefest of explanations about the shooting and Jeremy's condition before her dad interrupted. "You need to get to the hospital. We've got Mia."

She reached for his weathered hand and gave it a squeeze. "Thank you."

"Go! We've got this."

Noel ran for the Laraby Center. Weaving her way around the students being interviewed by local police, she spotted the table where they had been sitting, all four phones still in the center. She covered the distance in a few strides, the commotion of law enforcement around her barely registering.

It had never made sense. How had they known so much about Jeremy? Right from the start they'd known where to find him. The picture taken after the debate had been meant to instill fear, but the forum had been a well-publicized event, no mystery there. How had they known he would be at the restaurant just two nights later, though? And the attempted burglary at her home? Where did that fit in? She supposed once they had the photo they could have found her with an Internet search. But how could they have timed the attack last Wednesday night so perfectly? She hadn't known when she would leave the building that night. Had they been watching her in the days after the debate? The thought made her skin crawl with an ominous shiver. And what about the carnival on Sunday or the coffeehouse today? That seemed unexplainable. She and Mia had walked in just minutes before the four o'clock meeting they'd discussed Monday night on the phone.

This ambush had taken time to plan. You could see that in its execution. And their demands seemed personal. All the pieces were there to figure it out, she just needed to put them in the right framework, she thought, searching under the table and pushing aside the legs of a chair to find her bag.

At least two of the men in that group were from Patrick's church. Mia had recognized Tanner from the meeting on Sunday, which made Noel recall the older man in the front row with her. Today, he'd been the one taking the video on his phone. Although she didn't believe Patrick Mueller was involved in any of this, it was possible that a more radical subgroup within his church had taken matters into their own hands, which left her wondering about the man she had been working with for the last two weeks. She shook her head. No, it couldn't be Dwayne. He had been standing by the service counter when the attack began, but he hadn't been a part of their group. Noel had watched him take the first relief shift during the CPR to save Jeremy's life.

He had worked as hard as all the rest, his compressions powerful and perfect like he had done it many times before.

Her hand closed on her bag, and she pulled it toward her. The answers were just outside her reach. She stood up and grabbed the four phones on the table. Holding onto her own, she slipped the others into her purse and used the chest strap to secure the heavier bag. Right now, she needed to get to the hospital.

A restraining hand on her shoulder made her turn. Detective Santino stood squarely in her path. She didn't have time for this.

"I need you to answer a few questions," he said, his gaze assessing.

"Not now, John, please." She kept her voice steady, forcing a calm she didn't feel. "I need to get to the hospital. I will answer any questions you have, but later."

His eyes narrowed as if weighing the decision to let her drive after the incident that had left the whole campus shaken. "Fine. I will come and find you in the surgical waiting area. He's going to be in surgery for hours, you know that."

Noel nodded. "Yes, but I want to be there when he gets out."

"More than friends now, I'm thinking." The detective stepped aside. "Anyone with eyes could see that coming."

The ache in her heart grew sharper at his words and she met his gaze. "Thank you. I'll see you later."

He lifted a hand, made eye contact with the officer stationed at the door, and then waved her through. When she finally cleared the science center, she raced for her car, groaning as she remembered that today she and Mia had parked at the far end of the massive lot that backed up to the open culvert system that drained water from the county highway.

She spotted a man ahead moving almost as quickly as she was, a briefcase bumping up against his leg with each step. All the oddities suddenly came together, even the contradiction in the study protocol. Anger pulsed through her, and her heartbeat increased with unbridled fury as she raced after him, confronting him as he reached for the door of his massive truck.

"How could you do this to him? He was your friend!" Noel shouted, stopping at the rear bumper of his car and squeezing the phone in her hand with rage. She watched as he shuttered a flash of anxiety behind a façade of disdain.

"Ms. Welsh, it's clear you are distraught after what happened. I'm on my way to the hospital to check on Jeremy. I assume you are doing the same given the nature of your relationship with him." David McMann pivoted toward her, shifting the briefcase to his other hand.

Noel drew in an angry breath, her fury growing at his theatrical pretense when he was the one who had set this all in motion.

"Did you think I didn't know?" David continued before she could respond, his tone dismissive. "I'd have had to be a blind man not to see the way he looks at you. He's in love with you, so what are you still doing here? Unless you don't feel the same way about him, of course."

He was trying to manipulate her, but she refused to take the bait. "You are the only one who could have known where he would be."

"I have no idea what you are talking about," McMann asserted, his eyes narrowing.

"You jammed our phones today and you've been bugging his office for weeks. It's the same technology, but one disrupts a signal and the other carries it." Noel saw the slight squint in his eyes at her words. "The police will find it when they search his office."

"Not if there's nothing to find."

A flash of satisfaction was gone as quickly as it appeared, and Noel knew he had already taken care of that problem. But with so little time between the incident and the arrival of the police, he hadn't just tossed the device in the trash. It had to be on him. She advanced on him, watching his fingers clench the briefcase handle. "You tried to run us down in a parking lot."

"I'm sure I was nowhere near that incident when it happened." He retreated a few steps to the front bumper.

He couldn't possibly outrun her with the weight of that briefcase, which made Noel wonder what else was in there as she tried to come up with a way to separate him from the evidence. Just keep him talking, she told herself. "You altered the study protocol in the final phase of the document's publication, didn't you? Just changed the words slightly so the inclusion of a subject who had any of the exclusionary criteria would not just disqualify them but would void the study. Taking a big chance, weren't you? Thinking no one was going to read it that carefully? I almost missed it as well. Almost."

His jawline tensed and his lips thinned as her needling picked away at his calm façade. "That's quite a theory. What could I possibly have to gain?"

The answer came to her in a wave of certainty. "To discredit the man who has been a thorn in your side since he was hired by the university for his Internet fame. And whose atheist beliefs have butted up against your growing fanaticism ever since. Did you seek out the Warriors of Righteous Deliverance or did they find you?"

The flash of rage in his eyes revealed the truth. Hate emanated from him. She inched closer to him, keeping her eyes on his face and not on the briefcase he carried.

Anger colored his face with a mottled, sweaty sheen, and spit flew from his mouth as he erupted. "He did nothing—nothing! — to get that job but take advantage of a social media following the university thought they could capitalize on." His breathing was ragged with rage. "They gave him a full professorship he didn't deserve and one it took me years to earn. I have worked my whole career to get what was handed to him. Now the university is about to name him department chair for Biology and Life Sciences, and all because he looks good on camera and knows how to talk a good game." McMann slipped a hand into his jacket and withdrew a small caliber handgun, the metal surface catching the waning sunlight and glinting with malice. "And none of it would have happened without you."

Just steps away from him and sandwiched between his truck and another equally big vehicle, she was in an untenable position and had little room to maneuver. She hadn't thought this through and now needed a distraction that was, she realized, as close as her hand. She raised the phone and turned the screen for him to see. The button at the bottom shone with its red glow. "Every word of your confession."

Driven by fury, he stepped forward to grab it from her, closing the distance between them. She spun away from him on the balls of her feet as if to keep the phone out of reach and at the same time tucked her knee up to her chest and unleashed a back kick that caught him squarely in the chest and propelled him backward with its impact. He hit the ground just beyond the front bumper, the briefcase forgotten, his arms flung wide as he landed on his back.

"Gun!" Noel screamed, knowing the police were still on campus and hoping someone would hear.

A heavy boot stomped down on McMann's wrist and he screamed as the gun fell from his hand. Dwayne kicked it away and then, with practiced skill, he flipped the older man over onto his stomach and pressed a knee into the base of his spine with his full weight behind it. He pulled David's wrists backward, securing the now immobile suspect on his belly.

Phone still in hand, Noel hit John Santino's number and followed the brief call by sending the voice memo she had just recorded to his phone. Within minutes they were surrounded by police officers and David McMann was in custody, the gun and the briefcase secured as evidence.

Knowing there was no avoiding Santino's questions, Noel reminded herself that Jeremy would not be out of surgery for hours. Although she chafed at the time it would take, she knew she could do nothing at the hospital. Jeremy's care was in the hands of a trauma surgeon now, and she needed to give the authorities the statements and evidence they would need to secure a conviction. She and Dwayne were separated and questioned. Glancing over at him, Noel was glad she had been right about this man who had become not only her partner in the clinical trial but also her friend.

Standing beside him after they had given their statements, she turned to him. "Thank you for the timely arrival."

"I was going to offer to drive you to the hospital and was waiting by your car. Good thing. Not that you needed my help." He looked down at her with a wide grin. "Nice move. I didn't know back kicks were part of your resume. Who taught you that one?"

"Jeremy did, just the other night, actually."

"You're a quick study, then, but I think I already knew that."

"And you have a few skills as well. You were in the military, right?"

"Did one tour straight out of high school. They trained me as a medic, but basic training is the same for everyone." Dwayne gave her an assessing stare. "Now do you need a ride to the hospital or are you good?"

"I've got this, thanks."

"You know we may be unemployed after this." Dwayne pulled his keys from his pocket.

Noel nodded. "They'll likely shut down the study, at least for a while."

"By the time I see you again, I'm thinking you could be a married woman." He rested a hand on her arm and gave a quick squeeze. "God bless you, Noel."

# CHAPTER TWENTY

Jeremy awoke to the sound of his brother grilling the surgeon about the vascular repair to his carotid artery and the length of the colon resection necessary to stop the abdominal bleeding. Although he appreciated his brother's advocacy, there was only one voice he wanted to hear and one face he wanted to see as he forced his eyes open.

"Welcome back." Noel stepped into his line of sight, her smile brilliant. She met his gaze and then brushed a stray lock of hair from his eyes. His pulse raced at the simple gesture, making an alarm sound on the monitor just beyond his sight.

Suddenly surrounded by doctors in green scrubs, he waited impatiently for them to finish their assessment. His thoughts grew clearer as he recalled the standoff at the coffeehouse. The surgeon finally stepped aside, satisfied with his patient's progress. Jeremy shifted his gaze to the foot of the bed where his brother waited with a grin of relief matched only by the fervor of his words.

"Good to have you back. You took your time about it," Will stated with a hint of fraternal sarcasm.

"Sorry. I got shot. Remember?" His voice sounded weak and his throat sore, but the words were clear.

"Oh, I remember. Nearly gave me a heart attack. Between you and my wife, I'm done with medical trauma in my own family! Can we please make it stop?"

"I'll do my best." Jeremy felt more like himself with this brotherly banter before he returned his attention to Noel. "How's Mia?"

"Shaky and traumatized, but safely home with Mum and Dad, thanks to you." Noel reached for his hand, avoiding the IV in his forearm and the A-line in his wrist as her fingers closed around his.

"Was anyone else hurt?"

"No," Will answered. "You were the only one."

"I have no doubt you two are the reason I'm still here. How bad was it?"

Noel and Will exchanged a glance, and Jeremy saw in their eyes a shadow of the fear they had faced to save him.

"You lost a lot of blood. The trauma surgeon told me the bullet missed your abdominal aorta by a centimeter," Will replied.

"CPR?" Jeremy asked, somehow knowing the answer.

"Yes, but we got you back on scene with the second shock just as the medics arrived."

"You are a handy guy to have around."

"I didn't do it alone," Will responded.

"I know." Jeremy shifted his gaze to the beautiful woman at his side. "It worked out just like Celeste said. You saved me."

"What did you see?" Noel asked, her eyes wide.

"I didn't see anything." Jeremy knew what she was hoping he would say, but he had experienced none of that. "I closed my eyes and your face was the last thing I saw, and now you're still right here with me."

"Which leaves you like the rest of us, little brother, having to believe in something you can't see. Accepting by faith what Noel has seen but few of us do. Did you do that, Jeremy?"

"I did." His eyes never left Noel's face. "When you said I didn't need to have perfect faith, I knew there had been a part of me that not only believed you but who wanted to believe it all. I didn't need to understand everything. I just needed to recognize that there was something out there—someone out there—who was smarter than me. And your words showed me the way, Noel."

Her smile faded in a wave of awe and her eyes glistened with unshed tears as she glanced over at Will.

"I'm going to give you two a minute," he said, leaving them alone.

"So you know what this means?" Noel leaned toward him, her eyes fixed on his, a lone tear escaping to run down her cheek. "Now you can marry me."

He lifted his hand and wiped the tear from her face. "Is that a proposal?"

"It is," Noel replied, no doubt or hint of levity in her tone. "The question is do you want to marry me, to be the father of our children, and someday the grandfather who gets to tell our remarkable story to a brood of grandchildren?"

"I do." Jeremy's heart ached with love for her. He was barely able to fathom the life that lay before him, one he had never dreamed of having and now was everything he wanted. "I want to spend the rest of my life thanking God for my beautiful tenacious wife." He tugged her hand, pulling her closer. "Thank you for never giving up on me. And for saving me."

"I think we saved each other," she whispered, her breath warm on his face before she kissed him.

# EPILOGUE

Noel stretched to her full height as dawn filtered through the A-frame's apex window and filled the loft with a soft glow. She had needed last night to herself before this day began and although her Mum had tried to convince her to stay with them, Noel had prevailed. Downstairs, she set the coffee brewing and moments later stood under the shower's warm spray, trying to decide if what she was feeling was nerves or anticipation. She settled on the latter as she brushed her teeth and combed through her wet hair. Smiling at her reflection in the steamy mirror above the sink, she pulled on a terrycloth robe before stepping from the bathroom. She had been waiting for this day most of her life: her wedding day, on the last day of this momentous year.

A knock sounded on the door as the aroma of strong coffee filled the tiny apartment. Noel smiled and covered the distance to the door in a few strides before pulling it open. Jeremy stood on the porch with his hands in his pockets and his shoulders back, a hint of a smile tweaking his lips.

"You do know it's bad luck for you to see the bride before the wedding, right?" Noel laughed, her words in sharp contrast to her actions as she pulled him into the apartment.

"I don't believe in luck, not anymore. And I needed a few minutes with you before this whole day of mayhem begins." Jeremy pulled her to him and held her in his arms. He inclined his head toward the long white sheath hanging from the rafters in the loft. "Nice dress."

Noel glanced back at the dress, so elegant in its simplicity. "It will look better on."

"Of that I have no doubt." Jeremy chuckled near her ear. "But the woman wearing it is all I care about. You could wear jeans and a sweatshirt and you would still be the most beautiful woman in the room."

"A bit laid back for what we have planned today, but thank you. I am looking forward to seeing you in a tuxedo. Another first for us."

"One of many," he said, eyeing her suggestively.

She grinned, choosing to ignore for the moment that tempting avenue. There would be plenty of time for that later. "What did you do after the rehearsal dinner last night?"

"I got a real-time look at the rigors of family life helping Will and Cherie get the girls to bed. Took them a long time to get to sleep. They are very excited about being flower girls today and about…" he paused for emphasis, "being big sisters."

"They're having a baby?" Noel exclaimed.

Jeremy nodded. "It was supposed to be a secret until after the wedding, but little girls don't know how to keep a secret very well. Looks like a honeymoon baby. Cherie's due in June."

"Four kids! They're going to have their hands full. Did Maddie and Scott get in okay?"

"Their flight from New Hampshire was delayed, but they made it in by midnight."

Noel watched a shadow play across his features. It was gone almost as quickly as it appeared and she knew he was thinking about the rest of his family. Tyler had called and talked to Jeremy, at least, to explain why he couldn't attend. His father had returned the RSVP with a simple check in the No box and nothing more. An e-mail from his mother a day later explained her inability to make the trip alone. And they had never heard from his youngest brother, Mitch, at all. These were just a few of many disappointments in Jeremy's life since the shooting on campus.

The biggest blow had come just hours after surgery when Noel had to tell him about David's betrayal. The arrest and indictment of the man Jeremy had believed to be his mentor and friend was devastating and offset only by his developing friendship with Patrick Mueller. The pastor had been shocked by the revelation that his church had unknowingly harbored members of such a violent group. The video of the shooting had gone viral, the views soaring into the millions. Jeremy's declaration of faith drew ire from his former fellow atheists and support from a vast community of believers who had shared it. He was more famous now than he had ever been, but all he wanted to do was get his research study back up and running. The IRB had halted the study until the protocol could be changed, vetted, and approved by the board after the semester break.

Filled with angst and self-blame for not having seen what was right in front of them, Jeremy and Patrick had found solace in each other, their friendship forged out of the remnants of a tragedy. As Jeremy recovered from surgery, the two had taken long walks together as prescribed by the surgeon. The power of fresh air and movement had proved healing not only for Jeremy's body but also for his mind, the former rivals hashing out a new path forward after crushing disappointment. Today Patrick would officiate at their wedding.

Stepping back from her embrace, Jeremy took her hands in his. "Before this day gets crazy, I have something for you."

Noel raised an eyebrow. "What could you possibly give me that would make this day any more perfect than it already is?"

"It occurred to me earlier this week that we had skipped a major part of the engagement ritual when you proposed to me."

"I did do that, didn't I?" Noel said, feeling proud of herself. "I didn't want you slipping away from me again."

"I'm never going to be any place but right here at your side." He met her gaze. "May I have your hand, please?"

She extended her hand to him as he reached into his pocket and withdrew a simple but exquisite ring, a single diamond in an elevated setting of white gold. He slipped it on her finger. "I wanted you to have this before we add the wedding band later today. Two circles of gold, a matched set, now and forever. Like us."

Noel's eyes filled with tears at his words. "It's beautiful."

"Mia helped me pick it out. She said you would want something simple and elegant."

"It's perfect. She knows me well after all these years as a family."

"And speaking of family," he said, pulling her to him. "I know you've been worried about me, about my family not being here today. I do plan to reconnect with all of them in the future, but if that never happens and if God never blesses us with any of the children we've been talking about, I want you to understand you will always be the only family I will ever need."

Noel brushed away the tears that blurred her vision, wanting a clear view of this man she loved with all her heart. Jeremy drew her over to the couch and they sank down onto the tiny love seat where it all began. The cushions took their weight as Jeremy wrapped her in his arms in this place where her memories had started to return, where together they had confronted her fears and moved beyond them to open the world of love and possibility that lay before them. His words whispered close to her ear sent a shiver of awe and anticipation through her. "I love you, Noel. I will always love you. You are my family now."

She'd thought her love for this man couldn't grow any bigger and yet her heart swelled, her love multiplying exponentially, feeling like she would burst with joy. Tears spilled from her eyes. She had no words. They all seemed inadequate to describe the awe that filled her chest as she lifted her head to meet his gaze.

"Those are happy tears, right?" he said, his eyes filled with the same devotion and awe that left her speechless.

She nodded. A wonder akin to reverence radiated through her and filled her whole being with a peace she had felt only once before. She reveled in this perfect moment, finally understanding in her core the meaning of the verse that would be read later today during the ceremony. "For a man shall leave his father and mother and be united to his wife and the two shall become one flesh." A concept so much bigger than a mere physical joining, it was the merging of two minds and two souls. "You are the only man I will ever love, truly my other half, body and soul."

The lines around his eyes grew deeper as he smiled that devastating grin that had held her captive from the first. "Soulmates."

"Yes, two souls destined to make this earthly journey together and blessed enough to make it a reality."

He blinked at her words and withdrew a folded note from his breast pocket. "Patrick gave this to me last night after the rehearsal dinner."

"I think you were his saving grace with your friendship and your interest in all he had to say."

"He's a good man and a good friend."

"So why did he give it to you last night?"

"I asked him the same thing. The funny thing is he couldn't have known what I was planning this morning but somehow it feels like we were meant to know this, on this day, and in this place."

"So what does it say?" Noel snuggled in closer to him as he unfolded the note.

"Eye has not seen, ear has not heard, nor the mind conceived what God has prepared for those who love him." Jeremy kissed the top of her head. "You may be one of the few people on earth who has seen and heard, but even you can't know what God has in store for us. And I can't wait to find out. You and me together forever."

# ACKNOWLEDGMENTS

Books have always been a retreat for me, a place of quiet and imagination. I enjoy immersing myself in the author's words as they build a story that entertains me and makes me think. I have endeavored to create that experience for you with Into the Light. If I succeeded in doing so, please consider leaving a review on Amazon or Goodreads to help others find their way to the same experience. Thank you for taking this journey with me. I appreciate your time and attention in a world where you have so many other things to do.

A few words of thanks to those who have helped this book on its way to resting in the hands of readers.

A first draft is just that, the first attempt at the story you have envisioned, a place to test the ideas that work and eliminate the ones that do not. You need honesty and encouragement from your first readers to make that happen. And mine are the best! Thank you to Kelly Anderson, Alli Anderson, and Mary Ellen Sullivan for helping me make the drafts that followed shine with clarity.

To my son-in-law, Matthew Stehle, for answering my questions about research studies and how they are conducted. I have taken some literary license with the facts to facilitate this story and any mistakes or inconsistencies are entirely mine.

A special thank you to my cousin, Jodi Daley, and West End Productions for producing the promotional video for Into the Light. What started as me reaching out to a cousin I hadn't seen in years, for help with the video for In This Lifetime, has now developed into a present day friendship and a lot of laughs. The blessing of family! One of God's great gifts!

A special thanks to Jonathan Camiolo, Susan Novalis, Mary Grace Yost, and Vinette Stegura for their reviews of Into the Light. Their words, some of which made me laugh and others which made me cry, made me eager to share them with readers.

And all my gratitude to God who called me back to writing after a long leave of absence. He reminded me that I had been given this talent for a reason and I needed to be using it, to give others a place of quiet retreat, a few hours with a good story, and a few thoughts about Him and His place in our lives. As other authors had done for me, it was my time to pay it forward. And so I shall.

# ABOUT KHARIS PUBLISHING:

Kharis Publishing, an imprint of Kharis Media LLC, is a leading Christian and inspirational book publisher based in Aurora, Chicago metropolitan area, Illinois. Kharis' dual mission is to give voice to under-represented writers (including women and first-time authors) and equip orphans in developing countries with literacy tools. That is why, for each book sold, the publisher channels some of the proceeds into providing books and computers for orphanages in developing countries so that these kids may learn to read, dream, and grow. For a limited time, Kharis Publishing is accepting unsolicited queries for nonfiction (Christian, self-help, memoirs, business, health and wellness) from qualified leaders, professionals, pastors, and ministers. Learn more at: https://kharispublishing.com/

www.ingramcontent.com/pod-product-compliance
Lightning Source LLC
Chambersburg PA
CBHW050340030726
47503CB00008B/2535

* 9 7 8 1 6 3 7 4 6 3 6 1 1 *